S0-BCQ-247

"Grow a backbone, Dhamari!" Tzigone snapped. "Thanks to you and Kiva, I can tell you from experience that it's possible to survive almost anything."

The wizard responded with a shriek of agony. Tzigone muttered a phrase she'd picked up on the streets and stooped beside him. Quickly she tucked her mother's talisman back into his hand. His screams immediately subsided to a pathetic whimper.

"I want you to survive," she told him. Her voice was cold and her eyes utterly devoid of the playful humor that had become both her trademark and her shield. "I'll find a way out of this place for both of us—and when this is all over, I'm going to kill you myself."

# Novels by
# Elaine Cunningham

## Songs and Swords

Elfshadow
Elfsong
Silver Shadows
Thornhold
The Dream Spheres

## Starlight and Shadows

Daughter of the Drow
Tangled Webs

## Counselors and Kings

The Magehound
The Floodgate
The Wizardwar

## Evermeet: Island of Elves

# The Wizardwar

## Counselors and Kings • Book III

### Elaine Cunningham

# THE WIZARDWAR

## ©2002 Wizards of the Coast, Inc.

All characters in this book are fictitious. Any resemblance to actual persons, living or dead, is purely coincidental.

This book is protected under the copyright laws of the United States of America. Any reproduction or unauthorized use of the material or artwork contained herein is prohibited without the express written permission of Wizards of the Coast, Inc.

Distributed in the United States by Holtzbrinck Publishing. Distributed in Canada by Fenn Ltd.

Distributed to the hobby, toy, and comic trade in the United States and Canada by regional distributors.

Distributed worldwide by Wizards of the Coast, Inc. and regional distributors.

FORGOTTEN REALMS and the Wizards of the Coast logo are registered trademarks owned by Wizards of the Coast, Inc., a subsidiary of Hasbro, Inc.

All Wizards of the Coast characters, character names, and the distinctive likenesses thereof are trademarks owned by Wizards of the Coast, Inc.

Made in the U.S.A.

The sale of this book without its cover has not been authorized by the publisher. If you purchased this book without a cover, you should be aware that neither the author nor the publisher has received payment for this "stripped book."

Cover art by John Foster
Cartography by Dennis Kauth
First Printing: March 2002
Library of Congress Catalog Card Number: 2001089471

9 8 7 6 5 4 3 2 1

UK ISBN: 0-7869-2728-3
US ISBN: 0-7869-2704-6
620-88548-001-EN

U.S., CANADA,
ASIA, PACIFIC, & LATIN AMERICA
Wizards of the Coast, Inc.
P.O. Box 707
Renton, WA 98057-0707
+1-800-324-6496

EUROPEAN HEADQUARTERS
Wizards of the Coast, Belgium
P.B. 2031
2600 Berchem
Belgium
+32-70-23-32-77

Visit our web site at **www.wizards.com/forgottenrealms**

# Dedication

To Peter Archer, who has the patience angle nailed
but is still two miracles short of sainthood.

**Entered into**
***The King's Lorebook,***
**on this the 22nd day**
**of the Redtide Moon,**
**in the 73rd year**
**of Zalathorm's Reign.**

*If cattle were bards, butchers would be villains.* This jordaini proverb reminds us that every tale is shaped by the teller. I am Matteo, King Zalathorm's newly appointed counselor, a jordain sworn to the service of truth, and Halruaa, and the wizardlords who rule.

Once, not long ago, I would have said these three masters speak with one voice. Now a hundred voices call my name, all of them compelling, many of them contradictory. Be that as it may. This is no time for introspection or philosophy— too many tasks lie before me. I will present my tale in straightforward fashion.

Halruaa's history begins in Netheril, an ancient northern realm famous for extravagant magic. Before Netheril's glory become her downfall, a group of wizards left their homeland and traveled far south, settling in a beautiful haven protected by mountains and sea. In this, our Halruaa, we have avoided the excesses of lost Netheril through elaborate laws and protocols, and through a series of safeguards. The jordaini, counselors to the wizard-lords, provide one of these safeguards.

We are an order of warrior sages, strong of mind and body, vessels destined to remain forever empty of Mystra's Art. The Lady of Magic has granted us no arcane talent whatsoever but rather has imbued us with a strong resistance to magic. Jordaini are identified before birth, taken from our families, and raised to know the art of warfare and the lore of our land. Lacking magic, we can advise our wizard patrons but can never coerce them. Nor can any wizard compel us. The secrets entrusted to us cannot be stolen or altered through magical means.

Additional laws and customs ensure the jordaini's faithful service. Ambition cannot tempt us, for we possess neither land nor title. We are forbidden indulgences that cloud the mind and discouraged from forming personal ties that might bias our judgment. Among the most powerful guardians of jordaini purity are the magehounds, wizards who serve as Inquisitors in the church of Azuth, Lord of Wizards.

Magehounds are granted spells and magical items powerful enough to pierce even a jordain's resistance. If a magehound declares a jordain unfit to serve, that jordain's service is over. If a magehound claims that a jordain is tainted by magic, this pronouncement is a sentence of death. Harsh indeed, but the trust between wizard and counselor demands absolute certainty.

Last spring a magehound, an elf woman known as Kiva, visited the Jordaini College. She passed judgment on Andris, the most promising student in recent memory. His "death" was carried out on the spot. Kiva, though, proved false. She spirited Andris away and used her position to secretly gather an army of magic-resistant warriors. She led them into the Swamp of Akhlaur, so named for the infamous necromancer who disappeared there two centuries past. Here lurked the laraken, a monster that fed upon magic. In my opinion, Kiva's intention was not to destroy the laraken but to unleash it upon the land. Her purpose, insofar as I can ascertain, was to wreak havoc upon Halruaa's wizards.

Kiva might have succeeded but for a young woman

named Tzigone, a street waif untrained in magical arts. Tzigone possessed a powerful raw talent for evocation. Her voice was the lure intended to draw the laraken away from its magical sustenance: a bubbling spring originating in a leak from the Elemental Plane of Water. Where Tzigone is concerned, however, things seldom go according to expectations!

Tzigone called the laraken and held it in her sway while we fighters attacked. We might have destroyed the monster, but it escaped through the gate leading into the Plane of Water just before Kiva moved this gate to some unknown place. This effort was greater than Kiva's strength, and by battle's end she clung to life by the thinnest of threads. I myself delivered her to the fastness of Azuth's temple, hoping the priests might revive her and learn the gate's secret location.

Kiva revived indeed. She escaped and gathered allies for a renewed attack upon Halruaa. She and the elves of the Mhair Jungle raided the Lady's Mirror, an Azuthan shrine and a treasury of rare spellbooks and artifacts. Other magical treasures were collected for her by a band of Crinti raiders—the "shadow amazons" of Dambrath, female warriors descended from human barbarians and drow elves.

Although it pains me to write this, Kiva's allies also included Andris, who learned of his distant elven heritage shortly after the battle of Akhlaur's Swamp. We jordaini know no family, and Andris was overwhelmed by the prospect of kinship. This, perhaps, led him to see honor in Kiva's actions where nothing of the sort existed.

Kiva must have had contact with wizards in neighboring lands, for her plans moved in concert with theirs. Though I hesitate to suggest Halruaan wizards were also in collusion with her, the actions of Dhamari Exchelsor, a wizard who befriended Tzigone, undoubtedly added to the chaos. (Let it be noted that Azuth's Inquisitors have examined Dhamari and have found him not guilty of conspiracy with Kiva.)

While these diverse events were unfolding, I searched for Kiva, fearing that the elf woman might open the gate and unleash the laraken. Andris, who awaits trial for treason, insists that Kiva's purpose was to destroy the ancient necromancer Akhlaur. She followed him into the Plane of Water expecting to prevail but not to return.

So Andris swears. I wish I could believe him. To Andris, Kiva was a hero who sacrificed her life to destroy every vestige of Akhlaur's dark reign. I have seen Kiva at work, and I do not believe anything good can be born of such hatred, such evil.

Whatever the truth of the matter, the former mage-hound was defeated. Once again, Tzigone thwarted Kiva's designs. Two doors were closed by the magic Tzigone triggered: the gate to the Plane of Water and a veil between our world and the Unseelie Court. As I write, Tzigone is trapped in that dark and unknowable realm. May Lady Mystra grant Tzigone grace and strength to survive until a way can be found to free her!

Despite our victories and our sacrifices, the turmoil Kiva set in motion was not easily quelled. The Crinti attacked in force from the north, and the fighters who engaged them were further harried by the Unseelie folk. An army of clock-work warriors was unleashed upon the royal city of Halarahh.

Any one of these foes might have easily been put down, but our strength was diminished by Kiva's earlier ploys. Divisions of militia were diverted to the western borders to guard against further incursions of hostile elves. As word of the laraken's defeat spread, many doughty wizards and adventurers disappeared into Akhlaur's swamp to search for treasure the necromancer reputedly left behind.

Even the season conspired to aid Kiva, for in the early summer, before the coming of the monsoons, piracy reaches its height. Halruaa's ships set sail to protect sea-going commerce and coastal towns, taking many of our best fighters. Halruaa's might is considerable, but it was thinly spread and sorely tested.

Now came the truly stunning blow. An invasion force from Mulhorand passed over the eastern mountains into Halruaa itself—*undetected by Halruaan magic.*

For the first time in nearly a century, King Zalathorm, the greatest diviner in the land, failed to foresee a coming threat. I cannot express how profound and devastating a blow this dealt to the Halruaan mind. Perhaps this was what Kiva had intended all along.

If this notion strains credulity, consider this: One of Kiva's allies, the creator of the devastating clockwork army, was Queen Beatrix, Zalathorm's deeply beloved wife.

I have nothing but admiration for my king, but in truth I must name Beatrix as Zalathorm's greatest weakness. Whatever she once might have been, she is no longer Halruaa's queen. Scarred within and without by terrible suffering, she has been steadily withdrawing from the world, seeking companionship only from the clockwork creatures whose creation she oversees.

Early last moon cycle, one of Beatrix's warrior constructs went amok. I fought and destroyed it but not before one worker was killed and several more were injured. In the time it took me to report this to the king, the clockwork monsters magically disappeared. The family of the slain worker was offered resurrection, the wounded given healing and redress. The matter might have been dropped, had not Tzigone intervened once again.

Tzigone can mimic voices with uncanny clarity and hold an audience in her hand with skill a bard might envy. Lately she left behind her life as a street performer to play the role of apprentice wizard, but her unsettled life has honed other, more questionable skills. Her fingers are light and nimble. She conjures entertaining half-truths as easily as a behir spits lightning. She walks like a shadow, climbs like a lizard, and smirks at the most formidable locks. Even the palace wards and safeguards could not deny her.

Tzigone slipped into Beatrix's workroom and with a magic mouth statue she recorded a most disturbing interview between the queen and Kiva. The elf woman came to Beatrix, commended her for her efforts, and took the metal monsters in preparation for the coming battle.

When Tzigone brought the statue to me, duty compelled me to inform Zalathorm of his wife's treachery. The queen awaits trial. This tragedy destroyed what might otherwise have been regarded as one of Halruaa's greatest triumphs.

Destroyed? Yes, I fear so. The invaders were repelled, and the floodgate was closed both in fact and metaphor. But the queen stands accused of treason. Although no one dares speak the words, everyone knows King Zalathorm is likewise on trial.

If the king knew of his queen's perfidy, he is as guilty as she. How could the most powerful diviner in all of Halruaa not see what was happening in his very palace? On the other hand, what if he truly could not? Is his power gone? Is this why he knew nothing of the invasion until Mulhorandi forces stood upon Halruaan soil?

All of Halruaa whispers these questions. If the cycle of history turns true, soon powerful and ambitious wizards will do more than whisper. No one has challenged Zalathorm's crown for nearly three generations, and the land has been at peace. In past times, though, Halruaa has known terrible wars of ambition, wars in which wizard fought wizard with spells of astonishing art and devastating power.

This brings my tale full circle and to another safeguard we jordaini provide. We are the keepers of the lore, and we spend the first twenty years of our lives committing Halruaan history to memory. Stories of wizardwars are the most fearsome we know. I pray daily to Lady Mystra that we Halruaans have learned from these oft-told tales and grown wise enough to avoid war.

Yet I cannot ignore this disturbing truth: if these prayers are granted, then we will be the first truly wise men in history.

# PRELUDE

In a dark moment of Halruaa's past, some two hundred years ago, a black tower stood near the edge of an ancient swamp.

Cages lined the walls of the great hall, a vast circular chamber encompassing the entire ground floor of the tower, which in turn was far bigger than its black marble exterior suggested. In these cages a bewildering variety of prisoners paced in frustration or slumped despairingly against the bars. Their mingled cries filled the tower, reverberating like echoes rising from the Abysmal pits. Red-robed apprentices calmly went about their business, either oblivious or uncaring.

In one cage huddled a small, bedraggled female, clad in a brief shift that did little to hide scars left by repeated magical experiments. She stared fixedly past the dwarf-forged bars, her eyes glazed with the knowledge of certain death.

Once known as Akivaria, a proud elf maid of the Crimson Tree clan, now she was simply Kiva, the necromancer's favorite captive and toy. Her heart had died the day the necromancer slaughtered her clan, but an unexpectedly deep reserve of stubbornness and cunning sustained her life. She had even survived the laraken's birth, a feat that surprised both her and her human tormenter. But today, at long last, it would end.

Kiva ventured a glance at the large, oval glass set into the bars of her cage, a window into a world of water and magic. Behind it raged a fearsome monster, a demon lured to the Plane of Water from the primordial depths of the Abyss. Twice the height of a man and as heavily muscled as a dwarf, it was purest evil encased in powerful flesh. Kiva knew the demon well—the wizard had captured and tormented it before—and memories of past encounters with the fiend filled her with terror and loathing.

The demon's massive fists pounded soundlessly on the portal. Like a water-bound Medusa, it was crowned with eels, which writhed furiously about a hideous, asymmetrical face. Their tiny fangs gnashed and snapped in counterpoint to the demon's silent screams. The necromancer commonly kept the demon imprisoned in magical limbo until the point of frenzy. Kiva never knew when the demon might erupt into her cage. This waiting was one of the wizard's crueler torments.

Kiva reminded herself of the experiment planned for that very night, one she could never survive, but even the promise of death brought little comfort. The joys of an elven afterlife were as far beyond her reach as her dreams of putting a knife in the necromancer's heart!

She craned her head, looking for the necromancer's favorite toy—a crimson gem that imprisoned the captured spirits of her clan. To Akhlaur, an elf's lifeforce was a source of energy, a thing no more highly regarded than the sticks of deadwood a kitchen wench might use to stoke a cook fire. For one of Akhlaur's elves, death offered nothing more than a new kind of enslavement.

The gem was not in its usual place. That meant that Akhlaur and his laraken were out hunting again.

A long, strident creak ripped through the cacophony. Kiva sat up, suddenly alert, and her resilient spirit grew bright with hope. The stone sentinels had awakened at last!

The necromancer's tower was guarded by undead armies, warded about with terrible traps and protected from wizardly incursion by the magic-draining hunger of the laraken. Never before had anyone fought through these defenses and triggered the twin gargoyles protecting the tower door.

Kiva struggled to her feet and pushed aside the mat of hair that once had been a lustrous jade. She clung to the bars and strained her ears for the sounds of battle. A distant clamor grew steadily louder until it settled around the stone warehouses imprisoning most of the necromancer's captives. The elf maid's heart leaped—many of her people languished in those prisons!

She heard the warehouses' stout oaken doors explode like lightning-struck trees. A chorus of elven song surged, then faded as freed prisoners fled into the surrounding forest. Joyous tears spilled from Kiva's eyes, though she herself did not hold much hope of rescue.

The tower's doors flew open and crashed into the wall. Two enormous gargoyles, similar in appearance to the water demon, stalked into the room. They took up ambush positions on either side of the open door.

After a moment of stunned disbelief, the apprentices quickly armed themselves with wands or fireball spells. One young man conjured a crimson lightning bolt and held it aloft like a ready javelin. Even the tower itself prepared for invasion. Bright lines of fire raced through the cracks between the marble ties, gathering power that would erupt in geysers of random, killing flame. Stone carvings stirred to life. Winged serpents peeled away from the ceiling's bas-relief and spiraled heavily downward. Black marble skeletons wrenched free of the grimly sculpted tangles that passed for art.

A hush fell over the tower as the captives awaited the coming battle with a mixture of dread and hope.

*Up, and quickly!*

The silent command rang in Kiva's mind like an elven battle cry. Perplexed expressions on the faces of the other captives suggested the message had come to all. There was powerful magic in the silent voice, magic untouched by the necromancer's malevolent amusement. That was enough for Kiva.

Hope lent her strength. She leaped and seized a crossbar, swung her feet up and hooked them over the bar, then pulled herself up and reached for the next handhold. Around the room other captives scrambled upward as best they could.

An angry gray cloud erupted in the midst of the tower with a roar like a captive dragon. It exploded into a torrent of rain. The force of the downpour threatened to tear Kiva from her perch, but she climbed doggedly, and a small, unfamiliar curve lifted the corners of her mouth as she perceived the attacker's strategy.

Steam rose from the floor with a searing hiss as the arcane waters met the necromancer's lurking flames. The apprentices stumbled back, screaming, throwing aside their magical weapons as they tried to shield their faces from the rising, scalding mist.

Instantly the cloud changed, compressing into an enormous, ice-blue blanket. It swept over Kiva like a ghostly embrace, then drove down into the scalding mist. Steam changed to delicate webs of ice crystals, which in turn crunched down into a thick, solid sheet of ice.

Stone and marble guardians froze, their feet encased in ice, the magic that animated them gone. One winged snake had not yet landed. Its wings locked in place as the ice-cloud passed over it, and it plunged down, exploding on impact and sending shards of black marble skittering across the frozen floor.

Only the twin gargoyles shrugged off the magic-killing rain. They thrashed about frantically, but they could not break themselves free of the icy trap. Someone else, apparently, could.

Neat cracks appeared in the ice around them, and the stone monsters rose into the air on small frozen squares like monstrous sultans on tiny flying carpets. Still struggling, they soared through the open door and landed with thunderous finality back in their accustomed places.

Kiva dropped back to the floor of her cage, ignoring the burning chill beneath her bare feet. She darted a quick look around for more defenses.

Several of the apprentice wizards lay dead, their bodies covered with a thick shroud of ice. Others were captured in ankle-deep ice, some shrieking in agony, others already falling into shock and silence. One young wizard had had the presence of mind to climb above the rising steam. He sat upon the shoulders of a marble skeleton, staring with stupid amazement at the limp crimson rope in his hand—all that remained of his splendid lightning bolt. A wild-eyed female apprentice stood halfway up the spiral stairs, frantically peeled away the budding twigs that had appeared on her wand, as if denuding the branches could restore the magic lost to the rain. She glanced up, briefly, as the invaders entered, then returned her attention to her ruined wand.

Several men in warrior's garb stalked into the room, their eyes scanning for further resistance. When they perceived none, they set about freeing the captives. A tall, strongly built man came to Kiva's cage, a man with a scimitar nose and a single long braid of dark chestnut hair. He took a small wand from his belt and lowered it to the skull-shaped lock securing her door.

"Don't!" croaked Kiva in a voice left raw by too many screams, too little song. She reached through the bars and seized the wizard's wrist. With her free hand she pointed toward the "mirror" and the suddenly calm and watchful demon.

The monster grinned in anticipation. Bloody saliva hung from its fangs in long strings.

"You cannot," Kiva repeated. "Disturb the lock, and you unleash the demon."

The wizard glanced at the drooling fiend. "Don't fear, child. We will not let it harm you."

"Lord Akhlaur will soon return! You cannot fight him and the demon both," she argued.

"Neither can Akhlaur fight two such battles. Has the demon any loyalty to him?"

*Loyalty to Akhlaur?* she echoed, silently and incredulously. "The demon is a prisoner."

"Then you need not fear its release. It will not be you or me whom the creature seeks. Just be ready to flee as soon as the door opens."

Suddenly the wizard's eyes clouded, as if he were listening to distant voices. After a moment his gaze sharpened, hardened. He spun toward his comrades. "Akhlaur comes."

They formed ranks, their wands held like ready swords or their hands filled with bright globes that coursed with the snap and shudder of contained power.

A tall, black-haired man strode into the tower. Rich black and crimson robes swirled around him, and he gazed about with the faint interest a courtier might display upon entering a ballroom. Behind him came Noor, his favorite apprentice, a doe-eyed young woman of soft beauty and ironclad ambition.

Cradled in Noor's hands was a ruby-colored crystal nearly as large as a man's head, sparkling with thousands of facets and shaped like a many-pointed star. It glowed, quite literally, with life. Kiva's gaze clung to the crimson gem with a mixture of longing and despair.

"Well met, Zalathorm," Akhlaur said with a hint of amusement.

The name startled Kiva. Even here, a prisoner in an isolated estate, she knew that name! She had heard stories of the wizard who was slowly bringing peace and order out of the killing chaos spawned by Akhlaur's rise to power.

A second shock jolted through her when one of the wizards broke from the group and strode forward. The great Zalathorm was a man of middle years and middling height. His hair and beard were a soft brown, a pallid color by Halruaan standards. Nothing in his face or garb suggested power. His hands were empty of weapons or magic. He stood a full head shorter than Akhlaur, and his somber, plain-featured face provided sharp contrast to the necromancer's aristocratic features. An image flooded Kiva's mind of a jousting match between a farmer's dun pony and a raven-black pegasus.

"I wondered when you'd get around to visiting," Akhlaur said. His gaze moved from Zalathorm and slid dismissively over the battle-ready wizards. His smirk sharpened into a contemptuous sneer. "*This* was the best you could do? Transformation into mindless undead could only improve this lot!"

A white-haired wizard spat out a curse and lifted his wand to avenge this insult. As he leveled it at Akhlaur, Kiva noted the expression of pure panic flooding Noor's face. The apprentice uttered a strangled little cry and flung out a hand as if to stave off the magical assault.

Light burst from the old wizard's wand. It veered sharply away from Akhlaur and streaked toward Noor like lightning to a lodestone. As magical energy flowed into the crimson gem, Noor's black hair rose and writhed about her contorted face. The old wizard's wand quickly spent itself, blackened, and withered to a thin line of falling ashes.

The magic came on, flowing until the wizard's outstretched hand was little more than skin-wrapped bone. Where there was life, there was magic, and Akhlaur's crimson star drank swiftly and deeply of both. The brave man died quickly, and his desiccated shell fell to the ice-covered floor with a faint, brittle clatter.

Stunned silence fell over the wizards. Only Zalathorm maintained presence of mind. He beckoned to the crimson star. The gem lifted out of Noor's slack hands and floated over to him. To Kiva's astonishment, Akhlaur did not intervene.

"You cannot harm me with that," the necromancer said, still with a hint of amusement in his voice.

"Nor you me," Zalathorm returned grimly. "With this gem, we entrusted our lives to each other's keeping."

The necromancer lifted raven-wing brows in mock surprise. "Why, Zalathorm! Take care, or I shall suspect you of harboring doubts about our friendship!"

"Doubts? I don't know which is the greater perversion: the use you have made of this gem, or the monster you made of the man I once called friend."

Akhlaur sent a droll glance toward his apprentice. Noor stood over the slain wizard, both hands clasped over her mouth and tears streaming down her lovely face. The necromancer took no notice of her distress.

"Tiresome, isn't he?" he said, tipping his head in Zalathorm's direction. "What can one expect of a man whose family motto is 'Too stupid to die?'"

Zalathorm lifted the gem as if in challenge, then swiftly traced a spell with his free hand. Every wizard in the room mirrored his deft gestures.

The room exploded into white light and shrieking power. Kiva dropped and hugged the floor of her cage as the tower wrenched free of its moorings and soared above the forest canopy.

Again she smiled, for the power of this casting was as great as any magic she'd endured at Akhlaur's hands. Moving an entire tower, a wizard's tower—*Akhlaur's* tower!—was an astonishing feat! Immediately she sensed Zalathorm's intent, and again she dared to hope.

When the tower shuddered to a stop, Kiva closed her eyes and inhaled deeply, as if she could draw the forest into herself. Senses she could never describe to a human told her where the tower now rested. Deep in the swamp was a rift carved into the land by a long-ago cataclysm known to the elves as the Sundering. The rift was a hidden place, a suitable tomb for Akhlaur's tower—and a place far from the laraken and its magic-draining power.

Kiva hauled herself to her knees and looked about for the necromancer. He stood crouched in guard position, brandishing a skull-headed scepter and an ebony wand like a pair of swords. Her throat clenched in dread, for she knew the spells stored in these weapons and knew Akhlaur could hold off magical attacks for a very long time.

Yet he did not strike.

Her gaze slid to the necromancer's face. A puzzled moment passed before she understood his wild eyes, his twisted expression.

*Akhlaur was afraid.*

Of course! The magical rain had stripped away even these powerful weapons! Akhlaur's confidence had rested upon his laraken and its ability to strip spells from other wizards and transfer them to its master. Now the tower had been removed well beyond the laraken's hunting ground, and no new magic flowed to the waiting scepter and wand.

Akhlaur's frantic gaze sought out his apprentice. "The laraken!" he howled to Noor, brandishing his scepter at the circling wizards in the manner of one who attempts to hold off wolves with a stick. "Summon the laraken!"

Kiva laughed. The sound was ragged, yet it rang with both hatred and triumph. Noor would not do as Akhlaur asked. The slain wizard had been her father—Kiva knew this in her blood and bones, just as she knew the spirit of the old wizard was now imprisoned in the crimson star, along with Kiva's kin. The anguish and guilt on Noor's face when the white-haired wizard died was as familiar to Kiva as the sound of her own heartbeat.

However, obedience to Akhlaur was a powerful habit. The girl's hands began to trace a summoning spell before she had time to consider her own will. She hesitated, and half-formed magic crackled in a shining nimbus around her as her uncertain gaze swept the room.

Several of the wizards had leveled their wands at her, ready to slay her if need be. All of them looked to Zalathorm, who held up a restraining hand and studied Noor with sympathetic and measuring eyes.

"Your father," he said softly, "was a hard man but a good

one. He believed magic carries a stern price. He came here to pay his daughter's debts."

Noor's eyes clung to the crimson star in Zalathorm's hands. "You will free them?"

"Yes," the wizard said simply. In a softer voice, he added, "I will grant them rest and respect."

Joy rose in Kiva like springtime. For a shining moment, she believed Zalathorm could actually free her, would free them all!

With a single, sharp gesture, Noor finished the summoning spell. Kiva had witnessed the laraken's summoning many times, and she saw at once that the spell cast was not the spell Noor had begun.

Power crackled through the tower, and the roar of angry seas filled the air. Rising above the surge was a keening, vengeful shriek. A shriek Kiva knew well.

She frantically backed away from the portal, flattening herself against the bars as she awaited the demon's release.

*Stand clear!*

Again the voice—the voice of the wizard who'd started to free her—sounded in her head. Kiva edged away from the bars. Bright energy jolted through them, and the lock's skull-like jaw went slack as it melted. Kiva tore at the door, not caring that the heated metal burned her fingers.

She stumbled away from the cage. Her retreat was unheeded, for the wizards' attention was fixed upon the creature bursting free of the shimmering oval and the open cage.

The water demon shielded its glowing red eyes with a dagger-taloned hand as its gaze swept the room. Red orbs focused upon the necromancer. Hatred burned in them like hellfire.

"Akhlaur," the demon said in a grating, watery voice, pronouncing the word like a foul curse. It sprung, impossibly quick, its massive hands arched into rending talons.

The wizard dropped his useless weapons and seized the creature's wrists. He frantically chanted spells to summon preternatural strength and killing magic. Zalathorm's wizards fell back as evil fought evil like two dark fires, each determined to consume the other.

Arcane power crackled like black lightning around the struggling pair. Akhlaur's luxuriant black hair singed away and drifted off in a cloud of ash. His handsome face blistered and contorted with pain—pain that fed his death-magic spells.

Suddenly the eels upon the demon's head shrieked and flailed in agony. One by one, they burned and withered, then fell limp to the creature's massive shoulders like lank strands of hair. Fetid steam rose from the demon's body, and green-black scales lifted from its flesh like worn shingles. Too furious to meet death alone, the demon forced Akhlaur inexorably back toward the portal.

The necromancer's hate-filled eyes sought Noor's face. He captured her gaze, then jerked one of the demon's hands, pantomiming a slashing motion. The girl's head snapped back, and four burning lines opened her throat.

Then Akhlaur was gone. In the mirror, the entwined figures of necromancer and demon rapidly diminished as they fell away from the glowing portal. Kiva felt a surge of triumph, then a sudden, gut-wrenching drop.

To her astonishment, she felt herself sucked into the Plane of Water with the necromancer!

Down she fell, sinking through a sea of magic, falling away from her forest, her clan and kin. Away from her past, her heritage. From *herself*. Falling too far to ever, ever return.

In some part of her mind, Kiva knew she was trapped in a dream. Two centuries had come and gone since Akhlaur's defeat. She awakened abruptly but not with the sudden jolt that usually followed an interrupted dream.

To her horror, she was falling still, tumbling helplessly through thin mountain air. The vision of Akhlaur's tower had been only a dream, but this nightmare was very, very real!

The elf flailed and tumbled, clawing at the empty darkness. Wind whistled past her and carried her shrieks away into the uncaring night. Stars whirled and spun overhead, mocking her with the long-lost memories of starlit dances in elven glades. Kiva felt no sorrow over her forgotten innocence—its loss was too old to mourn. As she fell toward certain death, her only regret was the unfinished revenge that had sustained her for two centuries.

A sudden blur of light and color flashed past her, circled, and dipped out of sight. Kiva struck something soft and yielding and felt herself received and cradled as if in strong, silken arms.

For several moments she lay facedown, too dazed to move, too stunned to make sense of either her fall or her rescue. After a while she raised her head and peered into the elaborate, swirling pattern of a carpet. The wind still whistled past her, but its passage no longer felt cold or mocking.

A flying carpet, then. Kiva felt about for the edges of the magical conveyance and rolled toward the safety of the middle. She cautiously sat up and found herself face to face with Akhlaur himself.

Two centuries of exile in the Plane of Water had taken its toll on Akhlaur. Lustrous black hair had given way to a pate covered with fine, faintly green scales. His long fingers were webbed, and rows of gills shaped like jagged lightning slashed the sides of his neck, but his expression of faint, derisive amusement was maddeningly familiar. For a moment Kiva heartily wished she'd left him in his watery prison.

"You are a restless sleeper, little Kiva," Akhlaur observed in an arch tone.

"Elves do not sleep," she reminded him, though she wondered why she bothered. Akhlaur was singularly uninterested in elven nature except as it pertained to his experiments.

"I trust you are unharmed by your little adventure?" he

asked, his manner a blatant parody of a master's concern for his faithful servant.

Kiva managed a faint smile, though she suspected Akhlaur had nudged her off the carpet in the first place just to enjoy her fall and her terror!

"It was . . . exhilarating," she said, imbuing her words with the dark irony Akhlaur so enjoyed. "All the same, I am grateful for rescue."

The necromancer inclined his head graciously, accepting her thanks as genuine. He had reason to think Kiva sincere. There was a death-bond between them, forged two centuries past so she could survive the laraken's birth. Kiva could not harm Akhlaur without slaying herself, and she counted on this to convince the wizard of her sincerity.

"Sleep," he instructed her. "We have much to do upon the morrow."

Kiva obediently curled up on the carpet and pretended to drift back into reverie, but dreams of the past dimmed before the great battle ahead.

During this battle, Akhlaur, the wizard who had come so close to conquering all of Halruaa, would fight not as her master but as her deadly and unwitting tool.

# CHAPTER ONE

$A$ small, swarthy young man glided like a brown shadow through a labyrinth of corridors far below King Zalathorm's palace. Dawn was hours away, and this deep place was lit only by the small blue globe in the young wizard's hand.

Moving with the assurance born of experience, he barely glanced at the ancient skeletons moldering in side corridors, silent testament both to the spirit of Halruaan adventurers and the wards guarding the land's deeply buried treasures.

He made his way to the center of the maze and stepped into a circle ringed with deeply etched runes. As he chanted in the ancient, secret language of Halruaan magic, the stone beneath his feet melted away, swirling downward like dense gray mist and reforming as a narrow, circling stairway.

Down he went, moving deeper and deeper into the heart of the land. With each step he intoned the specific arcane word required. He respectfully avoided treading upon the blackened spots marking the final resting places of wizards whose memories had faltered.

At the foot of the stairs was a great hall, lined on each side by a score of living guards. Here gathered many of Halruaa's great necromancers, keeping watch over secrets last whispered by lips long ago faded to ash and memory. They nodded to the young man as he passed, giving the deference due to the king's messenger. None of them suspected the true identity of the black-eyed, brown-skinned youth.

The disguised wizard stopped before an enormous door and bowed to the ancient, cadaverous archmage who guarded it. He handed the old man a scroll.

"A writ from the king," he said in the lilting accents common to the coastal islands.

The archmage glanced at the missive, then lifted his rheumy gaze to the messenger. "By the king's command, we must answer your questions with the same candor we would offer him. I swear by my wizard-word oath it will be so."

The youth inclined his head in respectful thanks. "I would know who raised and commanded the undead army during the battle against the Mulhorandi invaders."

The guardians exchanged uncertain glances. "The king himself is acclaimed for this victory," the archmage ventured.

The messenger snorted. "When did the king become a master of necromancy? Tell me who among your ranks could have done such a thing."

The old man's lips thinned as if to hold back the answer he was sworn to give. "It is beyond my art," he admitted at last. "No one in this room could cast such a spell. We can all raise and command undead, certainly, but not in such numbers! If the king did not cast this spell, then his equal did."

"Who is equal to the king?" asked the disguised wizard, imbuing his voice with a mixture of indignation and concern, such as a faithful young messenger might express.

"I assume you speak rhetorically, as did I," the archmage hastened to add. "For who could be the king's equal?"

*Who indeed?* The wizard swallowed the wry smile that tugged at his lips. The old archmage's parry was as deft as any swordmaster's, but in truth many wizards were beginning to wonder if perhaps they might prove to be the king's equal. The guardian's question might have been rhetorical, but it would not long remain in the bloodless realm of rhetoric.

The wizard bowed his thanks and gestured toward the door. The archmage moved aside, clearly eager to end this disturbing interview.

Massive, ironbound doors swung inward on silent hinges, untouched by mortal hand. Torches mounted on the walls flared into life, revealing a circular room with several doors but no floor other than a gaping pit. Faint but fearsome howls wafted up from untold depths, carrying a faint charnel scent and the promise of oblivion.

The wizard stepped into the empty air, counted off several paces to the left, and strode confidently across the void. He passed through three other magically trapped rooms before he came to the place he sought.

This final chamber was empty but for the ruby-hued crystal floating in the room's center. Shaped like a many-pointed star, it burned with its own inner light and filled the room with a crimson glow.

The wizard let his disguise melt away, revealing the mild, middle-aged face of the man who had claimed the crimson star more than two hundred years ago. He dropped to one knee and began the difficult process each visit demanded: emptying his mind of thought, his heart of sorrow and guilt. When at last the silence within matched the profound stillness of the chamber, he rose, lifted his eyes to the gem, and spoke.

"The heart of Halruaa seeks counsel," King Zalathorm said softly.

In lean words Zalathorm described the battle spells that just two days before had siphoned the fluids from hundreds of living men to create an enormous water elemental, then raised the desiccated men into an undead army.

"What wizard, living or dead, might have cast such a spell?" he concluded.

He tuned his mind's ear for the silent response, the familiar, elfsong voices of sages long dead. They spoke in a single-note chorus of wordless, overwhelming terror. Waves of emotion swept over him like an icy storm, stealing his breath. Stopping his heart.

Crushing pain enveloped Zalathorm's chest, sending him staggering back. He fell heavily against the chamber's only door, unable to move or breathe. For long moments he believed he would die in this room.

Finally healing magic, more ancient even than the sages' remembered fear, pulsed from the crimson star.

The king's heart leaped painfully, then took up its normal rhythm. Slowly his agony receded. Once again, the crimson star had preserved its creator.

Once again, it had given Zalathorm an answer he could find nowhere else. The gem was undying history, centuries of experience preserved in eternal immediacy. In all of Halruaa's long history, Zalathorm knew of only one wizard who could inspire such terror in the time-frozen sages' hearts. Though no word had been given, Zalathorm had his answer all the same.

Somehow, Akhlaur had returned.

# CHAPTER TWO

The streets below King Zalathorm's palace teamed with life, even though the sun barely crested the city's eastern wall. Matteo stood at the king's side, listening as Zalathorm received a seemingly endless line of supplicants.

It was Matteo's first day as King's Counselor, and already he was fighting off the urge to fidget like a schoolchild. The king had charged him with the defense of Queen Beatrix. Why not let him get on with it?

Matteo could not understand the king's insistence on honoring his custom of granting daily audience. In these extraordinary times, mundane routine seemed as out of place as a witless sheep among unicorns!

Reminders of the recent battles were everywhere. Laborers still cleared away the debris and rubble cluttering the king's city. The pyres in the burial gardens outside the city walls burned steadily. Professional mourners sang themselves into rasping silence, then yielded their places to others. Their keening songs soared up into the smoky clouds, commending the spirits of fallen Halruaans to the gods and their bodies to the sky.

The Halruaans were a proud and defiant people who mingled mourning rituals with extravagant victory celebrations. Students at the mage schools were sent home until after the new moon. Merchants and artisans closed their shops before highsun and did not reopen after the sunsleep hours were past. Street performers sang ballads and acted out tableaus; fireworks dazzled the night skies. Somber, hardworking Halruaans, wizards and common folk alike, devoted themselves to defiant celebration, as if to thumb their noses at ubiquitous Death.

Outside the palace, the familiar song of the street began a swift crescendo and took on a faintly dissonant note. Zalathorm nodded to Matteo. Glad for the diversion, the young jordain went to the window to see what was going on.

As always, a throng waited outside, hoping for audience with the king. The scene had a festival air. Street vendors came to display their wares, and wandering performers kept the crowd entertained. Matteo quickly averted his eyes from a young juggler, for the lad's deft hands and carefree grin reminded him too painfully of his friend Tzigone.

His gaze slid over the dancing bear that plodded and whirled like a corpulent matron, and settled briefly upon the drovers hawking exotic beasts. Beaming parents handed their children up for rides upon camels from the Calimshan deserts or an enormous three-horned lizard from the jungles of Chult or an aged and rather threadbare unicorn. There was even a young elephant, an animal seldom seen in Halruaa. Two small, shrieking children clung to the gaudy red and yellow litter on the animal's broad, gray back.

Matteo's eyes darted back to the elephant. Its long trunk lashed back and forth, as if swatting away an attacking swarm. He looked closer and realized this was precisely what the animal was doing. Several people had taken to pelting the unfortunate creature with fruit and morning cakes.

He turned back to Zalathorm. "One of the drovers has brought an elephant. The crowd is attacking it, perhaps because the animal is native to Mulhorand and a reminder of the invaders."

A scowl darkened the king's face. He rose from his throne and stalked toward the window, gesturing for Matteo to follow. Courtiers parted as the two passed, watching with furrowed brows as the king broke his own unbending custom.

Zalathorm led the way to a hidden stairwell, where narrow, winding steps spiraled down to the street. These he took at an astonishingly brisk pace.

"With respect, sire, may I ask your intentions?" Matteo called as he jogged after the king.

Zalathorm stopped and shot a glance back at his counselor. "The people outside the palace are waiting for me to settle disputes. This particular one isn't going to improve with age."

Matteo would have argued the wisdom of marching into the middle of a street disturbance, but he assumed the king had his reasons. He followed quickly, loosening the peaceties on his daggers as he went.

By the time they reached the street, the situation had devolved into chaos. The elephant whirled this way and that, lunging at its circle of tormenters with short and astonishingly swift charges. Two wizards had cast spells of levitation to lift the terrified children out of the boxlike litter. They were floating, kicking and wailing, toward the frantically outstretched arms of their parents.

Several more wizards advanced on the animal. Small balls of crackling, bluish energy flew from their outstretched hands and exploded against the elephant's hide with sharp, sizzling pops.

Matteo immediately sensed their strategy: Back the elephant into a walled garden, where it could be easily contained. The animal, though, was too panicked to cooperate. Emitting shrill, trumpeting cries, it began to rear and pitch like a bee-stung stallion.

"Idiots," muttered Zalathorm.

Since their miniature lightning shockballs were not putting the elephant into retreat, the wizards began to hurl larger missiles. A small barrage of many-colored lights hurtled toward the terrified animal.

The king lifted both hands and slammed his right fist against his left palm. Immediately the missiles struck an invisible wall and were deflected off at a sharply climbing angle, ascending the sky like festival fireworks.

One of these missiles, a bolt of energy shaped like a slim crimson javelin, glanced off the magical barrier and came around in a tight turn, like a fish changing directions in a swift moving stream. It hurtled directly, unerringly, toward the spellcaster who had disrupted its course.

Matteo's response was part training, part instinct. He leapt in front of the king, his hands lunging for the shaft of the magical javelin. The weapon scorched through his clenched fist—only his deeply inbred resistance to magic kept the thing from burning down to bone.

Even as his fingers closed on the shaft, he twisted his wrist slightly, not trying to stop the weapon so much as to shift it off course. The magic weapon turned broadside but kept its course. Matteo's right arm jerked free of its shoulder joint in a searing, white-hot flash of pain. He hurtled backward, still holding the crimson bolt, and slammed into a courtyard wall.

Matteo tossed aside the dissipating weapon and reached for his left-handed dagger, ready to protect the king if need be, but in the brief moment it took him to blink away the dancing stars from his vision, Zalathorm had moved to stand beside the elephant.

The king stroked the animal's bristled gray hide in a soothing manner. When the drover came up to take the reins, Zalathorm spoke a few quiet words. Matteo could not hear what was said, but he noted how the color leeched from the drover's face. The man backed away, ducking his head repeatedly in quick, nervous bows.

Zalathorm's gaze swept the quiet, watchful throng. "Many are the tasks before us. Halruaa is equal to them all, so long as our energies are not distracted from the real work at hand. Those of you who require the king's judgment may wait in peace. Those who came seeking spectacle have been satisfied and can go their way."

Though the king spoke calmly, his voice reached the outskirts of the crowd. Some of the morning revelers slipped away, others reclaimed their places in line with subdued faces.

Matteo returned to Zalathorm's side, cradling the elbow of his injured arm in his left hand. "Fine speech," he murmured. "Many are the tasks before us—and what better way to illustrate this than for the king and his counselor to tend the well-being of a pack animal?"

The king sent him a sharp glance. "If pain prompts you to sarcasm, by all means let us repair your shoulder immediately."

Matteo managed a small bow. "My apologies, sire. Though I thank you for you kind thought, healing spells and clerical prayers have about as much effect upon a jordain—"

"As flattery has upon a mule," Zalathorm broke in. "An analogy, mind you, that I find surprisingly apt."

He took hold of Matteo's arm and gave it a sharp twist and a sudden, precise shove. Pain exploded in Matteo's shoulder and skittered along his limbs and spine. As suddenly as it came, it was gone but for a deep, dull ache.

Matteo rolled his shoulder experimentally. "Amazing. I doubt a jordaini battlemaster could have done better."

For some reason, Zalathorm found that amusing. "High praise indeed!"

He strode toward the palace wall and the stairs, which had suddenly reappeared in a new location. Matteo followed.

"If I may ask, what did you say to the elephant drover?"

"Jaharid? I told him I calmed the elephant by speaking with it mind to mind. I reminded him the elephant is an intelligent, perhaps even sentient beast, and suggested that since he could bear witness to many of Jaharid's less-than-legal activities, it behooved him to treat the animal with courtesy and respect."

Matteo took this in. "The elephant told you these things?"

The king sent a quick, amused look over his shoulder. "Our large, gray friend did not offer an opinion concerning Jaharid's business practices. Few elephants are well versed in Halruaan law."

"I see. You know this Jaharid, then."

"Never set eyes upon the man. A simple divination spell yielded his name, along with an interesting image: Jaharid bartering with a Mulhorand pirate for a baby elephant. If you'd had dealings with the Mulhorandi, would you want them brought to light? Mark me, Jaharid will treat the animal well and give it no cause for complaint."

Matteo considered this. "According to what I know of the Art of divination, this seems an unusual insight. Divination is the study of the future."

The king lifted one shoulder dismissively. "The seasons pass and return. The future can often be read in the patterns of the past."

Though the words were prosaic, they sent an image jolting into Matteo's mind: Tzigone, deep in trance as she sought her own earliest memories, accidentally moving past her own experiences to witness events occurring long before her birth. Zalathorm, it seemed, had unconventional talents of his own.

"You are more than a diviner," Matteo observed.

Zalathorm stopped and turned. "I am king," he said simply. His lips twisted in a wry smile, and he added, "At least for the moment."

He waved away Matteo's attempted protests. "No wizard has stepped forward with a challenge, but it is only a matter of time. We both know this. Your former patron, Procopio Septus, stands tall amongst the waiting throng."

Matteo secretly agreed. Still, "Sire, you know I am sworn not to reveal one patron's secrets to another."

Zalathorm sent him an inquiring look. "Did I ask you to? Procopio is ambitious. I need no jordain to tell me what my own eyes perceive."

"Of course not, my lord." Matteo hesitated, then asked the question that had been harrying him since his appointment. "Forgive me, but why exactly *do* you need me? I have lived twenty-one summers, hardly enough time to gain the wisdom a king's counselor requires."

The king smiled faintly. "Surely you've heard the whispers questioning my fitness to rule. Do you agree with them?"

This question startled Matteo, and the answer that came to mind stunned him. Zalathorm waited for him to speak, studying him with eyes that needed no magic to measure a man.

"I'm not sure," Matteo said at last.

Zalathorm nodded. "Therein lays the answer to your question. An older, wiser jordain would have told me what he thought I wished to hear."

"If I offend, I beg pardon," Matteo began.

The king cut him off with an upraised hand. "If you apologize for each outbreak of candor, we'll have little time to speak of other matters. Honesty is a laudable trait, but let's agree now that it's best appreciated long after the advice is given."

This blunt speech conjured in Matteo's mind an image of Tzigone's pert face, her expressive mouth twisted in exasperation at his inability to add "interesting color" to the truth, her big brown eyes cast skyward. Matteo swallowed the sudden lump in his throat and banished the wistful smile from his lips.

"Perhaps you disagree?" the king inquired.

"Not at all, sire," he said, inclining his head in a small, respectful bow. "Indeed, I have heard that sentiment expressed before."

❧

By highsun, all the petitioners had been heard. The street song dimmed to a somnolent murmur as the residents of Halarahh sought shelter from the midday heat. Sunsleep hours were both custom and necessity in this sultry land.

The king and his counselor, however, did not take time to rest. Matteo followed Zalathorm through a maze of corridors and up winding stairs, past armed guards and magical wards guarding the high tower where Queen Beatrix was imprisoned.

Her small chamber was comfortably appointed but as starkly white as a greenmage's infirmary. The walls were freshly whitewashed and the carpet quilted from thick pelts of lambskin. White satin cushions heaped the bed, and a long settee had been covered in white-embroidered silk. Here sat Beatrix in profound stillness, immobile as the metal constructs that had been her passion and her downfall.

Despite her captivity, the queen was gorgeously gowned in white satin and cloth-of-silver. An elaborate wig of white and silver curls framed a face as pale as porcelain. Her dark eyes were kohl-rimmed and enormous, startling against the unnatural pallor.

Zalathorm stooped to kiss the snowy cheek. "You are well, my lady?"

After a moment, she responded with a faint nod.

The king sat down beside her and took one of her small, still hands in his. "You are here by my command. In this I had no choice. But I believe nothing that has been said of you."

The queen lifted her eyes, not quite meeting Zalathorm's gaze. Though she stared blankly past his shoulder, she lifted her free hand and gently touched his cheek. Overcome, Zalathorm captured the small hand and pressed it to his lips.

Though loath to intrude, Matteo stepped forward. "My lady, do you remember Kiva visiting you, taking away the clockwork creatures?"

"Kiva," Beatrix repeated. Matteo might have taken this response for a simple echo but for the uncharacteristically grim note that had entered the queen's voice.

Matteo crouched down so his eyes were level with hers. "You are accused of conspiring with Kiva, and building the clockwork creatures on her command. Were you enchanted?"

"Not by Kiva."

Matteo and Zalathorm exchanged puzzled glances. The queen seemed unusually lucid, but this pronouncement was unexpected. "By whom, then?"

"Not who." A cloud passed over Beatrix's face, dulling the faint light in her eyes. She withdrew her hands from the king's grasp and folded them in her pristine lap.

"If not whom," Matteo persisted, "then what?"

A hint of animation returned to her painted face, and she glanced toward him. "Yes."

"Yes?"

"Yes. What."

Matteo puzzled this over. The light broke suddenly. "You were not enchanted by a person but by a thing?"

After a moment, Beatrix nodded.

Finally, progress! Matteo sent a triumphant glance toward the king. The expression on Zalathorm's face sent him rocking back onto his heels.

The king stared at his wife, his countenance deadly pale and stamped with horror. He slipped onto his knees and buried his face in the queen's lap. His words were faint and choked with emotion, but Matteo caught something that sounded like, *"Gods above, what have I done to you?"*

After a moment, Matteo went to the door and tapped softly. The guard let him out, and he stood quietly in the hall until the king rejoined him.

"Sire, disturbing though this interview was, we made progress. We should continue."

Zalathorm shook his head. "You will get nothing more. The moment has passed."

"Before it did, you learned something important."

"Yes." Zalathorm cleared his throat, then spun away and stalked toward the tower stairs.

Matteo fell into step and waited, but the king did not elaborate. After several moments, the jordain gave up any pretense of patience. Stepping into the king's path, he rounded to face him and affixed him with a challenging stare.

"With respect, my lord, you command me to defend the queen but tell me nothing that might aid in her defense!"

To Matteo's surprise, the king dropped his gaze first. "Magic is not the solution to every problem. Sometimes it creates as many problems as it solves. I was not aware of one of these problems until just now. There is nothing more to tell you." He held up a hand to forestall Matteo's ready protest. "Nothing, at least, that is not held in silence by powerful enchantments and wizard-word oaths."

The jordain stood his ground for a few moments more, then fell back with a sigh. A wizard-word oath was sacred, unbreakable. This was not a matter of choice. As a consequence of swearing "by wind and word," the lips of a Halruaan wizard were magically sealed.

So there it was, then. Matteo's difficult task had taken a downturn into the realms of impossibility! He had twenty days to uncover a secret the king could not speak, a secret a nation of wizard-lords had not uncovered.

Twenty days, and each passing day left Tzigone alone, abandoned in a place of horrors beyond Matteo's imagining.

After a moment, he realized the king was studying him. "You are thinking of your friend," Zalathorm stated gently.

Matteo managed a faint smile. "I did not think any but a magehound could plumb a jordain's heart."

"She is her mother's daughter. Such women are capable of inspiring joy and pain in great and equal measure. I do not know a way to release your friend," he said, shrewdly anticipating Matteo's next question, "but may I make a suggestion?"

"Please!"

"Follow your heart where it takes you. Perhaps the daughter's secrets will shed light upon the mother's."

Matteo seized the king's arm, bringing them both to a stop. "Do you foresee this?" he said eagerly.

The king pulled away and fixed him with a searching gaze. "Can you conceive of any circumstance, jordain, in which you would willingly, even gladly violate an oath? Regardless of the cost to you, or the gain to another?"

Matteo hesitated, then shook his head.

"Then you are the better man. Once before, I paid love's price in honor's coin. I would do so again if I could free Beatrix. Since I cannot help the queen, I will bless the man who can and bear any cost to myself as a bargain."

Before the jordain could respond, Zalathorm simply disappeared.

With a deeply troubled heart, Matteo accepted the truth of his task. Zalathorm was as much a prisoner as either Beatrix or Tzigone, and the jordain's task was to free Halruaa's king.

Even if that meant destroying him.

# CHAPTER THREE

Deep, silvery mist—mist so thick it came just short of rain, so pale and chill it resembled shape-shifting ghosts—swirled a slow dance through the dismal landscape. The deep moss shrouding the conical fairy mounds was as sodden as sponge, and moisture dripped from blighted trees in maddening, oddly syncopated rhythms.

A small, battered figure huddled in the dubious shelter of a small stone cave, her thin arms wrapped around her knees. The cave, dank and cold though it was, offered at least the illusion of protection, and as Tzigone was finding out, in this place, illusion was a very powerful thing indeed.

One figment of Tzigone's imagination snuffled at a small, dark carcass. The griffin, though nearly as insubstantial as the mist, had fought at her command, and with beak and talons like those of an enormous eagle it had sent the Unseelie folk into retreat.

Her tormenters had left behind the body of a fallen comrade. Tzigone forced herself to study the torn and broken thing, hoping to find some vulnerability in her strange captors. The dark fairies were so quick that her eyes could not fully perceive them.

The dead fairy was closer to four feet than to Tzigone's five. Though Tzigone's form was waiflike, barely recognizable as female, she felt positively robust next to the delicate creature. Its skin was raven-black, its features even more narrow and angular than an elf's. Small, oddly shaped wings—crumpled but still beautiful—draped from narrow shoulders. They were of a strange, translucent black under which a rainbow of colors seethed and shimmered. The fairy's long, oval head had no hair and needed none. The eerie beauty of the creature discouraged any comparison to humans. The Unseelie were what they were, and they were terrible beyond imagining.

Tzigone allowed her gaze to slide away, hoping the creature nosing at the dark fairy's corpse would be gone by the time she glanced back.

It was not. In this place, nightmares refused banishment.

The monstrous illusion was like no living creature she knew. Matteo had told her when she accidentally conjured it that first time that no one had seen such a beast for nearly three hundred years. The long-extinct griffin had a monstrous draconian body, leathery, scantily feathered wings, and a primitive avian head. A thick mane surrounded its neck, and it crouched on powerful leonine haunches.

The monster plunged its wicked beak into the carcass and shook its head sharply. Flesh came free with a sickening, wet sound, followed by the snap of fragile bone.

Tzigone shoved her fist against her mouth and tried to replace horror with gratitude. After all, the misty griffin had given her a brief respite from the dark fairies and their relentless torment—torment that was mostly illusion but no less painful for that.

Somehow the Unseelie folk managed to get into her mind and heart. They tormented her with all the things they found in the dark corners and all the things her busy imagination could conjure. The monstrous griffin proved that sword could cut two ways.

Her nimble mind danced ahead to thoughts of escape. There had to be a way out of this gray world. She and Matteo had fought the dark fairies before, and it was apparent that Matteo knew little about their foe. That was a bad sign. In Tzigone's opinion, Matteo knew more than the gods had forgotten. If he couldn't deal with the Unseelie folk, what chance had she?

On the other hand, Dhamari Exchelsor had known how to open the veil between the worlds. Obviously there was a spell, and Matteo would find it.

"Dhamari," she murmured, suddenly remembering that he shared her exile. She rose painfully to her feet, gingerly testing her chilled limbs. After a few tentative steps, she set out to find the treacherous wizard.

She walked for a long time through the swirling mists. Finally, disgusted and weary, she kicked at a giant toadstool and watched the spores rise in an indignant cloud. At this rate, she'd never find Dhamari. If she could conjure illusionary creatures, why not a pack of hunting hounds?

That notion didn't appeal. During her street days, Tzigone had been chased by canine guardians too often to hold much affection for them. Besides, summoned creatures could be dangerous and unpredictable, even in the world she knew. She remembered the owlbear that had savaged her fellow travelers—and she fiercely banished this line of thought. Such memories could be deadly here. Instead she conjured an image of Dhamari's panicked face as she dragged him with her beyond the veil.

A faint, inchoate whimper nudged her from her reverie. She opened her eyes just in time to keep from tripping over the wizard.

Dhamari Exchelsor lay curled up like a newborn mouse. His sparse hair was soaked with perspiration, and his wide, glazed, staring eyes spoke of unending nightmares. The wizard was trapped in his own mind, tortured by his own misdeeds. Tzigone couldn't think of more fitting justice.

Justice or not, in this state Dhamari was of no use whatsoever.

With a sigh, Tzigone sank down beside the comatose

wizard and placed one hand on his shoulder. He was nearly as cold as the mist. She chaffed his hands and noted the chain threaded through his fingers. Curious, she tugged at the chain. A small medallion slipped out of his clenched fist, a simple, familiar-looking ornament fashioned from mist-dull metal.

Frowning, she felt around in her boot, where she'd last put her mother's medallion. It wasn't there. Somehow, Dhamari had taken it from her.

She yanked the precious trinket out of the wizard's hand. Dhamari's body jerked convulsively, and his mouth stretched into a rictus of anguish.

"This protected my mother against you and your agents," she murmured, understanding what ailed the wizard. "When you've got it, it protects you from yourself, which is probably the only reason you've survived this long."

On the other hand, the medallion also offered Tzigone a key to the past and the answers that might be hidden there. Surely anything she learned through her emerging powers would be more honest than anything Dhamari might tell her.

Just a little while, she decided. She closed her hand around her mother's talisman. Using the memory exercises Matteo had taught her, she sank deep into the past.

*The city of Halarahh lay sleeping beneath a coverlet of mist, oblivious to the young woman who ran the walkways atop the city's thick, stone walls. Swift she was, with slim, tawny limbs and an effortless gait that brought to mind a young doe. The watchwizards who kept the predawn guard nodded a respectful greeting as she passed, for Keturah's name was known in this city of wizards. She was small of stature, lithe and quick as a dancer, with an abundance of glossy brown hair and large dark eyes full of laughter and secrets and magic. . . .*

Tzigone jolted back to consciousness. This was her mother, seen more vividly than Tzigone could remember her! Quickly, eagerly, she thrust aside the epiphany and went back in, deeper, past the misty impressions into Keturah's own perspective. Dimly, in some corner of her mind, Tzigone realized she had *become* Keturah. Her hand tightened around the precious talisman, and she gave herself fully to the vision.

Tzigone/Keturah rested her elbows on the carved wall and began to hum as she gazed with contented eyes over the city, the heart of her beloved land and the home of the reclusive King Zalathorm. From her vantage, Keturah claimed a view a hawk might envy.

The sun edged over the highest peaks of the eastern mountains, fading the sapphire clouds of night to silvery pink. To the south, far out over Lake Halruaa, dense, gray storm clouds grumbled like titanic dwarfs roused too soon from their beds. The city itself awakened quickly, offering no arguments to the coming day. Carts and horses clattered purposefully toward market. Mist rose from the public gardens, jasmine scented, and with it wafted the lilt of young voices as singing maidens gathered dew for potions to court beauty and love. The brisk cadence of their song sped the task, for even in this, the coolest season, the sun's warmth came on quickly.

Keturah watched as sun-loving creatures began to emerge with the dawn. Winged snakes, brilliant as ropes of gemstone, took to the air. Orange and yellow lizards darted up the walls on broad, sticky finger pads. In the moat beyond the city wall, a roar like that of a bull crocodile lifted into the sky. An answering call rumbled from the gardens that flourished in the shadow of the great wall.

A concerned frown furrowed the wizard's brow. She ran down the flights of stairs leading down the inside wall and into the public garden. She stopped at the edge of a pond and began to sing in a clear, rich alto—a voice lovely in its own right but also full of magic's lure.

In response, a large reptilian snout thrust up from the pond. Golden eyes slashed with obsidian pupils fixed upon the singing wizard. In moments the creature undulated out onto the shore, revealing a behir, a beast more fearsome than a crocodile, more delicate than a dragon. Four pair of legs framed a long, serpentine body covered with scales of cobalt blue. The neck was long and graceful, and slender horns flowed back from a long, pointed head. Behir were as highly prized as swine in this city, but instead of bacon and ham and sausage, the exotic reptiles were apportioned for magical components and scrimshaw. It was a custom to which Keturah could never quite reconcile herself.

The behir paused uncertainly on the shore. Tiny blue sparks crackled around it as the creature snuffled, taking in the scent of Keturah's magic.

Her melody softened into a lullaby. Crystalline fangs flashed as the behir yawned hugely. The creature circled twice, like a drowsy hound, then lay down with its snout cradled on its foremost paws. The sizzles of magic faded as the behir sank into deep sleep.

Keturah kept singing, but she threw her hands out wide and began the gestures of a powerful spell of diminution. Each sweep and flow of her hands brought them closer to her center, and with each, the behir also diminished in size. Her casting continued until the twelve-foot creature was no bigger than a dragonfly.

She picked up the miniature behir and placed it on her shoulder. Instinctively the behir's tiny claws dug into the linen of her tunic. She set off for home, planning as she ran how and where to set the creature free.

Keturah stopped a few paces away from her tower and marveled, as she often did, that this estate was hers. Encircled by a wall was a series of fine buildings: servants' quarters, a guesthouse, a bathhouse, even a stable. Lush gardens were fragrant with flowering herbs and bright with the morningsong of birds. The crown of her estate was the wizard's tower, a tall, six-sided structure of green-veined marble, enrobed with flowering vines and topped by an onion dome roof of verdigris copper.

At five-and-twenty, Keturah was young to have such a grand home, but she was a master in the art of Evocation, a school of magic highly regarded in Halruaa and the most uncommon of magical talents. There was much demand for her time, and she was paid accordingly. The tower was hers in exchange for tutoring Dhamari Exchelsor, the only son of wealthy electrum miners and wine merchants. Keturah did not like owing her home to a single student, but this was common practice. Apprentice fees were steep. A truly gifted student never lacked for teachers, but aspiring wizards of moderate talent expected to pay dearly for their training. Dhamari's talents were modest indeed.

To his credit, he worked hard. Unlike some of Keturah's male apprentices, Dhamari showed no interest in her or in his fellow apprentices. Nor did he pester the servant girls. He was always proper, always polite and respectful. Keturah would have thought him cold but for his fascination with the newest apprentice.

She sighed, troubled by the turn her thoughts had taken. Kiva, an acolyte of the Temple of Azuth, had recently been sent to Keturah as part of the obligatory training in every school of the magical Arts. Kiva was a wild elf, a rarity in this civilized land. Her golden eyes reminded Keturah of a jungle cat, and Keturah suspected the elf was every bit as unpredictable.

Of one thing Keturah was certain: Kiva was a bad influence on Dhamari. He was intrigued by creatures of legend and dark magic, and the exotic Kiva seemed to inflame his imagination with possibilities. Of late he'd been asking Keturah for spells that would allow him to call and command creatures, as she did, but Dhamari had little talent for this particular type of evocation—or any other, for that matter. Very soon Keturah would have to encourage him to seek a new master and explore other schools of magic. The very notion filled her with nameless relief.

Keturah shrugged off these thoughts and strode through the outer gate. She stopped cold, frozen as surely as if she'd been halted by an ice dragon's breath.

Her neck prickled, and waves of gooseflesh swept down her arms. A second chill shuddered through her as her mind acknowledged what her senses had perceived: some dark and foul creature had invaded her home!

She began to chant a spell of discernment. Tendrils of bilious green mist—the manifestation of a powerful magic-seeking spell—twined through the air. Grimly she followed them into the tower and up the winding stairs. A sudden cacophony exploded from a room high above, and the mist was no longer necessary to guide her onward.

She sprinted up the final flights and raced toward the main laboratory. The heavy wooden door was closed, and it bulged and shuddered under the assault of some unknown power. Keturah summoned a fireball and held it aloft in one hand. With the other hand she threw open the door, leaping aside as she did.

The door crashed into the wall as a tangle of heaving, writhing vines spilled out into the corridor. Billows of smoke followed, bearing the acrid scent of sulfur.

Though Keturah could not see into the room, she could pick individual notes from the racket: glass vials shattering, fire crackling, priceless spellbooks thudding against the walls, furniture clattering as it overturned. A man's grunts spoke of pain and exertion, and a beautiful, bell-like soprano voice lifted in keening chant. Above it all rang a shrill, insanely gleeful cackle that tore at the ears like fingernails on slate.

"An imp," Keturah muttered. She left her fireball suspended in air like a giant firefly and began to tear with both hands at the vines blocking the entrance. "The idiots have summoned an imp!"

She managed a small opening and struggled through. For a moment she stood taking stock of the chaotic scene.

A richly dressed young man stamped frantically at a smoldering carpet. His boots smoked, and his thin face was frantic with terror and smudged with soot. He lofted his dagger with one hand, slashing futilely at the creature circling him like an overgrown gnat.

His attacker was a particularly nasty imp with a body the size of a housecat, enormous batlike wings, a yellowish hide, and a hideous face dominated by a twisted and bulbous nose.

The imp had been busy. The tapestries and drapes showed the assault of its claws, and the ripped edges smoldered from its touch. As the imp circled Dhamari, it spat little bursts of scalding steam, cackling with delight at the young man's pained cries.

Kiva stood over a potted lemon tree, chanting a growth spell. This was clearly not the elf woman's first attempt at containing the imp. The center of the room was dominated by an ornate cage fashioned from the vines of a flowering herb—an ingenious spell but for the fact that the cage door stood ajar. Imps were notoriously difficult to contain.

Keturah hissed out a sigh of exasperation.

Dhamari glanced up and caught sight of his mistress. Guilt and relief fought for possession of his face.

"Praise Mystra! Keturah has come."

His exclamation distracted the elf from her spellcasting. Kiva whirled toward the wizard, and the expression on her strange, coppery face changed from concentration to accusation, as if Keturah were somehow responsible for the rampaging imp.

"Do something!" the elf snapped.

At that moment, Kiva's future at the tower came to a certain end. Keturah set her jaw and reached into the bag tied to her belt. She removed a bit of powder wrapped in a scrap of silk—a charm of the sort any prudent evoker carried as a safeguard against a miscast summoning. This she tossed into the imp's path.

The silk dropped away and the sparkling powder stopped in midair, spreading out into a translucent wall. Batlike wings backbeat frantically as the imp tried to evade, but the wall caught and held it like a fly in sap. The creature struggled and shrieked and cursed, but nothing availed. Finally it fell into seething silence, yellow chest heaving as it eyed the wizard with murderous rage.

"Be gone," Keturah said quietly. As quickly as thought, both the creature and its magical prison disappeared.

The wizard turned to study the cause of this debacle. Kiva, despite her spell battle with the imp, looked as poised and polished as a queen. The elf was clad in a fine green gown and decked with matching gems. Her dark green hair had been skillfully coaxed into ringlets, and each curl glowed with the color and sheen of jade. Subtle paint enhanced her exotic features, and a complex perfume, green and wild and somehow disturbing, mingled with the scent of the plants that transformed the room into an exploding jungle. The elf was more than a hand's breadth taller than Keturah yet so delicately fashioned and exquisitely groomed she made the young wizard feel coarse and common. In Kiva's presence, Keturah often had to remind herself she, not the elf, was mistress in this tower.

"So you conjured an imp," she said coolly. "Deliberately?"

Dhamari and Kiva exchanged glances. "Yes," the young man admitted hesitantly.

"I see." Keturah swept one hand toward the wild, wilting foliage. "This, I suppose, is banishment that reverses this summoning?"

"You know it is not," the elf replied in equally cordial tones. "You have not seen fit to teach the necessary banishment spells."

With great effort, Keturah banked her temper. "Necessary indeed! It is unspeakably reckless to cast a spell, any spell, that you cannot counter. You didn't even carry a protective charm, did you?"

Dhamari hung his head, but Kiva merely sniffed, as if to mock so obvious a question.

"Both of you have forgotten several primary laws of evocation," Keturah continued. She ticked them off on her fingers. "Don't cast magic you can't counter, don't summon creatures you cannot banish, and never, ever summon any creature you can't handle."

*"A creature I can't handle,"* Kiva echoed, pronouncing each word with incredulous precision. "My dear Keturah, I've *handled* monsters far more imposing than a smelly yellow imp!"

Keturah held her apprentice's glare for a moment. She peeled the tiny, sleeping behir from its perch on her shoulder and carefully placed it on a branch of the lemon tree. "Very well, then," she said calmly. "If you're as knowledgeable as you claim, subdue this creature."

The elf glanced at the lizardlike creature and sent Keturah a look that, had it been on a human face, might have been called a smirk. Her delicate, coppery fingers reached for the tiny reptile.

Lighting bolts sizzled out of the behir, blackening Kiva's fingertips and sending her green hair dancing around her face like leaves in a sudden wind. She snatched back her hand, drawing her breath in a quick, pained hiss. The gaze she turned upon Keturah was coldly furious and utterly inhuman.

"You baseborn cow," she said softly.

A shiver coursed along Keturah's spine, for the contrast between the beautiful voice and the malevolent tone was chilling—as if she'd heard her death knell tolled upon fairy chimes.

She quickly pushed aside this dark fancy. "A wizard's reach must never exceed her grasp, Kiva, and a wizard's pride must be balanced by skill and knowledge. Remember this lesson, and the behir's sting will be well worth the pain. It is also your last lesson," she continued briskly. "You have until sunset to make arrangements with your temple and quit this tower. We will not meet again."

For a long moment the two females locked stares. Kiva broke away first, dipping into a deep and mocking bow. "If you say so, *mistress*, then it must be true." She turned and left the room, moving through the tangle of foliage with the sure, silent step of a jungle creature.

Keturah watched her go, her face troubled and thoughtful. Now she had one more culprit with whom to deal, and her anger returned in full measure as she rounded on the white-faced youth.

"If you wish to continue in this tower another day, Dhamari, you will give me your pledge, by wizard-word, never again to work such a spell!"

It was a harsh condition, but Keturah did not think it unjust. Such oaths were never asked or given lightly. There was no provision for regret or disavowal. No wizard could ever be foresworn, even if he dearly wished to be—not even if doing so would save his own life.

None of this seemed to concern the fledgling wizard. His boots still smoked from stamping out the imp's fires. His face was particolored like a painted harlequin's: pale on one side and on the other red from the bursts of scaling steam. His dark eyes were unfocused by pain and limpid with terror. As the implication of Keturah's words seeped through his distress, relief swept over his face like a healing tide. He took one of Keturah's hands in both of his and dropped to one knee.

"Mystra is merciful, but no more so than you!" he said fervently. "The Lady's blessing upon you! I was certain you would discharge me from the tower as you did Kiva."

"So I shall, if you do not swear. Kindly rein in your joy," she said tartly as she tugged her hand free. "What I ask of you is no small thing!"

"As you say, mistress," he agreed, but so great was his relief that he did not seem particularly abashed by the scolding. He rose to his feet and took a golden medallion from around his neck. On it was his sigil, a magical rune that was his signature and far more. This he gave her—a symbolic act showing he was quite literally in her hands. He pushed back his sleeves, closed his eyes, and held his hands aloft in an attitude of spell casting.

"By word and wind, sun and star, by the sacred flames of Lady Mystra and the magic She grants me, I swear that never in this life or any to come will I summon a creature I do not understand and cannot control." His eyes popped open, and he turned an earnest gaze upon Keturah. "This oath I swear gladly and freely, as I will any other you require of me!"

Sincerity shone in his eyes and rang in his tones. "It is enough," she said, relenting. She sent him to summon the gardener to clear away the vines and flowers. He left her presence swiftly, as if lingering might change her mind.

Left alone, Keturah started to sort through the mess. She returned two spellbooks to an empty shelf and began to kick through the vines in search of the rest. Her lips set in a grim line as she noted a burned and crumbled page entangled in the foliage. She freed the scrap of parchment and smoothed it out, hoping it was not from one of her precious books.

A glance told her it was not. Most of the page had been burned away, and what remained was brown and crisp at the edges, but she could make out a few oddly shaped characters. The markings were entirely unfamiliar to her: sharp, angular, elegant—yet somehow full of menace.

Keturah blew away some of the soot and ash and gave the scrap a closer study. She didn't recognize the spell or even the language, but she thought the markings looked vaguely Elvish. Full of foreboding, she left the laboratory for her private library, a small room housing the treasures inherited from her last master. From a hidden wall safe she took a large, slim volume.

The book was an artifact, the most valuable thing Keturah

owned. There were only two pages in it, electrum sheets hammered thin and perfectly smooth. On the left page was etched a blank scroll, and the right-hand page depicted an oval mirror and a smaller scroll. Each page was bordered by a complex design that upon careful inspection appeared to be fashioned of thousands upon thousands of runes, markings too numerous and tiny to be identified separately. According to Keturah's master, nearly every known spell was included in the tangle. The book could reveal the origin of any spell, and sometimes the identity of the wizard who had created it. Keturah had never tested the claim, for the price of such magic was high.

She set to work with a diamond-tipped stylus, painstakingly etching the strange runes onto the electrum scroll. When satisfied she had reproduced the spell fragment faithfully, she stood the open book upright on the table, angled so page faced page. She took a small candle made with costly spices and placed it between the pages, lit it, and began the words and gestures of the complicated spell. The silver-white sheen of the electrum "mirror" faded, to be replaced by clouded glass and a shadowy, featureless face. The scroll beneath began to fill with small, precise Halruaan runes.

She leaned close and began to read aloud.

"The spell is incomplete, and one of the runes is reversed and turned widdershins a quarter circle. The spell is likely Ilythiiri in origin. No wizard's visage comes to the mirror's call, but this much I, The Book, can say with certainty: the spell fragment is ancient beyond reckoning. Do you wish The Book to attempt a translation?"

Keturah leaned back and blew out a long breath.

*Ilythiiri.* The very word held terror, though it named a people gone from Halruaa since time out of mind. Ilythiiri was the name sages gave to the southland's dark elves, the ancestors of the evil drow.

Ilythiirian magic—by wind and word, what was Kiva thinking!

Keturah hurried to her treasure room to fetch gold and gems needed for the next level of inquiry. She closed the book to erase both scrolls, then opened it and recopied the spell fragment and the spell for translation. The treasure she placed in a small cauldron, along with a chunk of beeswax and an assortment of magical powders. She placed the cauldron on the banked coals of her hearth. When the wax melted, she poured the whole of it into a candle mold and waited impatiently for the spell candle to set. She set it alight and watched as the treasure melted away with the candle, lending power to the spell. New runes etched themselves onto the electrum page. As she read, Keturah could feel the blood drain from her face drop by drop.

The spell fragment spoke of the Unseelie Folk: dark fairies that haunted the mountains of Halruaa, mysterious creatures of such unfathomable evil even the drow were said to fear them. The rune that had been reversed and twisted was a charm of warding against these deadly fey folk.

"A warding reversed," she said slowly. "So the spell Kiva cast was not a warding but a summoning!"

Sweet Mystra! This explained why Dhamari had hesitated when she'd asked if they'd summoned the imp deliberately. The summoning was deliberate, but the imp's appearance had been a mistake, and a lucky one. Keturah was not certain she could have handled the dark creatures her students had intended to evoke!

The Lady be praised, neither Dhamari nor Kiva was skilled enough to breach the boundaries between the world they knew and the hidden realm of the Unseelie Court. Keturah was not certain she herself could do so, and she had no desire to seek an answer. Dhamari would not try again: she had his wizard-word bond on it. But Kiva . . .

Keturah leaped up from the table and looked around frantically for the scrap of parchment—important evidence if Kiva's ambitious were to be curtailed. The elf woman was a fledgling magehound. Keturah was not so young and idealistic to believe the Azuthans would rule against one of their own on her word alone. The clerics of Azuth, Lord of Wizards, were a minority in a land devoted to Mystra and were jealous guardians of their god's prestige and position. Most Azuthan priests were good men and women, but when faced with wizardly interference they became as defensive as cornered wolves.

Keturah's eyes fell upon the brown-edged scrap, nearly lost in a tangle of wilting vines. It had fallen from the table while she worked her spells of inquiry. She dropped to her knees and reached for the parchment.

Her fingers closed around a puff of green mist. It swirled through her fingers and wafted up to touch her face, and with it came a deep, green scent that was all too familiar. The mist abruptly disappeared, leaving Kiva's perfume lingering in the air like mocking laughter. . . .

Tzigone dragged herself from the vision and glared at the writhing, cowering Dhamari. Because illusion had such power in this place, she swore she could still smell the elf woman's perfume and the stench of sulfur in Dhamari's clothes.

She shook the wizard, shouting at him in an attempt to raise him from his self-inflicted torpor. He only shied away from her, flailing his hands ineffectually and pleading with her not to impale him with her horns.

"Horns," she muttered as she rose her feet.

For a long moment she watched the wretched man, a terrible person caught in a swamp of his own misdeeds. The urge to kick him was strong, but she shook it off.

"Grow a backbone, Dhamari! Thanks to you and Kiva, I can tell you from experience that it's possible to survive almost anything."

The wizard responded with a shriek of agony. Tzigone muttered a phrase she'd picked up on the streets and stooped beside him. Quickly she tucked her mother's talisman back into his hand. His screams immediately subsided to a pathetic whimper.

"I want you to survive," she told him. Her voice was cold and her eyes utterly devoid of the playful humor that had become both her trademark and her shield. "I'll find a way out of this place for both of us—and when this is all over, I'm going to kill you myself."

# CHAPTER FOUR

The waning moon rose unnoticed over the streets of Halarahh, its light shrouded by somber clouds rising from the pyres. Two dark-clad men slipped through the darkness to the wall surrounding the green-marble tower.

Matteo followed as Basel Indoulur—a powerful conjurer and the lord mayor of Halar, Halarahh's sister city—moved confidently up the wall. The portly wizard climbed as nimbly as a lad, finding handholds and crevices in the smooth marble that the jordain's younger eyes could not perceive. But then, Basel had known Keturah very well, and probably had reason to know the tower's secrets. What surprised Matteo was how well the man could climb and how much pleasure he seemed to take in this small adventure despite the seriousness of their purpose.

For the first time, Matteo saw a similarity between the wizard and Tzigone, who had been Basel's apprentice—and who was perhaps also his daughter. Matteo suspected that Basel might be *his* father, as well. Raised at the Jordaini College with no experience of family, Matteo nonetheless felt a bond between himself and these two disparate rogues, a bond as binding upon his heart as truth itself.

The two men clambered over the wall and walked

with quick-footed stealth through gardens fragrant with herbs. Dhamari, who had taken over the tower after Keturah's exile, had been a master of potions, and the narrow paths leading to the tower were nearly obscured by dense growth. The intruders made their way to the base of the tower without incident and stood for a moment eyeing the vines that seemed to erupt from the green-veined marble.

Basel caught Matteo's eye. With a rueful smile, he dropped his gaze pointedly to his own rounded belly.

"I'm twice the man I was last time I climbed this tower. Unfortunately, I mean that quite literally. Are you sure we can't use the front door? What place in all Halruaa is denied to the king's counselor?"

"None, provided I wish to have my actions scrutinized by the city council. Dhamari is a casualty of war. He named Tzigone as successor to his tower, but she is also missing, and she has not named an heir. Until the Council of Elders rules on this matter, the tower will be sealed against magical intrusion. If we disturb the wards on the doors or attempt to enter the tower through magical means, Procopio Septus will hear of it."

"Ah." Basel's face hardened. "Better a knife at my throat than that man looking over my shoulder." He glanced at Matteo. "I know he was your patron."

"Never apologize for speaking truth. For what it's worth, Tzigone held a similar opinion of our lord mayor. She called him 'Old Snowhawk.' "

"Among other things, no doubt. Well, let's get this over with." Basel began the chant and gestures of a spell.

Matteo had seen wizards employ cloaking spells before, but this was the first time he'd seen years peeled away by magic. Basel's face narrowed and firmed. Jowls lifted and disappeared, and the ravages cause by middle-aged resignation and too much good living faded away. But his twinkling black eyes were unchanged by the removal of a few lines, and his black hair was still plaited into dozens of tiny, bead-decked braids.

Basel winked at the staring jordain. "Dashing, wasn't I?"

Matteo responded with a wan grin. In truth, he had been searching the wizard's younger countenance for some reflection of his own face. Basel's features were rounded, while the jordain's face had been fashioned with bolder strokes: sharply defined brows, a determined chin, and a narrow nose with a decidedly convex curve. Matteo's hair was lighter, too—an unusual deep chestnut with flashes of red. At nearly six feet, he was tall for a Halruaan and considerably taller than Basel. Only their builds were somewhat similar: broad through the shoulders, with deep chests and well-muscled limbs.

The jordain was not the only one to note this resemblance. Basel winked again. "Let this be a lesson to you. See what can happen when you stop your daily weapons training? For good measure, I'd suggest you stay away from aged cheeses, red wines, and sugared figs."

Matteo tugged experimentally at the thick tangle of flowering vines. "If this venture fails, shall I include that advice in your eulogy?"

Basel snorted. "Since when was sarcasm included in a jordain's rhetorical studies?"

The young man shrugged and began to climb. Wizards' towers were protected by magical wards, but as Matteo had learned from Tzigone, mundane methods often proved more effective than counter spells. Even so, the method of entry into Keturah's former tower grated on his conscience. There was little about his friendship with Tzigone that did not.

By Halruaan law, Tzigone was a wizard's bastard, an unwitting crime that brought disgrace or even death. She was also a thief and a rogue, yet Matteo, who was sworn to uphold Halruaa's laws, shielded her at every turn.

Women, it would seem, tended to complicate life on a rather grand scale.

Basel hauled himself through an open third-floor window and dusted off his hands. "No sense climbing any higher. The place is deserted."

"Dhamari's servants don't seem particularly loyal," Matteo observed.

Basel's artificially young face turned grim. "With very good reason. Come."

He led the way up tower stairs to Dhamari's study. Matteo entered and scanned the vast chamber. It was like most other wizards' workrooms, but for an enormous corkboard stretched along one wall—a butterfly collection, from the looks of it. He went closer, and as he studied the creatures pinned to the wall, his distaste deepened to horror.

Dhamari had not drawn the line at butterflies. Tiny chameleon bats were neatly displayed alongside a desiccated fairy dragon and a tiny, mummified sprite. Several empty pins were thrust into the cork. Matteo pulled one and studied the fleck of translucent, papery blue that clung to it.

He showed it to Basel. "This looks like a scale from a starsnake's discarded skin."

The wizard muttered an oath. "I would give ten years off my life to know when and how Dhamari got that skin."

Matteo nodded, understanding the wizard's point. Twenty years ago, Keturah had been condemned as a murderer for her ability to summon these dangerous creatures. It was a rare ability, and after she fled, no one had thought to look for guilt elsewhere.

"How could both Tzigone and I have misjudged him so thoroughly?"

Basel reached into a small bag at his belt and took from it the talisman Dhamari had given Tzigone. "I've done a number of magical tests, and discovered that this is not Keturah's talisman but a copy—a very good copy, but one entirely lacking magic. At first, I thought the magic had faded after Keturah's death."

A logical assumption, except Keturah was not dead. Noting the bleak expression in the wizard's eyes, Matteo heartily wished he were free to tell Basel all.

"The original holds a permanent spell, very powerful, which protected the wearer from a particular person and all those who worked in his behalf," the wizard concluded.

"In Keturah's case, that would be Dhamari," Matteo mused. "Is it possible Dhamari kept the original talisman, using it as protection *against himself?*"

Basel whistled softly. "I wouldn't have thought the little weasel capable of such cunning, but that would explain how he concealed his real character and motivations."

"Why?"

"Ambition," Basel said shortly. "Shortly after Keturah took on Dhamari as an apprentice, she overheard him boasting that he would become both an Elder and an archmage. She told me this because she found it rather odd and quite out of character. Dhamari was a man of modest talent, and he seemed to understand and accept this. But enough talk. Let's find out how he got as far as he did."

They fell to work, searching the workshop and libraries for anything that might shed light on the spell Dhamari had given Tzigone—the spell that had hurled them both into the Unseelie Court.

Matteo quickly discarded scrolls describing poisons and transforming potion, lingering instead over anything that dealt with elven magic. This seemed prudent, as Kiva had played a part in Dhamari's goals, or perhaps vice versa. Finally, in the very bottom of a deep chest, he unearthed a moldering tome embossed with slashing, angular runes.

His heart danced wildly as he realized the significance of those runes. He strode over to Basel, carrying the spellbook with the same care and repugnance he would show a deadly viper.

"Ilithiiri," he said, handing the book to the wizard. "I have read legends of Halruaa's dark elves, but I never imagined that artifacts, even spellbooks, might have survived so long."

Basel placed the fragile tome on a reading table and began to page through it. After a few minutes, he drew a small parchment roll from his tunic and began to copy the dark elven spells.

"Is that wise?"

The wizard glanced up. "Is it wise to drink snake venom in hope of curing another snake's bite? If the ancestors of drow elves and Crinti bandits can help me counteract what Dhamari has done, I'll hand my entire fortune over to their accursed descendants!"

Matteo thought of Andris, imprisoned for aiding the treasonous Kiva. "Can any good come of evil?"

Basel sniffed and kept copying. "I could stick my head in the sand and pretend evil doesn't exist, but all that would do is present my arse as a convenient target."

"But—"

The wizard glanced up, his eyes sharp. "Do you want to help Tzigone, or don't you?"

As Matteo held the challenging gaze, his own stern conscience mocked him. "I'm coming to realize moral choices are often difficult and seldom clear-cut," he said at last.

Basel grunted. "I'll take that as a yes. Why don't you keep looking while I copy these spells."

Matteo held his ground, determined to tell the wizard what little he could. "Queen Beatrix will stand trial at the new moon. Did you know King Zalathorm has charged me with her defense?"

The wizard's eyes narrowed. "Yes, I heard. Why do you mention this now?"

"Since we are working together to free Tzigone, it seemed reasonable to ask your advice in this other matter."

"I don't envy you your task," Basel said bluntly. "Some of the artisans who built the clockwork creatures came forward to identify the ruins. Magical inquiry determined that all of these artisans worked for the queen and no one else."

"Yes." This was one of many disturbing facts Matteo's search had turned up.

"Perhaps you can prove Queen Beatrix intended no harm, no treason."

"I'm not sure 'intent' is relevant here. In recent years, the queen has not shown herself capable of logical thought. Also, any defense of this sort will be countered with stories of madmen and their acts of destruction. Halruaan history has its share of such tales. None of these insane villains escaped justice, nor will Beatrix if this argument is presented as her only defense."

"Perhaps you can prove her work was misused. Under Halruaan law, if a wizard creates a spell and a destructive spell variation is created and cast by a second wizard, the first wizard is held blameless. Beatrix made the clockwork creatures, but Kiva took them away and used them as warriors. If Beatrix had no understanding of Kiva's intentions—and it is likely she did not—perhaps she is protected by this law."

"If Kiva were available for magical questioning, this might be a reasonable defense."

Basel thought for a moment. "Have you considered the possibility that Beatrix's state of mind is the result of an enchantment?"

Matteo remembered the look on King Zalathorm's face when Beatrix said that she'd been enchanted—not by a *who,* but a *what.*

"This will be difficult to prove," he murmured, thinking of the oaths that bound Zalathorm to silence.

"Has the queen been examined by magehounds? By diviners?"

"She has. They can find nothing either to condemn or exonerate her. There seems to be a magical veil over the queen blocking any sort of inquiry."

A veil the king could not dispel, he added silently. He wondered once again why Zalathorm would put so important a task of divination upon the shoulders of a magic-dead counselor.

"You look troubled," Basel observed.

Matteo shook off his introspection. "It is a perplexing matter, but I thank you for your council. You have a solid grasp of Halruaan law, as I would expect from any former jordaini master—"

He broke off abruptly, but Basel's wide, startled eyes announced that the cat was already in the creamery. The wizard quickly composed his face and settled back in his chair.

"Apparently you have a good many things on your mind! Is there any particular reason for inquiring into my past employment, or are you inclined to fits of random curiosity?"

For a moment Matteo debated whether to follow this path. The need to know won out over propriety. "Yesterday, after the king named me counselor, you said we had matters to discuss." His heart pounded as he waited for the wizard to admit what Tzigone had hinted and Matteo suspected: Basel was his natural father.

The older man's expression remained puzzled. "I was speaking of Tzigone's rescue."

Matteo felt an unreasonable surge of disappointment. Not yet ready to let the subject drop, he asked the wizard what he had taught.

"Defense against battle wizards. Why?"

"That is a particular interest of mine. In the future, perhaps we could discuss it? That is, if you remember much from your years at the Jordaini College."

The perpetual twinkle in Basel's eyes dimmed. "Isn't there a jordaini proverb about memory being a curse as well as a blessing?"

"I don't think so."

The wizard's smile was brief and bleak. "There should be."

Basel's words followed Matteo into the palace dungeons. Just days before, he had delivered a prisoner to this place—a fellow jordain, and his oldest friend. The memory of that felt very much like a curse.

The corridors were uncommonly quiet and dark, and the light of Matteo's torch seemed to push uncertainly at the darkness. He rounded a corner and almost stumbled over a large, huddled form. He stooped over a particularly burly guard and touched his neck. Life pulsed beneath his fingers, faint but steady. Only a very skilled fighter could drop an armed man without harming him. That meant Matteo's quarry had passed this way.

The jordain stood and walked cautiously toward the archway leading into the next corridor. He dug a handful of flour from his bag and tossed a bit of it at the arch. No telltale streaks of light appeared amid the brief flurry of powder.

The jordain frowned. As queen's counselor, he'd made a point of learning palace defenses. This door should have been warded with a powerful web of magic.

He bent down and ran his hands over the smooth stone floor. There was a faint, gritty residue on the stone, a crystalline powder mingling with the flour. Matteo sniffed at the crystals clinging to his fingers and caught a faint, sharp scent.

"Mineral salts," he muttered. He rose and headed toward the eastern dungeon at a run.

Andris's cell was far below a mineral spring that served the palace bathhouse. Over the years, water had seeped through dirt and stone and left almost imperceptible deposits on the walls. Mineral salts were simple and common but powerful in knowledgeable hands. Certain witches used salt to contain magic within boundaries or to ward off magical attacks. Wizards used crystals to focus and amplify magical energy. Crystals could also scatter such energy. Mineral salts, hundreds of tiny crystals scattered in just the right place and at precise times, could disrupt certain spells. Andris possessed such knowledge.

After the battle of the Nath, Andris had yielded himself up to Matteo willingly, almost remorsefully. Why was he trying to escape now?

Matteo sprinted to the cell. As he'd anticipated, the door was ajar. A large key drooped from the lock, and two senseless guards sat propped up against the bars. He picked up a water pitcher from a large trestle table and dashed the contents into the guards' faces. The two men came awake sputtering.

He seized one of the guards by the shoulder and gave him a brisk shake. "Your prisoner has escaped. Tell me, how was he brought in?"

"The gargoyle maze," the guard muttered, massaging his temples with both hands.

"Sound an alarm, and send guards down the main gargoyle corridor. Tell them to extinguish the torches behind them as they go. They are to veer off into the moat passages and allow themselves to be heard doing so."

The guard struggled to take this in. "That leaves the long corridor unguarded."

"Leave that to me," Matteo said.

He got the men on their way. The trestle table was cluttered with gaming dice and empty mugs. He swept these aside and picked up the unattached table top. He balanced it on his head and walked quietly toward the end of the main gargoyle corridor—which, not incidentally, came close to the grated sewer tunnels, and the dungeon's best hope of escape.

The corridor was dark, and the faint smoky scent of extinguished torches lingered. Matteo kicked the heavy oak door at the end of the hall, closing it and throwing the hall into impenetrable blackness. He moved forward several paces until he found a crack in the stone paving, then eased the table down and wedged it into the crack. Letting the table lean toward him, he put his shoulder to it and waited.

His keen ears caught the sound of a light-footed man running barefoot. He braced himself just before someone hit the tabletop at a dead run.

Immediately Matteo threw the table forward and hurled

himself with it. Despite the double impact, the table jounced as a man pinned beneath struggled to free himself. Matteo's seeking hands found the man's throat.

"Be still, Andris. Don't make this worse than it already is."

There was a moment's silence, then a raspy voice inquired, "Matteo?"

"Who else would guess that you'd be counting off paces in the dark?"

A moment of silence passed, and Andris let out a muted chuckle. Matteo released his grip and rolled off the table. He tossed it aside and helped the winded prisoner to his feet. "Eighty-seven paces," Andris said. "Another five, and I would have slowed down for the door. You couldn't have backed up just a little, I suppose."

"The thought crossed my mind. Briefly." Matteo threw open the door, and faint light filtered in. Andris's translucent form was nearly invisible in the gloom, and he looked more ghostly than ever. His face, always angular, was gaunt and drawn.

He's slipping away, Matteo realized. The grief and dismay this realization brought surprised him. By now, he thought he'd be inured to the pain of losing his friend. He swallowed his dismay and leveled a stern look at the former jordain.

"Why were you attempting escape?"

"It's not what it seems. Though this might be difficult to believe, I was looking for you."

Matteo folded his arms. "Here I am. Here I would be, had you merely asked the guards to summon me."

"Do you think I didn't try?" Andris retorted. "They insisted the king's counselor has better things to do than listen to a traitor's prattle."

Matteo could see the logic in that. "I should have left instructions with the guards."

Andris shrugged. "You're here now. By the way, congratulations on your new office. I can think of no man more worthy of the honor."

"Please, keep repeating that thought," Matteo said dryly. "If words truly have power, they might turn that sentiment into reality. Now, what did you want to tell me?"

"I heard the guards speak of the battle against the Mulhorandi invaders," Andris began. "Was it true, what they said about the necromantic spells?"

"They could hardly have exaggerated."

"Who cast them?"

Matteo's brow furrowed. "To the best of my knowledge, the king did."

"Has he said so?"

The jordain considered this. "He hasn't denied it."

Andris gripped Matteo's arm. "What I'm about to say might be difficult to believe, but hear me out. Before I left the Jordaini College to rejoin Kiva, someone sent a blink bird to alert me to books hidden in my chamber. One of these books dealt with jordaini ancestry. I learned the name of my elven forebear. A name you know well."

"Kiva," Matteo said slowly. "She could be hundreds of years old, a living ancestor. That was why you cast in with her!"

"It was one of the reasons, yes, but that is a tale for another time. The other book was a grimoire, the spellbook of Akhlaur. Akhlaur the *necromancer.*"

"Gods above! Are you saying that spell was in the book? That it was a spell of Akhlaur's creation?"

"That and more. Matteo, Akhlaur is alive. He is *back.*"

Matteo stared at him in silence. "How is that possible?"

"I don't know, but it's the only logical explanation. Kiva had the spellbook for a while, but she was gone before the spell was cast. Any Halruaan wizard would be quick to claim such a feat. Zalathorm has neither claimed nor denied it. I suspect he has come to the same conclusion I have. He's allowing people to think what they will as he prepares for the inevitable confrontation."

Matteo's head whirled as he tried to assimilate his friend's grim logic. He didn't wish to believe it, but neither could he refute Andris's words. He blew out a long breath, then drew one of his daggers and took a bit of flint from his bag. A single deft movement produced a spark and set a wall torch alight. That accomplished, he turned to his friend.

"I think you'd better tell me everything you know."

Andris nodded. "Years ago, before Akhlaur began his rise to power, three young wizards, friends from boyhood, created a powerful artifact. This artifact was a symbol of their friendship. It joined them, lending the strength of all to each. This they did in response to dangerous times, for all three were active in Halruaa's defense. In youthful arrogance they called themselves the Heart of Halruaa. The artifact would protect them and their descendants, creating a legacy of guardianship."

Matteo jolted as he recalled a conversation with Zalathorm in which the king had hinted of powerful magic protecting the "Heart of Halruaa."

Andris noted this response. "What is it?"

"Not long ago, Tzigone and I were attacked by thugs and taken to an icehouse. Between us, we dispatched most of the men. The dead and wounded simply faded away. King Zalathorm told me that when the Heart of Halruaa is concerned, either the threat or the threatened are removed from danger. A similar thing happened when clockwork monsters went amok in the queen's workshop."

The ghostly jordain's eyes went wide. Matteo lifted an inquiring brow, but Andris shook his head.

"Never mind—a fleeting and unformed thought, not worth speaking. I suspect you came here to ask me to help you retrace Kiva's steps, to determine what role she played in the queen's downfall."

"That is true."

"I'll help you. In exchange, you must help me destroy the Cabal."

A burst of startled laughter escaped Matteo. "As if the two impossible tasks currently before me were not sufficient! Andris, I don't even know what the Cabal *is!*"

"I just told you."

Matteo sobered. "The artifact? The Heart of Halruaa?"

"Well, it's good to know that palace life hasn't made your wits less nimble," Andris said dryly.

"That does make a certain macabre sense," the jordain mused. "Yet all my life I've heard tales of a secret group of wizards who supported and controlled the Halruaan government in mysterious ways. You're saying there's no truth to these tales?"

Andris's faint smile held a world of bitterness. "Sometimes truth can be found only in layers of irony."

"If that's not a jordaini proverb, it should be," Matteo retorted. "How do you know these things?"

"I read Akhlaur's grimoire," he reminded Matteo. "I know why the artifact was created, and I know what it became. It must be destroyed."

Matteo regarded his friend for a long moment. "Once, I would have taken any course of action on your word alone. Forgive me, but those days have passed."

The ghostly jordain nodded. "Fair enough. You saw how the laraken drained the life force—the magical essence—of all the elves it encountered."

Matteo averted his eyes from Andris's translucent form. "Yes."

"Where did that magic go?"

He blinked, then frowned. "I assumed the laraken consumed it, as we do food."

Andris shook his head. "The laraken was only a conduit. The stolen life-forces are contained in the heart of an ancient, magic-storing gem."

"You're sure of this?" Matteo pressed.

"I saw a similar gem in the Khaerbaal Swamp. I brought it to Kiva. She shattered it. I saw the elven spirits, captive for centuries, released. Never have I seen such joy! Whenever following Kiva weighed heavily on me, I thought of that moment and my part in it."

Matteo nodded, understanding at last what had motivated his friend.

"Will you help me?" Andris pressed.

Still he hesitated. "You wish to destroy an artifact that supports King Zalathorm's reign."

"Why not? Wasn't it you who told me that no good can come of alliance with evil? You also spoke of conflict between a jordaini's three masters: truth, Halruaa, and the wizardlords. It is time for the truth to be told, and you may have to choose between your patron and the good of Halruaa."

Perhaps this, Matteo mused, was what Zalathorm had intended. Perhaps this Cabal was the mysterious "what" that held Beatrix under enchantment.

"I will consider," he agreed. "In exchange, give me your word that you will not escape. Swear this upon your elven honor."

Something bleak and cold thawed in Andris's eyes. "I didn't think you understood what that meant to me."

"I don't, entirely, but I'm learning the importance of heritage."

He extended his hand, and they clasped wrists like comrades never parted. "You won't come to regret this," Andris vowed.

"No need. I regret it already," his friend retorted, only half in jest.

The corridor ended in a locked gate. Matteo raised his voice to hail the guards. A small battalion promptly clattered up. Matteo singled out the man wearing a commander's insignia.

"You will release this man," he stated.

The guard bristled. "On what authority?"

Matteo merely lifted one brow, an imperious gesture that prompted Andris to swallow a smirk. The guard dipped his head in a nervous bow. "I do not presume to argue with the king's counselor, but this man just tried to escape!"

"I obtained his word that he will not escape from me. Did you?"

The guard opened his mouth, then closed it in a thin-lipped grimace. "No," he said after a moment.

Matteo nodded pointedly at the door. The guards set about unchaining the locks and removing the magical wards.

"You do that very well," Andris murmured as they strode down the corridor. A hint of his old twinkle had returned to his translucent hazel eyes, and shades of their former camaraderie added an amused edge to his voice.

Matteo sent him a sidelong glance. "My skills seem to be improving. I never thought the day would come when I could outsmart Andris. And with a trestle table! It is said that a man is equal to the weapon that fells him."

The ghostly jordain snorted. "Go ahead. Enjoy the moment."

"I intend to! At this rate, I will soon be able to best you in battle."

Andris's smile returned in full. "As a wise man recently observed, keep repeating that thought. If words truly have power, they might eventually turn into reality."

# CHAPTER FIVE

The aroma of strange herbs filled the air, and the soft music of reed flutes and long-necked stringed instruments followed Matteo down the corridor of the greenmage's domain, a wing of the palace where the palace servants and courtiers sought healing.

Matteo paused at an open door and gazed for a long time at the big man who lay, propped up with pillows, in a narrow bed. Themo, Matteo's jordaini friend and classmate, was finally awake after a long and unnaturally deep slumber. His eyes were open and focused, and he gazed out the window with a reflective air.

Matteo tapped on the doorframe. "The king's counselor, come to call," Themo said without looking over.

A smile pulled at the corners of the jordain's lips. "How did you know?"

"You're the only one who knocks. The greenmages burst in at all hours like rampaging orcs."

"At least you haven't lacked for company." Matteo came in and set his gift, a small bottle of golden haerlu wine, on the bedside table.

Themo seized the bottle and pulled out the cork with his teeth, then took a long pull. He wiped his mouth on the back of his hand.

"You were speaking of orcs and their manners?" Matteo teased in a dry tone.

The big jordain shrugged. "I'd better hammer while the forge burns and the iron is hot. You know how the jordaini masters can be about wine."

Matteo sat down in the room's only chair. "You seem resigned to returning to the Jordaini College."

"Have I any choice?"

The question was rhetorical, but Matteo answered it anyway. "Follow your heart, and become a warrior rather than a counselor."

Surprise widened Themo's eyes. "This is possible?"

"It is uncommon, but not entirely unknown. A dispensation from Zalathorm would free you from your vows." Matteo looked keenly at the somber-faced man. "I thought you would be pleased by this prospect."

Themo threw aside the covers and paced over to the window. He propped his hands on the sill as if he could not bear, unsupported, the weight he carried. "I'm not sure I'm meant to be a warrior."

"That's a strange sentiment from the best fighter to come out of the Jordaini College this decade."

The jordain let out a short burst of humorless laughter. "Truth, Halruaa, and the wizard-lords," he reminded Matteo. "You might be doing well for yourself in the last two categories, but seems to me you're falling a bit short in truth-telling. How many times have you pinned me? How many times has Andris gotten his blade against my throat? I'm the biggest among us, sure, but the best?"

"You have something Andris and I lack. You fight with passion, even joy."

He turned away. "So do the drow."

Matteo blinked in surprise, but then he saw the sense of it. "The dark fairies saw your love of battle, and turned it against you. That's what overcame you, and what causes you to doubt yourself still. They twisted it, Themo."

"Not by much," the big man responded. "During that battle, I relived every mistake I've ever made, and every dark secret I have. That wasn't all—it was like I was responsible, personally, for every wrongdoing in Halruaa's past."

Fear, bitter and burning, rose in Matteo's throat like bile. If Themo suffered so in a short battle with the dark fairies, how was Tzigone faring in the Unseelie Court? Until now Matteo had been able to temper his concern with memories of her quixotic sense of honor. Tzigone was no paladin, but she had courage and a good heart.

Yet if Themo could be tormented by knowledge of history, how much more torture could be extracted from Tzigone's gift of reverse divination? She could relive the past, bringing it back as vividly as a storytelling illusionist.

"Sorry, Matteo. Those who step in rothe piles shouldn't wipe their feet on their friends' carpets."

Matteo looked up sharply, startled by this odd and unfamiliar proverb. "Pardon?"

"I didn't mean to pile my troubles onto your shoulders," Themo rephrased, misunderstanding Matteo's sudden, somber turn.

He shrugged. "No magic, no penalty," he said, speaking a phrase they'd often used as lads. These chance-spoken words triggered an inspiration. As boys, they'd fought like a litter of puppies. Some of Matteo's fondest memories were the moments he and Andris and Themo and their jordaini brothers had spent pummeling each other into the dust.

"Palace life will be the ruin of me," he complained, patting his flat stomach. "Too much wine, not enough exercise. I'd be grateful for a practice match."

He noted the tentative interest dawning in his friend's eyes. "It would infuriate the greenmages, which would no doubt raise your spirits," he added.

"There's that," Themo agreed with a fleeting smile. The big jordain reached for his tunic. He pulled it over his head and buckled on his weapons belt. "Better go out through the window," he commented, glancing toward the open door.

Matteo followed him, climbing over the low windowsill into a courtyard garden. He glanced around the "battle-field." Low, soft, green moss grew underfoot, sprinkled with tiny, yellow flowers. A fountain played into a shallow fishpond in the center of the courtyard. The trees that shaded the garden had been trimmed so that the lower limbs were well out of reach.

He drew his sword and raised it to his forehead in salute. Themo mirrored the gesture, then fell back into guard position.

Matteo made a short, lunging feint. The big jordain wasn't fooled. He shifted onto his back foot and came back quickly with an answering attack. There was no weight behind it, though, and Matteo easily parried. The first, tentative exchange finished, they broke apart and circled.

"You are less familiar with a sword than with the jordaini daggers," Matteo commented. "Shall we change weapons?"

Themo grinned. "Feel free. I don't mind the extra reach."

As if to demonstrate, he brought his sword up in a high arc, swishing above Matteo's head. This left his chest unprotected, but Matteo was not tempted to attack. Despite his size, Themo was cat-quick, and coming within his longer reach would be foolhardy.

Instead Matteo ducked and spun, moving in the direction of Themo's swing. Rather than parry, he struck his opponent's blade, speeding it on its sweeping path and putting Themo slightly off balance.

The big jordain recovered quickly and brought his elbow back hard. Matteo leaned away from the blow so that it just grazed his tunic, then danced nimbly aside.

Themo came on with a series of jabbing attacks, which Matteo met in quick, ringing dialogue. They moved together, skirting the edge of the fishpond.

Matteo noted the glint in his friend's eyes and reviewed his memory of the courtyard's layout. The fountain was but two paces behind him. For a moment Matteo was tempted to allow his opponent to back him into the water. He quickly discarded this notion. Even if the ruse was lost on Themo—and that wasn't likely—Matteo had always thought deliberately losing a match was a lie told with weapons rather than words.

He shifted to his right and spun away. Three quick steps brought him up behind Themo. He swept his blade in, level to the ground and turned so the flat of it would smack the big jordain on his backside.

Themo took the taunting blow, then with a speed astonishing for his size he whirled and seized a handful of Matteo's tunic. He threw himself back, dragging the smaller jordain with him.

They went down together with a resounding splash. Matteo pulled away and got his feet beneath him—and promptly tripped over one of the pots that held water lilies.

The big jordain planted a hand on Matteo's chest and shoved. Down he went again. When he came up, sputtering, Themo was already out of the pond, grinning like a gargoyle.

"A wise fighter uses the terrain," his friend reminded Matteo.

The smaller man waded toward his opponent. "I didn't expect you to take the fight into the water."

"You should have." Themo lunged again. Matteo ducked under the attack and came up hard, knocking the sword aside with his blade and following with a punch just below the ribcage. Themo folded with a resounding "Oof!"

"Good one," he congratulated in strangled tones.

Matteo used the brief respite to climb out of the pond. He lunged suddenly, his sword diving low. The big jordain leaped over the blade and stepped back. His sword traced an intricate, circular pattern, a mixture of challenge and bravado.

On Themo came, his weapon leaping and flashing. With each blow, his grin broadened. His dark eyes sparkled with reborn joy as Matteo met each attack and responded in kind.

After many moments they fell apart, gasping for air.

"I won," Themo said in a wondering tone.

Though the match was a draw, Matteo did not disagree. What Themo had lost was his once again. Matteo made his farewells and spoke a few placating words to the thin-lipped greenmages who had gathered to observe the mock battle. As he left, he heard Themo's teasing responses to his healer's scolding, words that quickly drew the heat from her words. The last thing he heard was the greenmage's laughter, sounding surprised and pleased and entirely female.

Matteo chuckled, pleased that Themo could indulge his non-jordaini inclinations. He would not be the least surprised if the big man headed to the port city of Khaerbaal at first opportunity to renew his acquaintance with a certain good-natured barmaid.

His smile faded quickly. Tzigone, the friend who needed him most, would not be so easily rescued.

Never had Tzigone been so weary. Gasping for breath, she sank to the ground, not caring about the sodden moss, not feeling the chill.

They had come again, the dark fairies. This time they had pulled from her the memory of the first few years of her life, after her mother had been captured and she had been a child alone. For years Tzigone had sought to recover these memories, thinking to find in them the key to who she was. Now she was grateful for the darkness that had shrouded them for so long.

Tzigone flopped onto her back, willing herself to breathe slowly and deeply. She had run for what might have been hours, fleeing from one terrifying memory only to find herself enmeshed in another. She might be running still, but her Unseelie tormenters had released her. If they ran her until her heart burst, they would have no more pleasure from her.

Seeking rest and escape, she traveled deep into her memory—past the traumas of a street child, past the time spent as daughter of a fugitive wizard. The secrets of her own life had been bared. If there was answer for her, a way out of this endless prison, it was not in her lifetime, but her mother's . . .

It was twilight, Keturah's favorite time, and the three young wizards with her seemed as happy as she to be out under the open sky. The four of them stood on the flat roof of the guesthouse, watching as the setting sun turned the storm clouds over Lake Halruaa into a dragon's hoard of shining gold and ruby and amethyst. Behind them loomed Keturah's tower, its green-veined marble gleaming in the fading light.

Keturah watched as the apprentices practiced a simple spell of summoning. Earlier that day, she had taught them to call the bats that emerged with the coming of night—tiny, chameleon bats that changed color as they wheeled against the sunset clouds.

The youngest apprentice, a girl not yet in adolescent bloom, had donned gloves of bright pink silk. A bat landed on her hand, hanging from her finger like an endearingly ugly fuchsia blossom. The girl's laughter was happy and excited—childhood's magic blended with that of her emerging Art. Keturah chuckled in sympathy.

A bell tolled from the garden below, indicating a visitor too important to ignore. Keturah signaled the students to continue and headed for the stairs to answer the summons.

Her visitor was an elf, an exceedingly well-favored male with coppery skin and a strikingly handsome face. But for his traditional white garments and the bright blue, green, and yellow enameling on his medallion, he might have been mistaken for either a warrior or a professional male courtier. Keturah knew him by name and by sight, as did most of Halarahh society. King Zalathorm might be reclusive, but the same could not be said of his queen. Fiordella enjoyed grand fetes and festivals, and she was frequently seen in the company of Zephyr, her favorite counselor.

Keturah put the gossip firmly out of mind and exchanged the expected pleasantries. As soon as she could do so without offending proprieties, she asked what service she could render her queen.

"No more than is required of all wizards," Zephyr observed sternly. "You will follow Halruaa's laws."

Keturah blinked. "How have I failed?"

"You are not yet wed."

"That is so," she said cautiously, "but I am young, and in no great hurry."

"You are six and twenty," he pointed out. "Wizards are required to marry before the age of five and twenty."

"I have never heard of that law," she protested.

"Most wizards are early wed, so it is seldom necessary to evoke this law. But a law it is, my lady, and you cannot flout it."

"I suppose not," she said, and sighed. "I will consult a matchmaker before moondark."

"There is no need. The match has already been made."

Keturah's heart seemed to take flight, only to reach the end of its tether and thump painfully back into place. "It is the woman's prerogative to initiate the match!"

"There are exceptions," he pointed out. "From time to time, it is determined that one wizard's lineage is exceptionally well suited to that of another."

"Determined? By whom?"

"The match was submitted to the Council of Elders and approved."

Ordinarily, suggested matches could be appealed, but if matters had gone that far, there was no undoing them.

"Who was chosen for me?" she said resignedly.

"Dhamari Exchelsor."

Disbelief swept through her like an icy wind. "That is not possible! He was my apprentice. It would be unseemly."

"He left your tower nearly a year ago," the elven jordain pointed out. "His current master deems him ready to test for the rank of journeyman wizard, generalist school. His specialty is the crafting of potions. He will not require your tutelage in the Art of evocation."

Keturah took a long, steadying breath. "When two wizards matched for marriage are already acquainted, it is custom to consider the nature of their feelings. Never did anything pass between us that should lead to marriage!"

"He has already agreed. The match is made and approved. It is done but for the wedding feast, which I understand is set for this very night." The jordain cocked his head and considered the clatter approaching Keturah's gate. "That would be the Exchelsor family. As mistress of this tower, should you not greet them?"

Moving in a daze, Keturah went out into the courtyard. Dhamari Exchelsor entered the garden, his expression strangely shy. Keturah took a small amount of comfort from this. If she was to be overwhelmed by events far above her control, at least she was not alone.

Dhamari was closely followed by his family and their retinue. They had a priest of Mystra in tow and servants bearing trays upon which were arranged the traditional marriage items: a silver chalice, a scroll, a small, jeweled knife. One of the servants held a robe of crimson silk that was richly embroidered and encrusted with gems. This she held out to Keturah, clucking indignantly over the woman's simple tunic and bare legs.

"Now?" Keturah murmured, sending a look of appeal toward the queen's counselor.

Zephyr shrugged. "Why wait? The matter is settled."

Moving like one in a dream, Keturah allowed the servant to help her into the robe, to tie the marriage cord around her waist.

She echoed the spells of binding and drank from the

chalice when it was given her. When they handed her the ceremonial knife and pushed back the sleeve of her robe to bare her wrist, she stood for a moment studying the pulsing life beneath her skin.

As if he feared what she might do, the priest quickly took back the knife and handed it to Dhamari. He nicked Keturah's wrist, then his own. They pressed them together, a symbol of bloodlines mixed.

When at last the ceremony was over, the Exchelsor clan erupted into loud celebration. Dhamari winced and sent Keturah a shy, rueful smile.

"You look as overwhelmed as I feel, my lady. If you desire a few moments' privacy to catch your breath, I will try to keep the revelers away."

She nodded, grateful for his understanding, and slipped off in search of a quiet corner of the garden.

Dhamari watched her go, then sought out the queen's jordain. He found the elf lingering by the front gate, watching the celebration with narrowed eyes.

"The thing is done and well done," he said.

"Is it?" Zephyr countered. "You came here well before the appointed hour, before Keturah learned the reason for this match. By law, she must be told."

"She will be, when the time is right. Leave it in my hands."

When the jordain hesitated, Dhamari pressed a small, coin-filled bag into his hand. "Our lady has no need of wealth. She is enriched by your faithful service," he said meaningfully.

"And the potions?"

"I am qualified to administer them." He paused for a wistful smile. "You have not seen the wizard Keturah in a temper. It would be best if she hears the full story from my lips and in private."

"As you say." Zephyr handed Dhamari a wooden box.

Dhamari opened the box and took from it one of many tiny vials. He emptied the potion into the contents of a gem-encrusted wine cup. "We will begin this very night," he assured the jordain. "You may tell your lady that all will go as planned."

An odd little smile touched the elf's face. "She will be gratified to hear this, I'm sure."

"And please, convey my regards and thanks to the queen."

That strange, secretive smile flickered again. "I will do that, as well," Zephyr agreed, "although at a somewhat later time."

He punctuated this cryptic remark with a proper jordaini bow, then he turned and disappeared into the night with disconcerting elven grace. Dhamari shrugged and took a small packet from a hidden pocket of his tunic. He ripped off a corner and spilled the powder into the wine. For a moment the liquid fizzled and bubbled, seething as it turned a hundred shades of crimson and purple and green. Then, suddenly, it settled back into the sedate, aged gold of fine haerlu wine. Dhamari smiled with satisfaction and went in search of his bride...

Fury, pure and searing, tore Tzigone from the past and jolted her back to herself. Around her lingered the faint shadows of the green tower, and the garden full of ghostly revelers. Tzigone's eyes sought her mother among the shadows.

"She didn't know," the girl murmured, thinking of the potions which had shaped both her mother's destiny and her own. "That son of a scorpion poisoned her!"

Fury filled her, focused her. Tzigone swiftly fell back into her vision of the past . . .

Keturah's respite was short-lived. A member of the Exchelsor family, a stout, matronly woman whose name Keturah had never heard spoken, pounced on her like an overweight tabby and dragged her into the midst of the feasting. The bride stood with her back to the garden wall, an untouched plate of food in one hand, watching the celebration with the bewildered detachment of an ancient, fading wraith spying on the living. By wind and word, she could not understand why these strangers were so pleased!

Her new-made husband came toward her, a wine goblet cradled in both hands. There was a strange glint in his eyes that made her skin crawl. Keturah was no stranger to the ways of men, and she knew full well the response her face and form evoked. She took the cup from him and managed a single sip. Her stomach roiled in protest, and she turned away so that he could not read her revulsion.

Dhamari's mother chose this moment to bustle over. Dressed in cloth-of-silver, a reminder to all of her wealth in electrum mines, she rustled like aspen leaves in a gale.

"Where is your steward, daughter? There are arrangements to be made and apprentices to dismiss."

"Dismiss my apprentices?" echoed Keturah blankly. "Whatever for?"

The woman tittered. "You must have drunk deeply if you've forgotten the moon of seclusion! Lady Mystra grant, you will soon thereafter devote yourself to a mother's duties. There will be no time for apprentices for years to come."

Ambition gleamed bright in the woman's eyes, shedding light on the family's collective glee.

The Exchelsor family had wealth in great abundance, and they did not hesitate to use it to get what they wanted. They'd given her this very tower as Dhamari's apprentice fee. Their son was accounted a wizard, but his talents were small, and he would never be famed for his mastery of Art. But if he wed a wizard of power and growing acclaim, he might sire a child who could do what he could not. With Keturah's help, Exchelsor could be known as a wizard's lineage. In Halruaa, that was the path to nobility.

But if her precipitous marriage had no more basis than a merchant family's ambition, why had the Council approved it? Keturah did not believe the Elders could be swayed by wealth alone. What hidden gift did Dhamari possess that might make a child of their mingled blood so desirable? What could possibly have brought this matter to the interest of Queen Fiordella?

She looked around for Zephyr, but the elven jordain was not to be found.

"Drink," Dhamari urged softly, nodding at the cup Keturah clenched. "I put a potion into it to help you sleep. When morning comes, we will begin to make sense of this."

Because his words so closely echoed her own thoughts, Keturah lifted the jeweled cup to her lips. As Dhamari promised, each sip brought her deeper into blessed lethargy. She was dimly aware of the increasingly raucous wedding feast, and of the rising moon, and of her guests' snickering jests as Dhamari caught her when she swayed and carried her into the tower.

Then Dhamari was gone, and there was only the young apprentice, her childish face worried and perplexed as she helped Keturah out of her wedding robe and into her solitary bed.

Maybe Dhamari was right, Keturah thought as she drifted into slumber. Perhaps with the coming of dawn, all of this would start to become clear. . . .

The eerie song of the dark fairies pulled Tzigone away from the memory, drawing her back into the frenzied terror she'd so recently escaped.

She pressed both hands to her throbbing temples. "These things don't know when to quit," she murmured. With difficulty, she brought to mind an illusion.

The faint glow of firelight brightened the mist, revealing a cozy tavern bedchamber and two inhabitants—a lad dressed in a farmer's clothes and a red-haired woman clad in flowing layers of black silk. She drifted closer and smiled at her suitor. Fangs, long and lethal, gleamed in the firelight. The boy backed away, tripped over a stool, and crab-walked frantically toward the door. Faster than thought—as fast as the dark fairies—the beautiful vampire moved to bar the way. Her delicate hands seized her prey and jerked him upright. For a long moment she held him trapped, savoring his terror. Then she lowered her head and fed. After a few brief moments, she tossed him aside. He fell to the floor, drained and still.

*"Blood is a pale thing next to the wine of fear,"* she whispered.

The illusion faded away, and with it, the dark fairies' tormenting song.

A smile ghosted across Tzigone's face. "The Unseelie have their faults, but no one can claim they can't take a hint," she grunted, and then sank back into her borrowed memories . . .

Mist swirled, then parted to reveal Keturah standing on a narrow balcony encircling her tower, a private place sheltered from the intense heat by the shade of the onion dome just above and shielded from curious eyes by the soaring height of the tower. Here she came often to walk alone.

A year and more had passed since Keturah's strange wedding. She no longer took apprentices, for reasons she feared to admit even to herself. Her most frequent companions were the creatures that came to her call.

The wizard propped her elbows on the wall and watched as a starsnake glided by on iridescent wings, looking like ropes of jewels against the sapphire sky. She began to sing, and her voice was strong and sure as it rose into the wind.

The creature winged past, heedless of her call.

Keturah's song died abruptly. She buried her face in her hands and drew a long, shuddering breath. This was not the first time that her magic had failed her. Over the past few moons, it had been growing increasingly unreliable.

For some reason she had kept these small failures from Dhamari. This was not a difficult thing to do. He spent most of his time working alone. Potions fascinated him, and he was absorbed with the creation of a spellbook that would ensure the fame of the Exchelsor wizards. Oddly enough, since their wedding he had done nothing else that might establish his lineage and legacy.

Their first days of marriage, the traditional moon in seclusion, had been a puzzlement to Keturah. By day they had walked on the shore, calling creatures of the sea and watching them splash and play in the cresting waves offshore. She had shown Dhamari the spells for summoning giant squid and teasing from them sprays of sepia that could be captured and used as a component for wizard's ink. They had spoken with selkies, watched the dolphins at play, but it seemed that they had once again become mistress and apprentice. Dhamari was polite, respectful, detached. He left her at the door to her bedchamber each night and returned to his studies.

This pattern continued after their return to Halarahh and to Keturah's tower. Dhamari was unfailingly courteous. They ate together each evening, and he poured exquisite wine from the Exchelsor cellars and engaged her in learned conversation. Their association was not altogether unpleasant, but neither was it a marriage. It was not even a friendship, and Keturah could not bring herself to confide to this stranger her concern over her waning power.

Keturah watched the starsnake disappear into the sunrise clouds. She hadn't been able to gather enough magic to get its attention, still less compel its will!

She cloaked herself with magic and with a wrap of flowing silk, then quietly made her way across the city to the home of the greenmage Whendura. There were many such physicians in the city, minor wizards and priests who had studied the magehound's art as well as divination and herbal lore. The common folk had their midwives and clergy, but a wizard's health was so bound up in Art that a special set of diverse skills was needed. Whendura was well respected, but her home was far from the fashionable coast, a location deliberately chosen to give clients a sense of privacy and security—or, as much as such things existed in Halruaa.

Whendura, a small, plump woman who looked as if she ought to be plying grandchildren with honeycakes, met Keturah at the door with a warm smile. She ushered her visitor up two flights of stairs to a small room, chatting cozily as she pounded herbs and mixed them with watered wine. Keturah stripped down to her shift and set aside all her spell bags and charms and wands, so that nothing magical might confuse the greenmage's tests. She drank the green sludge Whendura offered, then endured a long list of questions and much magical poking and prodding.

At last Whendura nodded and began to gather up her wands and crystals. "So much magic within you," she said respectfully. "It is a great gift that you give Halruaa!"

Keturah frowned. "I don't understand."

The greenmage's busy hands stilled, and a flash of compassion lit her eyes. "Don't fret over it," she all but crooned. "It is often so. The potions can bring confusion."

"Potions," Keturah echoed without comprehension. "Confusion?"

Whendura gave her a reassuring smile. "It will be different when the babe is born," she said gently as she continued to gather up her tools. *"May Mystra grant,"* she added under her breath.

Keturah realized that she was gaping like a carp. "Babe? What babe?"

It was the greenmage's turn to be astonished. "You are not with child?"

"No," she said flatly. "It is not possible." How could it be, when her "husband" had never once crossed the threshold of her bedchamber?

"Then why have you come for testing?"

"I told you," Keturah said impatiently. "My magic is diminishing in power and reliability. To whom should I come but a greenmage?"

Pity and comprehension flooded the woman's face. "It is always so, for a jordain's dam. Do not look so shocked, child," she said, clearly distressed by what she saw in Keturah's face. "You were told all of this, but sometimes a woman loses memory along with magic."

The truth slammed into Keturah with the force of a monsoon gale. She was being prepared to give birth to a jordain!

Keturah forced calm into her reeling mind and brought forward what she knew of such things. Though jordaini births did occur unaided from time to time, it was more often a rare and highly secret procedure, involving potions that stopped the hereditary transfer of magic from mother to child.

So that was the reason why Dhamari was content to leave her at her door each night! Their match had been granted because it had the potential of producing a jordaini child. Keturah thought of the spiced wine they drank during their shared evening meal. No doubt he'd been slipping her potions to shape the destiny of their eventual child. He would not risk disrupting the process before it was completed.

Why would he do such a thing? Never was this fate imposed upon a woman without her knowledge and consent!

Wrath, deep and fierce and seething, began to burn away her confusion. The parentage of the jordaini counselors was held in secret, but great honor was afforded wizards who gave a counselor to the land. It was a sure way for a wizard to advance in rank and status, and none need know the reason. Despite the vast power of Halruaa's magic—or perhaps because of it—many children died in infancy. A potential jordain was taken from his mother's arms and listed in the public records as a stillbirth, lost among the many babes born too frail to carry the weight of Halruan magic. Never would the parents know the name or the fate of their child, and never would the public know why certain wizards acquired rare spellbooks, choice assignments, or even positions on the Council of Elders.

All this Keturah's friend Basel had told her late one night, shortly after the death of his wife and newborn child. His description of this secret process had carried the bitter weight of a confession.

Keturah heard the greenmage's voice in the next room and the soft, mellow chimes that opened the scrying portal. She crept to the door, pushed it open a crack, and listened.

"So great a sacrifice!" Whendura said, speaking into the scrying globe. "If Keturah has lost this much memory so soon, I fear her mind will not survive the birth of the child."

"You did well to contact me. I had not realized it was so bad with her." Dhamari's voice floated from the globe, resonant with earnest concern. "Childbearing does not come easy to Keturah. In the morning she wants no one near her. Sometimes her sickness lingers until highsun. Is there no potion that can relieve her suffering?"

The ringing sincerity in his voice made Keturah want to shriek with fury.

"You know there is not," the magehound said sternly. "She cannot take any magical potion of any kind, for fear of altering the delicate balance and harming the child."

Keturah's eyes widened as a grim possibility seared its way into her mind. Dhamari knew her devotion to Halruaa. If she were chosen as a jordain's dam, she would find a way to accept her fate. Yet he had made sure that she knew nothing of this.

"Keep my lady with you," Dhamari went on in his gentle voice. "She is too confused to travel alone. I will come presently and collect her."

Keturah hurried to the window. A tall iron trellis covered with pale lavender roses leaned against the wall, leading down into the greenmage's garden. As she eased herself out and began to climb down, she blessed Mystra that Dhamari had never had much talent for travel spells. He would have to depend upon their stables. The ride to the magehound's home and back granted Keturah some time.

Once she reached the ground, she conjured a travel portal and leaped through it. She emerged not in her own home but in the public gardens, near the pool where she had found the blue behir nearly a year ago.

For a moment she considering attempting another gate spell but was afraid what the next random location might be. She set off on foot, hoping that the sedate mare Dhamari usually rode kept to its usual, plodding pace.

After what seemed an eternity, she reached her tower. She raced up the stairs to gather a few belongings and seek some answers.

"Mistress."

Keturah stopped on the stair landing and whirled, regarding a woman with a face similar to her own, yet somehow coarser and lacking in symmetry.

"What is it, Hessy?"

'Did you see Whendura the greenmage this morn?"

Keturah blinked. "Yes. What of it?"

"She is dead. I heard it cried in the marketplace." Hessy swallowed hard. "It is said she was killed by starsnakes."

"A starsnake? At this hour? Unless she climbed one of the bilboa trees to accost one in its sleep, that seems unlikely."

"She was attacked in her own tower. They say there must have been at least three of the snakes."

Dread began to gnaw at Keturah, giving way to growing certainty. The winged snakes never ventured within human dwellings. They were also fiercely solitary creatures, capable of bearing young without need for another of their kind. They avoided each other assiduously—never had she seen more than one of them in the same place. Though starsnakes had a high resistance to magic, no natural starsnake would attack a wizard—unless compelled to do so by a powerful spell.

Keturah began to see the shape of Dhamari's plan. He could not allow the sympathetic greenmage to become Keturah's ally for fear of what the two women might together discover. Keturah would be confined to her tower, under Dhamari's care, until the birth of the valuable child. Then she would be turned over to Halruan law—if indeed she survived the birth with her mind intact—and the child would be Dhamari's to control. No doubt a magehound would detect some spark of magic in the babe, and the child would be rejected by the jordaini order. Everyone would regard this as a tragic waste and look upon Dhamari with great sympathy.

Oh, but he was clever! The only flaw in his plan was Keturah was not yet with child. He probably had spells prepared to entrap her long enough to remedy this lack.

"It was Dhamari who found Whendura, I suppose." Her voice was harsh as a swordsmith's rasp. "Or what little was left of her?"

Hessy nodded, and her eyes confirmed Keturah's unspoken suspicions. "The militia are questioning her servants about who came before him. He has not been truth-tested for her death. The militia did not deem it necessary, as he is a maker of potions and not a wizard known for his ability to summon such creatures."

"Unlike his wife," Keturah said bitterly. "Yes, Dhamari can be very convincing."

"They will test you," Hessy said hopefully. "They will learn the truth."

Keturah shook her head. "He has been giving me potions that confuse magical inquiry. Whendura thought I was with child, and she is among the best greenmages in the king's city. The council will wait until after I have given

Dhamari a child. By wind and word, that I will never do!" she swore. "Let the mangy whelp of a rabid jackal find me if he can!"

The servant hesitated, then pressed a bit of bright metal into Keturah's hand.

"Wear this talisman wherever you go," she whispered urgently. "It will tell you when Dhamari is near, or those he sends."

Keturah stared at the servant in puzzlement. "This is a rare and costly thing. How did you come by it?"

The girl attempted a smile. "You pay me well, and my needs are small. I saved every coin I could, hoping that when the time came, I could see you safely away."

"When the time came?"

"I clean his lab," Hessy said flatly. "I have seen the spells he creates. Forgive me for not speaking of what I knew!"

Many wizards enspelled their servants and apprentices to keep them from betraying secrets. Even so, Hessy's concerns were for her mistress's safety and not her own. Words utterly failed Keturah. She opened her arms, and Hessy rushed into them. For a moment the two women stood clasped in a sisters' embrace.

Keturah pulled away and walked to the open window, chanting a spell as she went. Hardly caring if the spell held or not, she stepped out into the wind . . .

Tzigone hit the ground facedown, landing with a spine-numbing jolt and a solid splat. She pushed herself off the mossy cushion and rose to her feet, wiping the moisture from her face. For a while she paced, waiting for the last lingering shadows of her vision to fade. When all she could see was the bleak expanse of rocky moor, she sat down with her back against one of the jagged standing stones that littered the dark fairies' realm.

So there it was—the beginning of her story. For years,

Keturah had evaded Dhamari's pursuit, finally falling into the hands of Kiva, the elven magehound. Somewhere in between, Tzigone had been born.

That was interesting, but Tzigone didn't see how it could help her get free of this place. She would try again . . . later. Right now she was bone-weary, soul-weary.

Even so, she gathered her small remaining strength and sank back into recent memory. When she opened her eyes, a tall, solid figure stood over her, arms crossed and an expression of fond exasperation on his face. The illusion of Matteo was nearly as ghostly as the form of his friend Andris, but Tzigone took comfort from the illusion of his presence.

She raised her eyes to his shadowy face. "Good news, Matteo. Dhamari is not my father."

*You're sure of this?* inquired the illusion with typical jordaini skepticism.

"Positive. I saw it in one of those past memory trances you taught me to do. The little weasel never even made an attempt at fatherhood. You'd think all those wands and chalices and crystal balls that wizards have lying around would plant the idea. The man has no appreciation for symbolism! He never once cast a spell, if you follow."

Matteo's misty visage furrowed. *No spells? But Dhamari is a wizard.*

Tzigone groaned. "I'll put this in terms a scholar can appreciate: either there was no lead in Dhamari's stylus, or he was just never in the mood to write."

A faint flush suffused the illusion's face. *You saw this?*

"There wasn't much to see, praise Mystra." The amusement faded from her eyes, and she studied Matteo for a long moment. "None of this is real, you know. Nothing here is real, anyway, and I wouldn't bet on whatever's happening back in Halruaa. Life is mostly illusion and wishful thinking, isn't it?"

*Yes.*

"You're the only person I've ever known who is exactly what he seems." She grinned fleetingly. "I'm sorry for all those times I called you boring and predictable."

*No you're not,* Matteo's illusion responded.

Tzigone chuckled. "Well, maybe not *all* those times."

She began to drift, and leaned back against the stone. "Stay with me for a while?"

*Always.*

Because this was the Unseelie court and because illusions had great power here, the answer Tzigone heard was what she needed to hear. As the exhausted girl sank toward sleep, she realized that truth, in its purest form, was quite different from fact. Matteo was worlds away, but he was truly with her.

The familiar warmth of her friend's presence enfolded her like a cloak. Drawing it around her, Tzigone settled down to sleep while she could.

The dark fairies would return soon enough.

# CHAPTER SIX

**T**wo figures strode across the swamp water surface, confident in the spells that allowed them to traverse the murky water as easily as a northman might cross a winter-frozen pond. Despite their reliance upon magic, both these travelers looked utterly at home in this wild place.

Kiva's coppery skin and jade-green hair proclaimed her a native of the jungles. The colors of her beauty blended with the lush foliage, and her movements held the subtlety of shifting shadows. The human's scaled, faintly green skin, the gills on his neck, and the webbing between his fingers suggested a creature well suited to places where air and water mingled.

The amphibious wizard halted, leaning on his staff as he rested. For several moments the only sounds were the voices of the surrounding swamp, the faint crackle of energy that surrounded the wizard's staff—a living but stiff-frozen eel, hard as mithral—and Akhlaur's labored breathing.

"The air is thin. Two hundred years in magic-rich water cannot be countered in mere days," he snapped at his companion, as if she had chided him for some weakness.

Kiva lifted her hands in a defensive gesture. "This jungle has always been difficult for humans. Surely you remember the last time you were here."

Akhlaur's thin lips curled in a sneer. "Not so difficult. The natives died as easily as those in any other place."

The wild elf bit back her outrage and kept her face calm. "When you are ready, we should move on."

They pressed deeper into the Kilmaruu Swamp, the site of Kiva's first great victory. Twilight gloom settled over the swamp as they neared a swift-running river bordered by deep gorges and spanned by the remains of a bridge fashioned from a single, enormous log.

Akhlaur regarded the skeleton of the three-horned creature sprawled across the blackened wood. His face took on a dreamy expression, as if he were lost in fond memory.

"Monsters from Chult—I'd almost forgotten that spell! Bringing them here was difficult but worthwhile. The wild elves had never seen such creatures before. Quite amusing."

"No doubt," Kiva said flatly. She pointed toward the opposite bank. "That way."

The necromancer eyed the apparently impenetrable forest wall. "It did not look so when last I came through. There were terraced gardens amid the trees."

"Two hundred years," the elf reminded him. "The jungle covers all and forgets nothing."

He sent her a sharp glance. "That sounds suspiciously like a warning, little Kiva."

"A proverb," she said mildly, "of a sort often spoken by the jordaini. During your exile, these sayings have infested the Halruaa language like gnats upon overripe fruit."

"So much for my gift to Halruaa," Akhlaur observed. "It is said that no good deed goes unpunished!"

Several responses came to Kiva's mind, all of which were almost guaranteed to kindle the necromancer's rage. She acknowledged his ironic proverb with a nod, then led the way across the log bridge. They crawled through the rib cage of Akhlaur's creature and passed into the forest. The wizard followed her down long-forgotten elven paths that no human, magically gifted or not, could ever see.

Night fell, and the path traced a steeply sloping hill. They skirted several ravines and pits—all that remained of the elves' outer defenses. Finally they stood within the crumbling walls of the ancient elven city.

Moonlight filled the courtyard, lingering on the blackened, vine-covered ruins.

Akhlaur looked about in dismay. "What happened here? Pillage I could understand, had it been widely known that elves lived in this part of Halruaa! But this was a hidden city. Certainly a few learned wizards suspected its existence, but sages and looters seldom drink from the same bottle."

"Not looters, Lord Akhlaur, but time. Time and Halruaa herself conspired in this destruction."

"I am not one for riddles," he warned.

She took a moment to choose her words. "The destruction of Halruaa's elves could not have been accomplished by one wizard, not even one as powerful as you. During your rise to power, all of Halruaa looked the other way and pretended not to know."

The necromancer looked at her as if she'd stated that most of the trees were green. "You are just now discovering the nature of humankind? Even those who consider themselves virtuous see only what they wish to see. *Especially* those who consider themselves virtuous! After all, illusions, once created, must be maintained."

"Yes, my lord," she agreed, though his observation made little sense to her.

A strange silence hung over the city as they worked their way over piles of crystalline rubble toward the treasure Akhlaur had left here.

Kiva stopped at the door of the elven temple, staring in revulsion at the scene before her. What had once been a place of great beauty and serenity now resembled an abandoned charnel house.

Bones lay in tall heaps. Long, delicate elf bones were tumbled together with the thick, yellowed remnants of humans, swamp goblins, even such creatures as birds and crocodiles. Many of the bones had been blackened and broken, probably by the explosion the clever jordain Andris used to break the charge of the undead creatures. Kiva wondered how long it had taken for the shattered, scattered remains to gather themselves and return to this place.

She glanced at Akhlaur. He nodded, and she stepped over the threshold.

The intrusion triggered defensive wards. Shudders ran through the piles of bone. With a horrible clatter, the undead guardians rose.

Elven bones skittered across the floor, cast aside as the other creatures took shape. Kiva's eyes narrowed, as if to hold back the gleam of triumph they held. The elves whose bones these were had passed far beyond Akhlaur's power.

The others, however, had not. A skeleton of gray stone, the unmistakably squat and sturdy frame of a long-dead dwarf, lofted a giant's thighbone like a club and stalked forward. The floor around the undead dwarf writhed as hoards of giant snakes and crocodilian skeletons undulated forward, their naked fangs grinning wickedly. Other skeletons marshaled behind this undead vanguard, some of them entire, some partial creatures that limped or hobbled or crawled toward the intruders.

The necromancer chanted softly, gesturing toward the advancing army, directing them to go here and there, as if he were a master of dance. The advancing wall of undead creatures parted, moving to face each other in two long lines.

A sharp crack rang through the temple as every bipedal creature snapped off one of its arms and held it aloft with the other, forming an arch to honor and welcome their master.

Akhlaur swept through the grisly arch to the temple's most sacred and powerful place. The elf followed, suppressing her disgust with great difficulty.

So much magic, and for what? Would humans never learn that just because a thing *could* be done, it did not follow that it *should* be? For all their complacency, their careful laws and customs, Halruaans had not fallen far from the tree of their Netheril ancestors.

Akhlaur stopped abruptly. For a long moment he gazed in consternation at the empty altar.

This was the most dangerous moment. All Kiva's wiles would be tested here.

The necromancer turned furious eyes upon her. "Where is the globe?"

Kiva just shook her head, as if she were too stunned to speak. "Stolen," she marveled at last. "It must have been stolen."

"What wizard could get near this place?"

She suppressed a sneer. Of course Akhlaur would assume that only a Halruaan wizard would be capable of such a feat! "None, my lord," she said hastily. "I heard rumors, though . . . "

"Speak!"

"There were tales of an army of magic-dead fighters. Jordaini, mostly."

An expression of extreme distaste twisted the wizard's face. "Again, these *jerdayeen*," he scoffed, using the old Netheril word for *court fool*. "Not one of my more successful experiments."

"Yet these fools have become highly regarded counselors in Halruaa." Akhlaur chuckled at her words, and Kiva added, "Even the king employs them."

Her tone was innocent enough, but her words had the desired effect. Speculation crossed Akhlaur's face, quickly chased by wrath.

"Zalathorm," he muttered. "*He* sent the jordaini in. He has the globe!"

Kiva nodded slowly. "It is possible. Who else could have known so much about your magic and about these elves?"

Who else indeed? she thought. For a moment, Kiva relived the flash of joy—an emotion she had thought banished from her heart forever—that she had known when Akhlaur's green crystal shattered and the trapped spirits within took flight.

Akhlaur turned and stalked back through the skeletal arch, muttering as he went. "Two globes missing, and with them all the magic they held! Thousands of spells, hundreds of life-forces—all that, stolen. By curse and current, Zalathorm will pay!"

A sly, satisfied smile crossed the elf woman's face. She quickly banished it. "You were so close, Lord Akhlaur. Had Zalathorm not interfered, you would have gathered the lion's share of Halruaa's magic into your hands. As you will yet do," she added hastily when the necromancer shot a glare over his shoulder.

"On that you may depend," Akhlaur grumbled. "I have other bases, other sites of power. They will be more than enough."

When they emerged into the ruined courtyard, he swept both arms wide. A shimmering oval appeared. Akhlaur stepped through—

And sank like a stone into miry water.

Kiva emerged from the magic gate behind him, walking lightly on the swamp water. She, unlike Akhlaur, had been expecting this wet reception.

The wizard shot out of the water and settled down beside Kiva, looking none the worse for his dunking. He looked about him in consternation. "What is this place?"

"You knew it as the Swamp of Ghalagar, my lord. Now it bears your name."

He nodded, remembering. "My tower stood here before Zalathorm and his wretched band of charlatans moved it. Where is the rest of the estate?"

"The prisons were there," Kiva said, pointing to a dense growth of flowering vine. "Where we stand, the gardens once grew. There was a leak, you see, from the Plane of

Water. A small trickle of liquid magic kept the laraken fed and kept the wizards out."

Akhlaur's pale green face brightened. "So my tower is undisturbed?"

"But for the gem I used to free you, yes." She paused for effect, then added, "I used an undine to retrieve it for me."

The necromancer's eyes narrowed. "Pray do not tell me my tower is under water!"

She shrugged apologetically. "Zalathorm dropped it into a deep rift. I am one of only three living souls who knows where the tower lies." Her words held a subtle barb, reminding the necromancer that two of his foes still lived.

Akhlaur scowled and looked around at the swamp. "Amazing, what the passing of years can bring."

"That is the fate of long-lived people, my lord. We bear witness to many things and endure great changes."

Akhlaur nodded, not understanding the parallel Kiva intended. She was still young, as an elf's life was reckoned, but during her lifetime one of the most terrible chapters of her people's history had been written. The wizards and loremasters did not acknowledge these grim truths, and the people of Halruaa neither knew nor cared.

Well, they would soon know.

They stood together for a moment, gripped in private and very different contemplation. Akhlaur shook off his introspection first. His keen black eyes scanned the landscape, settling on a large, black stirge busily gorging itself on the corpse of a fhamar, a hairless swamp marsupial. The feeding insect resembled a monstrous mosquito, but its body was nearly as large as a housecat, and its black-furred belly tight with stolen blood. A weird humming melody rose from the feeding monster.

"That will do," Akhlaur said, and began to chant.

The stirge grew rapidly, almost instantly. In an eyeblink, the imbedded snout elongated into a deadly javelin, and the extra length thrust the suddenly much-larger creature higher into the sky. The stirge-song snapped off abruptly. Akhlaur's chant filled the sudden silence.

The insect turned its multiple eyes toward the wizards. Its enormous wings began to whir like wind through aspens, and it soared with deadly intent toward Akhlaur.

The necromancer held up a hand. The stirge stopped in mid air, as suddenly and completely as if it had slammed into an invisible wall. Akhlaur made a small circling gesture with his hand, and the hovering stirge slowly turned its back.

"Have a seat," Akhlaur suggested, pointing toward the monster's feet. The creature had back-turning talons, which curved into a basket-like shape.

Gingerly Kiva eased herself into the offered "seat." Akhlaur settled down beside her and spoke a command word. The gigantic stirge lurched into the air with a speed that stole Kiva's breath.

The stirge took off through the jungle, tilting this way and that as it worked its way through the thick canopy. Branches parted to let them pass, bright birds flew squawking in startled protest. Kiva directed the way with a terse word when needed, clinging tightly to her grotesque perch.

At last the stirge settled down near a long, narrow pool. Kiva leaped away and brushed flakes of dried blood—the creature was not a tidy eater—from her hands and arms. Released from the spell that bound it, the creature hummed off, rapidly shrinking back to normal size as it went.

Akhlaur studied the water for a long moment. He lifted both arms high and began to chant the spell that had created the enormous water elemental during the Mulhorandi invasion. The surface of the pool shimmered, then tons of water leaped upward to take new shape.

A manlike creature, thrice the height of an elf, sloshed toward the shore. Akhlaur continued to chant, this time forming a spell of evaporation. The creature faded into mist, which rose, wraithlike, into a thick, roiling gray cloud. Thunder rumbled in its belly, and lightning flashed impatiently.

"That lowers the water level considerably." Akhlaur said, looking well pleased with himself. "Where shall I send the cloud? Khaerbaal? Halar?"

"The king's city," Kiva suggested, choosing her words deliberately. "Send it to Halarahh."

Akhlaur smiled like a shark and pointed toward the east. The cloud darted away, intent upon dropping its burden upon Zalathorm's city. The necromancer glanced expectantly at Kiva.

"A marvelous spell, Lord Akhlaur," she obliged. "I have never seen its like!"

"Nor, I daresay, has anyone in Halruaa. For two hundred years I have lived and learned in a world of liquid magic."

Kiva's lips twitched. "Then I trust this summer's rainy season will prove unusually interesting."

The necromancer chuckled, pleased by the elf's dark humor, then set to work, giving Kiva one task after another as if she were some green apprentice or even a serving wench. She accepted her role without complaint. Playing servant to Akhlaur was nothing compared to all she had already endured—and a small price to pay for her long-sought revenge.

An unseasonably fierce storm raged outside the windows of Basel Indoulur's tower. Wind shrieked through the king's city like unholy spirits, and steady gray rain made memories of sunny days seem as distant as childhood dreams. Basel Indoulur considered the storm an appropriate backdrop for his studies.

He sighed and pushed away the book, a rare tome borrowed from the man who had succeeded him at the Jordaini College. Basel had fought the Crinti bandits in his youth, though he knew little about these shadow amazons beyond his personal experience with hand-to-hand tactics. But the more he read, the more Basel became convinced that the key to this matter lay with the drow-blooded raiders. The otherwise fearless Crinti dreaded the dark fairies. This suggested the shadow amazons possessed useful information.

Basel rose and began to pace. His long-time rival, Procopio Septus, was an avid student of the Crinti, as he had demonstrated in his recent victory against them.

A victory that, in Basel's opinion, was perhaps a little too timely and convenient. Perhaps it was time to shake the lord mayor's tree and see what fell out.

An hour later, Basel Indoulur lifted his goblet and beamed at his host. "To the hero of the hour, master of storm elementals. The spell components for that grand feat must have cost a small fortune! But no sacrifice is too great for Halruaa, and other songs by the same minstrel."

Procopio Septus pretended to drink his wine and tried not to glare at his visitor over the goblet's rim. Try as he might, he couldn't decide what to make of Basel's visit. The portly conjurer—with his jovial airs and obvious love of good living—was, on the face of things, an easy man to dismiss. However, those who followed Halruaan politics knew him to be a fair, even wise ruler of the city of Halar. Many wizards, particularly of the conjuration school, owed their training to Basel Indoulur. He was never without at least three apprentices. Procopio marveled that Basel had not yet replaced Tzigone, the troublesome little wench whose contributions to the recent battle had carried far higher a cost than any Procopio had incurred.

In fact, Procopio had known nothing but gain from the recent invasion. Scandal had dogged him in the months since Zephyr, his elven jordain, had been executed as a traitor and a collaborator of the magehound Kiva. After Procopio's successes in the Mulhorandi invasion, this had been all but forgotten. The people of Halarahh stood solidly behind their lord mayor, proud of his magical feats and military success. More than one wizard had come to him quietly, hinting that perhaps the king was not quite what he once had been, subtly suggesting that perhaps it was time for a man of Procopio's talents to come into his own.

Yet Procopio could not forget that he had achieved these heights through a number of hideously illegal actions. He searched Basel's round face for any hint of a smug, knowing smile. Was it his imagination, or did those twinkling black eyes hold a malevolent gleam?

"You are not here solely to drink my health," he said bluntly.

Basel placed a hand over his heart, pudgy fingers splayed. His expression of contrition looked genuine. "You are weary of speaking of your victories. I should have realized this, knowing you for a modest man. Forgive me, but yes, I came here laden with questions. I have always found there to be much confusion in the aftermath of battle."

Procopio heard the warning in these words. Though Basel might be an odious little toad at present, years ago he'd earned a name as a competent battle wizard. He was subtly waving his own colors, reminding Procopio that he had the experience to see what others might miss.

The diviner rose. "I will show you something that may answer many of your questions."

He led his visitor to his gaming room. Here stood several tables, each with a different elaborate terrain representing historic battlegrounds. He went to the table that depicted the mountainous northern region known as the Nath, the site of his victory against the Crinti.

A word from Procopio sent hidden drawers around the table springing open. Thousands of tiny, animated figures leaped from the drawers and hurled themselves into battle.

Tiny skyships floated above a valley filled with miniscule warriors engaged in fierce hand-to-hand combat. Streaks of colored lightning darted from the miniature skyships. Basel's eyes widened as they settled upon a tiny ship with gaudily colored sails, upon which were painted voluptuous winged elves in a rather advanced state of undress.

"Yes, that is indeed your *Avariel,*" Procopio assured him. "You see before you the battle we recently shared. With these tables, these toys, I can reenact battles again and again, testing different strategies and scenarios. Over the years I have learned much."

Procopio took a wand from his belt and waved it over the table. Some of the figures melted away, and others took their place. Many of the warriors were tiny, gray females.

"Crinti," he affirmed, noting Basel's thoughtful nod. "They have been a particular interest of mine. No one else, to my knowledge, has made such a study of the shadow amazons."

"So your knowledge of the Crinti rose from your interest in war games?"

"None of my choices are entirely random, my dear Basel," Procopio said, punctuating his words with a patronizing smile. "You forget that I am a diviner. It is my art to see what another man does not."

His words, like Basel's, held a subtle warning. The foolish conjurer chuckled and slapped Procopio on the back, as if he were congratulating an old friend on a jest well told.

"So you keep telling me," he said with jovial humor. "It's a fine position you find yourself in. If no one else can see all these mysteries you keep hinting of, who could possibly dispute your claims?"

Procopio responded to the teasing with a faint smile, but he could not bring himself to give more than terse responses throughout the rest of the conversation. Finally his lack of cordiality pierced even Basel's well-padded armor, and the portly nuisance took himself off to bedevil another.

The diviner went immediately to his study, clenching in one hand a bright yellow bead from the end of one of Basel's ubiquitous braids. A simple spell had coaxed it free, and another had brought it to Procopio's hand. With this personal item, he would make short work of finding out Basel's secrets.

Procopio spent the rest of the afternoon in mounting frustration, studying his scrying globes for something he might use against his foe. Basel Indoulur was remarkably free of enemies, even grudges. Procopio brought up images, one after another, of the conjurer's former apprentices. A smile came to each face when Procopio subtlely nudged thoughts of their former master into their minds. It was the same with Basel's servants, his city officials, his fellow wizards. It seemed that none of Basel Indoulur's acquaintances had anything against him but Procopio himself.

Inspiration struck. Procopio gathered his own animosity into a single, focused energy. This he sent into a blue-black globe, soaring out across all Halruaa to seek its own reflection. When the globe began to clear, and a scene to play before him, a slow smile spread across the diviner's face.

Impossible though it might seem, there was another who hated Basel even more than he did.

In the aftermath of any victory, there is mourning as well as celebration. Much of Halruaa's grief found voice in grand and solemn ritual, but all across the land, private tears were shed, and silent oaths made.

One of the most beautiful old villas in all Halarahh was the Belajoon family estate. Ancient and sprawling, it was home to four generations of wizards and several family branches. As did most Halruaan buildings, this villa held it shares of secrets.

In a chamber far below the oldest mansion on the estate, an old man knelt before a glass vault. In it lay his greatest treasure, his young and adored wife Sinestra. She was dead—killed not in battle but by mysterious magic.

Guilt mingled with Uriah Belajoon's grief. He was well beyond his prime, and his name would never be included among the ranks of Halruaa's great wizards. Other than his wealth and his absolute devotion, he had little to offer a woman such as Sinestra. But there were other wealthy men in Halruaa, and Uriah had noted well how many a man's eyes followed Sinestra. He had given her a protective charm, a gem that would bring her directly home if any other man should touch her.

Home she had come. Uriah had found her in their bed, her too-still face strangely changed. He knew her, though, from the ring she wore and by small hidden marks that he hoped only he might recognize.

Sinestra's death had revealed a startling secret: her beauty had been lent her by magic. This Uriah had never suspected. Granted, he was not the most powerful of wizards, but Sinestra had been his apprentice, and he'd never sensed unusual strength in her gift. The wizard who'd molded Sinestra's face into that of a goddess must have possessed a level of Art beyond Uriah's comprehension.

Perhaps Uriah's lack of wizardly skill had killed her! Perhaps his small, protective spell had turned a greater wizard's brew into poison. This thought tormented him until he could no longer bear it.

He hauled himself to his feet and went off in search of an Inquisitor, a specially trained wizard attached to the temple of Azuth. Few wizards were as adept at ferreting out the origins of spells as was a magehound.

Before dark he returned with a tall, thin man whose petulant expression left little doubt concerning his opinion of this errand. Uriah suspected the man would not have come at all but for the reputation of the Belajoon clan. The magehound expected lavish compensation, but that expectation didn't improve his opinion of his benefactor.

Uriah was long past caring how other Halruaans measured him. He led the man to Sinestra's tomb and left him to do his work. He lingered at the far corner of the chamber, however, watching intently as the magehound cast his spells of inquiry.

The expression on the magehound's face turned from impatience to incredulity. Finally he lowered his silver-and-jade wand and turned to Uriah.

"I have grave news indeed."

The old wizard steeled himself to hear that his spell, his ineptitude, had caused the death of his beloved Sinestra.

"There is a spell upon your wife so that another man's touch will return her to your side."

Uriah confirmed this with a single nod.

"The man who touched her was Lord Basel Indoulur."

For long moments, wizard and magehound regarded each other, neither quite able to take in the truth of this. Finally emotion began to rise in Uriah's heart. There was fear—for Basel Indoulur was a noted conjurer—but fear paled before his fury. With this anger came a murderous resolve.

"You are certain of this?"

His voice was steady, grim. A wary expression—a shadowy version of respect—entered the magehound's eyes.

"Beyond doubt. What would you have me do with this knowledge?"

The old wizard considered. He would avenge Sinestra, of that he was certain. The problem was his utter lack of ideas concerning how to proceed!

He took a heavy, gold chain from around his neck and handed it to the magehound. "For now, keep this knowledge close. When the time comes, I will call upon you to bring inquisition. You, and no other."

The magehound's eyes flashed with ambition. In these uncertain times, Halruaans searched for traitors in every well and under every bed. If he could deliver as powerful and canny a wizard as Basel Indoulur to judgment, his fame would be assured!

He inclined his head to Uriah, favoring the minor wizard with a bow usually exchanged only between men of equal rank and power.

"As you say, Lord Uriah, it will be done."

The wizard waited until his guest left, then flung himself upon the curved dome of Sinestra's tomb and wept. Each tear watered his hatred of Basel Indoulur. Surely an opportunity to strike would come, even to a man such as he! If it did not, he would find a man who had greater power and a better chance of success.

His Sinestra was dead. One way or another, Basel Indoulur would pay.

# CHAPTER SEVEN

A band of warriors followed a small, green-clad wizard, a half-elven woman who moved through the swampy jungle like a cat. They followed closely, their faces grim and their eyes constantly scanning for some new danger.

In the canopy overhead, a bird loosed a burst of maniacal laughter. The peeping of hidden tree toads brought to mind a bevy of malevolent sprites, tittering behind tiny hands as they plotted mischief. A prowling jungle cat—a clanish creature more cunning and deadly than a mountain wolf—roared out an invitation to hunt. From the surrounding forest one feline voice after another picked up the refrain until the very trees seemed to vibrate in time with the death-promising song.

The largest man in the group, a distant cousin to the wizard, threw down his machete. "Only fools enter the Swamp of Akhlaur, be there a laraken here or not!"

The half-elf stopped and turned. Despite her diminutive size, she possessed an aura of power that froze the fighters in mid-step. Like her men, she showed signs of hard travel in sweltering heat. Her black hair hung in limp strands around slightly pointed ears, and her large, almond-shaped eyes were deeply shadowed in a gaunt and heat-reddened face.

"Do you call me a fool, Bahari?" she said with deceptive calm.

He stared her down. "Thirty of us entered this place. Seventeen remain. How many more need to die?"

Her chin lifted, and her dark eyes narrowed. "I gave my wizard-word oath."

"I'm sure your father's wife was very impressed by this," he sneered. "You are quick to serve a woman who despises you."

The half-elven wizard turned away. "I would not presume to know Lady Charnli's heart. Nor should you."

"I know her better than I want to. No matter how this ends, she's not likely to reward either of us, and she'll never thank you."

The wizard shrugged and turned her attention to the path ahead. The jungle vines grew thick, and enormous, softly glowing green flowers nodded amid the tangle. One of the flowers, a large but tightly furled bud, tossed and bucked wildly, as if it contained a frantic bird struggling to free itself from a soft-shelled egg. Muffled peeping came from within the flower.

The wizard raised her machete and carefully sliced the flower from its stem. A tiny, golden monkey tumbled out, flailing and shrieking. She dropped her machete and caught the little creature, then jerked back her hand with a startled oath as the monkey sank its needlelike teeth into her thumb. Off it scuttled, scolding the half-elf as if she had been the source of its misery all along.

Bahari lifted a sardonic eyebrow in silent comment on the nature of gratitude. He retrieved his machete and hers from the jungle floor and handed her one with a courtly bow—a mockery of the proud Halruaan family that excluded them both.

With a hiss of exasperation, the half-elf turned her attention back to the flowering vines. The lovely plants were carnivorous and grew where carrion was in great abundance. Oddly enough, only a few bones were entwined among the vines.

She studied the area carefully. The vines grew from the stumps of thick, much-older canes. A long, yellowed bone drew her eye. She eased it out of the old roots, moving her head to one side to avoid a snapping blossom.

The wizard stood and showed the warriors a human thighbone. "Not Zilgorn. This man has been too long dead. But this place has been recently disturbed—these vines are new growth on old stems. We go on."

The men groaned, but they stood aside as the wizard cast spells to wither away the dangerous vines. They made short work of snapping aside the remaining dry twigs and stepped into what appeared to be a large, deeply shaded clearing.

Bahari lit a torch. Flicking light fell upon heaps of marble, all that remained of a once-fine structure pulled down by the passing of time and the inexorable green hands of the jungle. Vines filled the room like a nest of sleeping snakes, nearly obscuring the remains of a temple of Mystra. They curled around the altar and twined through the skeletons of warriors who had died with their weapons in hand.

Two of the men made signs of warding over their hearts.

"This must have been the Mystran shrine on the old Ghalagar estate," the half-elf mused. "My mother spoke of it. Her people lived beneath these trees long ago, before the Ghalagar clan lost these lands and changed their name to Noor."

The wizard turned to leave, pulling up in sudden surprise when she came face to face with a glassy statue of an elf woman. Her eyes filled with deep sorrow, and as she backed away she chanted a few keening words in the Elvish tongue.

"Necromancy," observed Bahari grimly. "The stench of death-magic clings to this place. Let's agree that this jungle is a fitting tomb for Zilgorn the necromancer and be done with it."

She shook her head. "Zilgorn was my half brother, no matter what else he might have been. We go on."

Somber and silent, the small band left the temple and followed a narrow, barely perceptible path sloping down toward the river. The sounds of swamp creatures grew louder—the grumble of great frogs, the roar of crocodiles, and the chittering of thousands upon thousands of insects.

Their quest ended at the banks of a river, and the strange sentinel standing at water's edge.

The husk of skin-wrapped bone suggested a tall, powerful man. Shreds of once-fine scarlet linen clung to the corpse, and long, black hair moldered about the fleshless face.

The half-elf approached and gingerly lifted the gold medallion that hung around the dead man's neck. She studied it for a moment, then nodded once in confirmation.

Bahari folded his arms. "So it ends. You knew Zilgorn's likely fate before you stepped foot into this accursed place."

"His mother is old. She should not spend her last years wondering what became of her firstborn son."

The fighter threw up his hands in disgust. His eyes narrowed, and in one cat-quick motion, he brought his machete up like a sword and lunged at the half-elf.

The attack was unexpected, but she was quick enough to roll aside. As she fell, she heard an unnerving crackle erupt from her half-brother's body. A shower of acrid brown dust burst from his desiccated chest—along with the brilliant green head of a swamp viper.

The mercenary traced a quick, circular movement with his machete, spinning the deadly snake around the blade and thwarting its lunge. He shouted to two of his men, then hurled the snake to the ground between them. They began wildly hacking at the creature with their machetes.

A small explosion rocked the clearing, and a glowing cloud burst from the mutilated snake. It hung for a moment in the heavy, humid air, quivering with gathering magic. Then a small storm erupted, and glittering green sparkles descended like bits of bright, lazily drifting hail.

"Zombie powder!" the wizard shrieked as she rolled to her feet and kicked into a run. "Don't breath in, don't let it touch you!"

Most of the men heeded her, clamping hands over their mouths and noses as they fled the descending hail. One fighter tripped over a root and fell. Glittering green limned him, and a bright light flared and died. Horrible spasms wracked his body, and his cries faded to a lingering rattle.

The others backed away in horrid fascination as their comrade rose, lurching toward them with a chunk of bloody snake clutched in one hand.

Surprisingly fast, he seized a comrade and clamped his hand on the man's jaw. Forcing it open, he stuffed the snake down the man's throat.

Again green light flared, and the second man expired in violent paroxysms. Two pairs of dull, glazed eyes turned upon their comrades and kinsman. Loyalties forgotten, the two men drew weapons and attacked.

The mercenary nearest them was too slow to understand, too slow to react. The newly made zombies fell upon him. He went down shrieking, clutching at the pumping stump of his sword arm. In moments he also rose, wielding his own severed arm as a bludgeon.

The half-elf slowed to a stop as she realized that none of her warriors kept pace. She turned and watched the riverside battle in horror and disbelief. She had no spells that might help—her art was the crafting of healing potions— but even to her unseasoned eyes, it quickly became apparent that this fight could have only one end. Each man who fell rose again, only to join the swelling ranks of his undead comrades.

"Flee!" she shouted to the survivors. "Flee or die!"

Bahari turned toward her. In a few quick strides he was at her side. He swept her up easily and slung her over his shoulder, taking off at a loping trot. The half-elf clung to his baldric strap, grateful that her warrior cousin proved loyal to the Charnli family despite his previous complaints.

Finally Bahari stopped. He casually threw the half-elf to the ground.

Startled, she rolled and looked up at her rescuer's face. His eyes were dull and glazed, steadfastly fixed upon something behind her. He dropped to one knee and bowed his head—or what was left of it.

With sickening understanding, the wizard gazed at the man's crushed skull. Her gaze followed the sound of other warriors dropping to the ground in obeisance. To her dismay, the entire party had followed Bahari to this place. Quaking, she lifted her eyes to the object of the undead warriors' veneration.

A tall, bald man regarded the small army with a thin smile on his green-scaled face. Then his black eyes settled on the half-elf wizard. He held out a webbed, faintly green hand. Another, smaller viper dripped from it like drool and slithered toward her.

She tried to flee, but her treacherous body refused to obey. Trapped in the waking nightmare, she could only scream helplessly as the viper slithered up the length of her body. Then the snake crawled into her mouth, and she could scream no more.

As the viper disappeared down her throat, a terrible chill spread through her, sped by waves of agonizing convulsions. Life slipped away like mist, leaving behind a strange, cold clarity. Every spell she had ever learned or cast stood ready in her mind, as quiescent as the undead warriors. She lifted her hand and gazed with horror at the transformation—the pale bronze color was fading to a sickly gray, and the skin on her delicate fingers had grown tougher than a dock worker's.

Frantically she drew a small knife from her belt and sliced at her own wrist. Blood welled, thick and dark, but the pulse of life was nearly gone. She could not even take her own life. It had already been taken from her.

"Not this," she croaked, her eyes imploring the strange

green wizard. "Kill me, but do not make me a lich!"

A sharp gasp drew the half-elf's eyes to the woman in the wizard's shadow. She was a wild elf, copper-skinned and crowned with lustrous green hair. Her golden eyes mirrored the horror that gripped the dying wizard.

The half-elf's gaze dropped to Bahari's discarded machete, then returned to the elf woman's face. "*Es'-Caerta,*" she pleaded, an Elvish phrase that defied translation, used only at the end of formal prayers blessing and beseeching the gods.

Whether the green elf understood or not, it seemed fitting to the half-elven wizard that this should be her last spoken word.

Without hesitation, the elf woman stooped and seized the machete. She threw herself into a spin, circling once, twice, to gain power and momentum. In the instant before the blade hit, the half-elf's eyes sought her savior's grim face, and her silent lips shaped the elven blessing one final time.

Kiva staggered to a stop, the bloody machete clasped in both hands. For a moment she regarded her handiwork: a neatly decapitated head, elven eyes closed in peace and a faint, contented smile upon bloodless lips.

The next instant she was hurtling through the air. Her back struck a tree and she slid to the ground.

When her vision cleared, she saw Akhlaur standing over her, his pale green face twisted in fury.

"Have you any idea what you've just wasted? You have deprived me of a servant as obedient as any of these fools but with an undying wizard's power!"

Using the tree as a support, Kiva pushed herself to her feet. "It's impossible to change another wizard to a lich!"

He dismissed this obvious misperception with a wave of one webbed hand and continued to glare, clearly waiting for some word of explanation.

But Kiva could think of no justification for her impulsive act—at least, none that Akhlaur would accept. "She was half-elven," she said at last, "and therefore not a worthy servant."

The necromancer's wrath faltered, and a strange, lethal amusement dawned in his eyes like a dark sun. "What of *your* descendants, little Kiva? Did you so disdain their human blood? Did you slay them, as well?"

A flood of emotions—feelings Kiva had thought long dead—burst free from some locked corner of her heart. She dropped her eyes to hide her loathing and hatred and shame. Any one of these responses could prove fatal.

Nor could she answer the necromancer's questions without stepping off another precipice. She had given birth, just once, before the laraken's spawning had destroyed all hope of further progeny. Her long-ago daughter had been half-elven, a scrawny, sickly thing barely clinging to life, almost completely devoid of magic. Akhlaur had never acknowledged his child by Kiva, but he had made good use of the girl. That sad little half-breed had been Akhlaur's first magic-dead servant, the germ of an idea that eventually became the jordaini order.

To Akhlaur, that long-ago daughter was the subject of a necromantic experiment, and nothing more. He would be insulted by any claim of kinship. Yet Kiva could not take a similar viewpoint without disparaging the child's human father.

No answer was correct. Any response could bring harsh reprisals. It was the sort of cruel game Kiva remembered from her distant captivity. But she was no longer that captive elven girl.

Her chin lifted, and her eyes cooled to amber ice. "My only living child is the laraken. It carries a portion of Akhlaur's magic. How could I possibly disdain that?"

For a long moment their stares locked. Then Akhlaur stooped and seized the half-elf's head by the hair. He lifted it and regarded it thoughtfully. "How old do you suppose she was?"

Kiva blinked at this unexpected question. "Forty, maybe forty-five years. Quite young for a half-elf, and about the same as twenty-five years of human life."

"Then I suppose there's little chance she achieved archmage status."

"It seems unlikely."

"Pity. I've a spell that requires the powdered skull of an archmage who died during the lich transformation."

Kiva shot him an incredulous look. "Is this a common enough occurrence to warrant its inclusion in spell components?"

"If the spell were common, it would hardly be worth casting." The necromancer negligently tossed the head into the pool, and tapped thoughtfully on his chin as he gazed out over the spreading ripples. "Well, no matter. There are other ways of raising the tower."

He gave a terse command to the undead warriors. They fell to work digging a narrow canal that would divert the water downhill to a nearby river.

"A small thing," Akhlaur said with a shrug, "but this river feeds the pool drowning my tower. The more water is removed from that pool, the easier the task of raising the tower. Perhaps I will return the tower to its original location. An unusually strong place of power, that."

Dark inspiration struck Kiva, a small repayment for Akhlaur's cruel game. She was not the only one whose past held moments of shame and defeat.

"Perhaps we should visit this place again before beginning such a massive undertaking. It is possible the laraken drained all power from that spot. If that is so, one place in this swamp is as good as any other."

Akhlaur considered, then began the chant for a magical gate. He and Kiva stepped through, to emerge near the mirky bog that had first welcomed them to Akhlaur's Swamp.

"This is the highest point in your former estate," Kiva said. She pointed to an obelisk, a standing stone deeply coated with moss and half submerged in water. "The tower stood there."

The necromancer studied the obelisk with narrowed eyes. "The power of this place is gone, but for a glimmer of magic clinging to that stone. Come." He cast a spell that would allow them to walk upon the swamp water. Kiva followed, knowing full well what they would find.

The translucent image of a slim, doe-eyed girl slumped by the obelisk, eyeing something beneath the water with a mixture of hopelessness and longing. The necromancer's eyes widened in recognition, then narrowed to furious slits.

"Noor!"

Akhlaur spat out the name of his former, treacherous apprentice as if it were a curse. The ghostly girl looked up. Terror suffused her face. She turned away, flinging up both hands to ward off the barrage of spells he hurled at her. Fireballs sped toward her, sizzling and steaming as they passed through the humid air. Black lightning flared from the wizard's hands, charring the moss covering the obelisk to ash. None of this had any effect on the ghost of Noor.

However diverting the sight of a thwarted Akhlaur might be, Kiva finally tired of the display and seized the necromancer's arm. "I do not think you can destroy the ghost, Lord Akhlaur. She died when Zalathorm claimed the crimson star. It seems likely that her spirit is somehow linked to the gem. You will not be able to avenge yourself upon Noor as long as Zalathorm holds the crimson star. The sooner the gem is destroyed, the sooner Zalathorm's power will be broken!"

The necromancer composed himself. In an eyeblink, his rage-twisted face smoothed out into its usual faint, supercilious smile. "Zalathorm's downfall would be delightful to behold, but why would I want to destroy the gem?"

Kiva noted the faint flicker of uncertainty in the necromancer's black eyes. "But you *could* destroy it, if you so chose."

The wizard's lip thinned into a tight line, and for a moment Kiva feared that she had overestimated his power. "It can be done," he said at last. "Three of us created the gem. Its destruction would also require three."

The elf's shoulders slumped. "Then you can't defeat Zalathorm."

"I didn't say that," Akhlaur snapped, stabbing one long finger in her direction. "The crimson star will be difficult to work around, but not impossible. I will rebuild my magical arsenal past anything Zalathorm can command."

Kiva turned aside abruptly, pretending to be absorbed by the fading outline of Noor's ghost. At the moment, her own dreams felt nearly as insubstantial.

For many long years, Kiva had assumed Akhlaur would want the gem destroyed, so that he and Zalathorm could fight toe to toe. It had never occurred to her that all three of the gem's wizardly creators would have to be in accord.

Such accord seemed beyond the grasp of those once-friends, long ago turned mortal enemies. One of these wizards, Kiva held firmly in hand, but Akhlaur was proving more difficult to control than she had anticipated.

Inspiration struck. Akhlaur did not actually claim the three *creators* must destroy the gem. He merely noted it took three. Kiva reviewed what she knew of the gem and its powers. It protected the three creators—and their descendants.

Their descendants! She knew three of these descendants all too well! Time and again they had evaded death and slipped through traps. If these accursed wizard-spawn could benefit from the crystal star's protection, perhaps they could also destroy it!

Kiva turned to the necromancer. "I need to go to the king's city to gather information that may prove useful."

The wizard dismissed his elven "servant" with an absent wave of his hand. Kiva quickly conjured a gate and stepped out into a prepared location—a deeply shadowed arbor in the public gardens of Halarahh.

She nearly stumbled over a young couple, common laborers judging by their dress, too absorbed in each other to notice her arrival. Kiva picked up the rude knife the lad had set aside. She brought the hilt down hard on the girl's head, then dispatched the suitor with a quick slash, taking care not to get any of his blood on the stunned girl. Kiva knelt by the girl and gave her head a quick, wrenching twist.

Kiva's victim was small and slim, and her gown looked to be a near fit for the slender elf. Since the girl had prepared for an assignation, she'd worn a cowl and cloak. This would provide cover for the elf's telltale hair. Delighted with this unexpected bounty, Kiva quickly claimed her prize. She quickly dressed herself in the dead girl's clothes and made her way through the deepening twilight to Basel Indoulur's tower.

A dark-haired young woman in an apprentice's sky blue robes opened the gate. For a moment Kiva felt that she was still regarding a ghost, so closely did the girl resemble the long-dead Noor.

"You are Lord Basel's apprentice? The Noor heiress?"

The girl smiled. "I am one of the apprentices, yes, but since I have an older sister I'm not likely to inherit. I am Farrah, second daughter of Ahaz and Beryl Noor. How may I serve?"

Kiva glanced over the girl's shoulder. "Actually, I came seeking another apprentice. A girl known as Tzigone."

The smile fell from Farrah's face. "Tzigone was lost in the recent battle. You must be newly come to Halarahh, for her story is sung at every corner."

At Kiva's urging, the apprentice repeated the tale. During a pivotal battle, when the Crinti threatened to overrun the Halruaan army and the dark fairies stood poised to pour through a portal and into the fray, Tzigone had not only closed the floodgate but had also dropped the veil between the worlds. She had sacrificed herself, binding her magic with that of other wizards to seal these gates.

Kiva remembered the jolt of power that had thrown her and Akhlaur free of the Plane of Water. So *that* was the source of it! She supposed she ought to be glad the timing of Tzigone's spell had coincided so well with her own, but all she could feel was fury. Once again, Keturah's little bastard had interfered!

Well, perhaps all was not lost.

"What of Tzigone's friend, the jordain known as Matteo?"

Farrah brightened. "Another hero. He lives and serves King Zalathorm as counselor."

A sharp burst of panic sizzled through Kiva, quickly mastered. "I know Matteo. He must be deeply saddened by Tzigone's loss. What became of his friend Andris?"

"He lives," the girl said shortly. "He awaits trial for treason, but I hear he was released to Matteo's keeping. Matteo wished to visit the place where Tzigone disappeared and took Andris as a guide."

More likely, Kiva thought grimly, he had something more productive than mourning in mind. If she and Dhamari Exchelsor could find a spell that parted the veil to the Unseelie Court, eventually other wizards would do the same.

If that occurred, the three wizard-spawn descendants would be together in one place. That simplified matters admirably.

Kiva fingered the knife hidden in the folds of her stolen cloak and contemplated her next steps. Even though the cowl covered her hair and ears, her face was unmistakably elven. Farrah Noor must not tell anyone that an elf woman had visited, asking questions about Tzigone and Matteo. There were few elves in Halruaa, and the appearance of one at this time and place would hint too directly at Kiva. She could either kill Noor or take the memory from her.

Murder was risky in Halruaa, for it led to magical inquiry. Even memory loss could be reversed.

The elf forced a smile onto her face and thanked Farrah Noor for her time and her kindness. She walked away from the tower and into a side street, where she watched until a sturdily built young man entered the tower by a side door. After a while, lamplight flickered in a room several floors above. Kiva made out the man's silhouette.

She closed her eyes and brought to mind his face and form, chanting a spell that would cast an illusion over herself. Clad in the young man's image, she sauntered over to the tower door and knocked.

Again Farrah came to the door. Her dark eyes widened in surprise. "Mason! What, forgotten your key again?"

To avoid telltale speech, Kiva went into a fit of coughing, nodding to show agreement. The girl stepped aside to let "Mason" pass. Kiva pulled the knife and waited while the girl shut and locked the door. When Farrah turned to face her assailant, when the shocked puzzlement in the girl's eyes turned to fear and supplication, Kiva struck.

Still wearing Mason's form, she cleaned the dripping blade on Farrah's robes and made her way up toward the tower room. Mason was already asleep, lying on his back and snoring like a sailor. Kiva took a potion of forgetfulness from her bag. This she poured into the apprentice's open mouth, drop by subtle drop. When the vial was empty, she dropped it on the floor along with the blood-smeared knife.

When Farrah's body was found and magical inquiries made, the magehounds would recover an image of the last face Farrah had seen, and they would discover her belief concerning her killer's identity. Mason, of course, would know nothing about the murder. His convenient loss of memory might be construed as self-preservation on his part, or as one layer of an elaborate deception. Either way, the situation would take some time to unravel.

Kiva intended to use this time well. She began the casting of another far-traveling spell. Before Farrah Noor's body cooled, Kiva would stand in the Nath, the wild northwestern mountains. By this time tomorrow, descendants of all three of the crystal star's wizard creators would be in her hands.

# CHAPTER EIGHT

Storm clouds rumbled over the wild mountains. Rain fell steadily, and an occasional sizzle of lightning cast brief illumination over the bleak terrain.

Kiva moved through the Nath like a shadow, aided by the keen night vision of her people. She kept alert, for her elf-blooded quarry also had vision well suited to darkness.

Years of acquaintance with the Crinti bandits had taught Kiva their patterns, their habits, their haunts. She quietly made her way through twisting passes and over tumbled stone to a hidden watch post. There stood a tall warrior, a shadowy figure with storm-gray skin and hair, her feet planted wide apart and her face lifted to the wild sky as if to defy the gods.

"Xerish," Kiva murmured, recognizing the Crinti scout. She reached into her bag and fingered its contents until she found the spell components she needed. Then she rose and shouted out a hail in the mangled, bastardized Elvish dialect the Crinti used with such pride.

The scout whirled, sword out and face wary. Her suspicion turned to joy when Kiva stepped out of her hiding place.

Xerish loped forward and swept Kiva into a crushing, sisterly embrace. "Elf-sister! I am so pleased you are not dead!"

"That gratifies me, as well," Kiva said with as much warmth as she could manage. She quickly extricated herself from the Crinti's arms and held out a small, deeply tarnished silver locket. "I have brought you a gift."

The Crinti took the trinket and examined it with interest.

"Open it," Kiva suggested.

Xerish found the clasp. Inside the locket was a crumbling lock of white hair. She lifted astonished eyes to Kiva's face.

"Relics," the elf said, confirming the warrior's unspoken question. "The only known remains of Mahidra, the warrior woman who founded your clan."

The Crinti quickly put the locket around her neck. Overwhelmed, she drew herself up and saluted Kiva, her fists thumping against opposite shoulders. "I will prove myself worthy of this honor, this I swear. My life is yours."

That brought a flicker of a smile to Kiva's face. "Tell me, how did we fare in the recent battle?"

The gray face clouded. "Badly. Many Crinti fell to the Halruaans, some fled the dark fairies. Scouts gather the survivors. We return to Dambrath before the new moon."

Kiva nodded as she took this in. "The camp is near?"

"An hour's run, maybe two. I will take you there."

Xerish broke into a long-legged trot. The elf easily fell into stride. When the conical mounts of the fairy hills came into sight, just a few paces away but shrouded in the rain and mist, Kiva fell back, gripping her knees and struggling for breath as if she had been winded by the run.

The Crinti circled back, her face puzzled. Kiva abruptly straightened, flinging out one hand and hurling a bolt of black and crimson energy at the bandit. The magic missile struck Xerish in the chest and sent her hurtling toward one of the mounds. She hit hard, her arms thrown out wide. There she stuck like a bug to flypaper, too stunned to draw breath.

Kiva took tools from her pack—a small hammer and four long, silver spikes. She ran at the stunned Crinti with the grim intent of a vampire hunter. Dull thuds resounded through the chilling rain as Kiva pounded the stakes through the woman's hands and ankles. Through it all, the magically trapped Xerish did not cry out. Crinti warriors did not acknowledge pain, but her strange blue eyes burned with bewilderment and betrayal.

Kiva rose and began to walk widdershins around the mount, chanting as she went. Finally she came around, held her captive's accusing gaze, and slapped her hands sharply together. Magic flared like black lightning, and the Crinti woman was sucked abruptly into the mound.

The elf waited expectantly as the dark spell ran its course. A life for a life—Kiva gladly doomed Xerish to the place Crinti feared more than death in exchange for a more useful being's freedom.

Finally the crackling energy erupted into a second explosive burst. Kiva closed her eyes and turned her head away from the sudden, blinding flair. When she looked back, a wretched figure cowered at the base of the fairy mound.

"No," Kiva said flatly, staring in disbelief at her prize.

The freed human was not Tzigone—was not even female! A Halruaan male crouched at Kiva's feet. His pale face bore a distinct resemblance to a hairless weasel, and his scant hair was plastered against his skull by sweat and blood.

Shrieking with incoherent rage, Kiva kicked the wizard again and again. He merely curled up, his arms flung over his head, his thin form shaking with sobs. A familiar talisman flew from his hand. He lunged for it, wrapping the chain around each finger and clutching the trinket as if it were his only link to life and sanity.

As, Kiva suspected, it truly had been.

"Dhamari Exchelsor," she said with loathing. "Why is it that whenever a spell goes awry, Dhamari is not far away?"

The weeping man suddenly went still. After a moment, he ventured a glance at his tormenter. "Kiva?"

There was a world of hope in that single word. Kiva grimaced. If Dhamari saw solace in her, he must be in very bad shape indeed!

But Kiva was ever willing to improvise. She crouched beside the wizard, crooning silly, soothing words. He took the flask she handed him and drank, hesitantly at first, then with great thirst and greater need. Finally she took the flask from his hands.

"You are safe, Dhamari. I have brought you back."

Kiva watched him slowly absorb this, watched as his eyes took focus and turned as hard as obsidian.

"Where is Keturah's bastard?"

The ice in Dhamari's voice startled her. She sat back on her heels and regarded him. He returned her gaze without faltering, and for long moments Kiva stared into a mirror of her own soul.

"Hatred," she said approvingly. "A thirst for vengeance. Where is the sniveling weasel I have known and loathed these many years?"

The wizard took her taunting without flinching. "He is gone, as who would know better than you? Together we learned why the Crinti dread the dark fairies. You know what happens to those who pass beyond the veil and return. I have been through a crucible. The dross has been burned away, and my heart's ambitions have been forged into steel."

"Like the drow before you," Kiva said, repeating the legend explaining the dark elves' absolute evil.

Dhamari actually smiled. "Even so. I am ready to resume what I set about years ago, before Keturah's escape and death set my plans awry."

"Yes, I believe you are," she said thoughtfully. "Before you continue your rise to immortality, there is one thing you should know. Keturah is not dead."

The wizard stared at Kiva. "How is this possible? You

yourself told me of her death! You brought me her talisman!" He brandished the chain with its small, simple medallion.

Kiva grimaced. "The Crinti are thorough. When they finished with Keturah, she was beyond recognition. They told me she was dead, and I believed them. No one who saw her then would have doubted it."

"But she is alive."

"More or less. She is now known as Queen Beatrix."

Dhamari stared at Kiva for a long moment, then he began to laugh without humor. "So Keturah, mistress of evocation, has become the mad queen of Halruaa! Odd, the little turns life takes."

His mirth abruptly disappeared. "So *that* is why the Council of Elders presented me with a bill of divorcement so soon after Keturah's disappearance! I had thought this a courtesy, for what wizard wishes to maintain any alliance with an accused murderess? It was Zalathorm's doing, wasn't it?"

"That seems likely," Kiva said, though it was nothing of the sort. Zephyr, her kinsman and her ally, had seen to this detail.

"So Zalathorm knows of his queen's past identity," Dhamari repeated, in the manner of one who was trying to stretch his mind around too large an idea.

"How could he not? Isn't he the greatest diviner in all Halruaa?"

Dhamari considered this, his face troubled. "If the king knew all that had passed between Keturah and me, I would not be alive today. Nor did he know of the Mulhorandi invasion. Is it possible that his powers of divination owe more to legend than reality?"

"Many wizards are asking that very question. I suspect you will find Halarahh to be an interesting place. Shall I return you to your tower?"

The wizard nodded. He rose painfully to his feet and limped through the magical gate Kiva conjured.

Left alone, Kiva considered the fairy mound. The spell

of substitution was difficult and expensive. She could not cast it again, not without many hours of study, days of rest, and spell components that were exceedingly difficult to come by. For the time being, Tzigone would have to stay where she was.

Kiva only hoped she could get to the girl before Matteo did.

Dhamari stepped out of the magic portal and into his own gardens. The dank chill of the Unseelie realms and the pelting rain of the Nath were nothing but unpleasant memories. Here in the king's city, stars gleamed overhead, and the soft night air was as sultry as a whispered promise.

He stood for a long time, breathing in the intense, green fragrance, grateful merely to be alive and free of the dark fairies. He did not regret what he had become during his torment—far from it—but he was just as happy to have the transformation done and over with!

His eyes swept over the gardens, lush and fragrant in the waning moonlight, then narrowed as they settled upon the gatehouse.

The gatekeeper was gone. Dhamari stalked to the tower and threw open the door, bellowing for his servants. Only silence greeted him.

Worry replaced ire. The wizard hurried up the stairs to his workshop. As he had feared, his laboratory had been disturbed, its contents sorted with a haste that suggested his "visitors" preferred not to be caught at their search. Dhamari set to work, methodically going through the tumbled vials and scrolls and books, noting which were missing. Most disturbing were the missing works on the Unseelie folk.

Someone was at work on a spell to free Tzigone. Why else would anyone take such things? Dhamari sincerely doubted anyone would go to such effort on *his* behalf!

A faint, sardonic smile twisted his lips as he recalled his own rescue. "I *thought* Kiva's welcome lacked a certain warmth," he murmured. "So Kiva still has a use for Tzigone. I wonder what that might be."

Dhamari had other, more immediate problems to ponder. He leaned back in his chair and considered the wreck of his library. The intrusion into his tower was not a thing lightly done. Halruaan law frowned upon those who despoiled a wizard's tower.

It occurred to him that the tower had been warded. If he'd been the first to enter the tower by conventional or magical means, his arrival had triggered magical alarms. He hurried to the window. Sure enough, several men in the blue-green uniforms of the city militia quick-stepped toward the tower.

Dhamari hurried to a hidden door that led to a passage set between two rooms. There he sat, listening to the sounds of the militia tromping through his tower. Their search was long and maddeningly thorough. When at last all was silent, he crept back out into his study and the problem that awaited him there. Someone knew far too much about him. But who?

The answer struck Dhamari like a fist. Surely the thief was none other than Basel Indoulur, Tzigone's self-appointed guardian and, most likely, her sire! Basel had flown his skyship into the dangerous Nath to rescue Tzigone. He had put his life at risk to aid Keturah after her escape. What was robbing a wizard's tower, in comparison?

"This could be a problem," he muttered. Once Basel heard of Dhamari's return—and he would—he was sure to follow Dhamari's every move like a hawk on a hare.

The wizard rose and began to pace. "What to do?" he said distractedly. A conjurer of Basel Indoulur's stature was too dangerous to ignore, and too powerful to take on directly. At least, too powerful to take on alone.

Dhamari hurried to his scrying chamber and settled

down before a large, amber globe. He quickly cast the spell that would seek out Kiva.

Agonizing minutes passed before the elf's face drifted into focus. As Dhamari opened his mouth to speak, he noted slender black spires rising from the ground behind Kiva. His jaw locked open in gaping astonishment.

"This is not a good time," Kiva said curtly.

Dhamari sputtered. "I should say not! Those spires—I have seen them sketched in a lore book. Why did you not tell me you were raising Akhlaur's tower?"

"Since I intend to share his treasures with every wizard in Halruaa, I'll post word of my progress in all the local taverns," she retorted.

A terrifying possibility occurred to Dhamari. In the moments before Tzigone had dragged him into the Unseelie Realm, he had caught sight of Kiva disappearing into the gate that led to the Plane of Water. If she had returned, who or what might have accompanied her?

"What of the laraken? What of Akhlaur?"

The elf's gaze slid to one side. "We will speak later. I must go."

"He's back, isn't he?" Dhamari persisted. "He's alive, and you have brought him back from exile. *This* is how you plan to depose Zalathorm? Kiva, that is like ridding a barn of mice by bringing in vipers! What will Halruaa become with that accursed necromancer on the throne?"

"Akhlaur will never rule Halruaa," she said softly, her eyes burning with hatred. "I swear it. Zalathorm's crown will pass to another."

Dhamari's astonishment swiftly transmuted to interest. "To whom?"

She lifted one shoulder impatiently. "Procopio Septus, most likely."

"The lord mayor is a powerful man," Dhamari allowed, "and respected among the Elders. But what wizard, or what two or three or twenty, could possibly stand against Akhlaur?"

"Do not trouble yourself. That is my concern."

Dhamari's only answer was a derisive sniff.

The elven face in his globe grew very still. "Never forget, Dhamari, that I freed you from the Unseelie court. I could very easily send you back."

He doubted this but was not interested in testing the matter.

"I have overstepped. As apology, please accept this information." He quickly told her about the missing spellbooks and Crinti lore and of his suspicions concerning Basel Indoulur. "I know this man, Kiva. He and Keturah were friends from childhood, perhaps more than friends. He might not be imposing to look upon, but he is dangerous."

Kiva hissed out an exasperated sigh. "I cannot take three steps without tripping over a Halruaan wizard! Something must be done to hold them off a bit longer."

Dhamari waited for her to elaborate. When she offered no further information, he went on to another matter. "If you hate Halruaa's wizards so much, why would you support Procopio Septus?"

She shrugged again. "Because he is ambitious, and because he is not Zalathorm."

Dhamari was speechless, dazzled by the dawning of new possibilities. "I suppose any other wizard would do as well?"

Kiva was silent for a moment, her amber eyes noting the birth of new ambition. "You have crossed me before, Dhamari. I won't forget that. But as long as you prove loyal, who knows what your future might be? My friends have sat upon the Council of Elders, become jordaini masters." She smiled briefly, unpleasantly. "My former mistress reigns as queen. Perhaps you'd like to reclaim Zalathorm's wife along with his throne?"

A warning bell began to toll in the back of Dhamari's mind. Kiva had spoken of Keturah as if she had recently learned of the woman's new identity, but was it possible that Kiva had had a hand in putting Keturah on Halruaa's throne? If so, to what purpose? There was much about his plans that Kiva did not know. Most likely the elf could make the same claim!

"You speak of powerful friends, but many of them are dead," he pointed out. "The queen is a madwoman, thanks to your Crinti barbarians. It seems to me that you're a dangerous friend to have."

"A far more dangerous foe. Measure the height of your ambitions, Dhamari. After you have compared the risks to the prize, we will speak again."

"Why wait? Tell me what I have to do."

Again Kiva darted a glance to one side. "Two things. First, strike up a partnership with Procopio Septus. Let him pull your wagon along until the time comes to discard him. I will send you a magic missive detailing his recent misdeeds."

"Good," Dhamari said, nodding. "Blackmail provides the foundation for a good many political relationships."

"Second, seek out wizards likely to support Zalathorm and destroy them. I must go." The coppery face winked out of the globe, suddenly and completely.

"Just two things," Dhamari muttered as he pushed away from the scrying globe. "Extort one of the most powerful wizards in Halruaa, and slay those who support the king. Mere trifles!"

He hurried to the shelf where he kept his message bottle. He set it on a table and sat down to wait.

Before too long, a scroll appeared inside the bottle—Kiva's message, magically sent. Dhamari eagerly shook it out and smoothed the parchment out flat. As he read, he began to chuckle with delight.

Oh, yes, Procopio would accept him as a partner. The lord mayor would have little choice. Dhamari had to admire the man's daring. Procopio had been clever indeed—perhaps clever enough to succeed in challenging Zalathorm, but it was one thing to challenge a king, and quite another to actually wear his crown.

Dhamari walked over to a mirror of polished bronze and regarded his reflection, thoughtfully brushing at his scant hair. He was not a handsome man, or an imposing one, or powerful—at least, not in the ways that Halruaa measured magical might. In fact, there was nothing particularly compelling about him.

The wizard shrugged. No matter. There was not a man alive who would not be vastly improved by the addition of a crown.

Kiva hurried back toward the rising tower. Fortunately, the casting was long and difficult, and it seemed unlikely the necromancer noted her inattention. Akhlaur still stood with his eyes shut, his webbed hands outstretched. The blood from the needed sacrifices pooled around his feet and seeped slowly into the ground.

The black tower glistened as it rose, slowly, like an obsidian elemental taking shape. Around it stood a silent horde of long-dead skeletal creatures, raised from the surrounding swamps to participate in this strange reincarnation.

As the tower rose, thousands of naked bones took on flesh and form. The water that had drowned the tower and its treasures seeped upward into the patient dead. Undying servants—not quite zombies, not quite water elementals—stood ready for their master's command. Ancient bone showed through translucent, watery flesh.

It was, Kiva had to admit, an ingenious way of ridding the site of much of the water. The drained pit would remain beneath the tower, providing space for dungeons and middens, and the warriors would help Akhlaur stake his claim.

She waited until the tower doors had risen level with the newly firm ground. Doors and windows opened by unseen hands, and desert-dry winds whistled through the tower rooms. At last the tower stood as Kiva had last seen it: an imposing work of Halruaan art, a peerless storehouse of necromantic arts, a place of horrors too well remembered.

Kiva added her applause to the listless, watery patter of zombie hands. "Never have I seen such a spell, Lord Akhlaur, or such an army! These warriors should be more than sufficient to drive away the attacking wizards."

The triumphant smile fell from the necromancer's face. "The tower is under attack?"

She fell back a step and brought a look of chagrin to her face. "I misspoke, my lord. No attack is underway, to the best of my knowledge, but raising the tower required an enormous amount of magic. There are wizards who might sense spells of such magnitude. Sooner or later, they will come to investigate."

The necromancer acknowledged this with a nod. "Obviously you have a suggestion."

"I do, my lord. With your permission, I will summon the laraken back to the Swamp of Akhlaur."

Akhlaur's black eyes narrowed. "How do you know this spell?"

"It is similar to the magic that summoned its parent, the water demon. I saw it cast often enough to burn it into memory." With effort, Kiva kept her voice level and calm.

The necromancer looked intrigued. "Few can learn spells by observation alone. You have always been among my best apprentices, little Kiva," he said, ignoring the fact that she had learned about this particular arrow not as a student archer, but as a target. "Very well, let us see what you can do."

Kiva smiled blandly. "Indeed you will, my lord."

A flicker of suspicion entered the wizard's eyes, then was gone. "The best of my apprentices," he repeated in a tone as mild as hers. "I am eager to see what other lessons I have inadvertently taught you."

She heard the warning in his words and noted the keen interest in his eyes. For the first time, Akhlaur seemed to consider the possibility that all might not be as it seemed. He did not look dismayed by that prospect— to the contrary. Nothing pleased him more than a cruel game, a hidden purpose.

The elf held her smile and silently promised to give the wizard all he desired and more.

# CHAPTER NINE

**M**orning crept over the Nath, fading the night sky to a dismal gray. The rain that had fallen steadily all night ceased with the coming of light, and mist rose like summoned spirits from the stony ground.

Slim gray figures moved through the swirling, land-bound clouds, preparing their horses, gathering supplies, bundling weapons plundered from the Halruaans and from their own dead. Shanair, the Crinti chieftain, sat her shadow-gray mare and watched as her decimated forces prepared for retreat.

One of the warriors cinched a thick bundle of bloodstained arrows to a tall bay stallion—a dead Halruaan's war-horse turned pack animal. She caught Shanair's eye and gave the chieftain a quick, fierce smile.

"Fine arrows, and each one wrenched from an enemy's body! This stallion will breed a hundred foals by summer's end. All will fetch a good price in Dambrath."

Shanair nodded, understanding what prompted the woman's boasts. They would return to their native land laden with plunder. They would have honor and wealth. As raiders, they had done well indeed. No one need speak of their deeper, failed purpose.

It would be good to return to Dambrath. Shanair glanced around the campsite, a relatively flat place carved high into the mountainside by a long-ago rockslide. The site was littered with boulders and nearly surrounded by jagged cliffs. Piles of tumbled rock squatted above them like tipsy, dwarven sentinels. A small, potable spring bubbled up from somewhere deep in the heart of the mountain, and a few shallow caves offered shelter from the elements. It was a highly defensible place, if not a comfortable one, but no fitting home for a Crinti warrior. Soon Shanair would again ride free over open plains.

The prospect gave her less pleasure than she expected.

A faint buzzing, like that of a captured wasp, came from a small leather pouch affixed to her belt. Shanair's gray face furrowed in puzzlement as she unbuckled the fasteners and drew a small, smooth, round stone from the bag.

*Elf-sister, I greet you.*

A familiar voice sounded in Shanair's mind, a lilting, bell-like soprano that lent rare grace and elegance to the rough Crinti dialect. Shanair knew only one person whose voice held such music. Clutching the stone, she slapped her heels into her horse's side and reined the beast away from the camp.

"Kiva!" she whispered. "We thought you dead!"

*Do you really think I would leave before the battle was over?*

Shanair, suddenly ashamed, glanced back over her shoulder at the bustling camp. She herself was preparing to do precisely that.

Her practical nature quickly reasserted itself. "What more can be done? The battle was fought. Many Halruaans died, but too many remain. We Crinti are too few to push them into the sea."

*The Crinti need not fight alone. The floodgate—*

"The floodgate is closed," Shanair said flatly. "We felt the magic shake the mountains. We saw the spring disappear."

There was a moment's pause, and the stone in Shanair's

hand surged with power. The Crinti, attuned to Kiva through some magic she did not understand, recognized temper flaring bright and quickly controlled.

*What I was about to say,* Kiva went on pointedly, *was that many magical treasures are buried around the site of the floodgate. Dig a circle around the place of the spring's origin, about seven paces from the center.*

Shanair shook her head before she remembered the elf could not see this response. "This morning, Xerish did not report. We tracked her to one of the dark fairy mounds. There she disappeared. This is no place for the Crinti."

This time the stone flared hot enough to burn Shanair's fingers. *Did you find another set of tracks, or are the Crinti not skilled enough to follow a true elf's trail?*

The venom in Kiva's words smarted worse than the burning stone. "One trail only," Shanair admitted.

*There were two trails leading to the Green Crone,* Kiva said, giving the Crinti name for that particular fairy mound. *Xerish failed me, and I sent her beyond the veil. Do as I say, Shanair, or you will find you have far more to fear than the Unseelie folk.*

The magical contact broke off abruptly, leaving Shanair stunned and enlightened.

"Elf-sister," she muttered in self-disgust. All this time, she had believed Kiva viewed her as a comrade, if not quite an equal. The Crinti dealt death with a quick hand. Though they were brutal and unforgiving of failure, no one among them would ever torture one of their own. Kiva had given Xerish to the dark fairies. Nothing could have painted the truth in starker colors than this.

Shanair and her proud people were nothing to Kiva.

She tugged on the horse's reins, turning it back around to the camp. After the recent defeat, the Crinti had retreated to the place where the floodgate had been hidden. Not only was it a defensible camp, but all the scattered Crinti knew it to be the fallback place. Each day had brought new stragglers. If Kiva spoke truth, there was enough magic in this place to send them all beyond the veil.

"Call in the sentinels and scouts," she shouted. "We leave this accursed place before the sun burns away the mists!"

Basel Indoulur stooped and peeked cautiously through the low, open door. The wizard who'd crafted Procopio's gaming tables was said to be an unusual soul, but the reality was odder than Basel had anticipated.

A stout, middle-aged female gnome ceased her work long enough to give him a cheery wave. "You'd be Lord Basel, then? Come in, come in."

He ducked through the door and exchanged pleasantries with his host. She was an odd-looking little creature, brown as a mushroom except for eyes of cornflower blue and a bright, rosy bloom on her plump cheeks and large, button nose. Her abundant brown hair was caught back in a blue kerchief, and a neat, white apron covered her kirtle. Although famed for her skill as an alchemist and artificer, the little wizard looked more like a cook holding sway in a miniature, well-managed kitchen.

After greeting Basel, she went back to a low table. Shelves above it were lined with jars filled with strangely colored powders.

"This has the look of an apothecary shop," Basel observed.

"That and more." The gnome winked at him, then picked up a miniature mortar and pestle. She began vigorously grinding at something pale gray and unspeakably foul smelling.

"Bat guano," she said cheerfully. "Very useful in creating explosions. Have some?"

She held out a small, paper-wrapped packet, much as a homey granny might offer a treat to a child.

Not wishing to offend, Basel accepted the odd gift. "You said I might have a look around?"

The gnome waved her hand toward a small side room. "All the Crinti lore is in there. Stay as long as you like. Don't worry about making a mess—I've already seen to that."

He thanked her and made his way over to the small room. Unlike the main chamber, this area was an untidy jumble. Tiny, carved figures tumbled about in various stages of completion. Piles of miniature limbs and weapons waited to be attached to tiny bodies. Fully assembled figures had been daubed with paint, but the detailed work that made them look like living things had yet to be completed. All the figures would eventually be enspelled into the almost-living toys Procopio Septus favored so highly.

A long table was heaped high with old books and shards of pottery. Basel reached tentatively into the pile. His hand brushed something furry, and he instinctively pulled back.

An enormous tarantula, its body nearly as large as a rat's, darted out at him, hissing like an angry cat.

Basel's battlefield nerve deserted him in the face of this unexpected foe. Letting out a startled shout, he seized a heavy tome and lofted it high over the attacking arachnid. He kept yelling as he brought the book down, hoping to drown out the sound of impact. His efforts were only partially successful.

"Mind the spiders," the gnome called cheerfully. "For some reason they tend to gather in that corner."

Basel regarded the splattered creature with disgust, then turned his gaze to his chosen weapon. Greenish ooze dripped from a cover embossed with slanted, spindly runes, which proclaimed the book to be a history of the southland's dark elves. He scraped the book clean with the packet of bat guano and settled down to read.

Hours passed, and Basel pored through one book after another. He pieced together scroll fragments and shards of spell-vessels of a sort not used for hundreds of years.

Finally he stood and stretched, thinking fondly of a fort-
night by the sea and perhaps a pilgrimage to a holy Mystran shrine. He would need something of this nature to
cleanse himself of the creeping, soul-deadening evil he'd
immersed himself in.

"Like crawling through a midden," he muttered, glaring
at Crinti lore. "If water seeks its own level, small wonder
that Procopio is so taken with such things!"

The gnome peeked around the doorjamb. "I'm for the
tavern. Found what you need?"

"Actually, no," he admitted. "I'm looking for an ancient
spell, probably created by dark elves."

A bit of the cheeriness faded from the gnome's face. "Well,
I suppose you have your reasons. There's a book or two in the
root cellar that might serve. Never had much use for them
myself, and they seemed right at home down there."

Basel followed her to a miniature kitchen. She kicked
aside a wooden door in the floor and disappeared down a
ladder. The wizard accepted things she handed up to him—
a pair of rutabagas for tomorrow's stew, some dried herbs,
a small bag of coin, and finally a book bound with black
wyvern hide, long ago faded to a dull, papery gray.

He thanked the gnome and began to turn the ancient
vellum pages—carefully, for they were fragile. By the look
of them, they had probably been written by some of the
first wizards from ancient Netheril. Basel struggled with
the archaic language and the even more ancient spells.

Finally he found one that quickened his heart and
chilled his blood.

A dark-elven spell opened a small gate to the Unseelie
realm, allowing one mortal to be substituted for another. It
was possible for both to return, but only if the would-be rescuer possessed rare clarity of character and a heart that
offered no foothold to the dark fairies' magic. The rescuer—
or the sacrifice, depending upon the outcome—must wear a
talisman containing, among other things, a lock of hair from
an ancestor, preferably a wizard of great prowess.

Basel grimaced. While this requirement would not be difficult for most Halruaans, it presented a real challenge for a kinless jordain. Yet Basel could think of no one but Matteo to whom he would entrust this task.

He copied the complex spell, working as quickly as he dared. He paid the gnome woman for her time and hurried to his tower, where a gate awaited that would take him to the floodgate's location—the place where Tzigone had disappeared and where Matteo was bound.

# CHAPTER TEN

**F**our men rode northward through the rugged
Nath, following the faint, twisting trail left by a dry
streambed. Although all four were Halruaan and
all were clad in the jordaini garb of white linen, it
occurred to Matteo that he and his friends presented a strikingly diverse group.

Iago, the small, slight man who led the way,
had seen well over thirty summers, at least ten
more than the three men with him. Themo was
the youngest, a bluff, cheery giant who was still in
many ways more a youth than a man. Andris was
taller than most Halruaans and wiry rather than
muscular. His coloring was unusual: auburn hair,
hazel eyes, and freckled skin that refused to
burnish in the sun. Hints of these colors remained, despite Andris's mysterious transformation during the battle in Akhlaur's Swamp. Despite
all, Matteo still considered Andris the best jordain
he knew.

Yet nothing resembling brotherhood passed
between Andris and the other two jordaini, who'd
accepted the ghostly jordain's presence only after
much argument and under protest. Even Themo,
who had counted Andris a boyhood friend, had
little to say to him.

As they neared the battle site, the expression
on Iago's face changed from wary to grim. He

reined his horse back and fell into step with Matteo's steed.

"I understand the need to trace Kiva's path. Andris has cause to know it better than any other, but perhaps you should consider his true purpose in bringing us here."

"Andris is still a jordain," Matteo said quietly. "He follows our code. I would stake my life on his word."

"And ours as well," Iago grumbled.

Eager to change the subject, Matteo turned to Themo. "You have not spoken of your plans. What will you do, now that you've been released from jordaini service?"

The big man gave him a fleeting grin. "I'd like to survive this trip." He lifted one shoulder in a shrug and gestured to the jordaini garments he wore out of life-long habit. "Truth is, I'm feeling more adrift than I expected to. The only thing I know is the jordaini order."

"The world is too wide for a single man's eyes to take in," Matteo observed.

"Just so. I don't need someone to do my thinking for me, mind you, but it's easier to think things through if you have some sort of reference point. Maybe I'll join the militia."

Matteo nodding approvingly. "There is great need for such as you."

He would have said more, but Andris placed a translucent hand on Matteo's arm. He pointed to a small muddy patch of ground just off the path, almost obscured by a tumble of rocks. There, barely discernable from horseback, was a faint footprint.

Matteo signaled a halt. He slid from his horse and went over for a closer look. The print was long and narrow, most likely a woman's foot, and the boot sole showed signs of repeated repair. A faint smear of blood appeared on a rock nearby, as if the traveler had stumbled and caught herself. Most likely, someone already wounded and weakened had passed this way, and recently. Neither the blood nor the muddy print was completely dry.

"Crinti stragglers," Matteo said softly. "Keep your weapons at hand."

Iago shot a disgusted look at Andris. "So much for his jordaini honor!"

Shrill, ululating battle cries rose from a dozen hiding places, coming at them from all sides and echoing off the surrounding mountains.

"The floodgate clearing," Andris said urgently. "It's nearby and gives our best hope of holding out against so many."

"How many would that be?" retorted Iago. "How large an ambush have you arranged?"

No one heard his objection, for they were already riding hard on the heels of Andris's mount. Iago kicked his horse into a run, following the other jordain up the steep, narrow path created by the streambed and into a clearing.

Andris leaped from his horse and put his shoulder to a large, rounded boulder. Themo came to help him. They rolled it into the opening made by the stream, and then piled more rocks on top. The makeshift dam would not stop the Crinti, but it would slow them down.

"Now there's only one way in," Andris said, pointing to the pass leading out of the clearing.

"And only one way out!"

A woman's voice, harsh and heavily accented, rang through the clearing. The jordaini whirled, just in time to see a large net spinning toward them from behind a precarious pile of rocks. The weighted net slapped into them and brought them down in a tangle of limbs.

Over a dozen Crinti warriors stepped from the shadows of small caves, planting themselves in a circle around the edge of the net and holding the jordaini trapped beneath. One of them, a tall woman with crimson tattoos encircling her upper arms, looked Andris over appraisingly.

"Elf-blooded or not, I did not think you would return. You have also spoken with Kiva?"

Matteo noted the stunned expression that crossed his friend's face, the flicker of confusion and indecision.

"No," Andris said shortly. "I didn't know she had returned."

"Then you brought the humans here on your own. Well done." The big Crinti pulled out a sword and slit open the net over Andris. She reached down and hauled him to his feet.

Her gaze skimmed her other captives. Her strange, blue eyes narrowed when they settled upon Matteo. "This one killed Whizzra. It was his woman who summoned the dark fairies."

"My friend," Matteo corrected.

Shanair laughed and cast a sly glance toward Andris. "And here is another of your 'friends?' You do not choose them wisely. This one betrays you, and the girl was not strong enough to master what she summoned. She is dead now, or gone beyond the veil, which is much worse."

She turned to her warriors. One of them had a large, powerful crossbow cranked and ready, leveled at Matteo's chest. The chieftain jerked her head in Matteo's direction. "Kill him first, but slowly."

The gray archer smirked and lowered her aim.

"Wait," Andris said. He pulled out his jordaini daggers. "I've known this man since boyhood. A crossbow is too swift and too kind."

He turned to Matteo. He flipped both daggers, caught them by their points, and sent first one then the other spinning toward the captive jordain.

The first dagger struck the ground near Matteo, neatly slicing through the tied ropes of the net. Matteo thrust his arm through the opening and closed his hand around the handle of the second, spinning dagger.

A risky move, catching a thrown dagger, but one the two of them had practiced together since boyhood.

Matteo sliced through the net and burst out into the clearing, drawing his sword as he came. He dropped into guard position, prepared to hold off the Crinti's blades as Themo and Iago struggled free.

As he moved, he saw Andris whirl and seize the

woman's crossbow. The jordain forced her aim up at the large, unstable rock formation that had hidden the Crinti ambush.

Boulders tumbled down into the clearing, bringing more stones with them. Andris hurtled forward, driving Iago toward a small overhang. The four jordaini flattened themselves into the scant shelter as the thunder and dust of falling rock filled the clearing.

"She was wrong, you know," Matteo shouted at Andris. The pale jordain sent him an inquiring look. "The Crinti chieftain. She said I do not choose my friends well."

A quick look of gratitude flashed in Andris's pale eyes. "Obviously she never met your horse Cyric."

The two jordaini shared a chuckle. When the avalanche ceased but for echoes carrying the grumbling thunder from mountain to mountain, they came cautiously out, swords ready.

Most of the Crinti had gone down under the tumbling stone. Some shifted weakly, others lay bloody and still. Only a few Crinti were left standing—odds the jordaini could reasonably face. The chieftain staggered to her feet, her wild, steel-gray hair crusted with blood.

"Another traitor," she said, eyeing Andris with disdain. She spat at the ground. "You are not worth fighting. *She* is not worth fighting *for*. We go."

The surviving Crinti turned and disappeared through the pass, swiftly melting into the hills.

"Shouldn't we give chase?" Themo asked.

Iago sent him a withering look. "Remember the battle cries that sent us scurrying into this hole? This was a small group. Most of them are out there. If they want to leave Halruaa, I say we let them."

He turned to Andris. "You have proved me wrong. See that you keep doing so."

"I'll do my best," the jordain agreed, "but I should warn you that despite my best intentions, I seem destined to betray those around me."

"A strange sentiment," Matteo protested, "from someone whose quick thinking kept us alive."

"I thank you for that thought, but remember that heritage plays a strange part in destiny."

"Then it's just as well we jordaini seldom know of our ancestry," Iago said curtly. "Do you think the Crinti was telling the truth about Kiva? Is she still alive?"

Andris sighed. "I don't know what to think. The spells cast during the invasion were right out of Akhlaur's spellbook. Few living wizards could cast them. To my thinking, the possibility of Akhlaur's return indicated that Kiva died in the Plane of Water. But Shanair spoke of Kiva as if her survival was a fact we both knew. She had no reason to lie to me."

Another tremor shuddered through the clearing. "Another rockslide," groaned Themo, eying the distance between the jordaini and their recent shelter.

"Worse than that." Matteo pointed to the center of the clearing. Cracks splintered the hard-packed ground, revealing glimpses of several strange items that had been dislodged by the tremor—a cat-headed statue carved in jade, a sword hilt forged from crimson metal, a strangely shaped rod.

"This is a natural site of power, made stronger by those hidden artifacts. Wizards use ritual to focus magic, but this is not the only way of doing so. Sometimes magic can be triggered by other strong energies."

"Like an avalanche," Iago said.

Themo nudged the discarded crossbow with his foot, then sent a sidelong glance at Andris. "Seemed like a good idea at the time, did it?"

Andris wasn't listening. He stared at the strange circle of light dawning in the clearing. It erupted in a sudden brilliant flare, then faded.

In its place stood a monstrous creature, easily twice Themo's height. Exaggerated elven ears slashed upward, framing a hideous green-scaled face. Living eels writhed about the monster's head, their tiny, fanged jaws snapping. Four massive arms flexed, making the monster look like a mutated wrestler preparing for attack. Each of the four hands sported curved talons as deadly as daggers. Thick, greenish hide armored the monster, and slightly luminous drool dripped from its bared fangs.

The monster's black eyes settled upon the stunned jordaini, and it threw back its head and let out a shrieking howl that spanned the spectrum of sound, at the same time a thunderous grumble and a raptor's shriek.

"Holy mother of Mystra," breathed Themo.

Iago drew his weapons. "Few men are granted their wishes. You wanted to fight the laraken."

"Obviously, I lied."

Despite his jest, the big jordain was pale as death. Matteo remembered Themo's recently confessed doubts about his worthiness as a warrior. Yet Themo pulled his sword and shouldered his smaller comrades aside, rushing in to take the first slashing blow of the laraken's claws. The other jordaini followed close behind.

Matteo gave a silent prayer for the men who had fallen in the last battle with this foe and those who were about to join them.

Basel Indoulur stepped from the shimmering magic of his transportation spell into a grim, gray world. The sun climbed sluggishly toward its zenith, looking faint and pale through its shroud of mist. He found himself nearly at the top of the mountain, looking down into a small, rock-strewn clearing.

The sight below chilled him. Four men battled a fierce, four-armed creature. The monster seized one of the men in all four hands and lifted him, struggling and kicking, to its waiting fangs. A glint of sun reflected from the man's hair, and auburn lights flashed like a premonition of spilled blood.

"Matteo," murmured Basel, his voice thick with grief and dread.

A smaller man darted forward, his sword angled high and braced like a lance. He threw himself at the monster, and his sword found an opening beneath the creature's upraised arm.

Its bellow of pain and rage shook the mountains. Hurling Matteo aside, the creature fell upon this new foe. Its two lower hands seized the man's sword arm at wrist and elbow. With a quick twist it snapped the arm like a reed, bending the forearm into an impossible angle.

The other men—a huge man in jordaini garb and one that looked more like a soap bubble than flesh and sinew—slashed at the monster with their respective weapons of steel and crystal. Matteo staggered to his feet, found his fallen sword, and rejoined the battle. All of them fought fiercely, clearly determined to rescue their comrade.

But the creature would not be cheated or deterred. Still holding the small man's mangled arm, the monster jerked him up high and used him like a flail to beat back his own would-be rescuers. Again and again the monster lashed out. The three jordaini dodged and rolled aside from each blow, but they were helpless to prevent injury to their captured comrade. In moments, the man was reduced to something that more closely resembled a broken doll than a brave jordain.

The monster backed away several paces. Each of its massive hands closed on one of the wounded man's limbs, and the creature threw all four of its arms up high. For the briefest of moments it held the man aloft, well above the reach of his comrades.

Then, with a ringing shriek, the monster threw its four arms wide and tore its victim apart.

All this happened far more quickly than the telling would take. Muttering an oath, Basel reached into his sleeve for a battle wand, one he had carried for twenty years. Leveling it at the strange monster, he chanted the spell that would loose stinging bolts of cold. He smiled as icy blue light streaked from the wand. Cold and ice were rare things in Halruaa, and Basel's enemies had seldom been prepared for such an attack.

He looked forward to seeing this one's response.

Matteo ducked under slashing claws, then lashed out high. His sword retraced a bloody line under the laraken's lower left arm—one of the monster's few vulnerable spots. Ichor flowed freely down the creature's side. Matteo dropped and rolled away, yielding his place to Themo. When the big man was forced to evade, Matteo came back in.

The two of them harried and worried the creature, like a pair of wolves snapping at a stag. Matteo tried not to think of Iago's fate or his conviction that they all would share it.

"Fall back," he snapped at Andris. His friend seemed more insubstantial than ever, little more than a shadow. The presence of the laraken obviously leeched away his strength. Yet Andris kept coming in, using his near-transparency as a means of slipping up behind the monster unseen.

Andris ignored Matteo and slashed at the laraken's tail. The monster shrieked and thrashed the wounded appendage wildly. One blow connected, sending Andris tumbling painfully over the rocky ground.

But Matteo and Themo made good use of the diversion. They moved out wide on either side of the laraken, swords flashing as they kept all four of the monster's hands busy and held well out from its body.

The creature wheeled this way and that, as if sensing its vulnerability.

The attack came from an unexpected quarter. A bolt of pale blue sizzled down from a nearby mountaintop, heading directly for the laraken's chest.

Matteo's first impulse was to leap between the monster and the magic. Instantly he checked himself—his resistance to magic was strong but certainly not absolute, and since he had never before seen a missile of this nature, he did not know if he could survive it.

Instead he threw himself at Themo, knocking his friend clear of the magic missile. They rolled together, swiftly breaking apart and coming to their feet in ready guard—just in time to see the missile find its target.

The blue light softened and spread as it approached the monster. A glowing haze enveloped the laraken and sank into its hide like water into a sponge. As the laraken absorbed the magic, its wounds closed and the muscles on its corded limbs swelled with renewed strength.

"It's healing," Themo marveled, staring at the monster. "What now?"

"We hope that whoever cast that spell isn't stupid enough to do it again," Matteo said grimly.

The laraken shrieked and came at them in a darting charge. Matteo set his feet firmly, lifted his sword, and prepared to die well.

Suddenly another fighter appeared between him and the charging laraken. With astonishment Matteo recognized Basel Indoulur. The portly conjurer stumbled and fell to one knee, dropped prematurely from a blink spell that had been intercepted and drained by the laraken's hunger.

"No magic!" Matteo shouted as he charged forward to protect the wizard.

The laraken slashed at Basel with rending talons. Matteo caught the laraken's wrist near the hilt of his sword and threw himself to one side. The laraken, expecting more resistance, was led slightly forward. Matteo only hoped Basel had the wit and instinct to use this moment to escape.

The wizard threw himself into a forward roll, going between the laraken's legs and coming up behind, a sword in each hand. The monster whirled and slashed.

Basel met the laraken's blow with one sword and brought the other weapon into guard position. Suddenly the at-guard sword lengthened, leaping up toward the laraken's unprotected armpit.

Matteo shouted a warning, but it was too late. To his astonishment, the sword dug deep into the monster's body, unaffected by the monster's magic drain. Basel released the impaling weapon and backed away.

The jordain smiled briefly as he realized what had just happened. He had seen such a weapon demonstrated once before. A deadly mating between a crossbow and a sword, it was a double-layered contraction fashioned of cunning levers and springs. A trigger sent the outer layer hurtling forward, effectively doubling the length of the sword.

Matteo charged the bellowing monster with a high, slashing feint, hoping to free an opening for one of the other fighters to drive the imbedded blade still deeper.

But the laraken ignored him. Its form began to waver and fade, much like the landscape when viewed through the shimmering filter of a magic portal. The creature gave one final roar and disappeared. The trick weapon fell free and clattered to the rocky ground.

Matteo picked up the blade and returned it to its owner. "A well-chosen weapon. Your style of fighting seems familiar."

"It should be. We trained with the same man. Vishna was my swordmaster well before you were born." Basel looked around the clearing, littered with rock and dead Crinti warriors. "You've had a busy morning. Who are these others?"

"Iago is dead," Matteo said softly. He eyes slid over the jordain's scattered remains and moved to the survivors. "Themo has a gash requiring stitching. Andris will have to speak for himself—his state is beyond my knowledge and understanding."

The ghostly jordain sat slumped on a rock, staring

with unseeing eyes at the place where the laraken had disappeared.

"I will tend Themo," Basel said softly. "You see what can be done for the other."

Matteo came over and placed a hand on Andris's shoulder. It seemed to him that his friend was no longer quite solid.

"She's alive," the jordain said flatly. "The Crinti spoke the truth. Kiva is alive."

Matteo crouched down to eye level. "How do you know?"

Andris cast a bleak look up at Matteo. "The laraken is back."

Basel glanced up from his work. "That's the problem with fighting monsters. It's rather like house-tending, in that it never seems to be done and over with. You spoke of Kiva's return. Why do you equate one monster with the other?"

"I saw Akhlaur's spellbook," Andris explained. "The necromancer created the laraken, but there are limits to his powers over it. He generally has an apprentice trained to summon the laraken, for he cannot. Who but Kiva could do this thing?"

Matteo blew out a long breath and sat down next to his friend. "Kiva, alive and aligned with Akhlaur! But how could she summon the laraken? You saw what happened to her last time she got too close to it."

Andris shook his head. "I have the feeling we'll find out far too soon."

# CHAPTER ELEVEN

The laraken was falling again. It flailed wildly, clawing at the swift-flowing stream of magic.

Then the magic was gone, and the laraken stood mired to its haunches in murky water. Familiar sounds and scents filled the humid air. The puzzled creature realized, without understanding why, that it had been returned to the place of its birth.

Suddenly the laraken was ravenous. The Plane of Water had yielded a steady, constant supply of magic. Here in the swamp, the monster would need to hunt. The laraken threw back its head and sniffed the air. A faint scent of magic, the spoor of its prey, lingered in the humid air. The laraken followed the scent as unerringly as a hound, stalking out of the mire and toward the borderlands of the swamp.

It crouched behind the thick trunk of a bilboa tree and peered at the straggling line of humans cutting their way through waist-high grasses. Magic clung to them like scented smoke.

The laraken's black tongue flicked out, tasting the air with reptilian pleasure. The male who led the group carried a sword decorated with a glowing gem and filled with magic—fairly glowing with it. The laraken drank the savory draught.

Abruptly the wizard stopped, his hand going to

the despoiled sword. Steel hissed as he drew the weapon, and he stared for a long, disbelieving moment at the dull, clouded stone in the hilt. He tossed the useless blade aside and shouted incomprehensible noise at his comrades. One of them, a woman wearing robes of jungle green, stepped forward and brandished a tall black staff.

In response, the bilboa trees began to stir like awakening titans. The ground shook as roots tore free of the soil. Ancient wood creaked as the ensorcelled trees stretched and flexed, trying out their first fledgling steps.

The laraken backed away, enthralled by this wondrous display. It ducked as a thick limb swept over its head in ponderous attack, and it began to drink. Leaves withered to brown ash as the living trees yielded up their magic-enhanced lives. The laraken shrieked with joy at the intoxicating magic flowing into its limbs.

The wizards threw down their weapons and fled in panic. The laraken reached out, draining their spells, drinking their essence. Giddy with magic, the creature did not at first notice the uprooted bilboa trees begin to totter and sway.

Down they went, moving at the slow, inexorable pace that characterizes nightmares. Living trees shattered beneath the weight of the toppling giants, and a shrill chorus filled the air as creatures that made verdant cities of jungle trees died along with their homes. The humans, those slain by the laraken's hunger and those yet alive, went down under the tangle of killing limbs.

The laraken scuttled back, dodging the upturning roots and the churning soil. A sudden swell of torn root caught it and sent it tumbling.

Pain lashed through the monster. Flying branches and unearthed rock tore at its hide as the humans' swords could not. The sated pleasure of the laraken's recent banquet faded as the stolen magic flowed into the healing process.

Quickly the glow of the magical feast faded. Far too quickly.

Suddenly the laraken understood. The spells, the stolen magic, were being taken away! That meant that He Whose Spells Could Not Be Eaten had also left the world of watery magic.

The laraken—not quite healed, ravenous to the point of agony—threw back its head and shrieked in despair.

Kiva watched as Akhlaur received the stolen magic. His long, black staff crackled with bluish light and gathering energy. His faintly green face was intent as he considered the nature of his booty.

"Druid spells," he said disgustedly, and tossed the eel aside. "The laraken will have to do better than that."

Despite his words, he seemed pleased. The laraken would quickly advance Akhlaur's rise to power, even if many of the spells it drank were of no use to its master. Whatever magic Akhlaur possessed was magic that another wizard did not.

"One thing concerns me about the laraken's return," Kiva said. "I am afraid its presence might drain away my hard-won spells. It did so once before." In a few words, Kiva told the necromancer how she had regained her wizardly magic and how the effort had aged her.

"You raided the Lady's Mirror," Akhlaur repeated, clearly amused. "I must say, little Kiva, your initiative is rather impressive."

The necromancer snapped his fingers, then plucked a small, glittering vial from the empty air. "All problems have solutions. You recognize this powder?"

The elf hesitated, then nodded. It was the same glowing green substance that had triggered the zombie transformation in the half-elven wizard's guard.

"There is a death-bond between us," Akhlaur went on, "which already gives you some immunity to the laraken. I can strengthen that bond. While I am not averse to taking your spells, it serves my purpose to keep you as a loyal servant."

Kiva pretended to consider this. "But what if I die, my lord? The death-bond between us is already as strong as it can be without binding both ways."

"Hence the potion," Akhlaur said with strained patience, as if speaking to a particularly slow and stupid child. "I have no intention of dying, of this I assure you! This potion will grant you a type of immortality. An elf can expect an unnaturally long life; this will ensure a lich transformation at the end of it."

"I had never aspired to such an afterlife," Kiva said, speaking for once with complete truth. Elves, particularly wild elves, viewed transformation into any undead creature as an unspeakable abomination and a fate to be avoided at any cost.

The necromancer took her words at face value. He motioned for Kiva's water flask and poured the potion into it. She accepted the flask eagerly and tipped it back. Remembering the terrible death throes of the half-elven wizard, Kiva gave a theatrical shudder and dropped to the ground. She thrashed and flailed, twisting herself into wild contortions—conveniently managing to spit out most of the tainted water unnoticed. By her reckoning, a sip would strengthen the death-bond sufficiently without preparing her for lichdom.

At last Kiva dragged herself to her feet. "And you, Lord Akhlaur," she said hoarsely. "Have you also taken this precaution?"

The necromancer gave her a condescending smile. "As long as the crimson star lasts, what power could possibly bring me down?"

"I have often pondered that very question," she said.

Akhlaur's face fell slack with astonishment, then darkened with wrath. Just as quickly, his expression changed to dark mirth. "The best of my apprentices," he repeated.

◉

Wizards from all over Halruaa gathered in the council chamber of King Zalathorm. The king's greatest magical treasure—at least, the greatest treasure of which people were aware—was a great, amber globe that could summon wizards from every corner of the land. Each wizard who achieved the status of Elder wore a golden ring set with a round amber stone. Using these artifacts, Zalathorm could summon a council at any time and could communicate with some or all of his faithful wizards.

The problem, mused Zalathorm wryly, was that few of these wizards were entirely as faithful as they wished to appear.

He looked out over the sea of waiting, respectful faces. Zalathorm was a powerful diviner, as adept at gauging the heart and purpose of a man as any wizard alive. The truth he saw behind many of those faces pained him to the soul.

"I have summoned you here to discuss the aftermath of the Mulhorandi invasion," he began.

Applause swept through the hall as wizards hailed their king for his role in the recent victory. Zalathorm cut the ovation short with a sharply upraised hand.

"Every man and woman here had a part in Halruaa's victory. Let us address the future. We have received word from Mulhorand. An ambassador seeks permission to offer terms of peace."

Silence hung thick in the crowded room. "What possible terms could they seek?" demanded a thin, querulous voice. Febir Khorn, a wizened man whose face wore every day of his ninety years, thumped his staff indignantly on the polished marble floor. His advanced years, longtime friendship to Zalathorm and absolute loyalty to the king purchased him the right to speak his mind at will. "If the Mulhorandi stay out of Halruaa, we will let them live. What more could they ask or expect?"

A chorus of huzzahs and approving laughter filled the hall. Zalathorm smiled at the indignant wizard. "It is my sincere wish that everything was as forthright as you, my friend, but, despite Halruaa's victory, several mysteries remain. These we must and will address."

His steady gaze swept the crowd. No one doubted that he spoke of his own queen, and her coming trial for treason. Many of the wizards dropped their eyes, shamed by their whispered accusations and speculations. It was widely rumored that Zalathorm's queen would never come to trial at all, that her misdeeds would be shielded by the king's power.

"The battle between the storm elementals provides a key to one such mystery," Zalathorm continued. "Procopio Septus turned back the attack, using a storm elemental fashioned in his own image. It is likely that the Mulhorandi wizard did the same. I propose that we have an artist sketch the Mulhorandi storm elemental and send it back to Mulhorand with their diplomat."

Procopio stepped forward. "The man is dead—killed when his elemental was vanquished. What benefit would this bring?"

"We will insist that the Mulhorandi supply us with the man's true name, as well as some of his personal belongings, so that we can pursue a full divination into his plans and purposes. If the Mulhorandi do this, we will seek no reprisals. If they attempt to shield this man for fear of exposing others involved in the invasion, we will retaliate with an attack on Mulhorand."

An astonished babble exploded. Halruaa had repelled many invasions over her long history, but never had she launched an attack upon another country!

"There is wisdom in tradition," shouted Procopio above the din.

Complete silence fell over the hall. This was the first open challenge to the king.

Zalathorm's steady gaze acknowledged the wizard lord's words for what they were. "You obviously think that tradition holds more wisdom than your king. Tell us why."

Such bluntness was rare in Halruaan society, and for a

moment Procopio looked disconcerted. He quickly gathered himself and responded in kind.

"Fully a third of Halruaan wizards and fighters were destroyed in the recent battles. Four hundred fell in the king's city alone. It is time to rebuild, not to extend forces already depleted."

Zalathorm nodded gravely. "Our losses were great, but would you have us cower behind our mountain walls, weak and timid in the eyes of the world? Why give our neighbors cause to consider another attack?"

A murmur of agreement rippled through the room. Procopio inclined his head in a slight bow. "You know your subjects well, my lord. You appeal to our pride, and we are indeed a proud people. There is an important difference, however, between pride and blind arrogance. The invasion—the first in more than a century!—demonstrated a serious weakness in our defenses. To deny this is folly. Making a scapegoat of one of the invading wizards might be satisfying, but it detracts from the larger problem."

Zalathorm's gaze did not waver. "The larger problem, indeed. In your opinion, Lord Procopio, was the recent threat against Halruaa from without or within?"

Procopio's lips tightened into a thin line, and several of Zalathorm's supporters nodded approvingly. This was a deftly chosen question, for the lord mayor could give but one answer.

"Both, my lord."

"Then we must pursue both. We will send envoys to Mulhorand. We must know more about the wizard who enspelled our borders and learn how he mingled the magic of Mulhorand with the hidden lore of Halruaa—and we must learn who helped him."

Zalathorm paused to give weight to that pronouncement. As his meaning became clear, stunned disbelief spread from face to face like a spell-borne plague. Revealing Halruaan magic to foreigners was the most egregious treason, the most unthinkable betrayal!

Yet, what else could have happened?

"I hesitate to speak of this," the king went on, addressing all the wizards, "for I see how your eyes slide to those next to you, weighing and wondering. Unlike most of you in this room, I have lived in a time when wizard fought wizard. We must avoid a return of those days. We must stand together, even as we root out weakness and treachery. I pledge to you, by wind and word, that all will be brought to light."

The silence enshrouding the room grew heavier. Zalathorm had given his wizard-word oath, even though his queen stood accused.

For a moment Zalathorm believed that he had averted the crisis of ambition and conflict. Perhaps reality reflected his young jordain's belief—perhaps truth was indeed the most powerful weapon to use in Halruaa's service.

But Procopio wheeled to face the assembled wizards, indignation and incredulity sharp on his face. "Are we all to submit to Inquisition? What sort of tyranny is this? What of the laws of Halruaa, the rights of her wizards?"

The utter lack of logic startled the king. "I do not propose to do away with either."

"Not openly, no," the wizard returned, "but magic and secrecy are like sword and sheath. A man who carries naked steel is more likely to use it. You speak of the dangers of wizardwar, yet it seems to me that you fan the flames! In casting suspicion upon every wizard in Halruaa, perhaps you hope to deflect it from known traitors and incompetent leaders?"

Mutters of protest mingled with muttered agreement. A woman in warrior's garb shouldered her way forward, her hand on the hilt of her sword. Wizards parted to let her pass. Rhodea Firehair was as tall and ruddy as a northern barbarian, skilled with both blade and battle magic. She came nearly toe to toe with the lord mayor, forcing him to look up at her considerable height.

"You go too far, Procopio," she growled.

The diviner inclined his head. "I pray you are right, Lady Rhodea. None of us wishes to see Halruaa torn by more conflict. But I see what is coming, *even if others do not.*"

Procopio's condemning words rang through the hall. He turned and walked from the room, his back to the throne. After a moment's hesitation, several more wizards followed or quietly disappeared.

Rhodea strode to the throne and took up a place at Zalathorm's left-hand side—the traditional position for a champion. Her sword sang free of its scabbard, burning with magic as fiery as her own hair. Blood-red light bathed the battle wizard as she raised the sword and slammed it sharply against the buckler strapped to her left forearm. A high, metallic note echoed out through the room like a battle cry.

"Zalathorm has spoken. Any who would challenge the king or his decisions must come through me," she announced over the grim music of her sword.

Deep silence ruled the counsel hall. Then, one by one, the wizards began to step forward with loud acclamations, some of which provided deliberate cover for those wizards who slipped quietly away. Already deals had been made and sides chosen.

With sinking heart and soul-deep sorrow, Zalathorm acknowledged the truth in Procopio's words. There was little difference, sometimes, between foreseeing a battle and causing one.

He did not need his divination magic to understand that a wizardwar had begun.

# CHAPTER TWELVE

Later that day, Rhodea Firehair stomped angrily into the vast, stone chamber that housed Halruaa's mint. She acknowledged the guards with a curt nod and submitted with ill grace to the spells of divination that each visitor, no matter how well known, was subjected to before entering.

Usually she acknowledged the wisdom of such precautions. It would not do to allow a thief or hostile wizard to slip into the mint. Much of Halruaa's wealth poured through this place. Rich ore came in by the wagonload, to emerge as the elegantly stamped skie that formed the basis of Halruaan currency.

She was in no mood, however, to endure the foolishness of her fellow wizards. The shameful display in Zalathorm's counsel hall left her sword hand itching for the feel of her weapon. The sword still glowed faintly red from the power that had fueled her indignant defense of her king.

Rhodea stopped by the cooling pool and plucked a fresh-minted coin from the water. The image of King Zalathorm, the only ruler Rhodea had ever known and the only one she intended to serve, gazed back at her.

She nodded curtly. "As it should be."

The wizard's mood improved as she walked

slowly through the mint. Here, all was as it should be. Stout, dour-faced dwarves shepherded their ore through the smelting process. Artisans labored with tiny tools, engraving plates for new coin. A tall, red-haired young woman argued loudly with the dragon keeper, her hands milling in furious gestures.

Rhodea smiled fondly. Her daughter, Thalia, possessed in full measure the family's passionate nature. Though she would never be a great wizard, the girl shared her mother's steadfast dedication to Halruaa. In time she would run this mint and run it well.

The subject of her ire was a half-elven wizard, specially chosen for his long life and his skill with magical creatures. Many years were required to raise and train a hatchling dragon and to learn the spells that kept the young creature relatively docile.

There was a jordaini proverb about the dangers of overdoing matters, something to the effect of chaining a dragon to do your cooking, yet the mint did precisely that. Risky, yes, but electrum ore was difficult to melt, and few things burned as hot as dragonfire.

Rhodea came alongside the arguing pair, who fell silent. "Greetings, Thalia. And to you, Pizar. Problems?"

Thalia glared at the half-elf. "The dragon is acting strangely. I told this . . . keeper . . . to review his spells of binding. He is too proud and stubborn to listen."

"I have reviewed them," the dragonmaster returned heatedly. "Of course the dragon is restless! She nears maturity. Soon we will no longer be able to control her at all. It is time and past time to return her to the wild! Another hatchling is nearly old enough for firebreath. It's better to suspend production of coin for a short time than risk both the dragon and the mint."

Rhodea nodded thoughtfully. "I agree. You have my permission to release this dragon as soon as the spells of transportation can be arranged. But do not release it into the Calimshan wastes, as usual. Mulhorandi recently sent some of their finest citizens to call. Perhaps we should return the courtesy."

Shocked silence fell over the contentious pair. They exchanged glances and began to grin like urchin conspirators. Rhodea chuckled and moved on.

She strode over to the main vat to observe the dragon. The creature was still young, no more than twenty feet long and covered with bright red scales. Mithril chains and unbreakable spells kept the creature secure during its brief servitude. The dragon seemed tame enough, breathing gouts of flame at the base of the enormous vat whenever the dwarves on the scaffolding above shouted for it.

Rhodea looked up. Four dwarves, working two to a wheel, turned the crank that stirred the simmering brew. Another dwarf stood on a lower level of scaffolding, adjusting the knobs that opened a circular hole near the top of the kettle. Gleaming silvery liquid poured down a long trough toward a smaller kettle, where still more dwarves scooped out the rapidly cooling metal and smoothed it into plates.

Much of the work was done by dwarves. They were the only creatures who could abide the intense heat. Even so, their bearded faces were nearly as red as Rhodea's famed tresses.

Suddenly a terrible stench filled the room, like that of a thousand well-rotted eggs. Rhodea spun, her hand clamped to her mouth, toward the source.

The dragon held its post, its eyes still magic-glazed into quiescence, its breath still coming in regular bursts. But the dragon's scales were no longer the clear, bright red of early adolescence but a verdant green. Its breath yielded not fire, but a noxious yellow cloud.

Rhodea gasped in astonishment. The sudden intake of foul air sent her into a paroxysm of coughing. The dwarves on the scaffolding were harder hit, coughing violently and teetering on their perch like drunkards. One of them lost his grip and fell into the molten ore with a terrible scream.

Bright droplets of liquid metal splattered the dragon.

Pain jolted the creature free from the protective spells. It began to roar and struggle. Its tail lashed, knocking the supports from under the vat.

The vast kettle tipped, sending a killing river of silver spilling slowly over the wooden floor. Wooden scaffolding burst into flame, and fire darted up the tapestries that softened the stone walls. In less than a heartbeat, the promise of wealth was transmuted into a death threat.

Rhodea reached for her Elder's ring, which would transport her immediately to the safety of Zalathorm's court. Frantically she sought her daughter.

Thalia stood too near the silvery lava. Rhodea would never reach her in time.

The wizard tore the ring from her hand and poured all her considerable strength into the family battle cry. Thalia spun toward the sound and instinctively caught the ring her mother hurled toward her.

Rhodea Firehair watched her daughter fade from the room, then turned to face the white wave of heat that preceded the killing flood. A warrior died with weapon in hand. Rhodea drew her sword and strode toward the light.

Word of the mint's destruction spread quickly, nearly as quickly as the molten ore and the fire that swept its wake.

Procopio Septus read the report again, muttering under his breath about incompetent fools, but in truth, he didn't understand how this thing could have come to pass.

Many of Halruaa's mages frowned upon the use of dragons in the smelting process. The creatures were as tame as dragons would ever be, hand-raised from hatchlings and warded with powerful protective spells.

"A visitor, Lord Procopio."

The wizard looked up, frowning. "I am not at leisure," he told his steward.

"He tells a most interesting tale," the man persisted. "He claims to have fought his way out of the Unseelie realm."

Procopio's jaw fell open. He knew of Dhamari Exchelsor's disappearance. He knew also that the wards on the wizard's tower had been breached. The militia had searched and found no one, but there was clear evidence of theft. The magical wards had not yet been examined to determine the identity of this thief—the Lord Mayor had higher priorities. It had not occurred to him that Dhamari himself might be the "thief."

He quickly mastered his surprise. "Let him come. I am in need of a bit of diversion."

The steward showed in a small, slight man. Procopio knew him only by sight and had always considered him an unassuming little man, hardly worth the time and trouble under ordinary circumstances.

Procopio exchanged the courtesies that protocol demanded. Even a great wizard was required to acknowledge lesser men, and Procopio was politically astute enough to court all men to some degree. Even a mediocre wizard could be a supporter, and at this pivotal moment Procopio needed every man and woman he could muster.

He smiled at the little man with a cordiality he did not feel. "I hear you have an interesting tale."

"Yes," Dhamari said dryly. "Your steward seemed to find it amusing. I don't suspect your credulity will stretch much farther. Be that as it may. I haven't come to discuss such things. I can tell you about the death of Rhodea Firehair, the self-declared champion of our *current* king."

Though the little wizard was being far from subtle, Procopio ignored the treasonous remarks. He steepled his fingers and gazed mildly over them at his visitor. "I have heard reports of the fire."

"Would you like to hear precisely what happened?"

"Please."

"Those who examined the ruins of the mint saw only the charred bones of a young dragon," Dhamari said without preamble. "It did not occur to them to inquire what color the dead dragon might have been."

"I fail to see the point."

"The dragon was shapeshifted from red to green. This detail will not be in any report you might read."

Procopio leaned back, beginning to see where this was going and, for the first time, truly interested in the little wizard's words.

"The raw ore came from an area with heavy mineral deposits. When the dragon was changed from red to green in mid exhalation, its fiery breath changed to gas. This mingled with the gases rising from the vat and formed a poisonous and extremely volatile miasma. I imagine the dwarves working over the kettle dropped like stones."

"You have a disturbing imagination," Procopio murmured. "Yes, I can envision the scene. The kettle knocked over, and the heat from the molten ore set the place afire. The gas incapacitated the workers, cutting off their spells and their escape. A grim but effective ploy, yet it has one rather large and glaring fault. Assuming you're right, the magic that would transmute red dragon to green would have to be a necromancer's spell of enormous power. Who could have done this?"

Dhamari spread his hands modestly. "As you may know, the Exchelsor family owns much of Halruaa's mining lands. Since I supplied the ore, getting a magical device into the mint was easy enough."

A burst of incredulous laughter escaped Procopio. "You were responsible for this spell?"

"If you will not believe me, will you listen to the only survivor? Like all members of the Council of Elders, Rhodea Firehair has a ring that will teleport her to Zalathorm's court in times of need. Her last, heroic deed was to hurl the ring at her daughter. She could not know that a rather similar magical device had been prepared to intercept any who might try to escape. Shall we hear what the little red-haired wench has to say on this subject?"

"By all means!"

Dhamari drew a small red globe from the folds of his robe and threw it to the floor. The crystal shattered, and a disheveled young woman staggered into the room.

She looked wildly around. Relief suffused her face when she recognized the lord mayor.

"Lord Procopio! Mystra be praised! You must summon help, and quickly! The mint is burning!"

Procopio rose and led the girl to a chair. "It has been already seen to, my dear. Please, tell me what happened."

He listened as Thalia Firehair told her story, which matched Dhamari's in most particulars. The little wizard took up a place behind the girl, patting her shoulder soothingly as she spoke in quick, broken phrases.

At last she fell silent. Dhamari met Procopio's eye. "Have you heard quite enough?"

The lord mayor nodded. Dhamari drew a knife and thrust it deep between Thalia's shoulder blades. He gave it a vicious twist, then shoved the dying girl to the floor.

"Bravely done," Procopio said coldly.

Dhamari shrugged. "She was a trained warrior, I am not. I have learned to work within my limitations. But let no doubt remain. Test me and see."

The wizard settled down in the chair Death had vacated and submitted to Procopio's divination spells. Several moments passed as Procopio cast one spell after another, not readily convinced even by his own puissant magic. Finally he could not deny the little wizard's claims.

"You did it," the diviner marveled. "But how?"

"I purchased a spell already created. All that was needed was a simple trigger word." Dhamari examined his fingernails, elaborately casual. "Did you know that Kiva first learned magic from Akhlaur, the greatest necromancer of his time?"

The implication struck Procopio like a thrown dagger. "Kiva gave you this spell? She still lives?"

The wizard chuckled. "I seem to be somewhat better

informed than the diviner who alone foresaw the Mulhorandi invasion. In fact, one might say that I am very, very well informed."

He handed Procopio a copy of the magic missive Kiva had sent him, a damning document that gave details of Procopio's recent collusion with the treacherous elf.

Procopio skimmed the parchment and threw it down. "What do you want?"

"An exchange, nothing more," Dhamari protested. "I admire your cunning and have no intention of hindering your quest for power with this unfortunate information. Indeed, I have information of my own to give you."

"At what price?"

"One you will not mind paying," he said slyly. "You want Zalathorm deposed. So does Kiva. So do I."

"Do you? What is this priceless information?"

"The king's queen, Beatrix, is something rather more than a mad wizard and a traitor to Halruaa, though one would think that would be sufficient. She is an accused murderess, an adulteress whose dalliances produced a wizard's bastard, and, last and perhaps least in any eyes but mine, my former wife."

Procopio rose so abruptly that his chair upended. "Beatrix and Keturah are one?"

"Yes, and it is likely the king knowingly took a fugitive criminal as his wife. If he did not know who and what Beatrix was, then he is a fool who has no business ruling a kingdom."

The diviner began to pace as new plots took form. Dhamari smiled. "I can see that this pleases you. Our first order of business, however, is to deal with a mutual enemy—Basel Indoulur, a man who could undo us both."

Procopio stopped abruptly and regarded his visitor with new respect. "You have a plan?"

Dhamari spread his hands modestly. "I was rather hoping you might."

"Basel has surprisingly few enemies. The only other I can find is Uriah Belajoon."

"Has he a substantial grievance?"

"I would not think so were I in his position, but the bereaved's wife was considerably more comely than mine," Procopio said dryly. "It appears that Lord Basel has murdered old Belajoon's pretty young bride."

A wide smile spread across Dhamari's face. "You have proof?"

"Not yet."

"It might not be needed," the little wizard mused. "If fact, it might be better not to trouble the Council with this matter. Uriah Belajoon is a strong supporter of the king. Goad him into taking his own vengeance, making him subject to Halruaan law, and we will have destroyed two more of Zalathorm's supporters." Dhamari glanced pointedly at the dead girl. "I will aid this with other attacks, as successful as this one."

"And in return?"

"For now, I would like my return held in secret. I carry magic that obscures my purposes, but I would ask of you additional spells to mask my presence, and a place where I might stay secluded. When the time is right, I will emerge—as a supporter of Halruaa's new king."

"Done."

Procopio extended his hand to the surprisingly resourceful little man. They clasped wrists, sealing a bargain with other wizards' blood.

# CHAPTER THIRTEEN

Dust still swirled through the clearing, and faint echoes of the deadly battle rumbled back to the jordaini from distant peaks. Matteo and his friends set about tasks that came in the aftermath of battle—tending the wounded, gathering weapons, honoring the dead.

Andris composed Iago's body as best he could, then he knelt at the dead man's side and gently closed his eyes. He began chanting a litany of the jordain's deeds and accomplishments, looking weirdly like a spirit come to welcome a brother to the next world.

Themo sat white-faced but stoic as Basel Indoulur stitched the gash on his shoulder. "Shame we don't have a priest handy," Basel murmured, his plump, jeweled hands moving with practiced skill. "This will leave an ugly scar, but we can close you up, and poultice the wound with a mold paste to keep it from festering."

The big man's face wrinkled in disgust, but he offered no comment concerning his treatment.

Andris rose and came to Matteo's side. "There is not enough dead wood hereabouts for a proper funeral pyre, and the ground is too hard and rocky to permit burial. Since there is no shortage of rocks, perhaps we should build a cairn, as the dwarves are said to do for their fallen kin."

Matteo's shoulders rose and fell in a deep sigh. "Iago's worse days were spent in the Nath. It doesn't seem right that this should be his resting place."

"Our horses have run off," Andris said patiently. "Most likely the Crinti have rounded them up. How could we bring Iago's body away with us?"

"By skyship," Basel put in. He deftly tied and tucked the ends of Themo's bandage and rose. "Before I left Halarahh, I sent *Avariel* ahead. I'm putting the ship at your disposal."

Matteo brightened. "That will help. In addition to everything else I must do, the king must hear that Kiva is alive, the laraken is back, and Akhlaur may have not only survived but even returned."

"If Zalathorm doesn't already know, we're in more trouble than we realize," Basel commented. "I understand your duties, but formalities will have to wait on matters that cannot."

The young man's eyes blazed with hope. "You found a spell to free Tzigone?"

"By Mystra's grace. And, as usual, the Lady's blessings are not entirely unmixed."

Basel quickly described the spell to Matteo. "I would go for her myself, and gladly," he concluded, "but my heart has enough dark corners to ensure failure. I can think of only one man who'd last in the Unseelie Court longer than a snowfall in a Halarahh bathhouse." When no understanding entered Matteo's eyes, Basel added, "I know only one man who values Tzigone's life as I do."

This time Matteo didn't hesitate. "If it's in me to bring her back, I will."

Themo jolted to his feet with a cry of protest. The effort proved too much for the wounded man; his face drained of color, and he all but dropped back onto the ground.

"Don't," he said through gritted teeth. "You saw what happened to me when we fought those thrice-bedamned fairies. What'll it be like in their world?"

"Perhaps Tzigone will tell you, once she returns," Matteo said quietly.

"But—"

Matteo sent Themo a look that froze the big man's protest in his throat. He turned back to Basel. "What about my jordaini resistance to magic?"

"There are exceptions to every rule," Andris put in with obvious reluctance. "Travel spells seem to be one. At Kiva's side, I walked across Halruaa in a single step."

"Kiva was a magehound," Basel reminded him. "Her spells would have more effect on you than a wizard's might. She is not, however, the only magehound in Halruaa, and the church of Azuth possesses certain artifacts that can bypass, at least to some extent, a jordain's magical resistance."

"Another magehound," grumbled Themo. "'*Some extent.*' This plan is shaping up nicely."

The wizard's shoulders rose and fell in a profound sigh. "I won't paint this picture with falsely bright colors. The risks are enormous."

"Not as high as the price of no action whatsoever. Is the spell ready?" A look of horror crossed Matteo's face as a grim possibility occurred to him. "Or was it absorbed by the laraken?"

Basel placed a reassuring hand on the young man's shoulder and pointed to a nearby peak. "When I realized what sort monster you men faced, I left my magical items up on the ledge there. No, the spell is not quite ready. We need to discuss one of the needed spell components."

The wizard hesitated. Matteo nodded encouragement.

"You need a lock of hair from an ancestor, a wizard of considerable power."

Matteo's gaze slid to the wizard's multitude of tiny black braids. A faint, wistful smile lifted the corners of his lips. "And you've come to give me the needed token."

Basel's brows rose. "I wish it were that easy! A jordain's lineage is not exactly common knowledge."

"Mine will not be spoken of lightly," Matteo said, holding onto patience with difficulty. "If you like, I will swear an oath to tell no one you are my father, but for the love of Mystra, let's get on with it!"

He wasn't prepared for the dumbfounded expression that flooded Basel's plump face. Matteo's heart plummeted as he realized his error.

"I see that I misspoke," the jordain said slowly. "Tzigone's most heartfelt quest was her search for family. She found my mother, so I assumed she took her apprenticeship with you because you were either her father or mine. It is known that your wife and child passed away in childbirth. That is often said of jordaini births. I thought—indeed, I hoped . . . " His voice trailed off into uncomfortable silence.

The conjurer gathered the shreds of his composure. "My wife did indeed bear a jordaini child, but the babe was a stillborn girl."

"You're certain of this?"

Basel's gaze was bleak but steady. "Beyond doubt. I refused to leave the room when the greenmage delivered the child. I held my daughter in my arms. With my own hands I lit her pyre. I am not your father, Matteo. Believe me, I would claim you if I could."

"And I you," the jordain said softly, "but let's speak of the world as it is, not as we wish it to be. I've learned that searching for a jordain's mother is not only futile, but harmful. We must focus upon my paternity. Tzigone told me my father was one of the masters at the Jordaini College."

"How did she find that out?" Themo demanded, looking both aghast and intrigued by this notion. This was not something jordaini discussed or pondered—such knowledge was considered beyond retrieval.

"She got into the birth records kept in the queen's palace."

"There you go. You're the king's counselor."

Matteo shook his head. "I don't have Tzigone's skill at

evading locks and wards, and the legal pathways to such knowledge are long and convoluted."

"There's another possibility," Basel said. "During my years as a jordaini master, I learned of a hidden book listing the jordaini ancestry."

"I have seen it," Andris said flatly.

Matteo brightened. "Did you read of my ancestry?"

The ghostly jordaini hesitated. "Mine was bad enough. Gods only know what swamp *you* sprang from." He punctuated his half-hearted jest with an equally wan smile.

"That is an evasion, not an answer," Matteo observed.

"With reason," his friend said softly. "Truths of this nature provide a dark mirror. I have learned that where family is concerned, each man must face his own reflection."

At that moment the clouds parted, and a wash of color swept over the rocky ground. Matteo glanced up. An enormous flying ship glided through the dissipating clouds, seemingly sped by the winged elves painted upon ship and sail. Sunlight filtered through bright, silken sails.

Basel's crew brought the skyship daringly close to the clearing. A rope ladder tumbled down. The wizard scampered up, amazingly nimble, and within moments a makeshift sling was lowered to raise the injured Themo. Matteo and Andris saw Iago's body aboard, then they climbed onto the skyship's deck.

They stood together by the rail, watching as the Nath fell swiftly away.

"It is fitting that Iago's ashes be scattered on jordaini land," Matteo commented as the skyship set course for southwestern Halruaa. "At least one aspect of this trip will end as it should."

"I'd reserve judgment until we learn what new thing has gone awry," murmured Andris as he nodded toward Basel. The wizard strode toward them, one hand steadying the large seabird perched upon his shoulder. His face was grim, and his eyes burned with wrath as well as something that might have been unshed tears.

"You should hear this," he said abruptly.

The wizard plucked a small feather from the bird and blew it from his palm. Immediately the feather dissolved into milky haze. Basel spoke an arcane phrase in Loross, the ancient language of Netheril and Halruaa, and the mist swiftly reformed into the shape of a stocky young wizard, a powerful looking man with muscles of the sort built by hours of labor.

The apparition bowed. "My pardon for this intrusion, Lord Basel, but I have grave news."

"This is Mason, one of my apprentices," the wizard interjected softly.

"I am sending this messenger from your tower in the king's city, for I cannot bring word to you directly. Farrah was found murdered in the front hall of the tower. The servants summoned the militia. I was shaken from sleep and brought to the magehounds for questioning." He hesitated for a moment, swallowing hard. "The knife that killed Farrah was found in my room, along with a vial from a potion of forgetfulness that erased the entire evening from my memory.

"I am innocent of this, Lord Basel, I swear it! There is nothing in me, no magic in all of Halruaa, that could compel me to do this thing. Yet the magehounds say Farrah died believing it was my hand that struck the blow."

The ghostly image broke off and passed a hand wearily over his face. "Please don't return on my behalf," he said in a softer voice. "Farrah is gone, and in deference to your position, I am allowed to remain under house arrest in your tower until you have time to address this matter. Tzigone needs your best efforts. The rest can wait."

His shoulder squared. "I suspect you will wish to carry the news to Lord Noor yourself. I should warn you that he is unlikely to believe in my innocence. Farrah and I have spoken of marriage. I have no wizard's lineage to offer, and Farrah's family considered my love an insult to their daughter and their family. They already think me a peasant and a knave. Defending me would only anger them. Let them say what they will. They can do me no further harm."

Mason's voice broke, and the image disappeared like a bursting soap bubble. The seabird leaped from Basel's shoulder and winged off toward the south.

Basel watched the avian messenger until it disappeared into the clouds. "I'll travel with you as far as the Noor estates," he said without looking back at the silent jordaini. "Their daughter was murdered while in my care." He started to say more, then shook his head and strode quickly away.

"Your friend Tzigone was their fellow apprentice. She seems to be near the center of every tangle we encounter," Andris pointed out.

"I've noticed that," Matteo said in a dry tone. "In Tzigone's defense, however, she does not create *all* the chaos that surrounds her. From the day we met, Kiva has never been more than two steps behind. I would be surprised if this murder proves to be an exception."

Andris abruptly turned his gaze on the landscape below. Recognizing his friend's need for silence and privacy, Matteo followed suit.

The rugged Nath was an unpleasant memory, and the fields and forests spread out beneath them were lush and green. Matteo leaned on the ship's rail, gazing down over his Halruaa with the fond eyes of a babe for its mother or a lover his lass.

The Noor estates bordered the Swamp of Akhlaur. A faint cloud misted the forest canopy like a net of delicate silver filigree crowning a wild elf's hair, or perhaps a cunningly spun web, ready to ensnare all who ventured too near. Both images brought to mind the memory of Kiva's beautiful, malevolent, elven face. A chill passed through Matteo, and he pushed away from the rail. He was not unhappy when Basel disembarked, and the skyship sailed away from the swamp and its memories.

By late afternoon, the sweeping lands surrounding

the Jordaini College came into view, and far beyond, a slim line of blue and silver sea. The skyship settled down upon a lake at the northern border of the jordaini estate. While Andris set about making Iago's funeral arrangements and summoning healers to care for Themo, Matteo went to the stables and selected a horse for the ride to the college.

He set a brisk pace, for sunset was not far away. At this hour the fields were bustling with activity as people harvested the endless round of crops, tended orchards, despoiled beehives of their sweet bounty, and cared for pampered livestock.

These lands were worked by commoners, Halruaan peasants who made their own livelihood while supplying the Jordaini College. As Matteo rode through, children tossed down their hoes to wave cheerily, obviously delighted for even this small diversion.

He did not find it amiss that a child should work alongside his parents, for his own youth had been no different. From before dawn until well after sunset, taxing lessons and hours of memory drills alternated with rigorous physical training. Rare was the moment spent without either a book or a weapon in hand.

Yet he also remembered time for play. A smile curved Matteo's lips as he rounded a bend in the dirt path and the river came into view. Year after year, melting snow from the highest mountains brought a rush of white water. Each spring's flood widened the ravine just a bit. Here an aged tree leaned over the water. A few young boys, naked as newborn mice, had hung a rope from a tree limb, and they took turns swinging out over the ravine and dropping into the water. Their hoots of laughter filled the air, interspersed with good-natured boasts and insults. This was a familiar scene, one often played out downriver among the jordaini lads.

But these boys could expect to learn a trade, wed a neighbor's daughter, build a cottage they might call their own, and raise children who would know who their parents were. For the jordaini, there would be no family. This was ensured by a final secret rite, a so-called "purification ritual" inflicted before they left for the wide world. Thanks to Kiva's machinations, another man had taken Matteo's place. The elf woman's experience with human males had left her believing that Matteo would disgrace himself and his order, given half a chance.

As Matteo rode through the jordaini lands, he searched the faces of every young man he passed. He didn't really expect to find the man who'd taken his place, of course, and after a while his thoughts shifted to calculating the odds against this occurrence. He was therefore surprised when his gaze fell upon a man whose hair was the same color as his, a dark and distinctive chestnut rarely seen in the southlands.

He reined his horse in for a closer look. The man was standing at the side of the road, gazing morosely at something in the high grasses. A low, wooden cart listed to one side on a broken wheel. Two piebald carthorses took advantage of the small disaster to nibble at the roadside meadow flowers.

The young man was tall and strongly built, much like Matteo in general size and appearance. On close examination his features were not all that similar, but the unusual richness of red in his hair drew the eye and cast a powerful illusion.

Matteo called out a greeting. "May I help you, brother?"

"Don't see how. The wheel splintered in that rut and the thrice-bedamned millstone tipped off the cart," the peasant grumbled. He glanced up, and immediately sank into the deep bow that showed proper respect for wizards and their jordaini counselors.

Matteo brushed aside the stammered apologies and asked the man's name.

A look of apprehension crept over the young man's face at being singled out in this fashion, but he didn't hesitate.

"Benn," he supplied. "Of village Falaria."

"All problems have solutions, Benn, and yours is easier than most. I see you carry an extra wheel," Matteo noted as he swung down from his horse.

"What fool wouldn't? The wheel's the least of it. Getting that millstone back in the cart—that's what I call a problem."

He looked surprised when Matteo peeled off his white tunic and began to drag the heavy wooden wheel off the cart, but he fell to work beside the jordain. In short order they had the new wheel in place, and then they stood side by side eyeing the millstone.

"Too heavy for two men," concluded the peasant.

Matteo's gaze fell upon a pair of long, stout oak oars lashed to the side of the cart. "Not necessarily. A Halruaan sage once claimed that he could lift the entire world, provided he had a lever long enough."

"Easy to say, hard to prove," Benn observed. "For starters, where would he stand?"

Matteo laughed and clapped him on the shoulder. "An excellent point. Let's see what we can manage, short of standing on the moon and using Yggdrasil, the Northmen's world tree, as a lever."

Together they rolled a likely boulder to use as a fulcrum. Ben guided the horses and cart into position, backing up little by little as Matteo used the oar to raise the millstone. At last he lowered one edge of the stone onto the low cart, then moved the fulcrum into position to lever up the far side.

When the task was done, Benn handed Matteo a goatskin of wine. Matteo tipped it back for a polite sip. As he lowered it, he noticed the peasant eyeing him appraisingly.

"No offense intended, my lord, but we might be mistaken for brothers."

Matteo was silent for several moments, not sure what good might come of taking the path this observation opened. "Perhaps, in certain lights and under certain extraordinary circumstances, we might even be mistaken for the same man."

The peasant nodded, accepting this. "I often wondered whose place I took."

His tone was matter-of-fact and without rancor. Matteo swiftly cut him off. "Don't say more."

"What harm? You know the story as well as I." He met Matteo's gaze with a level stare. "No, I see that's not true. You're packed with more questions than my sister's five-year-old son."

"You may have been enspelled not to speak of this."

"Doesn't seem likely. I told my Phoebe when I asked her to wed, and here I stand. If it sets your mind at ease, I don't have much memory of the before and during. Afterwards, the gatekeeper came to see me. Made me promise to 'foreswear vengeance,' which I guess is a fancy way of saying I should let sleeping dragons lie. He also said the man whose place I took had no part in it and would half-kill anyone who did."

Matteo gave a grim nod of agreement. After a moment, he ventured, "Are you treated well here?"

The peasant pointed toward a snug cottage, just over a stone bridge that crossed the river. Well-tended fields surrounded his domain. A small flock of goats grazed on a hill, and a pair of rothe calves gamboled in the paddock.

"If I hadn't been brought to the Jordaini College, my years would have been spent in another man's field. See what I have here. The jordaini hold title to the land, but it's mine to work as I see fit."

Benn shrugged. "My Phoebe pines for babes from time to time, but we two have a fine life together. She is mistress of her own home. She makes her cheeses and sells them to the jordaini for a fair price, and she's a good hand with weaving. I bought her a fine loom for her bride's gift," he said with pride. "How many men can claim that?"

The jordain's answering smile was genuine. "Few men achieve such contentment. Your happiness lifts a burden from my heart. It surprises me, though, that the guard could produce so much ready coin. A good loom is a costly thing."

"Oh, wasn't the guard. 'Twas a master paid me off."

Matteo's heart thudded painfully. "Would you know him if you saw him again?"

The young man snorted. "Not such a chore. An old man, but tall—about the height of you and me. Had a beak like a buzzard. This sound like anyone you know?"

The jordain nodded, for he could not force speech through his suddenly constricted throat. There was only one master who fit that description—his favorite master, an elderly battle wizard, and the last man in the Jordaini College whom Matteo would have suspected of involvement in this grim chapter. The last man he would have suspected of conspiring with Kiva.

With a heavy heart, Matteo mounted his horse and kicked it into a run. As he galloped toward the college gates, Andris's words rang in his mind:

*Some truths are like dark mirrors.*

Seeking his reflection in this particular man's face, if it came to that, would be a difficult task indeed.

Tzigone sank down onto a large stone, too exhausted to walk farther. She stared out into the mist—a constant, chilling presence that never seemed to recede a single pace no matter how far she walked. There was no edge to that mist, at least, none that she could find.

She was reaching the edges of her endurance. This morning she'd had to cut a new notch in her belt just to keep her trousers up. Time passed strangely here, but she suspected that several days had passed since her last meal. Though she'd rationed herself sips of water like a dwarven miser doling out gold, the waterskin she'd brought from Halruaa was empty.

She idly tossed pebbles into a small pool, watching the ripples spread. Fierce thirst urged her to throw herself at the water, but her days as a street performer had left her with a wealth of cautionary tales. Many a story warned of mortals passing through strange magical realms, only to be trapped forever if they ate or drank.

Tzigone gathered her remaining strength and sank into the deep, trancelike concentration that preceded her borrowed memories. Each day, it was easier to slip into her mother's past, perhaps because she herself was close to sharing her mother's fate.

That uncharacteristically grim thought dissipated in a flash of sunset color and sweeping winds. In this memory, Keturah was riding a flying wyvern! A small grin of anticipation lit Tzigone's face as she fell completely into her mother's memory, once again *becoming* Keturah in a vision more vivid than any dream.

Keturah dug her fingers between the blue-black scales of the wyvern's back and leaned low over the creature's sinuous neck. The thunderous beat of batlike wings buffeted her, and the dense forest below sped by in a verdant blur.

The young wizard clung desperately to her perch and to the magic that had summoned the wyvern. She could sense the malevolent will of the dragonlike creature, alternately puzzled and angered by Keturah's gentle compulsion.

Submitting was difficult for the creature, and cooperation impossible. Each downbeat of the wyvern's wings lifted them lurching into the sky, and each short glide was a stomach-turning drop, for the wyvern simply did not think to adjust its flight for the extra weight of a passenger.

A furious shriek burst from the wyvern. Keturah looked up, startled, as a shadow passed over her. Above soared an enormous griffin, wings outstretched. It glided in majestic circles as it took measure of the wyvern and its rider.

Keturah's reluctant mount banked sharply and began to climb, its rider and her magic completely forgotten. The wizard began to sing another spell, but the creature's vengeful shrieks and the keening of the wind blocked her efforts as effectively as an archmage's counterspell.

The wyvern's long, barbed tail whipped toward the griffin like dark lightning. The griffin shied back, rearing in midair. Its massive, white-feathered wings backbeat furiously, and its taloned forefeet and leonine paws thrashed at the air as it struggled to avoid the attack.

A bolt of energy flashed from the griffin's direction, sizzling into the wyvern's side. With a shriek of pain, the wyvern veered away. Keturah noticed for the first time that the griffin carried a rider—a slight young man, deeply browned by a life spent between sea and sun. As their gazes locked, the startled expression on his face told Keturah that he had been equally unaware of her.

It was a moment's contact, quickly broken by the erratic flight of the wounded wyvern. Now utterly beyond Keturah's control, it circled back for another attack. The wyvern dropped into a hurtling dive, coming just below the enormous winged lion. As it passed under the griffin, the wyvern threw itself into a rolling spin, swinging its poison-tipped tail like an enormous flail.

Suddenly Keturah was falling though the air. Another burst of magic darted from the griffin, catching her and slowing her flight to a slow, gentle drift.

Gratitude surged through her, and amazement. The young griffin rider had saved her, and at considerable risk to himself. Wyverns viewed griffins as natural enemies, and Keturah's erstwhile mount seemed intent upon tearing this one from the skies. The rider, if he wished to survive, would do well to save his spells for his own benefit!

As she floated down, Keturah craned her head back to watch the battle. Again and again the wyvern struck, snapping and stinging at the great lion-bird. As she had feared, many of the attacks got through. Maintaining the feather-float spell was obviously limiting the young wizard's defensive power.

The forest canopy rose to meet Keturah. She drifted through the small upper branches, then seized a handhold and began to climb down.

Meanwhile, the storm of feathers and scales raged overhead, growing ever closer and more frantic. The shriek of the griffin mingled with wyvern roars. Trees rustled and branches cracked as the gigantic creatures plummeted toward the ground, locked together in final combat.

Keturah flattened herself against the tree trunk as the enjoined creatures tumbled past her. Their descent was a long, sickening series of lurching drops and crashes, followed by a more horrible silence.

She half climbed, half slid down the tree. The great creatures lay at the base of the tree, locked together in an embrace so fierce that Keturah envisioned them taking the battle to whatever afterlife awaited them.

Keturah quickly forgot such thoughts when she saw the griffin rider. He was still strapped into the saddle. Blood poured from a cut on his scalp. One leg was bent at an improbable angle.

She quickly loosed the straps and ran her hands lightly over his neck and down his spine, then gently probed his skull. Nothing other than his leg seemed broken, praise Mystra, so she carefully dragged him away from the giant beasts.

All that night, she alternated between tending the wounded man and gathering enough wood to keep a circle of fires burning. The fire was a risk—Dhamari's latest hound was not far off her trail—but a small thing compared to the risks this young man had taken on her behalf.

Keturah did not have to summon strange and dangerous creatures that night to ward off her trackers. Creatures came of their own volition, answering the lure of fresh meat in great supply. In a summoning as complex as any that gathered humankind together, the scavengers roared and howled the invitation to dine. Then—again, far too like the Halruaans for Keturah's comfort—they fell to snapping over the scraps.

In all, the night was long and grim, and not a moment passed that Keturah expected might be her rescuer's last. The voices of the scavengers seemed to call his name, as well.

To her astonishment, the young man's eyes opened shortly before dawn. For several moments they followed her movements as she dipped a cloth in her tiny kettle and placed it on his forehead.

"I'm alive," he observed grimly. It seemed to Keturah that he was neither surprised nor pleased by this realization.

"You're lucky. I've seen fewer wounds on a defeated army."

He hauled himself painfully into a sitting position and regarded her thoughtfully. "Do you have experience with the military, or is that a figure of speech?"

Her lips twitched. "If you're asking if I'm a camp follower, the answer is no. I must say, though, that I find it admirably optimistic for a man in your condition to ask."

She expected the youth to be mortified. Instead, he responded with a surprisingly deep chuckle.

"It's been many years since anyone accused me of optimism!"

It was on the tip of Keturah's tongue to mock his choice of words—after all, her rescuer-turned-patient looked to be even younger than she—but something about him stayed her teasing comment. She studied him for a long moment. "You are wearing a magical disguise," she decided.

Astonishment flooded his face. "It should be undetectable," he said ruefully. "Gods above, the spells involved are complicated enough!"

"That explains a few things," Keturah mused. "Some of the spells you tossed at the wyvern were far beyond most wizards of your apparent years. Maintaining such a disguise can be distracting even without the feather-fall spell, for which I thank you. I suppose that's how you were overcome during battle."

"You're too kind," he said dryly. "Actually, to the best of my recollection, I think I was knocked senseless by a passing seabird. The stupid thing couldn't maneuver around the battle."

Keturah burst out laughing. "A man whose magic defies wizardly scrutiny, who rides griffins and casts spells like the king himself, downed by a clumsy pelican!"

After a moment the man's lips twitched. "I suppose the situation has a certain ironic appeal." His smile faded quickly, and he regarded her for a long moment. "Well?"

"That's a deep subject." She shrugged at his blank stare. "Sorry. That was one of my father's favorite jests. No wonder he never made much of a living as a bard."

"You're not going to ask me my true identity?"

Keturah shrugged again. "If you wanted it known, you wouldn't have conjured a disguise. If it's all the same to you, I'd just as soon dispense with introductions all around."

"Your secrets are your own," he agreed. "As far as I'm concerned, we were both born this morning. We have no life but that which lies before us." This prospect seemed to please him. His smile, boyish and frank, loosened some of the bonds around Keturah's heart.

"I like the sound of that."

"As do I." He glanced down at his splinted leg and sighed. "It appears that we'll be in this forest for quite some time. What shall I call you?"

"Something exotic, I think. Hmmm. Vashti?"

He snorted. "Only if you want me to envision you wearing purple veils and dancing with finger cymbals."

"No then. Simanatra? Chelis? Lissa?" With each suggestion his expression of mock horror grew. Keturah threw up her hands in feigned disgust. "Since you're so picky, why don't you name me?"

He considered her for a long moment with eyes that seemed to scan her soul. Finally he took her hand and lifted it to his lips.

"You're Beatrix," he said softly.

*The mists of memory swirled, and Tzigone's vision picked up many days later.* Keturah and the young wizard stood at the mouth of a cave carved into the heart of a living bilboa tree. Their eyes were fixed upon each other's faces as if they sought to memorize what they saw, and their hands were clasped in the manner of lovers loathe to part.

"Before you go, there are things you must know," Keturah said.

Her lover shook his head. "I know your heart. Your laughter is the music dearest and most familiar to me. What else is there to learn?"

"We have been wed for two days, but we have yet to speak of bloodlines."

*In some far corner of Tzigone's mind, joy flickered and burned bright. So this man was her father and her mother's true husband! She should have known her mother would not be so careless as to condemn her child to the fate of a wizard's bastard.*

The young man nodded. "Very well, then. I am a diviner, but I also possess a power not officially recognized by the Council, a power of mind rather than ritual."

"Psionics," Keturah said, her face troubled. "I have read of it. I studied the art of evocation, but my magic also has a feral streak. My father, who was a bard, once told me there were sorcerers in my mother's line."

Her husband lifted his brows, but he did not seem displeased. "Any child of ours will be a wild thing indeed!"

Keturah's smile faltered. "I was wed before, to a man who was never a true husband."

"So you told me. If there was no true marriage, you are not legally bound to him."

"I know that," she broke in. "There is more. He secretly gave me potions to ensure a jordaini child, potions altered with dangerous herbs. This is the legacy I might pass to your children."

The wizard lifted her hands to his lips. "Life is shaped by many things, sweet Beatrix. Choice is far more important than heritage. We will teach our children to choose wisely."

Keturah sent an arch gaze around their hidden camp. "And we are such experts on this matter?"

"Of course. Did we not choose each other?"

As the lovers moved into a farewell kiss, Tzigone eased her awareness away. She could not intrude upon this shared sweetness, even if they were her parents. *Especially* since they were her parents!

The vision left her filled with soft joy and an illuminating glimpse into how her strange magic came to be.

Tzigone drifted slowly back, moving through the faded years. When she came fully to herself, she was so exhausted that her eyelids felt too heavy to lift. The intense vision had taken more strength than she had to spare. Tzigone did not regret it. With a happy sigh, she pried opened her eyes.

A circle of dark faces surrounded her. Several Unseelie folk regarded her solemnly, like ravens preparing to feed upon the magical repast she had unwittingly provided. Horror flooded her as she realized that the dark fairies knew all that she had learned.

Tzigone seized a still-smoldering stick from her dying campfire and leaped to her feet. She spun in a circle, driving back the ethereal-looking fiends.

The fairies fell back, nimbly avoiding her attack. Before she could turn full circle, however, they darted back, leaping onto her and bearing her down to the ground.

There was no time to cast an illusion to fight them and no strength left for such magic. Tzigone went down under the vicious onslaught, feeling the burn and sting of dozens of small, spiteful wounds.

Now the true attack came. A long-hidden memory stirred, emerging from that dark place where Tzigone hid a girlhood spent in the streets and shadows. She smelled the fetid breath of drunken men and felt several pairs of rough hands. She heard the rip of her own small garments.

This had happened before—the attack, the helplessness, the terror. Gods above, she remembered it all.

Then came memory of a quick, acrid stench, like the scent of lightning come too close. Tzigone remembered struggling free of her attackers and running for the safety of the trees. It had never occurred to her to look back. Now she knew what she would have seen.

Two of the dark fairies were dead. Several more twitched in short, jerky spasms. Their glowing black eyes were clouded and glazed by the surge of magic that had burst from childhood memory. The surviving fairies darted away from this unexpected attack, moving too quickly for mortal eyes to follow.

The author of this devastation was almost as surprised as the dark fairies. Without design, without thought, Tzigone had summoned killing magic—as she had done once before as a child.

She recalled her mother's long-ago words and the stories she had heard since of common men and women who suddenly unleashed uncommon power. Magic came naturally, and sometimes unexpectedly, to those born of a sorcerer's bloodline.

Tzigone stumbled back from the grim scene and sank to the ground. The exhausted sorceress—for such she truly was—sank into dreamless oblivion.

# CHAPTER FOURTEEN

Matteo entered the Jordaini College by the north gate and rode directly to the training fields. Though the sun was little more than a crimson rim above the western mountains, Vishna was still at work with his jordaini charges. Several pairs of small boys trained with short wooden staffs, learning the routines of attack and parry that prepared them for the traditional matched daggers.

The old wizard glanced up, scowling at this infraction of rule. Horsemanship was learned in the arena and on the surrounding trails. The training fields were to be kept level and free from debris.

When Vishna noted the rider's identity, his ire changed to consternation. He swiftly mastered both emotions and clapped his hands sharply. The sparring jordaini boys lowered their weapons and came to attention.

"That is enough for today," he said with a smile. "Go to the evening meal before the cooks come at us with cleavers, angry that we've scorned their handiwork."

The jovial tone was familiar to Matteo, as was the slight twinkle in the old battle-wizard's eyes. It seemed to him, though, that Vishna's cheer was decidedly forced.

When the boys had left, Vishna strode over to

Matteo's horse. "Perhaps you and I could walk together, before it grows too dark for this old man's eyes."

Matteo swung down and gave his mount a light slap on the rump. The horse trotted gladly off for the stables, and the jordain fell into step with his former master.

Neither spoke until they entered the deeply shaded riding paths. Faint moonlight filtered through the trees, and lightning beetles greeted the night and each other with flirtatious winks of light.

Finally Vishna broke the silence. "Some time ago, I advised you to hone your skill at evasion, if not falsehood. Do you recall that?"

"Vividly."

Vishna smiled faintly. "You were not pleased by this advice. Court life has not dimmed your principles. Truly, I'm glad for it, but though you need not lie, you should learn not to wear truth on your face. I've known you since your birth, Matteo, and the questions you've come to ask could hardly be plainer had you tattooed them across your forehead."

The wizard lifted one hand and traced a complex gesture. Years faded away, and his thin, wiry frame thickened and took on muscle. The exaggerated curve of his nose softened, and his thin, gray locks grew thicker, more lustrous. Even in the faint light, Matteo could make out a familiar, rich shade of chestnut.

"This is my true form," Vishna said in a voice that was suddenly fuller and more resonant.

Matteo nodded slowly, trying to accept the truth he saw in the wizard's face. The resemblance between them was too striking to ignore. This, then, was the man who had sired him.

"The story is long." Vishna began to walk again, a long warrior's stride that matched Matteo's favored pace. "You know me as a battle wizard, and so I am, but I'm far more powerful than I pretend to be and far older. Many years ago, there were three of us, friends from boyhood, united in our love of Halruaa and our infatuation with magic."

Matteo stopped dead, staring at his mentor—his *father*—in horror. "You, Zalathorm, and Akhlaur."

"You know the tale?"

"Andris put it together. It was you who gave him the books, wasn't it?"

The wizard was silent for a long moment. "Truth unspoken can fester. This story has been too long untold. Zalathorm and I lived long past our expected years, in part because of the protection given us by the crimson star. I chose to live quietly, taking a number of names and living out several lives. This incarnation, Vishna the jordaini master, is only the latest."

A grim thought occurred to Matteo. Perhaps the resemblance between him and Benn could be explained in the most obvious fashion. "Do you have other children?"

"None living, no."

"What of your children's descendants?" Matteo pressed.

The wizard sighed. "There is one. He will bear no children, and I am glad for it. It is better that the bloodline ends with me."

The enormity of this revelation rocked Matteo back on his heels. Vishna had known that his own blood flowed through Benn's veins, and yet he had allowed the peasant to take Matteo's place at the purification rite. Perhaps he had even arranged this travesty!

"Yet you must have married," Matteo said coldly. "A strange choice for a man determined to end his own line."

"A life as long as mine grows lonely," the wizard replied, "but I did not act entirely without responsibility. Twenty-two years ago, I married a wizard whose bloodline suggested she could bear a natural jordain. Do you know that term?"

"A child born with jordaini potential without the intervention of potions."

"Yes. There are risks, which I assume you also know, but this course seemed safe enough. In fact, my wife's pregnancy was uneventful. Childbirth is never easy—you know that perhaps one birthing in three results in death to either babe or mother."

"Yes."

"This is especially true when great magic is involved, and one of the reasons why wizard bloodlines are so carefully regulated. My wife's mind shattered under the strain of childbirth."

Vishna fell silent for a long moment. "The parentage of any jordaini child is not known to the order, but I determined that I would know my son."

"So you supported the falsehood that your wife and babe died in childbed and came to the Jordaini College."

"About that time, Basel Indoulur decided to leave. His story is not mine to tell."

"I know it already. His daughter was stillborn, as jordaini females usually are."

Vishna's eyebrows rose. "Basel has confided in you. That simplifies my tale. The short of it is that his position became open. As a jordaini master, I could keep close watch on my son."

The wizard stopped suddenly and reached out to clasp Matteo's shoulders. "Before I continue, you must swear you will do nothing that might bring harm to the elf woman Kiva."

"Most people believe that Kiva died when the floodgate closed," Matteo said, choosing his words carefully. "Have you reason to think otherwise?"

The wizard shook his head impatiently. "Alive or dead matters not. I cannot continue this story unless you swear."

Reluctantly, Matteo did so. He would have to trust the gods and the laws of Halruaa to deal with Kiva as she deserved.

"Kiva was one of the prisoners in Akhlaur's tower. I freed her from a cage. She was a tiny thing, little more than a child and incredibly ill-used. I did not recognize her when we met years later, but she remembered me."

Matteo began to understand. "You tried to atone for the wrongs done to her by your former friend and partner."

"Guilt is a powerful thing," the wizard said with deep regret. "I swore by wizard-word oath to help her destroy the residual evils left behind by Akhlaur's reign. That seemed not only harmless but worthy. By the time I realized Kiva was not the helpless victim she purported to be, I was constrained by my oath and Kiva's magic from working against her."

"So you had to require a similar oath from me before continuing. Otherwise, even telling this story could be construed as a betrayal."

"Yes." The wizard sighed. "I view many of my actions without pride. My most egregious error was helping Kiva recruit jordaini students. I learned too late that she had a special grudge against the jordaini order."

Matteo could not trust himself to speak. This man, his own father, had betrayed his jordaini brothers.

"Although trapped by my vows," Vishna continued, "I tried to do as little harm as possible. When I intercepted Andris's thesis about the Kilmaruu Paradox, I realized he had an excellent chance of undoing the mess Akhlaur had left in the Kilmaruu Swamp. So I presented Andris to Kiva as an extremely talented battlemaster, one ideally suited to cleaning up after Akhlaur. I didn't think Kiva could hurt Andris."

"Why not?" demanded Matteo.

"I was stunned by Andris's 'death' and realized how wrong I'd been about Kiva," went on Vishna, as if he hadn't heard the jordain's question. "I was deeply relieved to learn of Andris's survival, but I felt responsible for what happened to him in the battle of Akhlaur's Swamp. Because I owed Andris some small measure of truth, I put before him books that would explain why Kiva did what she did."

"These books—can you say more of this without breaking your oaths?"

The wizard shook his head. "I would not speak of them

even if I could. The knowledge in those books turned Andris to Kiva's side."

"No. He might have descended from Kiva's line, but it seems to me that choice is more powerful than heredity."

"You and Andris, good men both, are proof of that," Vishna said, punctuating his comment with a sad smile. "You are the son of a coward and he the seventh-generation descendant of a mad elf woman and the monster who was once my friend."

Yet another bolt of shock tore through Matteo. "Andris is a descendant not just of Kiva but also of Akhlaur?"

Vishna's eyes widened. "You did not know this?"

"Andris didn't tell me—at least, not in so many words." Finally Matteo understood what Andris meant when he warned that he seemed destined to betray those around him. For months, he had been laboring under the heavy weight of his perceived fate.

Matteo stared at the wizard as if into a dark mirror, but he felt no kinship with the man he had once loved. Vishna's blood might be his. Vishna's choices were not.

"There is enormous peace in confessing this story and in acknowledging, if just between the two of us, that you are my son. A sad chapter is closed, and we can begin anew."

The selfishness of that statement floored Matteo nearly as thoroughly as the man's admitted cowardice. He stepped back, avoiding the wizard's offered embrace.

"Once we spoke of the Cabal," he said. "You denied that it existed."

A turmoil of indecision filled Vishna's eyes. "Perhaps the descendants of three old friends can set things aright. Perhaps I can yet leave a legacy of honor. I will tell you what I know."

Suddenly he began to change. The years flooded back, and the robust middle-aged warrior was once again the aging wizard Matteo had long known. But the process did not stop. More years sped by, and the spare flesh on the old wizard's bones withered. His eyes turned to fevered black pools in a face gone papery thin and gray as death. Before Matteo could move, Vishna fell to the ground, his frail body contorting in the final throes of a death long cheated.

"A lichnee," Matteo breathed, recognizing the grueling transformation of living man to undead wizard. "Goddess avert, you are becoming a lich!"

*"No!"*

The single word rattled out in a whisper, but it held a world of horror. This clearly was not Vishna's intent! Somehow, his fate was being imposed—a sentence of living death in payment for a final act of courage. According to everything Matteo knew of magic, this should have been impossible.

He swept the dying man up in his arms and ran toward the college, shouting for assistance. Curious students flowed from their dwellings, then shot off with typical jordaini obedience to fetch their masters.

The wizards who answered the summons could do no more than Matteo to stop the mysterious process. Finally, they shook their heads and stepped away, as they might to avoid a leper.

Vishna reached out a palsied hand toward Matteo's dagger.

The jordain hesitated, understanding what the wizard had in mind. Matteo had been taught that life was sacred, but better a quick death than the slipping away of the soul and the slow-creeping madness that overtook undead wizards. He pulled his dagger and curved his father's frail fingers around the hilt of the jordaini blade.

To Matteo's surprise, Vishna lifted the blade to his hair and sliced off a thin gray lock. This he handed to Matteo. He struggled to form words.

"Basel," he croaked. "Three. Legacy."

Matteo nodded reassuringly as he deciphered this message. Obviously Basel had contacted Vishna, his old swordmaster and successor, to enlist his help in Matteo's search for an ancestor's talisman. *Legacy* was also clear enough, for Vishna had agreed that destroying the Cabal would be a means to atone for his mistakes. But *three*?

The jordain's eyes widened as he made the connection. Three wizards had formed the crimson star, and Vishna had suggested that three descendants were needed to undo this grim legacy. Akhlaur, Vishna, and Zalathorm. Andris, Matteo, and—

*Goddess above!* This had been a day for revelations, but none stunned Matteo more than the notion of "Princess Tzigone!"

Vishna made a feeble gesture with his free hand, indicating that he wanted Matteo to leave. Their eyes clung for a moment, and then Vishna laboriously moved the blade to his throat. His unspoken plea was clear: he did not want his son to see him die by his own hand.

With deep reluctance, Matteo rose to honor the old man's last wish. As he strode quickly away, he glanced down at the lock of hair clenched in his hand. It was no longer thin and gray, but a deep, lustrous chestnut.

Back at Akhlaur's tower, the necromancer and the elf watched as a pair of skeletal servants stirred a bubbling kettle. Unspeakably foul steam rose as the remains of several ghouls boiled down to sludge. A half dozen vials stood on a nearby table, ready to receive the finished potion. On the far side of the room, several of Akhlaur's water-fleshed servants struggled to control a chained wyvern. Three of them clung to the beast's thrashing tail, while a fourth darted about with a vial to catch drops of poison dripping from the barbed tip. From time to time, one of the undead servants was pierced by a wing rib or a flailing talon, and the fluids surrounding the old bones drained away like wine from a broken barrel. Still more undead servants busied themselves with mops, cleaning the stone floor of their comrades' remains.

Kiva observed all this with a calm face and well-hidden revulsion. The tower and the forest beyond were filled with the clatter of undead servants. Kelemvor, the human's Lord of the Dead, probably had livelier company than this!

Suddenly an aura of flickering, blue-green faerie fire surrounded Akhlaur. A speculative smile touched the necromancer's thin lips. He dug into his voluminous sleeve and produced a tiny, ebony box. The glowing aura grew brighter and more condensed as it focused upon the box, then began to shrink as if it were slipping inside the little cube.

"A spell cast long ago is finally bearing fruit," Akhlaur announced with great satisfaction. He began the rhythmic, atonal chant of a spell of summoning.

"He is creating a lich," Kiva murmured with a mixture of horror and relief. She had seen Akhlaur prepare this phylactery many years ago and feared he had prepared it for his own transformation!

She held her breath as she waited to see what unfortunate wizard would come to the necromancer's call. An ancient man, little more than skin-wrapped bone clad in too-large jordaini garments, began to take shape on the stone floor. With a start, Kiva recognized the ruins of the wizard who had freed her from this very tower some two centuries past—and who had done her bidding for nearly twenty years.

At last the soft radiance faded into the cube, and the elderly wizard lay in seeming death.

"Remember the last time Vishna entered this tower?" she warned. "He was a powerful wizard. He will be a formidable lich."

Akhlaur brushed aside her concerns. "When Vishna revives in his new form, he will be completely under my control," he declared. He smiled horribly. "Together, we will pay a call on our old friend Zalathorm."

☙

The king sat quietly in a lofty tower chamber, watching his long-beloved wife with despairing eyes. He had lost Beatrix before, and so great was his joy in their reunion that he failed to question too closely the circumstances of her return. That haunted him now, though he was not certain what he might do differently, if given the chance to return to that point in time.

Beatrix sat with her hands folded in her white-satin lap, her vacant, painted eyes gazing at the window. Zalathorm wondered what she saw. Despite all his powers of divination, he had never been able to see beyond the veil that separated them. Magic he could not dispel clouded his queen's mind. The crimson star, the Cabal of whispered legend, protected itself and its creators with veils of secrecy or even madness.

It was the sort of "protection" Zalathorm would not wish upon his worst enemy. Not that he needed to—his worst enemy survived by the power of the same artifact that sustained Zalathorm's own life, his reign.

Perhaps because his thoughts lingered on the artifact, Zalathorm felt a surge of familiar power running through him like a sudden fever. Protective magic burned through his senses, as well as a desperate struggle for healing. There came the wrenching snap of a life bound to him, cut suddenly and brutally free.

"Vishna," he murmured, sensing his old friend's death. "How is this possible?"

Beatrix turned an incurious gaze upon him. The king stooped to kiss her pale cheek and hurried away. He quickly resumed his magical disguise and, as a brown-skinned youth, descended into the dungeon to consult the Cabal.

For a long time he stood silent before the crimson star, studying the glowing facets for an explanation of what had befallen his friend. Finally he dropped to one knee and quieted his sorrowing thoughts.

"The heart of Halruaa seeks counsel," he murmured. "Tell me, is Vishna among you?"

The only response was profound silence. He received no sense of his life-long friend from the crystal.

"So Vishna is truly dead," Zalathorm said quietly, wondering why he could not quite accept that truth. It seemed to him that something of the wizard lingered—perhaps nothing more than an echo of their collective magic, but something.

He turned back to the crystal, for another question demanded answers. Ambassadors from Mulhorand had yielded up the name of the wizard whose spells had shielded the recent invasion from view. Unfortunately, it seemed that nothing remained of Ameer Tukephremo but his name. The wizard had died in the invasion, his body lost, and his home and possessions destroyed by fire. Nothing remained that would aid Halruaan wizards in divination.

Zalathorm found that far too convenient for credulity.

Nevertheless, he projected a mental image of the man's face and a description of the cloaking spell that had shielded the invasion. If there was, as he expected, Halruaan magic mingled in that casting, the elven sages would detect it. After all, Halruaan magic descended from ancient Netheril, whose earliest mages were taught by elves. Despite the enhancements—some would say corruption and abominations—that Netherese wizards added to this magic, the roots of their tradition were decidedly elven.

His suspicions were quickly confirmed. The elven sages recognized the touch of Halruaan magic but could not identify the caster.

Zalathorm considered this puzzle as he made his way through the labyrinth to the exit and back to his palace. When divination would not serve, there were other ways to smoke out treachery.

Logic was foremost among them. Who was in a position to act, and who stood to gain? His thoughts drifted to Procopio Septus, who seemed exceptionally well versed in the magic of the eastern lands.

As the king neared his private rooms, he noted the small, white flag tucked into a bracket mounted near the door. Though a diviner of Zalathorm's power could easily sense the presence of most living beings, the jordaini's magic resistance made them difficult to perceive. It was custom and courtesy for a jordain to give notice of his presence.

Matteo was back already from the Nath. Zalathorm quickened his pace.

The young jordain rose when the king entered the room and sank into a deep bow. "My lord, I have much to report."

No preamble, none of the niceties of Halruaan protocol. Zalathorm nodded with approval. "Get on with it."

"The laraken has returned. My jordaini brothers and I battled it in the Nath. All would have died, but the monster was magically removed from battle. This suggests that Kiva may have returned from the Plane of Water, and possibly Akhlaur as well. The necromancer's spellbook contains a spell of dehydration similar to that cast against the Mulhorandi invaders."

"The spell was Akhlaur's," the king agreed. "There is no doubt in my mind. His tower has been raised—I've sensed a disturbance in the magic that hid it from treasure seekers."

The jordain smiled faintly. "Lord Basel said this report would be unnecessary."

"Basel?"

"Lord Basel met us in the Nath and put his skyship at my disposal."

"Good thinking. From now on you shall have your own ship. Have the steward see it to. What more?"

"I'm going after Tzigone. Lord Basel has found a spell that should serve. Its casting requires a lock of hair from one of my ancestors. I spoke with my father."

"Ah." Zalathorm looked at him keenly. "This saddened you."

"Deeply. I knew the man all my life. He was one of my jordaini masters. He taught me all I know of battle magic and watched over me from my earliest years. Yet I knew him as my father only on the day his life ended."

The king looked startled. "Vishna! Of course you're Vishna's son—now that I look for it, the resemblance is plain. I felt his death. Tell me why it coincided with your meeting."

Zalathorm listened as the jordain related Vishna's story. "A lich transformation. So that is why I sensed his essence still lingering. It's trapped somewhere, changing and gathering strength, awaiting a return to Vishna's body. Gods above!" he shouted, slamming one fist against the wall, "how could Akhlaur do this to a man he once called friend?"

"I fear he is not finished with Vishna," Matteo said quietly. When the king sent him a quizzical glance, the jordain added, "Akhlaur is a necromancer."

"Necromancers can command the undead," Zalathorm said in despairing tones. "As long as Akhlaur lives, Vishna will never be allowed to die."

# CHAPTER FIFTEEN

Matteo stood at the base of the fairy mound into which Tzigone had disappeared. Basel Indoulur's skyship hovered overhead, but the wizard and Andris had come down into the Nath with him. Basel stood ready to cast the spell, a magehound's jeweled wand in his hand and an uncharacteristically grim expression on his round face.

Matteo glanced from the wizard to the ghostly jordain and back. "I'm not sure which of you is paler," he quipped.

"I'm not the one casting the spell," Andris responded. "Lord Basel has the responsibility of sending you in. My only task is welcoming you back." He spoke stoutly, refusing to acknowledge the possibility that Matteo might not return. The two friends clasped wrists, then fell into a brief embrace.

Matteo stepped back and nodded to Basel. The wizard began the chanting of the spell. It was a complex thing, a strange and jagged melody that sounded sinister even in Basel's pleasant, untrained baritone.

A high-pitched, eerie wind began to whistle through Matteo's thoughts, swiftly growing into gale force. The powerful wind drove him back toward the conical hill. Yet the gathering storm was for him alone—the winds did not touch the other men. Andris lifted a translucent hand in farewell.

Suddenly the Nath was gone, and Matteo was hurled into a chill, gray world. He hit and rolled, quickly coming up into a battle-ready crouch, his jordaini daggers drawn and ready.

There was no need—he was alone. In fact, as he scanned the rock-strewn moor around him, Matteo saw no other sign of life. There were no birds crawling across the pewter-colored sky, no scurrying voles amid the dull grasses, not even the hum and chirp of insects.

Yet strange images seemed to swirl through the air, and voices lurked beneath the silence. There was more to this place than Matteo's eyes could perceive—he was certain of that. The magic here was so thick, so foreign to Halruaan magic, that even he could perceive its presence.

He wondered, briefly, what he might see through the eyes of a dark fairy. This misty moor was some sort of magical antechamber, no more real than a dream.

The ground beneath him was damp and thickly covered by moss, and as he walked the spongy surface seemed to absorb his energy. Certainly it slowed his steps. The mist thickened, until he could see no more than a few paces ahead. He called Tzigone's name, but sound did not seem to carry much farther than sight could reach.

Suddenly, as if from nowhere, a solid fist flashed into Matteo's face. There was no time to evade, so he took the punch, turning his head with the blow rather than bracing against it. He seized a handful of coarse linen and pulled his assailant down with him. They were evenly matched in size, and for several moments Matteo struggled to pin the man. When he did, he gazed down into a furious face, one disconcertingly like his own.

"Benn," he said in astonishment, recognizing the young peasant.

"Why did you bring me here?" the peasant demanded.

Guilt surged as Matteo considered this question. Was it

possible that he had truly dragged the young man into this grim place? Had his jordaini resistance to magic distorted Basel's spellcasting?

The man began to struggle. "Haven't you and yours done enough?"

"It was not my choice," Matteo said earnestly. "I never meant you any harm."

"How many people have to pay for your jordaini honors?" inquired a soft, almost toneless female voice.

Matteo released Benn and staggered to his feet, stunned by the sudden appearance of the small, listless woman he had met but once. He quickly inclined his head in the traditional bow of respect to a wizard—for this is what his mother had been, before his birth had reduced her to this state.

"My lady, you took your own path," Matteo said respectfully. "I regret where it has brought you, but the choice was never mine to make."

The woman's eyes seemed to stare right through him. "It is cold here," she muttered, as if she had heard nothing Matteo said.

He moved closer. "Vishna never told me your name," he said softly.

A puzzled expression crossed her face, bringing another stab of guilt and pain to the young jordain's heart. His birth mother had lost so much of herself that she could no longer remember her own name!

Another possibility occurred to him. Perhaps his mother did not know her name because *he* did not know it. Tentatively he reached out to the small woman. His hand lowered to her shoulder and went through. She was no more substantial than the mist.

Matteo whirled toward the peasant. Benn was gone. Indeed, he had never truly been there.

The jordain took a long, unsteady breath and considered his situation. These disturbing encounters were illusions somehow plucked from his own mind. Apparently the Unseelie folk had no trouble bypassing his jordaini resistance!

On a logical level, Matteo knew he bore no guilt for his mother's decision or for the children lost to the young peasant and his wife. These were choices made by others. Vishna had often warned him not to take responsibility where there was none, telling him that it was a form of pride.

Pride, Matteo suspected, could be his downfall here.

He held out his hands, fisted them, and turned them this way and that. His own form seemed nearly as wraithlike as that of his unfortunate mother. A moment of panic gripped him. If he could not count on his strength and his warrior skills, all was lost!

Pride again, he realized. As a jordain, he had dedicated his life to developing the strength of mind and body, but here, logic had little footing. And strength? Matteo lifted a hand to his jaw. It ached from the blow Benn's image had dealt him. Here illusion ruled. The calm, pragmatic certainty of a jordain was as out of place here as the white robes of Mystra on a tavern doxie.

Soft, mocking laughter sang softly through the mists, coming at him from all sides. Matteo snatched out his daggers and whirled this way and that, watching for the attack. No dark fairies came, and as he considered the sound, he realized that the voices sounded more mortal than fey, that they were all the same voice. The laughter was a young man's, deep in pitch and derisive in tone.

With a sudden jolt, Matteo recognized the sound of his own voice. His disembodied thoughts had taken wing and were mocking him.

"Calm certainty," he said, repeating in disgust the description of himself. This was as much an illusion as anything he had encountered! For nearly a year, since the day Kiva had entered his life and shattered his assumptions, he had been wracked with doubts about the jordaini order. He was no fit jordain, no matter what comforting lies he told himself.

A sudden bright truth came to him—a moment of epiphany that turned a year of turmoil on its head. Perhaps certainty was not the *reward* of faith, but the *opposite* of it! Perhaps faith meant keeping on, despite doubts. He had done that, and he would continue to do so. His doubts did not invalidate his life's task; paradoxically, they confirmed it.

The laughter died away. Matteo permitted himself a smile at this small triumph, then marshaled his thoughts and focused on his lost friend. If the mind was so powerful in this place, perhaps he could conjure Tzigone by force of will.

He almost tripped over her small, huddled form. With a glad cry, he sank to the ground and gathered her into his arms.

The jordain was not prepared for the jolt of power that sizzled over him. Somehow, he managed to keep his hold on the girl. The strange magical surge enveloped them both, sending their hair crackling around their faces and scorching their garments. The tattered remnants of Tzigone's apprentice robe blackened and steamed, but she herself seemed unhurt. Matteo blessed the jordaini resistance that protected them both.

Tzigone's enormous brown eyes searched Matteo's face, registering but not quite accepting his presence. She looked dazed, and her smile was a faint ghost of her old insouciant grin.

"Mind if I smoke?" she said, batting away the curling wisps that rose from her singed clothes.

Perhaps it was surprise, perhaps the tension of their surroundings, but Tzigone's remark struck Matteo as wonderfully absurd. He laughed aloud from the sheer delight of having his friend back.

The wry half-smile dropped off Tzigone's face. "I knew it," she muttered, disconsolate. "You're an illusion.

The real Matteo has less sense of humor than a slug."

"Somehow, I can't be offended," he said, still grinning.

"Tell me about it," she grumbled. "Goddess knows, I've tried!"

"It's me," he insisted as he framed her small face with both hands, "and I can prove it. Do you remember when we were chased by the wemic?"

A smirk tweaked her lips. "You thought wemics could climb trees, seeing that the bottom half of them is lion. Would you be frightfully disappointed, dearest illusion, to learn that griffin kittens can't purr?"

"Do you remember this?" he persisted. Before she could respond, he bent down and gently kissed her lips. Nothing of this nature had ever passed between them— surely she would have to know this was no memory-conjured illusion.

Tzigone's eyes widened, and a familiar, urchin grin spread across her face like a quirky sunrise. "It *is* you! It has to be! Who else could possibly believe a kiss like that would be worth remembering?"

She hurled herself into his arms, clinging to him with a fervor that belied her teasing words.

The Unseelie mists deepened around them, and the chill seemed to sink into Matteo's bones. With sudden certainty, he realized that the magic had indeed slipped inside him, trying to find something to twist and control and torment.

Suddenly he was intensely aware of the girl in his arms in a way he had never been before. The heat and the need were compelling, disturbing.

He searched his heart for the truth of this. There had been moments when he was intensely aware of Tzigone as female, and he had felt an occasional twinge of intrigued curiosity. But that was not the heart of their friendship.

This triumph was short-lived, for a sudden heaviness settled upon him—the obsessive weight of the debts that first shaped and defined their relationship. He glanced down and noted Tzigone regarding him with an equally troubled expression. On impulse, he decided to turn this latest test into a joke.

"You take your debts seriously," Matteo reminded her. "If I get you out of here, the price will be an entire year without any infraction of Halruaan law."

She wriggled out of his arms. "Before you talk about price, you need to see something."

Matteo followed her through the mist, keeping close on her heels for fear of losing her.

She stopped abruptly and turned to him. "Dhamari is gone. I think I know why." She stepped aside, giving Matteo a full view of the mist-veiled horror.

A Crinti woman sat propped against a steep-sided conical mound, her head lolling to one side. Her face was black with dried blood. Where her eyes had been were dark, empty holes.

"She tore them out with her fingernails," Tzigone said dully. "Whatever she saw here was more than she could face. Dhamari is gone, and she is here. It was a trade, Matteo. A *trade*. I won't take my life at the cost of yours."

"That's not how it will be," Matteo said sternly. "We are here together, and together we'll leave. We have to trust in that and in each other."

A silvery sword clattered to the ground between them, sending them both leaping back in surprise. Matteo recognized the sword as the weapon Tzigone had stolen from a swordsmith shop the day they'd met and later hidden behind his horse's saddle. Possession of a stolen sword had earned him a night in the city prison.

"Which one of us did that?" he wondered, pointed to the sword.

"Does it matter? The small betrayals add up," Tzigone said, her usually merry voice troubled. "How many times have I stolen your medallion?"

"Four or five," Matteo said dryly.

She shook her head and held up a jordaini emblem, a silver disk enameled with yellow and green, slashed with cobalt blue. "Twenty years on the streets isn't something easily forgotten, Matteo. Sooner or later, I'm going to cause more trouble for you than either of us can handle."

Matteo disagreed—he trusted Tzigone, and he searched his mind for something that might convince her she was worthy of this trust. Even as the thought took shape, a clatter of hooves and a bad-tempered whinny erupted from the mist.

He watched, open-mouthed with astonishment, as a tall black stallion trotted toward them—a horse that some irreverent stable hand had named "Cyric" after an insane and evil god.

"Lord and lady!" Tzigone exclaimed. "All that thing needs is glowing red eyes!"

The horse whickered and blew as Matteo stroked his ebony muzzle. The horse was warm and solid to his touch, not like the illusions the dark fairies had shaped from his stolen thoughts. "You're no nightmare, are you, Cyric my lad? I must admit, however, that when you snort like that I always expect to smell brimstone."

Tzigone eyes narrowed as she regarded the jordain and his favorite mount. "You're actually fond of that beast."

"Indeed I am! Cyric has thrown me, nipped my shoulder, and once when we were traveling he kicked over my lean-to and deliberately passed water in my cooking kettle."

"What's not to love?" she muttered.

"Yet he would run himself to death if I needed speed, and there is no horse alive that I'd rather trust in battle. Cyric is capable of a deeper, more profound loyalty than any creature I know. Any, perhaps, save one."

He slapped the stallion's rump and sent it running off into the mist. "You followed me into Akhlaur's Swamp and fought the laraken, though you had no way of knowing it would not leave you an empty crystal shell. You are here in this place because your friends and your Halruaa were threatened, and you gave yourself in their place. You and Cyric are two of a kind, Tzigone."

"Well, a girl can't hear *that* too often," she said dryly.

"There is nothing more powerful than friendship—and no friend I would rather have," he said earnestly. "That power has a magic of its own."

Tzigone's eyes brimmed. She dashed away tears with the back of one grubby hand and pointed. Matteo turned. The mist parted to reveal a moss-covered, conical hill. A shimmering oval beckoned them.

Her face froze, her smile shattered. He followed the line of her gaze. A swift-darting swarm approached, a small army of dark fairies apparently bent upon holding their captives in this misty netherworld. There was no way the two friends could reach the portal in time.

Matteo pressed one of his matched daggers into Tzigone's hands and drew his sword. They hardly had time to fall into position, back to back, before the dark fairies fell upon them.

Tiny knives flashed, too fast for the eyes to follow. Matteo felt the stings, shallow and taunting. His sword flashed out again and again, trying in vain to drive them back, and he moved his dagger in swift, complex defensive patterns.

So quick were the fey monsters that they easily darted in and back, working around each of his strokes and lunges, stabbing at him again and again yet always keeping beyond reach of his blade. Pain flooded over Matteo, but pain more like intense sunburn than anything a knife might inflict.

He glanced down. His white garments were flecked with blood from hundreds of pinpricks, and his forearms appeared to be covered with a fine rash.

At this rate, it would take a very long time to die.

He felt Tzigone step away from him, and quickly he

moved back into position, determined to keep her back covered.

"Let me go," she insisted, circling around as if to evade his protection.

Matteo easily moved with her, his sword and dagger flashing. "Forget it," he informed her curtly.

She hissed in exasperation and spun, nearly as fast as the fairies, delivering a sharp kick to the back of Matteo's knee.

He only faltered for a moment, but that was enough for Tzigone. She darted away. The Unseelie folk followed her like vengeful shadows.

Before Matteo could regroup, a flash of power lit the misty realm. He threw up one hand to protect his eyes.

When he could see again, he stared in astonishment at the charred bodies of several of the dark fairies. The rest had scattered—or maybe this was the sum total of their attackers.

The dark fairies were smaller than he had expected and so strangely beautiful that he almost regretted their fate. A terrible keening song rose from beyond the mist as the Unseelie folk bewailed their dead.

"They can die here," he marveled.

"So can we," she retorted as she scanned the mist for the next attack. "You didn't by any chance bring iron with you?"

"Basel said it can't be done," he said in bleak tones. "Iron weapons won't cross over the veil."

Tzigone's eyes narrowed as she considered this. "Not if you follow the rules, it won't. Call Cyric again."

"I didn't call him the first time."

"Sure you did. You're better at it than I am—that was the most convincing illusion I've seen yet."

"That's impossible! I'm a jordain!"

Even as he spoke, Matteo realized the truth of her words. He could *see* magic in this place, sense it in a way that powerful wizards and elven magi were said to do. The

Weave, the magic Mystra spun and sustained, was as foreign to him as air was to a fish, but perhaps this place knew magic of another sort.

"The Shadow Weave," he said. "It *does* exist! And I can sense it, even use it!"

He seized the girl's shoulders and turned her to face him. "Shortly before I left the Jordaini College, we received word of a new sort of magic sifting into the Northlands, perhaps even into Halruaa. It is said that the goddess Shar created another source of magic, one that has nothing to do with Mystra. Sages suspect that she experimented in isolated lands, perhaps in other planes of existence. This place of mist and shadows may be one such realm!"

Tzigone looked skeptical. "Fairies have their own gods. Didn't they have anything to say about this? They just stood by and let this Shar set up housekeeping?"

"This is not the Unseelie Court," he explained, "but a corridor between their world and ours. Nothing is real here. I suspect that the dark fairies have no power to hold us—perhaps they are protecting their own borders, as we do ours! Illusion is all-powerful here. It may be that people who stumble in are trapped simply because they believe they can't leave."

She frowned as she tried to sort all this through. "So you're telling me that you're some sort of wizard, after all."

"*No!* Well, perhaps," he amended. "The jordaini are vessels empty of Mystra's Art. It is possible that this void makes us uniquely suited to the Shadow Weave."

Tzigone shrugged. "You're usually right. What interests me most at the moment is the notion that we could leave any time. Now would be good for me."

A faint glow dawned in the nearby mists as another gate took shape. The faint keening of fairy song surged in alarm, and small black streaks hurtled toward them.

Matteo put two fingers to his lips and blew a sharp, shrill whistle.

The clatter of hooves announced Cyric's return a moment before the black stallion leaped from the mist and charged the attacking fairies. The illusionary stallion proved fully as evil-tempered and loyal as the original. Cyric plunged into the advancing horde, screaming with equine rage. The horse reared up, lashing out with his hooves.

"Iron horseshoes," Matteo murmured with satisfaction as he drew dagger and sword. "You can cast spells here— magic of many sorts is present. Transmute these to iron."

Tzigone raced through the words of a spell. The weapons grew heavier, and their shining metal turned as dull as the mist.

"Well done," he said as he handed her the iron dagger.

"Cyric and me," Tzigone said, holding up two entwined fingers.

Several dark shapes outflanked the stallion and sped toward them. Tzigone dropped into a knife-fighter's crouch and slashed out. For a moment a dark fairy female stood revealed, stunned into immobility by the unexpected presence of an iron weapon. Then Tzigone lofted the dagger and pressed the attack. Though slowed and weakened by the poisonous metal, the fairy still possessed the speed and agility of any swordmaster. The grimy little sorceress and the small, fey being circled and slashed, one determined to reach the portal and the other equally set upon barring the way.

Matteo fell into guard position, scything a path with his iron sword. He and Tzigone backed slowly toward the glowing portal. Finally Tzigone threw the dagger at the nearest foe and gave Matteo an ungentle shove.

They turned and ran the last steps to the magical portal. Together they leaped through, landing on ground that felt blissfully solid and hard.

He picked himself up and looked for Tzigone. Basel had already swept her up into a crushing embrace.

Andris came over to Matteo's side. "It is said that those

who enter the Unseelie court come out being what they truly are," he said softly. "What did you see? What did you learn?"

Matteo's gaze swept the Nath, searching for some sign of the Shadow Weave. He did not see its magic as he had in the Unseelie corridor. Not sure whether to be disappointed or relieved, he shrugged. "I am simply a jordain, nothing more."

The girl came over to Matteo, beaming, but pulled up short when her gaze fell upon the nearly transparent Andris.

"Nine hollow Hells! What's he doing here?"

"Andris is a jordain, pledged to the service of Halruaa. He is helping me tend several tasks of great importance."

"Isn't that cozy?" Tzigone folded her arms. "Last I knew, you two were going at each other with swords and looking pretty damned serious about it. Last I heard, he was working with Kiva and the Crinti."

"We've come to an understanding," Matteo said.

The girl shook her head. "I don't think you've got another Cyric here, Matteo."

Andris attempted an ironic smile. "Shall I take that as a compliment?"

"You can take it to hell and back, for all I care," Tzigone told him. "In the meanwhile, keep out of my way."

The ghostly jordain bowed and walked quietly away. Matteo started after him, then decided his friend would prefer solitude.

"You're wrong about Andris," he told her softly. "He is a good man, with perhaps too strong a sense of his destiny."

"Maybe." She tucked her arm through his and sent him a crooked smile. "You do have an annoying habit of being right."

"I have an annoying habit of being blind," Matteo said.

Tzigone pulled away and propped her fists on her hips. "You want to repeat that for people who don't speak jordaini?"

"Andris was right—those who pass the veil see themselves as never before. I didn't realize how large a part pride played in my life. Now I see it at every turn, and it is not an attractive sight."

"You're proud," she agreed, "and that's like saying Sinestra Belajoon, one of the most beautiful women in Halruaa, is vain. The way I see it, you're both entitled."

"Pride directs the focus inward. I look to Halruaan lore for answers. You are much more flexible than I. Without your quick thinking, we might not have fought our way through the dark fairies."

Her eyes went wide. "Who showed me how to recover memories? That came in very handy. Who was it who told me I was a wizard and urged me to learn about my magic?"

Matteo sighed. "You would have found your way to these things in time."

"I'll bet you tell a corpse the same thing. 'Don't worry about this minor defeat, my good fellow—I'm sure you would have picked up that sword sooner or later.' " She gave a wickedly precise imitation of Matteo's speech. "Would it salve your jordaini pride if I played the part of a swooning maiden?" she asked in her own voice.

The image was so ludicrous that Matteo couldn't help but smile. "It might."

"Well, forget it. Now that we're back, what are you? Still a jordain?"

He considered that. The sharp contrast between the shadowy plane and the world he knew had muted his perception. The ability to *see* magic had faded, yet there was something. . . .

"I suppose that depends upon your definition," he said.

"Jordain," she recited helpfully. "A prissy, arrogant know-it-all who can drone on about any subject at all until his listeners start bleeding from both ears. Someone who couldn't bend a law in a gale. An old maid who only knows enough about fun to keep me from having any."

Matteo's lips quirked. "That does sound familiar," he agreed.

Tzigone nodded and returned to his arms. "Then tell me this: Why am I so glad to be back?"

# CHAPTER SIXTEEN

Sunrise colors painted the sky as *Avariel* flew swiftly toward Halarahh and the modest villa that Basel kept in the king's city. The skyship swept over the city, slowing and settling as it approached the small tower.

Tzigone, who had bathed and dressed in blissfully clean garments, stood at the rail, taking in the vivid scene as if the heat of the Halruaan sun and the brilliant colors of sea and city could burn away memories of a grim, gray place. Suddenly she leaned over the rail and pointed.

"What in the Nine bloody Hells is that?"

A faint pollen-yellow aura surrounded the wizard's tower.

"The building had been magically sealed," Basel explained, his face suddenly somber. "With all that has happened, I did not have a chance to tell you of Farrah Noor's death. Mason has been accused. Since there is some uncertainty in the testing, he is allowed to remain in the relative freedom of my tower."

Tzigone's brown eyes went enormous with shock. "That can't be true! Mason would never hurt Farrah. They were lovers, you know. He was insanely giddy over her."

"If you are called to speak for him in court, I would suggest choosing different words to express their mutual affection," Matteo advised.

"Farrah's dead," she repeated, trying to take this in. "That doesn't seem possible. How did it happen?"

"From what I understand, she was killed with a knife, which was later found in Mason's room."

"That's thin," Tzigone scoffed. "What do the mage-hounds say?"

"Mason remembers nothing at all about her death, and they can't retrieve memories he doesn't have. He will be held in the tower until the more puzzling aspects of the situation can be resolved."

"Such as the militia, Lord Basel?" inquired Matteo, pointing to the guards at the gate.

The wizard grimaced as he took in the detachment of uniformed soldiers encircling the tower grounds. "We haven't men to spare on such foolishness."

They landed *Avariel* at the nearby skypond—one of the shallow, man-made lakes that provided convenient docking for the flying ships—and hastened on foot to Basel's villa. To their astonishment, the militia captain signaled to his men, and the guards barred the gates with crossed halberds.

"My apprentice shows considerable talent for wizardry, but at his current level of skill he hardly merits this level of security," Basel said coldly. "It is neither law nor custom to isolate a man held in house arrest. You have no reason to hold me from my own tower on Mason's behalf."

The captain bowed. "This does not concern your apprentice, Lord Basel. Begging your pardon, lord, but I have a writ for your arrest."

The wizard took the parchment and studied the runes. After a moment he rolled it up and handed it to the guard. "Very well. This is my apprentice, Tzigone. She is to be given free access to my tower, to come and go as she pleases."

"As you say." The captain signaled again, and two guards flanked the wizard.

Matteo stepped in and held the captain's gaze with an imperious stare. "Is Lord Basel to be taken in without benefit of counsel?"

After a moment, the man stepped aside and motioned his men to do the same.

"What can I do to help?" Matteo asked Basel softly.

"You've more important things on your plate. I'll send to Halar for one of my own jordaini counselors."

"At least tell me the charge!"

The wizard glanced at Tzigone. "I am accused of Sinestra Belajoon's murder."

The girl's jaw fell slack with astonishment. She snapped it shut and quickly caught up. "Sinestra is dead, too? How? Where?"

"I can't answer how, but the where is plain enough. She was in my tower, searching your room."

"Of course she was," Tzigone said clearly and distinctly. "Sinestra and I were friends, and she was looking for me. But of course you knew that. It's not as if you would mistake her for a thief, or anything like that."

Basel leaned closer. "Child, this is not the time to spring to my defense. Say no more until we have opportunity to speak. There are things about Sinestra you should know."

"Tell me now," she urged.

The wizard glanced toward the guards, who were becoming visibly restless. "Sinestra was once Keturah's servant," he said, speaking softly and quickly. "I knew her. We helped your mother escape after she was condemned as a murderer. You cannot afford to become entangled in this. Now, go back to the tower. We will speak when we can."

Basel stepped back and motioned to the guards. They reformed ranks, and he fell into step with them. Tzigone watched him go, her face stunned.

"Not good," Matteo fretted. "This gives Basel an apparent motive."

She spun and stalked back toward the tower. "Basel didn't do it. He wouldn't do anything remotely illegal."

"Well," Matteo hedged. At Tzigone's prodding, he told her that he and Basel had slipped into Dhamari's tower and had taken from it a number of valuable spells and books.

"But he got them for me, right?" Tzigone persisted. "To research the spell that freed me?"

"So?"

"Then he did no wrong. The tower was Keturah's before Dhamari stole it. I'm Keturah's daughter and heir. Whatever Basel took was mine. He didn't do anything wrong, ever, and I'll tell that to everyone who'll listen. Let's go."

She changed directions again, hurrying toward the city palace. Matteo matched her pace. "Tzigone, you will never get into the council chamber!"

"Why not? Who's going to stop the queen's jordain?"

"I am counselor to Zalathorm now," he corrected.

"Even better!"

Matteo sighed and pulled her to a stop. "I will bring you on one condition: You listen and say nothing. Until all is known, your tendency to add interesting facts to the truth could create complications."

She gave grumbling assent. They walked in silence to the pink marble palace and walked unhindered into the council hall.

The vaulted room was dominated by a vast marble table shaped like a half moon. Thirteen members of the Council of Elders sat around the table's curve, their faces grave at the prospect of hearing charges against one of their own.

Matteo and Tzigone found a seat in an empty upper balcony and watched as an Inquisitor of Azuth began the spells of testing.

The magehound was a tall, black-haired woman, fussily clad in the green and yellow robes of an Azuthan inquisitor and decorated with far too many gems. No doubt she wished to appear important and grand. Even her gestures had a theatrical extravagance that set Matteo's teeth on edge. He could imagine the vicious satire Tzigone would enact after the trial!

With a flourish, the magehound took out a silver rod and placed it against Basel's forehead. "The charge brought by Uriah Belajoon is true," she announced in ringing tones. "Basel Indoulur was the man who touched Sinestra and triggered Lord Belajoon's spell."

"That may be so," Basel said evenly, "but I merely closed the woman's eyes. She was already dead, slain by magic I did not cast."

Tzigone leaned out over the railing, her eyes fixed upon the man seated in the very center of the group of Elders. "Damn! There's old Snow Hawk. That can't be good."

Procopio Septus fit the description in every particular. He wore his prematurely white hair cropped close, which drew attention to a strong curved nose and black eyes like those of a hunting hawk. Matteo knew there was no love lost between Procopio and the accused wizard.

"He is the lord mayor of the king's city," Matteo reminded her. "He often hears accusations and sits in judgment. If there is to be a trial, it will go to the full Council of Elders."

Tzigone sent him a look of incredulity. "There will be a trial, all right. He hates Basel."

Matteo wasn't so sure. Procopio was a canny man. He was unlikely to remand a case to the Council of Elders unless he was certain it could be won.

He watched his former patron with great interest. Procopio listened gravely as the magehound cast spells that would recreate the last moments of Sinestra's life. She spoke of Sinestra and Basel talking in a tower chamber, Sinestra overcome by a spell, dying in terrible convulsions.

"Did Lord Basel create that spell?" asked Procopio.

The magehound hesitated. "That is impossible to say, since the object of the spell cannot be tested. Basel touched her, and she melted away."

"Was he the man who *killed* her?"

"I cannot say," she repeated, speaking with exaggerated precision. "The vision is not conclusive. Lord Basel was responsible for triggering the spell. That much I can tell you. The rest you must learn by other means."

Procopio Septus rose. "Let us review what little we know. Sinestra Belajoon came to Lord Basel's tower. She was killed by some malevolent magic, the author of which remains unknown. Lord Basel closed her eyes, and his touch triggered a spell that removed her to her own home. Her husband, Uriah Belajoon, conducted the funeral rites before bringing accusation against Lord Basel. Does that fit the particulars?"

He glanced from Basel to the magehound to the aging, portly man who sat in the accuser's chair. All nodded.

"Very well then, Lord Basel is free to go." He lifted one hand to cut short the Belajoon wizard's protests. "Halruaan law is very clear on this matter. When murder is suspected, magical inquiry must be conducted at once. After the body is destroyed, it is impossible to question the dead."

Uriah Belajoon's face turned purple with wrath, but he chopped his head once in curt acceptance of the sentence. He watched as Lord Basel walked from the chamber, his eyes burning with hatred.

"Old Snow Hawk is up to something," Tzigone mused. In a single, swift movement she rose from her seat and headed for one of the tapestries decorating the walls.

Matteo lunged for her and got a handful of air for his efforts. He peeled back the edge of the tapestry and looked up. She was climbing it, finding handholds in the weave. Her passage would be unnoticed from the other side, for the tapestry hung a bit away from the wall, attached at the top to a marble ledge. This ledge ran the length of the corridor and down several halls. It was wide enough to provide Tzigone a pathway, and high enough to hide her as long as she kept low.

With a sigh, Matteo abandoned thought of pursuit. He would, however, mention this possible security lapse to the palace guards. Most likely, they would laugh behind his back at the seeming absurdity of it.

That, he mused, was precisely why Tzigone had survived as long as she had.

Tzigone edged along the marble ledge, wiggling her way like a serpent. From this vantage, she could see the entire hall and most of the exits. Procopio Septus left through the south hall, on the heels of a throng intent upon finding shade and refreshment before the sun rose high and the sunsleep hours started.

She followed him through increasingly narrow city streets, moving like a shadow. Finally she tired of this and climbed a rose trellis to the roof above. She ran lightly over the roofs and dropped back down several houses ahead.

Procopio slipped into a dark doorway. After a slight hesitation, Tzigone followed. The door locked behind her with a sharp click, though no hand touched the bolt. She threw herself under a richly draped table just as a chandelier flared to life. A rainbow of colors filled the room as light streamed through the multicolored crystals that draped the ornate lamp.

The wizard gestured, and the rope holding the chandeliers lengthened, lowering it to his height. He considered it for a moment, then plucked a yellow crystal. This he tossed into the air.

The gem hung for a moment, then swiftly grew into a large, translucent bubble, slightly golden in hue. Its surface rippled slightly, and Dhamari Exchelsor stepped into the room.

Tzigone gritted her teeth to hold back an exclamation of dismay. The emerging wizard looked no more pleased than she.

"You have broken the terms of our agreement," Dhamari said.

Procopio extended his hands, palms up. "How so? You requested a place of concealment. What better than your own demi-plane? No wizard will find you there."

The little wizard conceded this with an ill-tempered nod. "I'm speaking of Basel Indoulur's hearing. I thought we agreed to handle this matter privately."

"I let him go," Procopio said.

Dhamari stared at him in disbelief. Understanding came, and a slow, wicked smile curved his lips. "Uriah Belajoon, denied justice, will have no choice but to take matters into his own hands. You know, of course, that he is not very powerful. He has little chance of killing Basel."

"Not on his own, certainly."

"Excellent," Dhamari crowed. "Basel would be difficult to convict: Uriah will not. Two more of Zalathorm's supporters out of the way."

"We are in accord," Procopio said.

Tzigone scowled in agreement—after all, insects usually did march in formation. She felt no surprise at learning that Procopio Septus harbored treasonous thoughts or that Dhamari was allied with him. The problem would be finding someone other than Matteo who would believe this tale!

Dhamari reached for the crystal. "I'll return to the plane later. There are some small matters I need to attend."

The diviner agreed and strode to a door on the far side of the room. Arcane light flared around the cracks, giving testament to a magic gate summoned. Dhamari slipped out the way Procopio had come in.

Tzigone gave him a moment, then followed him down a tree-shaded lane. She scooted up a scarlet beech tree and ran lightly along one of its massive limbs, keeping just ahead of the wizard. There were few people about at this hour, for the sun was high and fiercely hot. Tzigone waited until there was no one in sight. She dropped from her perch, seizing Dhamari's tunic and dragging him into the narrow divide between two shops.

Seeking escape, he fumbled for his crystal. Tzigone was quicker. She seized his hand and gave it a sharp twist that brought him down to one knee. Dhamari looked up at her and gasped in astonishment. Before he could let out his breath in a shout, Tzigone bent low and drove a fist into his belly. He folded, and a familiar glint of silver hung from his neck.

Her mother's talisman.

Tzigone lunged for it. The wizard slapped her hand away and seized her wrist with his other hand.

Sorcerous energy poured from the angry girl. To her astonishment, it merely collected in a circle on Dhamari's wrist.

He released her and rose to his feet, holding up one arm to display a copper bracer. "Your mother had a temper, too," he said smugly. "I collected some interesting wards, just in case."

Tzigone threw both hands high in a dramatic flourish of spell-casting. Instinctively the wizard lifted his hands as if to ward off the attack. Instead, Tzigone stepped in and brought her knee up hard.

A high-pitched wheeze gusted from the wizard. For a moment he looked at her with undisguised hatred. Tzigone could almost see the gnomework gears turning in his mind as he sought the vilest curse possible, the most wounding words. Nothing could have prepared her for what he said.

"Your mother is alive."

He spoke with such certainty that Tzigone almost believed him. The world shifted weirdly beneath her feet.

"I would know if she were alive."

"How could you, when even *she* doesn't know?" Dhamari taunted. His gaze slid down her, and his lip curled in a sneer. "I must say, you are the most unlikely princess I have ever beheld."

Tzigone froze in the act of denying this. Beatrix—this was the name her unknown father had bestowed upon Keturah. *Queen* Beatrix?

"As you may have heard, the queen will be tried for treason in a few days." Dhamari paused for a chilling smile. "The queen might be exonerated of the charge of treason by reason of her very apparent insanity, but the court will be less lenient if it becomes known that she has another, murderous identity."

"*You* killed that greenmage!" Tzigone threw back. "You killed her, and painted Keturah as the murderer!"

Dhamari looked nonplussed, "How do you—" He broke off abruptly, visibly gathered himself. "Why do you say that?"

She looked him over, then snatched a glove from his belt. "This is deerskin."

The wizard clucked softly. "My dear child, if you think that proves anything, you're as mad as your mother."

"You summoned the deer using one of Keturah's spells," Tzigone went on, "and you held it trapped and helpless while you shot it. It took four arrows. You're not much of a marksman," she added as an aside, then resumed her telling. "The man who tanned the leather lives on the Exchelsor family estates. He has four fingers on his left hand and he wears an eye patch."

The color drained from Dhamari's face during this recitation. "What does this mean?"

"It means that I can divine the past rather than the future. In the dark fairies' realm, I spent a lot of time looking into Keturah's past. I can't tell you what a relief it was to learn that you could not possibly have been my father."

The wizard's pale face took on a dull red flush. "Let me remind you that a vision induced by dark fairies is hardly admissible testimony. Nor are you a credible witness. I suspect that you can't be magically tested for veracity—your resistance to magic is too strong."

All of this was true. Even so, Tzigone kept her taunting smile in place. "You *can* be tested, can't you? If you take a single step against me or mine, I'll come after you with witnesses who have credentials the gods might envy."

He stared at her for a moment. "A sword at your throat, a sword at mine."

Tzigone shrugged. "It'll do for now. Now get out of my sight."

She watched him go, then sprinted off toward the public gardens. There were hidden pathways through the giant trees shading the city, and Tzigone knew them all. Such knowledge, combined with her magical resistance, gave her access to any place she cared to go. Not even the king's palace could hold her out. She quickly made her way to Matteo's room and found it empty. Gritting her teeth, she remembered his recent promotion and set a path for the room once occupied by Cassia, the king's last head counselor.

She slipped into the room. Matteo was in earnest conversation with the ghostly jordain. Both men looked up at her approach—at this point, she was too angry to soften her footsteps.

"Is it true?" she demanded.

Matteo studied her face for a long moment. For some reason, he did not have to ask what she meant. "Yes."

Tzigone took a long, calming breath. "How long have you known?"

"A few days. I learned of it the day after your disappearance. I would have told you before this, had I been free to do so." He stopped and considered his words. "No, that's not quite true. I would have told you regardless, before—"

"Before it was too late," Tzigone finished. Before Queen Beatrix, formerly known as Keturah, was executed for treason.

The jordain nodded.

Andris looked from one to another, his translucent face both puzzled and wary. "Perhaps I should go. I'll call the guard to take me back to my cell."

"No," Matteo said sharply. "You can stay with me until your trial is over or go wherever you like."

He turned to Tzigone. "Shall I take you to her?"

She nodded and fell into step. They passed through a labyrinth of palace halls and climbed the highest tower, one hemmed about with magical wards and accessed only by a narrow, winding stair. Guards—both human and magical—were stationed in small alcoves cut into the walls, hidden places that appeared suddenly, and, Tzigone suspected, changed places randomly. No one who climbed these stairs knew when they would confront a guardian, or what sort. The queen was well protected—and Halruaa was well protected from the queen.

Finally they paused before an ironbound door. Matteo gestured to the guards, who unchained the locks.

Tzigone leaned against the doorframe and studied the queen. Beatrix sat in a narrow chair, her hands folded in her lap. Incurious brown eyes, deeply rimmed with kohl and enormous in a small, painted faced, gazed back. There was no recognition in them.

Tzigone waited for her thudding heart to slow to a pace that permitted speech. She glanced at the slit of window. The day had passed swiftly, and sunset colors stained the skies.

"It is nearly night, Your Majesty, and time to prepare for sleep."

When the queen made no protest, Tzigone took a basin and filled it with water from a heated cistern. She found a soft cloth and knelt beside the queen. Playing the part of a handmaid, she gently removed the cosmetics from the queen's face.

Without the white paint, Beatrix looked smaller, younger, and far more beautiful. She did not, however, resemble the mother Tzigone remembered or the woman she had glimpsed in her vision.

"There must be a magical illusion over her," Tzigone said. "I'm going to dispel it."

Matteo began to warn her, but not soon enough. Tzigone's spell quickly stripped away the cloaking magic.

Her eyes filled with tears. The face before her was not recognizable as Keturah—was barely recognizably human. Skin and flesh had been flayed off, and what remained had been deeply burned by fire and acids. The woman had no ears and not much of a nose. On that horrific face, the elaborate white and silver wig was a mockery, like gems on a corpse.

Without thinking Tzigone reached to remove the wig. The queen seized her wrists with a surprisingly strong grip.

"No," she said quietly.

Tzigone's heart shattered. This simple gesture convinced her as nothing else could have. She backed away, dipping in a bow. "Good night, my lady."

She turned and fled the room. Matteo followed. He found her on the stairwell, sitting with her face turned to the wall and her arms encircling her knees. He settled down beside her and waited.

"I should have known better than to touch her wig," she said at last. "My mother had beautiful hair. Even now, she can't bear for anyone to see her without it."

"So you believe it's true."

Tzigone lifted one shoulder. "Why wouldn't I? You've never lied to me. Of course, you haven't exactly been lavish with the truth, either."

He started to reach for her, then pulled back. "What will you do now?"

"Hmm?" She glanced up at him. "I'm heading straight for the tower. You have my word on it," she added in a sharper tone when Matteo lifted a questioning brow.

He nodded and walked her to the nearest exit. As Tzigone sped into the twilit city, she blessed Matteo for his particular brand of logic. He assumed she would return to Basel. It never occurred to him to ask her *which* tower!

❂

Pebbles crunched under Uriah Belajoon's feet as he crept through the garden surrounding Basel Indoulur's tower. He considered casting a globe of silence but regretfully abandoned that idea. A yellow haze clung to the tower, the mark of warding against magical intrusion. He wouldn't risk discovery. Too much rested on surprise. He would have but one chance.

He crouched behind a flowering hibiscus along the main path and not far from the tower door. His fingers tightened around the hilt of a dagger. Magic would be perceived, but who would expect a single man to come to the mighty conjurer's domain armed with little more than a table knife? Sooner or later Basel would pass, and he would die.

Uriah waited as the moon crept above the rooftops of the king's city. Finally his patience was rewarded. The fat little toad who had killed his beloved Sinestra emerged from the tower and slipped into his garden. Basel Indoulur stood gazing up at the moon and the seven bright shards that followed it through the sky, as if the answer to some great puzzle might be written there.

A heavy sigh escaped the wizard. To Uriah Belajoon's ear, it held the weight of conscience. He gripped the dagger, slowly raising it as the hated wizard began to stroll down the path.

As Basel drew alongside the hibiscus, Uriah poured all his strength into a single lunging attack. For a moment, he was airborne and invincible—a wolf attacking a rival, a young warrior defending his lady, a god avenging evil.

The next, he was lying on his back and marveling at how the moonshards danced and circled.

"Lord Belajoon," said a surprised, familiar voice.

Uriah's eyes focused upon Basel Indoulur's face. A sense of failure swept through the old man, and the crushing weight of futility gripped his chest like a vise.

There was nothing more to be done. Sinestra was gone,

and gone also was the dream of vengeance that had sustained him. On impulse, he snatched up the fallen knife and placed it over his own heart. He gripped the hilt with both hands and prepared to plunge it home.

The crushing pain intensified, and the weapon slipped from suddenly nerveless fingers. Waves of agony radiated from Uriah's chest into his arms. He could not move, he could not even curse the wizard who took this from him.

Dimly he sensed Basel drop to one knee. The portly wizard seized the knife and tossed it aside. He struck Uriah's chest hard with the heel of one hand, placed his ear against the old man's chest, then struck again.

Uriah watched these efforts as if from a great and growing distance. He understood the truth of his death and the nature of Basel Indoulur's efforts. Suddenly it did not matter to him that the wizard he hated still lived and that he seemed determined to pummel life back into Uriah's body.

The old wizard turned his eyes toward the moonshards, remembering every bright legend he had ever heard about what might await him and believing them all. The lights grew and merged, filling his vision with brightness.

Tzigone crept through the streets toward the Belajoon mansion, intent upon retrieving something that had belonged to Sinestra. Basel was free today, but that was no guarantee against tomorrow.

One thing puzzled her—why hadn't Sinestra's death been investigated? Usually magehounds were called at once. Once the murderer was revealed, the remains were promptly cremated and the ashes scattered so that no further inquiry could be made. By law and custom, the secrets of Halruaan wizards died with them.

The ancient, sprawling mansion was amazingly easy to enter. All the lights were dimmed in mourning, and the windows were open. This spoke volumes about old lord Belajoon. Halruaan custom was to close all windows—an old superstition, based on the idea that open windows beckoned the spirits of the departed and tempted them into lingering. Apparently Belajoon wanted to hold onto his wife as long as he could!

Magic wards protected the windows and skittered across Tzigone's skin like delicate insects as she climbed over the sill. She slipped through the quiet house toward a room ablaze with candles. Sinestra's room had been left untouched, almost like a shrine.

Shaking her head at the old man's fond foolishness, Tzigone set to work. She found a small silver brush with a broken handle, tossed negligently into a drawer. This was important—whatever Tzigone presented for testing had to appear to be discarded. No magehound could legally test a stolen object.

As she picked up the brush, a bit of folded paper caught her eyes, something tossed into the drawer and forgotten. She lifted one edge of the packet and recognized the oddly colored powder Sinestra had taken from Procopio's tower.

"Don't touch that," advised a male voice behind her.

Tzigone leaped and whirled, coming face to face with Matteo's friend Andris.

He caught the packet she'd inadvertently tossed into the air and leaned away from the small puff of dust that escaped it. "You really shouldn't take this. If Lord Belajoon realizes the loss, they'll look for the thief."

"He probably doesn't know she had it. She didn't know what it was," Tzigone explained, feeling rather dazed and stupid. It had been a very long time since someone had crept up on her! "For that matter, *I* don't know what it is."

Andris folded back the paper and showed her the

powder. "This particular shade is known to artists as 'mummy brown.' Once it was precisely that—a pigment made from the ground remains of mummies. It has not been used for years, of course, but was fairly common during a period when northerners were given to exploring and despoiling the Old Empires."

Tzigone lifted one eyebrow. "I can see why you and Matteo get along. Why did you follow me?"

"Actually, I didn't." He cleared his throat. "I came to help Lord Basel, on Matteo's behalf."

"Now I know you're lying. Matteo wouldn't have sent you here."

Andris's ice-green eyes narrowed. "Did he send you here?"

"Good point," Tzigone admitted. After a moment, she added, "Did you find anything?"

Andris moved over to the wall and tapped lightly on a carved panel. It slid aside silently to reveal a hidden passage. He shrugged aside Tzigone's incredulous stare. "The original designs for nearly every mansion of note are in the jordaini libraries."

She whistled softly. "If you're ever in need of a partner, I might be available."

They made their way down a series of hidden stairs and halls. Finally Andris led her into a deep-buried chamber. The room was round and empty but for a long, glass box resting on a marble table. Uriah Belajoon had entombed Sinestra under glass.

Tzigone edged closer. Her friend had changed from a raven-haired beauty into the woman Tzigone had once glimpsed in a magic-dispelling mirror.

"She does look a bit like my mother," she mused.

"Keturah," Andris remembered. "Kiva spoke of her in the Swamp of Akhlaur."

Tzigone nodded, but her thoughts were elsewhere. She placed one hand on the glass and sank deep into concentration, seeking the spell that killed Sinestra. Its nature was familiar enough—a particularly virulent silence spell often placed upon servants—but try as she might, Tzigone couldn't feel who had done the casting. The person was powerfully, magically shielded from her sight. Tzigone felt a faint echo of her mother's magic.

"Dhamari," she said, pronouncing it like a curse.

# CHAPTER SEVENTEEN

Andris and Tzigone had no problem entering the palace, for Matteo had listed them in the guardhouse book. They were ushered through with an extravagant courtesy that Tzigone would have found amusing had she been in a brighter mood and more congenial company.

"*Friends of the King's Counselor,*" she muttered in a dead-on imitation of the guard's obsequious tones. "I'm surprised there's no medal to go along with that title."

"Yes, I rather expected someone to pull out a sword and knight us."

Tzigone shot a surprised glance at the translucent jordain. His tone matched hers—bemused humor, untainted by envy over Matteo's position.

She considered the puzzle Andris offered. "You two have been friends for a long time?"

He shrugged. "All our lives, but considering our relative youth, I'm not sure that qualifies as a 'long time.'"

"So why did you go over to Kiva?"

"Those are two separate lines of occurrence," he said evenly, keeping his eyes straight ahead.

Tzigone made a rude noise. "Mineral-rich soil enhancers—rothe manure sounds pretty good when you put fancy words to it, doesn't it?"

A fleeting smile touched the jordain's lips. "You

have a knack for finding the salient point. For a long time, I tried to convince myself that one thing had nothing to do with the other." He glanced at her. "I suppose you know my story."

"I've heard it. I just don't understand it."

"We Halruaans are raised with a strong sense of heritage and destiny. It was you who told me I was elf-blooded, so it should come as no surprise to learn there are blood ties between me and Kiva."

"That explains *part* of it."

"Not all," he agreed. "For a while, I thought Kiva's goals justified her methods. Admittedly, there was the battle itself. As a jordain, the most I could expect was to advise wizards on tactics and watch from afar."

"Which is why Kiva snatched you in the first place," Tzigone concluded. "Matteo says you're the best to come out of the Jordaini College in years. Better even than he is."

Andris sent her a wry grin. "Honest to a fault, isn't he?"

"I've noticed that." She stopped at the door leading to Matteo's chambers and appraised the jordain. "I think I could like you," she said, her voice sounding surprised even to her own ears, "but that won't stop me from killing you if you turn against Matteo again."

He didn't smirk at this announcement, as many men might have. Tzigone was waif-thin, and her head didn't reach the jordain's shoulder. She was unarmed, and he was a skilled fighter who carried several fine weapons. He had been trained in methods of combat against powerful wizards. She wore light blue robes that marked her as a mere wizard's apprentice. Yet he appraised her with the same intense scrutiny that she focused upon him.

"Then Matteo is doubly protected," Andris said at last, "for I will extend to you that same courtesy."

Tzigone nodded, satisfied. The door opened, and Matteo's eyes shifted from her to Andris. "You two look uncharacteristically earnest. I don't suppose this bodes well."

"The good news is that Sinestra Belajoon was never cremated," she said without preamble. "The bad news is that Dhamari Exchelsor is in the city, and he knows about my mother."

Matteo muttered a barnyard epithet and turned to Andris. "Forgive me for leaving you without a word of explanation, but these are not my secrets to share."

"You don't need to explain anything to me," Andris protested, but his eyes lit up at the inferred trust.

Matteo briefly clasped his friend's shoulder, then he and Tzigone set off down a long corridor. He slid her a sidelong glance. "You and Andris seem to be on better terms."

"You might say we have an agreement." When Matteo sent her an inquiring glance, she shrugged and elaborated: "We set boundaries around when and why we'd kill each other."

"Ah. An important step in any burgeoning acquaintance," he said in a dry tone. "Tell me of Dhamari."

Her face grew troubled. "Kiva must have brought him back across the veil. He hasn't the skill to manage that kind of spell. Where are we going?" she asked abruptly as they took a turn into a wide, marble corridor.

"Zalathorm's council hall. He must hear at once that Beatrix's secret is not as well kept as we'd hoped."

"This will hurt the king," Tzigone noted, considering this aspect for the first time. "Zalathorm has been Halruaa's mortar for a very long time. Without him holding the wizards together, things could get very messy."

"I don't think we can stop that from happening," Matteo said quietly. "Nor do I think we should try to hide the truth in an attempt to prevent trouble. Truth has a way of coming out, and those who try to hold it back are the first to be swept away."

They walked quietly into the vaulted marble chamber that was the king's council hall and waited in an alcove while a trio of angry wizards presented complaints to the king. All were connected in some way to the slain wizard

Rhodea Firehair. The Council of Elders had ordered an inquisition into their affairs. All three protested. They were heavily invested in important magical research. Magical inquiry at this time, they insisted, could open their secrets to other wizards and bring financial ruin.

"Never mind the ruin a wizardwar could bring," Tzigone muttered darkly. She looked up to find Matteo staring at her. "What?"

"The good of the king, the fragile peace." He shook his head. "You did not ponder such things before."

She shrugged and ran her fingers through her short, tousled, brown hair to tame it somewhat. "I've never had an audience with the king before, either." She caught the hem of Matteo's tunic as he turned toward the throne. "Does he know about me? That I'm the queen's daughter?"

Matteo hesitated. "He learned this not long ago, yes."

"Will he let me walk out of here? Halruaa's laws don't exactly embrace people like me."

"Zalathorm is a lawful king, but he is also a powerful diviner. If he acted upon everything he knew about his subjects, he would soon have no kingdom to rule."

"Cynical, but probably true." She blew out a long breath and tried not to dwell upon the things Matteo was so obviously not telling her. The man had no talent for lying—he couldn't even hold something back without looking pained.

That was one of the reasons she trusted him and why she followed him into the throne room of Halruaa's king.

Zalathorm's gaze flicked toward the newcomers, then slid to his seneschal. The blue-robed man immediately strode over to the guards, who ushered out the still-angry wizards with promises of a swift resolution. He followed them out and shut the chamber doors, leaving the two young people alone with the king.

Matteo dipped into a low bow, which Tzigone imitated deftly and precisely. It occurred to her, too late, that a jordain's bow and an apprentice wizard's were two very different things. The king didn't seem to notice, but Matteo's expression—quickly mastered—couldn't have been more horrified if Tzigone had drop-kicked the king's favorite hunting dog.

The jordain hastily cleared his throat. "Your majesty, this is Tzigone, apprentice to Lord Basel."

Zalathorm rose from the throne and took her hand. "Welcome, child. How can I serve the hero of Akhlaur's Swamp?"

"Tell me about my mother," she blurted out. From the corner of her eyes, she saw Matteo blanch at this egregious broach of protocol. Most likely, a string of fancy phrases was required before getting to the point.

To her surprise, the king merely nodded. He led the way to an alcove with several chairs and waited until all were settled.

"Where would you like to begin?"

"Did you know her before she left the city, her tower?"

"No," the king said. "I had heard her name, of course, for Keturah was considered a master of evocation and a wizard likely to ascend to the Council of Elders at a remarkably young age. But in the years preceding Queen Fiordella's death, I had become something of a recluse."

"How did you meet?"

"A chance meeting during her exile. She presented herself as a wizard tired of magic's demands and in need of solitude."

"That's it?" Tzigone said incredulously. "You had no idea who she was? What she was accused of doing?"

Zalathorm hesitated. "I could discern that she possessed a good heart. I did not inquire into her name and past."

Tzigone leaned back and folded her arms. "And years later, you married her."

The king looked to Matteo with lifted brows. "I did not tell her, my lord," the jordain said hastily.

"I didn't think you had. So the queen's secret is known."

"How widely, I cannot say," Matteo admitted, "but it

seems likely that this and more will be brought to light in Beatrix's trial."

Zalathorm merely nodded and turned back to Tzigone. "Yes, I married your mother in a public ceremony years after our first meeting. She came to Halarahh in the most extraordinary of circumstances—the lone survivor of a brutal Crinti raid, her beauty and her memory lost beyond recall. The council was so delighted by my decision to wed and so charmed by Beatrix herself that they were remarkably accepting. The history provided by the magehound Kiva was considered enough. Even I accepted this as truth, not having reason to suspect otherwise."

"That seems incredibly careless for a monarch."

"I agree," he said evenly, "and while I offer no excuses, consider this. When I met your mother, I had been king for nearly fifty years. Queen Fiordella had recently passed away. She was the fourth queen to share my throne. All were political marriages, of course, for how many people in Halruaa marry to please themselves?"

"Enough was enough," Tzigone concluded.

Zalathorm smiled faintly. "My thoughts precisely. The Council of Elders did not agree. After Fiordella's death, there was considerable discussion concerning whom I should wed next. Some of our more 'modern' wizards were even clamoring for a hereditary monarchy, such as those in the northern kingdoms. You can imagine the furor this notion inspired."

Tzigone nodded sagely. "Every female wizard in Halruaa went strutting around with her wizardly bloodlines tattooed across her cleavage, hoping to catch your eye."

Matteo put a hand over his eyes and groaned. The king, however, chuckled at this image. "Their methods were slightly more subtle but not by much." He quickly sobered. "The issue of marriage was only one of many. I had reigned long and lived far longer. Too long, in fact.

"Life is a priceless blessing," continued the king, "but three hundred years weighs heavily upon a man. The years bring the same cycles, repeated with minor and predictable variations. Generation follows generation, each asking the same questions and making the same mistakes. After centuries devoted to Halruaa and her magic—especially to the art of divination—it seemed to me that nothing could ever surprise or delight me again."

"Then you met my mother," Tzigone concluded.

"Yes." He met the girl's eyes squarely. "She was worth a kingdom then. She is worth it still. Don't fear any harm the truth might do to me or my reign. I suspect the truth will be kind to Beatrix—and to Keturah, as well."

"It might not be so kind to you," she said bluntly. "Beatrix was married before."

"Dhamari Exchelsor—"

"I'm not talking about him," Tzigone broke in. "She had a real marriage, to some young man who fell off a griffin. I can see into the past," she explained, noting the king's dumbfounded expression.

The king collected himself and glanced at a water clock, a tall glass cylinder filled with many-colored floating balls. He grimaced and rose.

"We will speak more of this at first opportunity. Lord Basel's hearing will begin shortly."

The two young people rose with the king. "But he was released!" protested Tzigone.

"Yes, in the matter of Sinestra Belajoon's death. Another wizard is dead. Uriah Belajoon died just last night, in Basel's garden. It appears that his heart gave out, but since this is the third death to occur in Basel's tower this moon, the council wishes to inquire more closely. Tzigone, if you know anything that might help Basel, I want you to present it."

A look of uncertainty crossed Tzigone's face. "You are said to be a talented performer," the king said. "It might ease your mind to speak as if you were playing a part."

"Not a bad idea," she admitted, "but the pink palace is a far cry from my usual venue. Nothing I've played in street corners and taverns hits the right note."

Zalathorm took her hand and raised it to his lips, a gesture reserved for great ladies. "Then create a new role. Face the crowd as one who knows in her heart she is daughter to a queen and a princess of Halruaa."

For a long moment Tzigone stared at the king, dumbfounded. Then she began to laugh—rich, unrestrained, bawdy laughter that shook through her like a storm. Finally her mirth faded, and regal hauteur swept over her face. She beckoned to Matteo.

"Come, jordain," she intoned. "We have much to prepare before I give audience."

She swept out like a starship in full sail. The two men watched her theatrical progress from the room.

"It is said that a king need never apologize," Zalathorm said, his eyes twinkling. "But judging from the look on your face, Matteo, I suspect I've just stretched that proverb to the breaking point."

That afternoon the pink-marble audience hall was filled to capacity with Halarahh's wizards. From his position behind the king's seat, Matteo searched the small crowd waiting before the dais and found Tzigone among those who waited to give evidence. Their eyes caught, and he gave her a slight, encouraging nod.

When the crumhorns sounded the resumption of council, Zalathorm glanced at the parchment before him and called upon Tzigone as first to give testament.

She climbed the dais and executed the proper bows to the king and the assembled dignitaries. "Before I speak in Lord Basel's behalf, I wish to advise this council of an emerging magical gift, one that has helped me find the evidence I will present. I have recently discovered a talent for reverse divination. I can see into the past with greater detail than is yielded by a legend lore spell."

A murmur of astonishment rippled through the crowd.

In Halruaa, magical skills were slowly and assiduously acquired. Sorcery was frowned upon, and "recent discoveries" of inborn talents were rare in their ordered society.

Matteo stepped forward. "I will attest to this. I have seen her go deep into memory and in doing so accidentally produce a memory that belonged to someone long dead."

A wizard of the Belajoon clan rose, a supercilious smile on his face. "Begging the jordain's pardon, but wasn't this girl a common street performer? How do you know this 'ancient memory' that so impressed you wasn't just another tavern tale?"

"This memory was powerful enough to conjure a visible illusion," Matteo said coolly.

"Lord Basel, her mentor, is a conjurer. No doubt she learned this trick during her apprenticeship."

"This occurred before Tzigone's training began," Matteo countered, "before her magical feats in Akhlaur's Swamp, before she had any notion of herself as a potential wizard. The image she conjured was a rare species of griffin, extinct for over three centuries. Few lore books contain any reference to such a beast. It is unlikely that a child of the streets would have access to such books. I was there at the time, and no one, no matter how skilled a performer, could have feigned Tzigone's astonishment. Her talent for reverse divination is a natural gift, and it is very real."

Tzigone faced down the wizard, who looked ready to argue with Matteo's assessment. "Give me something to hold, and I'll tell you its history."

"Here!" A woman rose in the balcony and tossed down a shining bauble. Tzigone deftly caught it and held it up for general inspection. It appeared to be an exceptionally fine opal necklace, with large, glowing white stones set in silvery filigree.

Zalathorm looked to the donor. "Lady Queirri Venless," he said, naming the wizard. "To the best of your knowledge, does this girl have reason to know the history of this necklace?"

"No. This I swear, by wizard-word oath," Queirri replied.

Tzigone turned her face toward the wizard, and her eyes took on a distant, unfocused expression. "You were twelve years old, wandering the forest near your home. There were hunters—poachers—setting up traps and lures. Curious, you hid and watched as they ran a baby unicorn into their traps and slaughtered it for spell components. You fled home with the tale. Your mother, outraged, had the poachers hunted down and killed. Their deaths have always weighed heavily upon you, and you still dream of the unicorn. You kept the horn and had it fashioned into this necklace. You wear it as a reminder that sometimes the price of magic is too high."

A long moment of silence filled the hall. "A fanciful tale from a two-copper performer," the nay-saying wizard sneered.

"Nevertheless, it happens to be true," Queirri said quietly. "No single living person knew the whole of this tale but me."

Zalathorm nodded. "I am convinced. Lord Basel's apprentice may speak for him, and her words will be afforded the same weight given to any diviner."

Procopio Septus rose abruptly from his place on the Elder's dais, his hawklike face blazing with indignation. "Respectfully, I must protest. Giving this . . . apprentice the same regard as a master diviner diminishes us all!"

A subtle murmur of agreement, barely audible, blew through the hall, cooling Tzigone's listeners as surely as an ocean breeze.

"One wizard's magic enriches all of Halruaa," Matteo said, repeating a common proverb. "No man is truly diminished by another's skill."

Procopio ignored this digression. "As lord mayor of Halarahh, I have a responsibility to uphold Halruaan law. By this law, no person who is under sentence of death can bear witness for or against another. It has come to my attention that Tzigone is the illegitimate daughter of the renegade wizard Keturah. By law, she was born under sentence of death."

Tzigone's chin came up. "I'm no bastard. My mother and father were wed."

Procopio snapped his fingers, and a sheaf of parchment appeared in his hand. "Here are papers of divorcement between Keturah and her husband, Dhamari Exchelsor. This girl was begotten by an unknown father well after this divorce."

"My mother married a second time."

"Did she? Whom?"

"A young man she met in the forest. He fell off a griffin, and she tended him."

"Does this hapless rider have a name?"

Her gaze faltered for just a moment. "I don't know his name."

The wizard's white brows rose. "An honest answer," he said with exaggerated surprised. "The fact is that there is no record of another marriage. A wizard's bastard, a magic-wielder of uncertain parentage—and especially one who 'discovers' unusual and unpredictable gifts—is a threat to Halruaa. By law, this threat should have been eliminated over twenty years ago!"

Basel Indoulur rose abruptly. "Keturah and I were friends from childhood, and remained friends after she was falsely accused and fled the city."

"Falsely accused?" Procopio broke in. "Not submitting to magical testing is as good as an admission of guilt!"

"Who was the Inquisitor of Halarahh at that time?" Matteo asked calmly. "Who would have examined Keturah?"

The lord mayor sent him a venomous glare. "How should I know? That was five and twenty years past."

"Six and twenty," Matteo corrected, "and the mage-hound in the city at that time was Kiva, an elf woman since convicted of treason. I can present documents from the Jordaini Council exonerating several jordaini whom Kiva had falsely condemned over the years."

"You're arguing that Keturah would have had reason to fear similar treatment? On what basis?"

"Kiva was an apprentice in Keturah's tower," the jordain said calmly. "Keturah dismissed her for reckless magic. Even if she knew or suspected nothing of Kiva's larger designs at that time, she had reason to know the elf woman's character and to believe her capable of taking vengeance."

Basel turned to face Procopio, and in his round face was the lean, hard shadow of the warrior he had once been. "You called Tzigone a wizard's bastard. In Halruaa, few words are as offensive or as dangerous as these." He paused to give weight to his next words. "On behalf of my daughter, I demand you give formal apology or face me in mage duel."

A furor broke out at Basel's words. Procopio had to shout to be heard. "This is absurd! Basel Indoulur cannot speak for this girl, no more than she can speak for him! No man under sentence can bear witness in another's defense!"

Matteo gestured for silence. "That is true, Lord Procopio, but no sentence has been passed against Lord Basel. This hearing is an inquiry, nothing more. Basel can legally speak for Tzigone."

"Who then can speak for him!" the wizard snapped. "A most convenient circle!"

He turned to face the sea of intent faces. "This is jordaini sophistry at its most absurd! This counselor would have us spin around until we are too giddy to remember the reasoning behind our laws. Perhaps he hopes we did not notice that in claiming paternity, Basel Indoulur admits aiding a fugitive wizard and thus adds to the charges against himself! Perhaps he hopes we forget that a child cannot be either the first or the only witness to speak in behalf of her parents. Are we to ignore all our laws?"

"Are we to ignore lawful challenges?" added Basel with pointed mockery. "If you fear to face me in mage duel,

Procopio, please say so plainly. I'm feeling a bit *giddy* from the effort of following your evasive remarks."

Chuckles rose from various corners of the hall, ceasing abruptly as Zalathorm rose. "All will be done according to Halruaan law," he said sternly. "This situation is unusual and requires careful contemplation. Permit me a few moments with my counselor." He motioned for Matteo and disappeared into a side chamber.

The jordain followed and shut the door behind him. "You actually fell off a griffin?"

"It's a long tale," the king grumbled. "When did you realize that Tzigone was my daughter?"

"Vishna mentioned the power of three—three descendants of the three wizards who created the Cabal. At the time, I knew that Andris had descended from Akhlaur and I from Vishna. My sire sent me off to rescue Tzigone. In context, it would follow that he considered her the third."

"I see," mused Zalathorm.

"Of course, the expression on your face when Tzigone mentioned the griffin confirmed it. How did this happen?" he demanded, making no effort to hide his frustration.

Zalathorm threw himself into a chair and sent a baleful look at his counselor. "In the usual manner, I suppose, though I doubt that's what you're asking."

Despite the seriousness of the situation, Matteo's lips twitched. "There is the final bit of evidence. That is precisely what Tzigone might have said. With respect, sire, how could you not know that you had a daughter?"

"It's simple enough. Shortly after we were wed, I left Beatrix—Keturah, if you will—for a few days, intending to go to Halarahh to renounce the throne. Urgent affairs of state detained me, and when I returned to explain I would need a bit of time to resolve matters in my past life, she was gone. I sought her, as did others. Beatrix was remarkably successful in eluding pursuit, as was her daughter after her."

"No jordain can be traced by magic," Matteo observed. "The potions given to Keturah protected them both."

"It's more than that. The crimson star watches over the Heart of Halruua—its creators and their descendants. That is how I learned of Tzigone's relationship to Beatrix. In vision, I saw her pulled into the Unseelie realm," Zalathorm explained. "Puzzled, I cast spells of lore-seeking, searching for any written information about Tzigone. Cassia's last few entries into the king's lorebook were most enlightening. As you know, my former counselor was not among the queen's supporters."

Matteo began to pace. "Let's consider the current tangle. Basel has claimed Tzigone, who is, in fact, your daughter. In the service of truth, you should claim Tzigone as your own, but this would discredit Lord Basel and almost certainly depose you, at a time when both of you are sorely needed. No doubt you are constrained from doing this by various oaths and artifacts."

"A bleak picture, but accurate," the king agreed. "But there are many roads to one destination."

He rose and returned to the chamber. All fell silent as he raised his scepter. "Sometimes laws shape the future, but more often they acknowledge changes that have already occurred. This debate has convinced me of need for a new ruling. Wizard-breeding has contributed to Halruaa's strength, but it is time to do away with these laws. How can any righteous nation punish children for the actions of their parents?"

The king's pronouncement fell into stunned silence. "Are we to breed like foxes and northern barbarians, with no more to guide us than impulse and proximity?" one of the Elders wondered.

Zalathorm smiled faintly. "I think more highly of Halruaa's people than that."

"Yet the Halruaan people and Halruaan law are inseparable!" protested another. "We are what our customs and safeguards have made us."

"Yet you cannot deny that we Halruaans are endlessly inventive. When law and tradition fall short, we devise new solutions." Zalathorm gestured toward Tzigone, still standing defiantly by Basel Indoulur's side. "Consider this young woman. Though untrained in magic, she charmed Akhlaur's laraken. There is little in Halruaan law and lore to explain that, but we have all benefited from her gift. There may be others like her among us. It is folly to condemn them out of fear and ignorance."

The king looked to Procopio Septus, and inclined his head slightly in the gesture one great wizard used to acknowledge another. "With all respect to both parties, it is my decree that Lord Basel's challenge be as if it never was. I declare Tzigone blameless in the matter of her birth. She may speak on Lord Basel's behalf."

Procopio's face went livid, but he had no choice but to return the bow and return to his seat. Profound silence filled the hall as the assembled wizards pondered the king's unspoken words.

Matteo drew in a long breath, impressed by the king's subtle solution. Zalathorm had quietly put aside more than a mage duel challenge—in allowing Tzigone to speak, he had repudiated Basel's claim of paternity without actually accusing him of falsehood. His purpose in removing the sentence against the bastard-born would be more puzzling to the listeners. Perhaps he was underscoring the false-ness of Basel's claim, perhaps it was a way of saving the girl without naming her true father. The debate would absorb the wizards, and leech some of their ire away from the new law. Zalathorm knew his subjects well!

The king nodded to Tzigone. She stepped forward, look-ing poised and almost regal. Her gaze swept the crowd. With the timing honed by years performing on street cor-ners and taverns, she waited until every eye was upon her and the silence thick with expectation.

"I saw Sinestra Belajoon's body," she said, speaking in rounded, ringing tones that filled the room. "She was not cremated according to Halruaan law and custom but kept under glass like a work of art or a trophy."

Shocked exclamations and muttered disclaimers rippled across the room.

"Is this possible?" the king asked Malchior Belajoon, Uriah's nephew.

He stepped forward. "It is, my lord. My uncle intended to honor the custom in time but could not bear to part with her so soon."

"Though I am not without sympathy," Zalathorm said gravely, "this is a serious matter. Accusations were spoken against Basel Indoulur days after Sinestra Belajoon's death. The law states that an accused murderer is entitled to confront the spirit of his victim. All assumed this was not possible. You allowed that assumption to stand."

Malchior's face darkened at this reproof, but he bowed to acknowledge the king's words. "My uncle employed a magehound to inquire into the cause of Sinestra's death. He was assured that Basel Indoulur was responsible for her death."

"He was responsible, all right," Tzigone agreed. "He asked a question she couldn't answer. Apparently she tried, even though there was a spell of silence upon her."

"Go on," said Zalathorm.

"I tried to divine that spell, trace it back. There is a protective veil surrounding the caster. I couldn't get past it, but I recognized it. It had the feel of my mother's talisman. Dhamari Exchelsor is wearing it."

"That is impossible," Procopio said flatly. "Dhamari Exchelsor disappeared into the Unseelie realm!"

"So did I," responded Tzigone, "yet, here I am."

For a long moment, she and the powerful wizard locked stares.

Zalathorm looked to his scribe. "According to law, Dhamari's tower would be warded against intrusion. Is there record of his return?"

The scribe cast a quick cantrip and picked up a big ledger. The pages rippled swiftly, flipping first one way and then the other, then the book snapped closed.

"None, sire."

Matteo noted the faint smirk that lifted one side of the diviner's lips. "If you have evidence of Dhamari Exchelsor's return, please share it," invited Procopio politely. "Until then, do not besmirch a wizard's name with accusations you cannot support!"

Tzigone swept a hand wide in a gesture that included the crowd. "Isn't that what we're doing here? Three people have died in Basel's tower: Sinestra Belajoon, Farrah Noor, and Uriah Belajoon. Basel knew them all, and he loved Farrah like a daughter. He tried to save Lord Uriah when the old man's heart faltered. These deaths are his tragedy, not his crime."

She lifted her chin, and her sweeping gaze seemed to capture every pair of eyes and lock them to hers.

Matteo drew in a quick, startled breath. In that gesture, he saw a shadow of Zalathorm's commanding presence. He glanced at the king, but Zalathorm's thoughtful gaze was fixed upon his unacknowledged daughter.

"Basel is innocent. This I swear this to you," Tzigone said, giving each word the weight of a royal pronouncement, "by Lady and Lord, by wind and word. Let any who wish to prove me false do the same."

No one spoke. No one moved. It didn't seem to occur to anyone that the challenge just thrown down had come from a waif with shorn tresses and an apprentice's blue robes. She took her seat, and the decision to release Basel was swiftly endorsed by a subdued council.

Matteo marveled at the irony of this. Had this taken place in a tavern, the patrons would have applauded and ordered another round. The wizards didn't seem to realize that Tzigone's persona was nothing more than a non-magical illusion cast by a talented street performer.

Or was it? He and Tzigone had just returned from a place where illusion and reality had no clear boundaries. Perhaps, he mused, things were not so different on this side of the veil.

Later that day, Procopio Septus made his way to the shop of a behir tinker, an artisan who made fanciful objects from a behir's colored, crystalline fangs. He listened with barely concealed impatience as the man demonstrated a musical instrument fashioned so that its strings were plucked by plectrums fashioned from multicolored fangs, enspelled so that the resulting sound could imitate nearly anything the musician wished.

"A marvelous toy, but I have no time for music," Procopio said flatly.

The tinker nodded and reached for a set of tiny, exquisitely carved spoons. "Perhaps a gift for a lady? These are in great demand."

"Yet you seem to have so many of them," the wizard said dryly. "Not quite the thing. A lamp, perhaps?"

The shopkeeper's brow furrowed. Before he could admit that he had none, Procopio nodded toward the crystal chandelier that hung in the rear corner of the room. The man's eyes widened in astonishment.

"I'll take that one," the wizard announced.

"Two hundred skie," the tinker suggested without missing a step. "A bargain."

Procopio dickered a bit, as custom demanded. The tinker settled on a price that might have been considered fair, had the lamp truly been his to sell.

The wizard examined his purchase, surreptitiously removing the yellow crystal from it. He gave the tinker an address of a quiet inn and asked to have it delivered and hung in a private room he maintained for one of his mistresses. It would not remain there long, of course. Given the pervasive nature of magic in Halruaan society, it was folly to keep a dimensional portal in one place for very long.

He made his way to the inn and took the crystal from a hidden pocket in his sleeve. A few words opened the portal, and Dhamari Exchelsor stepped into the room.

"What news?" he asked. Procopio related the events in a terse, factual manner.

"Let me tally this score," Dhamari said incredulously. "Uriah Belajoon is dead, and Basel Indoulur is not. Where is the 'help' the old man was supposed to receive?"

"Late in coming," grumbled Procopio. "But some good did follow. Malchior Belajoon, nephew to Uriah, has seen opportunity in his uncle's death. The Belajoon name is on every Halruaan's lips. To a clever man, notoriety is as good as fame. He sees himself as Zalathorm's successor and is gathering supporters."

Dhamari smiled. "Excellent. You do not wish to be seen as the only contender for the throne."

"Once the first sword is unsheathed, other wizards will step forward, either to support a powerful contender or to make claims of their own. Few of them will get far."

"So you are setting up straw men to be knocked down. Including Malchior, I suppose."

"Including Zalathorm," Procopio corrected. "Your task is to ensure that wizards who stand against Malchior die, making him appear more formidable than he truly is. Let Malchior gain support, until he appears to be the primary challenger to Zalathorm's throne."

Dhamari nodded. "To even the slate, I should see to the demise of some of Malchior's supporters, as well. Then when *Malchior* falls, he will appear to be one of many. You can then argue that the mighty, benevolent Zalathorm has been reduced to dispatching lawful challengers like a back-alley assassin."

"Well reasoned," Procopio agree. He looked keenly at the little wizard. "You can accomplish this?"

"I can. The time I spent enjoying your hospitality yielded some excellent spells, ones that should prove difficult to detect."

The conspirators talked for several moments more before Procopio slipped away. When Dhamari was alone, he took his scrying globe and summoned the image of a beautiful elven face.

A slow smile spread across Dhamari's face as the spires of Akhlaur's tower came into view. Zalathorm would fall indeed, but not by Procopio's machinations. The coming carnage would be far beyond the lord mayor's proud expectations, and when it was done, even a man of Dhamari's stature would stand very tall indeed.

# CHAPTER EIGHTEEN

That evening, after another fruitless and frustrating visit to the queen's tower, Matteo returned to his private chambers. He was not surprised to see Tzigone awaiting him, sprawled comfortably, if not elegantly, on a velvet settee. He stopped short, however, as a second figure rose from a high-backed chair.

"King Zalathorm," he said in surprise.

"Close the door, please," the king said. "There is something more to be discussed, and I would rather not do so in full hearing of passing servants."

Matteo shut the door and came to sit near Tzigone. He took her hand and held it firmly.

She sent him an incredulous look. "That bad, is it?"

"Just watch," the jordain said tersely. He nodded toward the king.

Zalathorm's visage had begun to change. The blurred lines of middle years gave way to taut, sun-browned skin. His features sharpened, and his frame compacted to the lithe form of a man half his apparent years. The robes of a Halruaan wizard-king changed into simple garments such as a young wizard out for adventure might wear.

Tzigone stared at this figure stepped from Keturah's memories. "The griffin rider," she said at last.

"Yes." Zalathorm sighed, and the weight of long years was in his eyes. "I admire Basel for what he did. Indeed, I envy him and wish I were free to do likewise."

Tzigone blew out a long breath. She stared at the king for a long moment, then absolved him with a wink. "Don't mention it. I mean that quite literally. Basel is my dear friend. He stood up before all the gods and half of Halruaa and implied that he was my father. You sort of glossed over it, and that was fine, but if anyone comes right out and publicly calls him a liar, I would be completely dragondung."

Zalathorm's brows shot up, and he sent an inquiring look at Matteo. The young jordain turned a deep shade of red.

"I believe that is a colloquial expression for extreme anger, my lord, one that holds connotations of something hot, steaming, unpleasant, and rather too large to deal with."

The king turned a wistful smile upon the girl. "Then I will leave matters as they stand. A dragondung sorceress is not something I care to contemplate."

"A sorceress," Matteo mused, staring thoughtfully at the girl. This explained a great many things.

Tzigone grinned and hurled a small honeycake at him. "Things change. Try to keep up."

He deftly caught the small sticky missile. A wicked impulse stirred, and he yielded at once. "While we're contemplating change, perhaps we should also consider a long-running debate in the Council of Elders concerning the nature of the crown."

She rolled her eyes and then glanced at Zalathorm, evaluating the silver circlet resting on his brow with a practiced eye. "Electrum and sapphires would be my guess."

"There's a faction in Halruaa," he continued, "that wishes to establish a hereditary monarchy."

Matteo let that shaft sink home. When Tzigone's eyes flew wide, and her face slackened with horror, he tossed back the honeycake. It struck the bemused girl on the forehead and stuck there.

The king passed a hand over his face as if to erase a smile, then sent a stern glare at Matteo. "Is that any way to treat the crown princess?" he said with mock wrath.

He rose, plucked the cake off Tzigone's forehead, and left the room. His footsteps quickly faded, along with a faint chuckle.

Tzigone licked her sticky fingers and looked thoughtfully at Matteo. "You know, I think I could get to like him."

"As you say, Your Highness."

Her eyes narrowed. Matteo responded with a bland smile. "Things change," he reminded her. "Do try to keep up."

Basel Indoulur strolled through the public gardens that lay between the city palace and his Halarahh tower. Sunset colors crept into the sky over the city, and the bright, complex perfume of a thousand flowers lingered in the soft air. The wizard took his time, for he was in no hurry to return to his lonely tower.

With no family of his own, Basel lavished time and attention on his apprentices, but Tzigone would not be returning to the tower for quite some time. Procopio Septus had seen to that. Now that she'd been publicly acknowledged as Keturah's daughter, her mother's tower was hers.

He sighed as his thoughts shifted to his other two apprentices. Farrah Noor was dead, and Mason, accused of her murder, was constrained by magic from leaving Basel's villa. The young apprentice was alternately morose and frantic, but he steadfastly maintained he'd had nothing to do with the girl's death.

Basel believed him, but Farrah's death had had dire and far-reaching impact on the uneasy wizards. In these uneasy days, the trial of one wizard for another's murder was like a match to oiled timber. The sooner they sorted through this tangle, the better. He wondered if perhaps Tzigone might be able to ferret out the true story from the potion bottle, as she had with the noblewoman's necklace.

Suddenly a bolt of orange light sizzled up into the sky and exploded like festival fireworks. Droplets of bright magic spread into a brilliant fountain and sprinkled down over Basel's tower.

The wizard broke into a run. He'd never seen such magic, but he suspected its purpose. A protective shield surrounded his villa, keeping Mason in until his fate was decided. It also kept people out, but no magic was inviolate—there were spells that could eat through this shield as surely as a black dragon's acid melted through a northerner's chain mail.

He burst through the arbor gates and sprinted down the street leading to his home. All the while, brilliant bursts of colored light exploded over his tower.

Clever, he thought grimly. Festival fireworks had been common occurrences since the recent victory. No one would find it odd to see them over Basel's tower, and he had apparent reason to celebrate. No one would suspect the true purpose of these lights until after the deed was done.

He pulled up short as three off-duty guardsmen sauntered out of a posh tavern. "Sound an alarm," he panted out, pointing up at the lights. "My tower is under attack."

The men exchanged puzzled glances, but they were not in the habit of arguing with wizard-lords. They executed the proper bows and set off at none-too-urgent a pace.

Basel rounded the corner to find his estate besieged. At least a dozen wizards ringed the walls, hurling one sparkling spell after another into the evening sky. All of them wore the Noor insignia, and many had the glossy blue-black hair common to Farrah's family.

Small, shimmering gates ringed his tower, standing ready to grant the attackers a quick retreat. With so many wizards against a single apprentice, no doubt they expected a swift and easy victory. Indeed, the glowing yellow aura surrounding the estate had worn as thin as a soap bubble. It shimmered perilously under the continuing magical assault.

"So it begins," Basel murmured as he reached for a wand in his sleeve. He leveled it at the nearest Noor wizard and unleashed a spell he'd never thought to wield against a fellow Halruaan.

Tzigone stood by the window in Matteo's chambers, gazing moodily out over the city. They'd just come from the tower. Her visit with the queen—she could still not equate that still, sad woman with the mother she remembered—had left her uncharacteristically subdued.

In the background, Matteo and Andris talked softly, planning not only the queen's defense, but Andris's as well. Matteo expected that his friend's alliance with Kiva would be forgiven in light of his service to Halruaa, both before and after his fall. Andris seemed less convinced of this. Tzigone suspected that in this regard, Andris was more on target.

A brilliant orange sunburst caught her eye. For a moment she watched as fireworks soared, blossomed, and faded. Suddenly the niggling uneasiness in the back of her mind exploded into realization. She whirled toward Matteo.

"That's over Basel's tower," she said, pointing.

The jordain looked up. "So it is. Basel is fond of festive things. He has reason to celebrate."

"He lost an apprentice," Tzigone retorted. "Basel loved Farrah—he wouldn't send up sparklers to mingle with the clouds from her funeral pyre!"

The two men exchanged glances, then came to flank Tzigone. "Cinibar rain," Andris said grimly, nodding to the descending orange sparklers.

"Most likely," Matteo agreed. Moving as one, the two jordain strode to the wall and took their weapon belts from the hooks.

"What? What?" she demanded.

"Cinnabar rain could dispel the magical shield the council placed over Basel's tower."

Tzigone dug into a small bag at her belt. "Meet me there," she said, and she hurled a handful of bright sand at an open window. The frame filled with shimmering light. Tzigone leaped through it.

She landed lightly in a battle-ready crouch just outside the walls of Basel's villa. Her eyes narrowed and swept the battlefield. Two wizards lay dead, charred beyond recognition. Basel tossed aside the spent wand and took another from his sleeve. As she watched, a thin stream of water erupted from it, splashed a spellcasting wizard, and arced up to intercept a lightning bolt of glowing cobalt blue.

Water and magical energy converged with a searing hiss. The blue bolt split in two. Half sizzled back down along the stream of water toward the wizard who had cast it, the other sped toward the water wand.

Before Tzigone could shriek out a warning, Basel tossed the wand to a nearby wizard and dived to one side.

Lightning stuck, simultaneously charring the discarded wand and the attacking wizard. A stench of burned meat filled the air, and two wizards—now nothing more than statues of coal—toppled to the ground and shattered into ash.

Keeping low, Tzigone ran over to Basel's side, dodging the bolts directed at him. Together they dove through a portal in the seemingly solid wall and rolled through to the garden side.

"Nice trick with the wand," she said. "With that timing, you should have been a bard."

Basel nodded absently and glanced up at the thinning shield. "We don't want to be in the open once that shield goes. Where the Nine bloody Hells is the militia?"

A distant percussion, the rustle of many feet running in

rhythmic formation, brought a sigh of relief from the wizard, but before he could speak, the soft yellow light of the protection spell began to flow downward, like melting treacle sliding over an invisible dome.

Basel took a wand from his belt and pressed it into her hand. "Farrah's family wants vengeance. Make them earn it."

Before Tzigone could protest, the wizard enfolded her in a quick embrace. She felt a touch nearly as deft as her own, and the cool pressure of a delicate chain around her neck. When Basel released her, a silver talisman glimmered over her heart, and her world began to blur and shimmer. For a moment Tzigone's world looked like two illusions cast into a single place. She could see the garden, and also the highest and most secure room in the wizard's tower.

She struggled against the spell like an insect caught in sap, desperate to stay where she was, to fight at Basel's side. But suddenly the world snapped back into focus, and she stood at the window of the tower armory in guard position, wand raised high and clenched in her fist like a ready knife.

Mason whirled toward her, relief and guilt struggling for possession of his countenance. "Lord Basel?"

"In the garden," she said grimly, and brought the wand down in a stabbing motion.

A dark line poured from the wand, quickly broadening as it went and changing into a swarm of fire ants. The winged horrors spun down toward one of the attackers. In moments they engulfed the wizard, who rolled shrieking amid the stinging cloud. His agony was brief. Death followed swiftly, and the fire ants scattered into the night.

Again Tzigone stabbed, and the wand spat another swarm at a wizard who was employing a spell of levitation to breach the wall. The fire ants surrounded him in midair. In response to his agonized screams, one of his kin hurled a small green bolt at the dying man. The magic struck the roiling black cloud, and the shrieking ended in a burst of magical energy. Green droplets fell to the garden, along with a faintly rattling hail of fried insects. Oddly enough, the spell of levitation survived. The corpse floated above his kin like a grim banner.

The wand yielded two more killing swarms. Tzigone tossed aside the spent weapon and looked around at the arsenal. Mundane weapons of wood and steel stood ready, and many conical, faintly glowing vials lined several shelves. A wooden rack held battle wands, lined up neatly as the swords. There was even a small ballista, mounted on wheels so it could be moved to any of the several windows.

"Load that," she snapped, pointing toward the giant crossbow.

Mason quickly put a bolt into place and cranked it back. She took one of the vials, fell quickly and deeply into a brief trance to check its nature and use, then gave a curt nod. She yanked the cork out with her teeth and fitted the vial over the bolt's point, securing it with a twist. The vials had been cunningly fashioned to fit over the points of the giant arrows.

Tzigone stepped behind the ballista and leveled it at a point just beyond the wall. Several Noor wizards converged there, their hands moving in unison as they mingled their magic in some great spell. She took a deep breath, held it, and pulled the ballista trigger.

The giant bolt hissed free and plunged down toward the spell-casting wizards. It shattered on the ground nearby, sending a tremor through the tower and a flash of orange-red light over the wizards.

Suddenly the light separated into three distinct, frantic fires. The conflagration spell caught all three, setting them aflame.

Tzigone's gaze snapped back to Basel. A faint glow around him spoke of a sphere of protection. Colored light rained down on him as two wizards hurled one colored bolt after another into the air directly above him. The portly wizard had already fallen to one knee, struggling to maintain the sphere as long as he could but unable to return the attack.

By now the militia were visible, coming at a dead run. Tzigone caught a glimpse of white among the blue-green uniforms and knew that Matteo came with them. He was, however, coming far too slowly for her peace of mind!

She looked to the enormous bilboa tree at the edge of the public garden, and began to sing. Her voice soared out into the sky, carrying into the complex city hidden among the leaves and branches.

The exploding lights reflected on enormous gossamer wings and scales the color of gemstones. Starsnakes, compelled by the sorceress's call, spiraled down from the glittering night sky. Two of them entwined a wizard in a sinuous, deadly embrace. His frantic, defensive spells slid off their scaled hides like water. A burst of energy sizzled through him. Tzigone glimpsed a blue-white flash of bone beneath the burning flesh.

She glanced back at Mason. "You should get out of here. Basel is drawing fire away from the tower to buy you time to escape."

As if they divined Basel's intention, the two wizards bombarding him changed tactics. The female advanced toward the tower, wand pointed toward the window framing Tzigone and Mason. The other kept the barrage of magical fireworks raining down on Basel's protective shield to keep the powerful wizard pinned down.

A ball of light began to grow at the end of the Noor woman's wand, expanding until it was wider across than the wizard's shoulders. Instinctively, Mason and Tzigone backed away from the window.

"That's going to hurt," Tzigone muttered.

At that moment Basel dropped the shield and pulled a throwing knife from a wrist sheath. The knife exploded into glowing crimson in his hand and spun toward the gathering sphere of destruction.

Basel's attacker kept up the barrage. Blue and gold rain

showered over the exposed wizard, searing into flesh and sending his oiled braids leaping into flame. Fire surrounded Basel, turning his countenance into that of a burning medusa. His eyes met Tzigone's frantic gaze, and he lifted his fingers to his lips as if to blow her a kiss.

The fireball exploded.

The magic, interrupted in its casting, spilled down over the wizard and flowed over the garden like lava. The tower shook as a second explosion shuddered across the burning magic, and the flame winked out. Nothing remained of the garden or any of the wizards who had fought there.

Tzigone was dimly aware of the sizzle of small fire spells, the clatter of weapons, and the shouts of fighting men. Several of the Noor wizards fled through their gates, but most were subdued by the militia.

Swift footsteps wound up the stairs to the tower. Matteo burst into the room, his eyes quickly scanning the scene.

Mason seized a sword and lunged. Almost absently, Matteo drew a dagger, parried the attack, and disarmed the man with a quick twist. He kicked the sword aside, shouldered past the burly apprentice, and went to Tzigone.

She fell into his arms and clung, dry-eyed and stunned. "Basel," she whispered.

"I saw."

Several uniformed men clattered into the room. Their eyes widened as they took in the arsenal. "Look at all this," one of them murmured in awed tones. "Lord Basel was expecting an attack."

Tzigone stepped away and placed a restraining hand on Mason's chest. The young man glanced into her face, then dropped the sword. Matteo faced down the man who'd just spoken.

"Don't be absurd. There's not a wizard's tower in all Halruaa that hasn't a room like this."

"They were after this man," Tzigone said, nodding at Mason. "I've seen a couple of those wizards before, come to visit Farrah Noor. Mason is suspected of her murder.

That was her family, and they were too impatient to wait for justice."

"Wizard fighting wizard," muttered the man wearing captain's braid. "This is a dark day, the first of many."

"The tower was besieged," Matteo retorted. "Basel's apprentices merely defended it. The law allows any man or woman to defend their lives and homes. Do not make this into something it was not."

He spoke with the guards for several minutes more. Finally they left to deal with the captured wizards and send messages to western Halruaa. Those who escaped would be rounded up and brought to trial.

When at last the militia left, Mason belted on a sword and began to gather up glowing vials.

"What, precisely, do you intend to do with those?" Matteo inquired.

The apprentice shot him a quick, grim look. "Basel is dead. I'm going after the Noor family."

"Put those vials down before you drop them," the jordain said sharply. "If you haven't the vision to see how far these flames could burn, at least consider the practical details. How far do you suppose you'd get in your quest for vengeance? You have not yet been absolved of Farrah Noor's murder. If you've an hour to spare, I'll list all the spells that could track you down in less time than the recitation of them would take."

The young man's eyes shifted briefly to the smoking, blackened garden. "So I'm to stay here."

Matteo's visage softened. "Come with me to the palace. You'll stay in guest chambers under guard until this matter is settled. Tzigone?"

"Go ahead. I'll follow you in a while."

The jordain hesitated, but he apparently sensed her need to be alone. The two men left the tower.

When all was quiet, Tzigone went to the window and leaned heavily against the sill. The charred gates stood open, and the magic that had encircled the tower was gone.

The interrupted fireball had melted rock and soil into a sheet of dark glass. In it was reflected a slim, shining crescent. She glanced up. The smoke still rising from the garden cast shifting patterns against the waning moon.

Tzigone stood there as the moon crested the sky, saying a private farewell to the man who had been her father, if just for one brief day. There would be no somber rites for Basel Indoulur, no formal funeral pyre such as honored Halruaa's great wizards. She suspected Basel would probably prefer matters as they were.

A soft, furtive sound pierced her reverie and sent her spinning around. She drew back, astonished, as her gaze fell upon Dhamari Exchelsor.

The wizard looked equally startled to see her. "What are you doing here?" he blurted out.

Her chin came up. "I'm Basel's apprentice, and by Halruaan law, his heir as well. I have every right to be here. You don't."

"Basel had no business in my tower, either," he spat out.

Tzigone lifted one brow. "*Your* tower? When you divorced Keturah, you forfeited legal rights to it. It's mine. Your belongings have been sent to the Exchelsor vineyard estates."

"Not all of them. I'm come to reclaim what Basel stole from me."

Her eyes narrowed. "You just happened to show up now. You were surprised to find anyone still alive in the tower."

"Unpleasantly surprised," he said, his eyes burning with hatred and his hand slowly drifting to a bag hanging at his belt.

"Did you know about this attack?"

"It was not a subtle thing," the wizard countered. His hand dipped into his bag and flashed toward.

Instinctively Tzigone threw up both hands. Magical energy coursed from her, ready to ward off the spell.

But the wizard knew her magic almost better than she did. No spell flew from his hand, but a tiny winged creature.

It exploded into full size, filling the room with rustling wings and thick ropes of topaz and emerald scales.

The starsnake flew at Tzigone, its jaws flung open for attack. She sang a single clear, high note, and the winged snake veered away, circling up toward the ceiling.

She kept singing, instinctively finding a strange, atonal melody that somehow matched the snake's frenzied, undulating flight.

In moments she felt the magic that entrapped the creature melt away. The starsnake shot out of the open window.

Tzigone stepped forward and drove her fist into Dhamari's slack-jawed face. He stumbled backward and fell heavily against a rack of edged weapons. Down clattered the swords and knifes, their keen edges leaving bloody tracks on the wizard's body.

Dhamari flailed at the falling blades, trying vainly to protect himself but making matters far worse than they needed to be. Each thrashing movement left another gash—in his panic, he was cutting himself to ribbons. Yet none of his wounds bled. Even in this, Keturah's talisman protected him from himself.

Tzigone reached down and closed her hand over her mother's talisman. "Enough," she said in cool, even tones. "Eventually, everyone has to face who he is and live or die with the results." With a quick tug, she broke the chain and tore it free.

The fallen wizard's body erupted into a crimson fountain, and his shrieks of rage and pain rang out into the night. In moments he lay limp and silent.

Tzigone put her mother's medallion around her neck and left the tower without a backward glance. It was time for her to take her own advice and face who she truly was.

Matteo slept not at all that night. Dawn crept over the city, and still he gazed at a moon grown perilously slim and frail. Moondark was only two days away, and when the moon was born anew, Beatrix would come to trial.

Andris's charge of treason might be forgiven. An obscure Halruaan law forgave offenders who did Halruaa a great service. Certainly Andris had done so many times over. Beatrix was another matter entirely. Matteo still had no notion of how to defend her, other than finding a way to shatter the Cabal—and with it, the king's most powerful shield. That path could only lead to chaos and unbridled wizardwar.

Last night's attack on Basel's tower was not a unique occurrence. More than one wizard had stepped forward to challenge Zalathorm's right and fitness to rule. Mage duels took place in street corners and city gardens as ambitious wizards strove to prove supremacy. Other wizards watched and chose up sides. Other illegal and more deadly forms of combat were becoming commonplace. Reports of spell battles and magical ambushes were daily occurrences. Just yesterday, three of the men who declared against Malchior Belajoon had disappeared, and no one could discern the magic or the spellcaster responsible.

A small pink dove fluttered to a stop on Matteo's windowsill. The bird cocked its head and looked at him expectantly. Matteo noted the small scroll case strapped to the dove's leg. He quickly removed it and shook out the bit of parchment. It was a note from Tzigone, asking him to come at once to Keturah's tower.

He hurried from the room, oblivious to the bird's aggrieved coos—such messengers were trained to wait for a reply. The green marble tower was not far from the palace, and the streets were still quiet under the fading night sky. Matteo sprinted down the street, intent on his goal. After the attack on Basel's tower, he suspected the worse.

He ran past a stand of flowering xenia bushes and didn't see the out-thrust foot until it was too late. He deftly turned the trip into a roll and came up in a crouch, daggers out.

Branches parted, and Tzigone's small face peered out at him. She gestured for him to join her. After a moment's hesitation, he edged into the small hollow.

"Procopio Septus is in the tower," she said.

Matteo's brows rose. "You're certain?"

"He just walked in." She shook her head in self-reproach. "I haven't had time to change the wards since I took over the tower."

He caught the implication at once. "Procopio knows Dhamari's wards! How could this be? A diviner might be able to see through some of them but certainly not all."

"I imagine Dhamari handed him the counterspells," she said grimly. "They're best of friends these days."

The jordain huffed. "You didn't see fit to mention this?"

"Do you want to hear what I have to say, or would you rather fuss?" she said sharply.

He held up both hands in a gesture of peace. "We'll come back to Procopio later."

"We always seem to," she agreed. "Anyway, last night Dhamari came to Basel's tower after you all left. He was very surprised to find anyone still alive. My guess is he knew the attack was coming."

Matteo looked troubled. "If he did, most likely Procopio knew as well. Proving that, however, will be difficult. Diviners are notoriously hard to read through magical inquiry."

"Maybe this will help." Tzigone handed him a small packet. "I got this from Sinestra Belajoon's room. She found it hidden in Procopio's villa."

"Oh?" he said cautiously.

Tzigone shrugged. "Sinestra had some notion about learning thieving skills. You might say she was my apprentice."

"Sweet Mystra," he groaned. "Twice-stolen proof is not much better than none at all."

"That depends on the proof. This is mummy powder."

Stunned enlightenment crossed Matteo's face. "Only the Mulhorandi embalm their dead. That suggests Procopio was in collusion with the invaders! On the other hand, per-haps Procopio got this powder from a northern grave robber. It was once used as a base for paint—"

"Too late," she broke in. "Andris already told that tale, and once was plenty. And really, do you see Procopio as a would-be artist?"

He conceded this point with a nod.

"Here he comes," announced Tzigone. "This should be fun."

Before Matteo could respond, Tzigone wriggled out of the bushes and headed for the tower. With a groan, he followed.

They met the wizard at the gate, his arms full of spell-books. He stopped short, and his expression was cautious but not alarmed.

"Shame about the invisibility spell," Tzigone said casu-ally. "The damn things just never seem to hold up, do they?" Her gaze skimmed the wizard, and she lifted one eyebrow in a politely inquiring expression. "Out for a quiet stroll? A mug of breakfast ale and a little loot and pillage?"

Procopio's face flushed and then hardened. "I am responsible for Halruan justice in this city, and these items will be needed for the queen's trial. I'm sure Dhamari Exchelsor would have wished it so."

"You're certainly in a position to know that," she shot back. "This was Keturah's tower before Dhamari stole her life. It's mine now, and everything in it. Don't think about poking around in Basel's tower, either."

"Two towers. Aren't you the ambitious one?"

"I have two parents."

"Both of them conveniently dead. In fact, many wizards have died of late." Procopio's black eyes narrowed. "Amaz-ing, that their killers are so hard to trace. It's almost as if the murderer was magically shielded from inquiry."

Matteo stepped between them, intercepting the wizard's challenging glare. "I don't like your implication."

"I don't give an Azuthan damn what you like or dislike,"

the wizard retorted. "You're a fool, Jordain, if you can't see beyond that pretty face to what lies within. Legend—legends in these very books—claim that dark elves slipped through the veil into Unseelie realms and came back as drow. What sort of monster did *she* become in the Unseelie Realm?"

Tzigone said quietly, "People become what they truly are."

"What, in your particular case, might that be?" sneered Procopio.

Her chin came up. "There's one way to find out, *wizard*. Meet me on the dueling field today at twilight."

# CHAPTER NINETEEN

For a long moment Tzigone's challenge hung heavy in the astonished silence. Then Procopio let out a startled laugh, which quickly settled into an arrogant smirk.

"This will be legal in every particular, so none can say I did murder. You, jordain, will bear witness the challenge was hers."

He started through the gate, chuckling. Matteo quickly moved into his path. "The books," he said simply.

Their eyes met in silent, furious struggle. Finally Procopio muttered an oath and let the priceless, ancient volumes tumble to the garden path. He stalked out without a backward glance.

Matteo turned to Tzigone, who stood regarding the books. "Right there is all the justification I'd ever need to squash him like a toad," she muttered.

"Tzigone, what in the name of every god were you thinking? Procopio Septus is one of the most powerful wizards in Halarahh!"

"I know." She glanced up. "Tell me what to do next."

He folded his arms and scowled at her. "Move to Cormyr?"

"You know what I mean. There's got to be a stack of customs and protocols for this sort of thing."

" 'This sort of thing' hasn't been done for many years," he retorted. "But yes, there are many defining rules. A challenge cannot be issued by a powerful wizard against one of considerably lesser rank. The spell battle challenge must take place on the old dueling field outside the city walls. I believe it's been used in recent years as pasturage for a herd of crimson zebras—racing stock, mostly."

"So I'll have to watch my step, in more ways than one," she said. "What else?"

"The Council of Elders must bear witness to the competition. Given Procopio's status, Zalathorm and Beatrix should be there as well." He broke off and rubbed both hands over his face. "Tzigone, what will this serve?"

She stood for a long moment, collecting her thoughts. "I can't be tested through magic. Not even Zalathorm will be able to take my word against Procopio. But if old Snow Hawk had anything to do with Kiva, if he had any part in Basel's death, he's going to die. It's that simple."

He shook his head. "No, it isn't. No one's going to die, because you're going to demand a mage duel."

"What fun is that?"

"I'm serious, Tzigone! The path that begins with vengeance leads to grief!"

"I'm not interested in vengeance," she said softly, "but destiny."

Matteo fell back, startled at hearing so grim a concept fall from her lips.

"Your friend Andris would understand." Tzigone raised a hand to cut off the jordain's argument. "Hear me out. Kiva's plans focused upon Keturah in some way I don't fully understand. When my mother's magic started to falter, Kiva passed my mother's task on to me."

"Even if that is so, why challenge Procopio?"

"Because of Kiva," she persisted. "She wanted this— wizard fighting wizard. Men like Procopio and Dhamari are feeding it. If they think they're going to get something out of it, they haven't been paying attention. Kiva might be crazy, but she's smart. She planned one diversion after another, whittling away at Halruaa's wizards, diverting attention, dividing our strength. The Mulhorandi invasion caught us on the collective privy with our britches around our ankles."

A faint smile flickered on Matteo's face, but his eyes remained somber. "Thanks be to Mystra for that last image! For a moment I thought myself listening to a somber Halruaan princess."

She bristled like a cornered hedgehog. "You think I'm challenging Procopio to prove something about myself?"

"Not at all. But I wonder if perhaps your challenge came from a sense of noblesse oblige. You are more Zalathorm's daughter than you realize."

Her eyes narrowed. "You weren't listening the other day. Basel Indoulur was my father, and he didn't trust Procopio any farther than he could spit rocks. Procopio wouldn't face Basel, and maybe that's another reason why this task falls to me. Enough talk," she said abruptly. "I'd appreciate it if you'd handle the details. I need to prepare for tonight."

Matteo opened his mouth to protest, then shut it with a click. Tzigone's argument had the desired effect—pointing out that any more time wasted detracted from her chances. He bowed slightly, keeping his eyes on hers— the formal salute of a jordain to a wizard of great power and rank.

With a jolt of unpleasant surprise, Tzigone realize that if she passed this test, that was precisely how she would be regarded.

"As you say, lady, it will be done," he said softly, without a hint of friendly mockery in his manner. "May Mystra guide and strengthen you."

Tzigone watched him go, one hand clasped over her lips as if to hold back a laugh, or perhaps a sob. At the moment, she wasn't sure which way to go. Matteo's formal farewell might sound absurd, but this was what lay ahead for them.

She shrugged. "I could always throw the mage duel and kill Snow Hawk later."

This excellent compromise, spoken only half in jest, raised her spirits considerably. She gathered up her mother's books and headed for the tower to prepare for the challenge ahead.

That night, as sunset color faded from the sky and the soft purple haze of twilight spread over the land, a great throng gathered at the western end of the dueling field. Artisans and minor wizards had been busy throughout the day. A makeshift wooden arena soared high over the field, and at the edge of the field a dais held chairs for the Elders and thrones for the wizard-king and his consort.

Beatrix was there, dressed carefully and elaborately in her usual silver and white. The only concessions to her coming trial were the pair of wizards who flanked her and the armed guards who surrounded three sides of the dais.

Tzigone came onto the field first. On Matteo's advice, she came out in a simple tunic rather than her apprentice robes. She repeated the challenge and listened while a herald read the lengthy rules of engagement.

Excitement simmered through the crowd as Procopio walked onto the field. He, too, was simply dressed, perhaps to downplay the vast difference between his rank and his challenger's. There would be little honor in besting a mere girl. When he executed the proper bows, he made a point of acknowledging Tzigone's heroics in the recent battles and in Akhlaur's Swamp.

The combatants moved to the center of the field and faced each other, staring intently into each other's eyes as they matched minds. Procopio's white brows rose when he perceived the size of arena Tzigone had in mind—the maximum allowed for their combined rank and status. A sly look entered his eyes as he perceived her likely strategy, and he conceded with a nod.

They turned, and each paced off half the length of the arena. That done, they again faced each other. A shimmering wall rose from the field, forming an enormous cube between them. That accomplished, the combatants moved aside to prepare defensive spells.

Matteo came to her side. "Any last words of advice?" she said lightly.

His brow furrowed in a conflicted frown. "Procopio Septus was my patron. I can't divulge any of his secrets, but I can remind you of things that are obvious to all. He is proud, he is arrogant, and he is short."

She studied him for a moment, then grinned in understanding. "I can work with that."

The crumhorn sounded the beginning of the challenge. Tzigone and Procopio took their places at the edge of the magical arena. When the final note sounded, they stepped in at the same instant.

At once Tzigone began to sing. Procopio waited confidently, arms folded and feet planted wide, his black eyes scanning the heights of the arena for the appearance of some conjured beast.

A small behir with scales of pale blue appeared on the dueling field, an unimposing creature that would have little effect on the wizard—except for its strategic position. The behir materialized between Procopio's feet.

The creature shook itself briefly, assessed its situation, and then attacked. Its small, slender head lunged straight up, and crystalline fangs sought a convenient target. A small sizzle of lightning-like energy jolted into its victim.

The wizard let out a roar of pain and fury. He kicked at the behir, which promptly let go. The little creature scuttled off, its six pairs of legs churning.

Tzigone dispelled it with a flick of her hand. "Proud, arrogant, and short," she said casually, "and maybe a little shorter than he was a few minutes ago."

The wizard snarled and called her several foul names. Tzigone shrugged. "Just be glad I insisted on a mage duel. Imagine if the behir hadn't been enspelled to do only subdual damage." She sent him an innocent smile. "Of course, I wouldn't be surprised if you were *subdued* for a very long time. . . . "

Procopio furiously conjured and hurled a fireball. His opponent clucked and responded with a scatterspell. The brilliant missiles met and exploded into thousands of small pieces, which drifted down in a bright, harmless shower, winking out to ash before reaching the combatants.

"Not much imagination there," she said, "but you are devastatingly handsome when you're angry. It's a shame that you're, well, *subdued*."

Wrath flared in his black eyes, then quickly banked. "This travesty will be over soon enough. You'll face me again, witch, without these walls and rules."

"That's what I'm counting on," she said, her lips smiling but her eyes utterly cold. "Back to the show. My turn."

She began to chant. A large, dusky creature took form in the center of the arena. The conjured wyvern's sinuous, barbed tail lashed angrily. It leaped into the air and described a tight spiral as it climbed to the top of the shimmering cube.

Procopio quickly countered, forming the spell for the storm elemental he had used to such acclaim during the Mulhorandi invasion. The arena shivered as wind lashed through it. The resulting clouds, tinged with color by the setting sun, flowed together, melding and shifting into the form of a giant wizard. The cloud form inhaled deeply and sent a gust of wind at the diving wyvern.

The gale struck outstretched wings curved taut in a hawklike stoop. The creature let out a startled shriek and went into a spin. It plummeted toward the ground, its batlike wings whipping so furiously that it seemed they would tear loose. The wyvern pulled out of the spin at the last possible moment and spread its wings wide, swooping so near the ground that the grasses bent and whispered as it passed over. The wyvern's deadly tail raked a long furrow in the ground.

Procopio's storm elemental reached out with a giant, translucent sword and sliced at the tail. It fell to the ground, twitching and writhing like a gigantic worm. The wyvern screamed. Dark blood boiled from the stump, and the great creature's wings slowed.

Tzigone made a deft gesture that released the conjured wyvern. It disappeared in a puff of mist. The poison-tipped tail made a few more blind attempts to find and stab the wizard, then it, too, melted away.

The cloud elemental stooped down and scooped Tzigone up in one hand. She pulled a dagger and slid it under the creature's thumbnail. The elemental roared—a sound like wind and thunder—and tossed Tzigone into its other hand, shaking the offended member.

Tzigone had never feared heights, but dread seized her as the elemental flung her from hand to hand. All the thing had to do was drop her, and Procopio's job would be finished. It was exactly as Matteo had feared: she did not have the mastery of magic to stand against a wizard like Procopio.

She quickly shook off the moment of despair and cast a simple featherfall spell. The elemental hauled her up and threw her with all its strength. Tzigone floated slowly down, touching the ground just short of the glowing wall.

With a grimace, she acknowledged that this was far too close. The first wizard forced out of the cube was declared the loser. She'd entered the arena hoping to humiliate Procopio but not expecting to win. Suddenly her goals shifted, her resolve settled.

She was a sorceress, like her mother before her. Although Basel Indoulur was the only father she held in her heart, in her veins ran the blood of Halruaa's king.

Tzigone stretched one hand toward one of the standards flying over the king's dais—a black silk flag with a firebird emblazoned upon it. The enormous arena encompassed the flag, and anything within it was fair game.

At her call, the firebird leaped from the silk and began to grow.

With each beat of its burning wings, the creature grew. Heat filled the arena, as the firebird circled Procopio's creature. The light from its wings reflected in the elemental, turning the clouds to brilliant sunset hues. The creature batted at its circling foe as it dissipated into colored mist.

Tzigone turned to Procopio and raised one brow, inviting him to take his next turn. She was not prepared for the look of astonishment on the wizard's face, swiftly turned to fury.

Procopio stalked over to the king's throne, shouldering past the barrier of shining magic. Tzigone, curious, followed.

"This was no just competition," he began furiously. "I did not issue this challenge but was honor-bound to accept. Yet I fight not one wizard, but two!"

Zalathorm regarded him coolly. "You accuse this young woman of cheating?"

"I accuse the king of intervening on behalf of his daughter!"

At that moment, Tzigone's suspicions were confirmed. Dhamari knew that Keturah and Beatrix were one, and so did Kiva. Procopio was surely aligned with at least one of them.

"I did not intervene in the spell battle," Zalathorm said quietly. "As for the other, I will not embarrass Lord Basel by directly refuting his claim."

"Basel is dead," Tzigone said flatly. "He was an honest man, but he lied to protect me. He would do anything for his apprentices, and when it comes right down to it, that's probably how he'd want to be remembered. If you want me to be his daughter, that's fine with me, but do whatever you need to do."

Zalathorm studied her with measuring eyes. Tzigone was not certain what he saw there, but an expression of resolve crossed his face. He rose from the throne and faced the whispering, puzzled crowd. All could see that something strange was occurring, but few had heard Procopio's claim.

Raising his voice, Zalathorm said, "Lord Procopio suggests that the fire roc summoned by this young woman was my spell and not hers. It was not. This I swear to you by wind and word. I do not work magic through another wizard and will not take credit for another wizard's work.

"Many of you believe I created the water elemental against the Mulhorandi from the fluids of living enemies and raised their skeletal forms as an army. I have never claimed this feat. It is important that all know these powerful spells were not mine."

His gaze swept the silent throng. With a quick gesture, he dispelled the shimmering magic of the arena. "This challenge has been made and met. I declare Tzigone, lawful daughter to Zalathorm and Beatrix, to be the winner."

The king silenced the sputtering Procopio with a glance. "You underestimated your opponent. You were so certain of her limits that you stepped beyond the bounds of the arena. By law, that is a default."

"Proud and arrogant," Tzigone repeated. She glanced down pointedly. "Not to mention, short."

Procopio's jaw firmed. He executed a choppy bow to Tzigone to acknowledge her victory and strode off—without the proper acknowledgements to the king.

"That one will come back to bite you," she murmured as she watched the wizard stalk away.

"It matters less than it did," the king answered, "now that I can leave Halruaa with an heir."

It was Tzigone's turn to gape and sputter. Zalathorm glanced pointedly at his seneschal. The man hurriedly moved a chair to the king's left side and ushered Tzigone to it. She sank down, feeling as though she'd reentered a world ruled by illusions.

Zalathorm rose and addressed the stunned and watchful crowd. "One challenge was made and met. I lay down another. I call upon the wizard who cast the great spells of necromancy against the Mulhorandi. I challenge him to battle—in the old way, without boundaries of magic."

The king gestured, and an enormous golden globe appeared, floating in the air before him. He placed one hand on it and repeated his challenge in ringing, metered chant, sending it to every wizard within the boundaries of Halruaa.

Again he addressed the crowd. "This land is on the brink of wizardwar. What will be done here could either burn out in a sudden flare or light a fire that could consume all of Halruaa. Gather all the forces of steel and magic and bring them to this place. I entreat all of you to put aside your personal ambitions and petty challenges. The wizard who cast this spell is formidable indeed. If I am not equal to the challenge I sent out this night, it might take the strength of every one of you to pick up the standard."

Far away from the dueling field, in the deepest part of Halruaa's deadliest swamp, Akhlaur and Kiva watched as the lich who had once been Vishna prepared his undead troops.

"He was a battle wizard," Akhlaur said with satisfaction. "The best of his generation."

Kiva forbore from observing that Vishna was among the wizards who had vanquished and exiled Akhlaur. "His plans seem sound enough. The battle will create a diversion. But the crimson star—"

"Enough!" snapped the necromancer. "The star aids Zalathorm and me in equal measure. It will not change the battle one way or another."

"Can Zalathorm be destroyed?" she persisted.

"Could Vishna?" he retorted. His mood suddenly brightened. "As a lich, Vishna will be a brilliant and loyal general. It will give me great pleasure to use Zalathorm's oldest friend to bring down his realm."

As the elf woman bit back a shriek of frustration, a golden light filled the clearing. Zalathorm's voice, magnified by powerful magic, repeated the challenge he issued to every magic-user in the realm.

Akhlaur's black eyes burned with unholy fire, and his gaze darted to his undead battlemaster. "All is in readiness?"

"It is," Vishna replied in a hollow voice.

"Gather our forces and weapons," he announced. "Quiet your doubts, little Kiva. The three will be reunited, and the crimson star will once again be mine to command!"

The crowd dispersed after the mage duel. Andris, who had been seated near Matteo behind the king's throne, walked silently toward the palace with Matteo and Tzigone, his crystalline face deeply troubled.

"Three of us," the jordain said at last. "We three are descendants of the original creators of the Cabal.

Tzigone elbowed Matteo. "Destiny," she repeated. "Maybe there's a reason we were all drawn together. Sometimes one person's task falls to another—or to three."

"What are we to do?" Matteo demanded.

"What I have intended all along," Andris said urgently. "We need to destroy the Cabal—the crimson star."

"Now, just as Zalathorm issued a challenge to any and all wizards who desire to take it?"

"Ask him," the jordain persisted. "If Zalathorm is truly a good and honorable king, he won't consider his life, even his throne, as a higher good than this."

Matteo was silent for a moment, then nodded abruptly. He made his way through the guards, Tzigone and Andris on his heels.

The king looked at him quizzically. Matteo leaned in close and softly said, "Andris is descended from Akhlaur."

Zalathorm's eyes widened. His gaze slid from his counselor to his daughter, then to the ghostly shadow of Andris. "I'll take you to it," he said simply.

Early the next morning, the four of them stood in a circular chamber far below the king's palace. The crimson star bobbed gently in the center of the room, casting soft light over them all. Andris's translucent body seemed carved from rosy crystal, and his eyes burned with fire that came from some hidden place within.

"I have tried to destroy this many times," Zalathorm said, "but one of its creators is not sufficient. Mystra grant the three of you success."

Andris pulled out a sword, lofted it with both hands, and threw himself into a spin. With all his strength, he brought the heavy weapon around and smashed it into the shining crystal. The next instant, his sword went flying in one direction and Andris in another. The sword, once released from his grasp, lost its glassy appearance and clattered heavily to the stone floor.

The jordain picked himself up. "Perhaps if we all strike at once," he ventured.

Matteo and Tzigone joined him and took up positions around the gem.

"From above," Andris cautioned, "so no one is struck on the backswing."

On Matteo's count, they all brought weapons down hard. Before they neared the artifact, the swords flew from their hands and clanged together, forming a tripod that hung in the air over the globe.

"So much for togetherness," Tzigone muttered, eyeing the enjoined weapons.

Andris paced around the artifact, his face furrowed in thought. "Let the princess try alone."

She made a rude noise, but she approached the gem slowly and touched tentative fingers to one of the starlike spires. For many long moments she stood silent, her deeply abstracted look changing to pain.

"So many," she said in a subdued voice. "I was a prisoner in the Unseelie court for a few days. These elves have been in captivity for more than two hundred years."

She eased her hand away and turned to the king, her eyes wide with understanding. "Keturah knows how it could be done! That's why Kiva wanted her all along—why she brought her here to the palace!"

She looked to Zalathorm for confirmation. "It is possible," he admitted.

Tzigone was already sprinting through the halls toward the queen.

The throng that gathered on the dueling field was far from the unified, disciplined host of Zalathorm's vision. Wizardlords and their retainers stood in separate ranks, eyeing their rivals. Each faction boasted wizards, clerics, and mercenaries. The spell battle against Zalathorm would be only the start. Anyone who successfully challenged the king would need all these supporters in order to defend his newly won crown against other contenders.

Procopio Septus, as lord mayor of the city, had at his beck the entire militia of the king's city. He strode along confidently, reviewing the ranks. Seriously depleted by war and confused by the turmoil among the wizards, the fighters looked uncertain of their purpose. The wizard at his side looked even less certain. Malchior Belajoon, would-be challenger to the king, measured the opposing ranks with worried eyes.

"Perhaps this is not the time to make my bid for the throne," Malchior ventured.

"The king welcomed all challengers. Your lineage is as good as his, and recent events have made painfully obvious that the king's powers are failing. What better time to press your claim?"

"I did not cast the necromancy spell!"

"It hardly matters. Zalathorm has issued a challenge, and he will be honor-bound to answer any who respond."

Again Malchior's gaze swept the gathering throng. "What of the king's plea for unity until the hidden wizard is unmasked?"

Procopio shook off this concern. Before he could speak, an enormous oval of shimmering black opened against the backdrop of forest, like a rift into a dark plain.

Warriors poured through, hideous undead creatures that reeked of decay and stagnant waters. The militia—as well-trained as any fighting force in the southern lands, veterans and survivors of the recent invasion—shrank back in horror.

The undead army swiftly formed into disciplined ranks. Their leader, a tall, gaunt wizard with livid bluish skin and a still-glossy mane of chestnut, strode from the gate and took up position.

As strange as this sight was, it did not prepare the stunned observers for what was to come. A small elf woman with long braids of jade-green hair emerged. Her cool, amber stare swept the wizards and seemed to linger briefly on Procopio's face. Then she stepped aside to yield way for an even more daunting apparition. A tall, thin man, robed in the necromancer's scarlet and black, stepped into the silence. In the bright morning sun, his pale greenish skin and faintly iridescent scales shone with a sickly glow—like some luminescent creature emerged from the sea depths.

Not a wizard there had ever set eyes upon the strange figure, yet all knew him for who he was. One of the most infamous wizards of Halruaa, whose name had been lent to a deadly swamp and scores of terrible necromantic spells, was not forgotten in a mere two centuries.

"Akhlaur."

The whispers seemed to coalesce into a single tremulous breeze. The necromancer inclined his head, an archaic courtly bow once performed by great wizards to acknowledge their lessers.

The gathered wizards exchanged panicked glances, no longer so certain that ridding the realm of Zalathorm was such a good and desirable goal.

Akhlaur had no doubts on that matter. "Zalathorm has issued challenge," he said in a deep voice that rolled across the field like summer thunder. "I have answered. Fetch him, and let it begin."

Kiva and Akhlaur retired to the rear of their ranks to await the king's response. The elf woman paced furiously.

"Troubled, little Kiva?" the necromancer asked.

She whirled toward him, flung a hand toward the dueling grounds. "Did you see all those wizards gathered to challenge the king? We should have let them! You know Halruaa's history as well as I. Her wizards might squabble, but they will unite against a single threat. Had you allowed Zalathorm to destroy these challengers one by one, your task would have been easier and its outcome assured! Now we will face them all."

Her vehemence and fury raised the necromancer's brows. "You fear for your safety," he said condescendingly, "and with reason. The death-bond ensures that if I die, so do you. I assure you, between the crimson star and my not-inconsiderable magic, we are quite safe.

"Yes," the necromancer continued, "all will go as planned. Nothing—least of all you—will interfere with this long-desired confrontation."

The elf stood silent for a long moment. "With your permission, I will watch your victory from the forest."

"As you will," Akhlaur said. Suddenly his black eyes bored into her. "Remember, you cannot betray me and live."

"I assure you, my lord," Kiva said with as much sincerity as she had ever brought to anything, "that this is never far from my thoughts."

Matteo and Tzigone paused at the door to the queen's chamber.

"What do you propose to do?"

"I'm making this up as I go along," Tzigone admitted. She walked softly into the chamber and dipped a bow before the too-still queen.

On impulse, she began to sing. The queen's gaze remained fixed and blank, but her head tipped a bit to one side as if she were listening. When Tzigone fell silent, Beatrix softly began to repeat the last song in a flat, almost toneless voice. Her voice strengthened as she sang. It was ragged from disuse and long-ago hurts, but in it was the echo of beauty.

Tzigone shot a dazzling smile at Matteo. She sang another song, and again the queen repeated it. Then Tzigone spoke of starsnakes, and the queen sang the little spell song that Tzigone had used to summon the winged beasts. On and on they went, with Beatrix responding with songs appropriate to various situations Tzigone presented.

"Well?" she said triumphantly.

"It makes sense," Matteo agreed. "Music and reason do not always follow the same pathways in the mind. A person who suffers a mind storm might not remember how to speak but often can still sing the songs learned before the illness. However, Keturah's voice no longer holds the power to cast magic."

"All she has to do is remember the song. I'll cast it."

After a few moments Matteo nodded. He left the room and spoke with the guards, who released the queen into his keeping. The three of them made their way down the winding stairs to the dungeon.

Matteo and Tzigone went first. He had committed to memory each of the spell words Zalathorm used during their descent and whispered each one to Tzigone—only a wizard's voice could undo the wards. She repeated each spell word as they moved together from step to step. It was a long descent, and by the time they reached the bottom both were limp with tension.

"For once that jordaini memory training came in handy," she murmured as she took off into the room.

A sudden bolt of energy sent her hurtling back into Matteo's arms. He sent her an exasperated look.

"Memory training," he reminded her. "There's no sense in having a jordain around if you don't make good use of him!"

Tzigone recovered quickly and sent him a teasing leer. "I'll remind you of those words at a more convenient time."

With a sigh, Matteo pushed her away and gave her a shove. "Three paces, then turn left."

They traversed the maze without further mishaps. Finally the three of them stood before the crimson globe. Andris and Zalathorm were still there. The jordain stood off to one side, watching intently as the king knelt before the shining artifact. Zalathorm rose and faced the newcomers.

"Akhlaur has returned. He awaits me on the field of battle."

Matteo looked uncertainly from the king to his oldest friend. "Much of Zalathorm's power comes from the artifact," he ventured.

"You told me it is impossible to fight evil with evil means," Andris reminded him. "What could be more wicked than leaving these spirits in captivity, when we might be able to free them?"

Zalathorm clapped a hand on the jordain's transparent shoulder. "That is the sort of advice a king needs to hear. Do what you must, and when the task is done, join me in battle." He glanced at Matteo. "When battle is through, I trust you will not mind sharing the honor of king's counselor with another?"

A wide grin split Matteo's face. The king smiled faintly. He stepped forward and gently touched his queen's face in silent farewell, then disappeared.

Andris looked to Tzigone. "What now?"

A whispered tune drifted through the room. Tzigone motioned for silence and listened intently to her mother's voice. The song was ragged, the notes falling short of true and the tone dull and breathy, but Tzigone listened with all the force of her being, absorbing the shape and structure of it.

Enchantment flowed through the song, revealing a subtle web around the glowing gem. Matteo stared at the gathering magic and recognized its source.

There was a defensive shield about the gem that no wizard could perceive or dispel. Someone, somehow, had crafted it from the Shadow Weave.

Matteo's nimble mind raced as he considered the meaning and implications of this. Kiva had studied the crimson star for over two hundred years. She had been Akhlaur's captive and most likely knew the secrets that kept the artifact inviolate against attack. Where had Akhlaur learned these secrets, some two hundred years ago? Knowledge of the Shadow Weave was only now creeping into Halruaa!

The answer struck him like a firebolt. Akhlaur had learned as Matteo had—in the shadowy antechamber of the Unseelie court. In doing so, he had become what he truly was. Vishna had wondered about his old friend's transformation from an ambitious wizard to a villain who saw no evil as beyond his right and his grasp. Here was the answer.

But why Kiva's interest in Keturah? Why the partnership with Dhamari?

Keturah could evoke creatures with a song. Spellsong was a powerful magic, one common to the elven people. Perhaps this was needed to form a bond with the elven spirits within. Then there was Dhamari, with his determination to summon and command the denizens of the Unseelie realm. He was an ambitious wizard but not a talented one. Perhaps Kiva had seen in him a fledgling Shadow Adept and encouraged him along this path.

Perhaps it was not three descendants who were needed, so much as three talents unlikely to occur in one person.

Matteo quickly took stock of his friends and their combined arsenals. "Tzigone, touch the gem. See if you can find some sense of Andris within it."

She shot him a puzzled look but did as he bade. Her face grew tense and troubled. "I can see the battle in Akhlaur's Swamp," she said. "Damn! I'd forgotten how ugly that laraken was!"

"Andris," prompted Matteo.

"He's here. Or more accurately, a part of him is." She withdrew from the gem and her gaze shifted from the ghostly jordain to Matteo. "What's this about?"

"Making contact with the spirits captured within. Andris is uniquely suited to doing this. The first step involved in multiwizard magic is attunement. That is his task. The casting of magic is all about focus and energy—the spell song you sing will no doubt be echoed by the elven spirits within."

Her gaze sharpened with understanding. "What about you?"

Matteo held her gaze. "Akhlaur cast a defensive web around the crimson star, made of the Shadow Weave. I can see it. Perhaps I can dispel it."

Andris's pale hazel eyes bulged. "You're a Shadow Adept?"

"I suspect that's overstating the matter," Matteo said shortly, "but it's close enough for our purposes. Let's get on with it."

"Those who used the Shadow Weave too often and too long can gain great power of magic, but over time they lose clarity of mind," Andris reminded him. "Whatever else you might be, you're still a jordain. You stand to lose the thing that most defines you!"

"Then let's do this quickly."

Tzigone extended both hands to the jordaini. Each took one. For a moment they stood together. Color began to return to Andris, flowing slowly back into the translucent form. Matteo nodded to Tzigone, and she began to sing the melody her mother had taught her.

The song seemed to splinter like light caught in a prism. It darted throughout the room, echoed and colored by a hundred different voices. The light in the crimson gem intensified with the power of the gathering magic.

Matteo brought his focus to bear upon the shadowy web. He reached out with his thoughts and plucked at one of the knots. It gave way, and two threads sprang apart. He reached for another and slowly, laboriously began to untie Akhlaur's dark magic.

The effort was draining, more exhausting than any battle he had known. Matteo's breath came in labored gasps, and the room reeled around him. Even worse was the loss of clarity. More than once he slipped away, only to be brought back by the stern force of his will. Each time, he felt like a man awakened from a dream, uncertain for a moment of where he was or his purpose for being here. Yet he pressed on. One more knot, he told himself. Only one. Now another, and so on, until the task is done.

Suddenly the web gave way. Light flared like an exploding star, and the artifact shattered.

Matteo instinctively dived at Tzigone, who in turn leaped to protect the queen. They went down together, and Matteo shielded them both from the bits of crystal hurtling through the room.

To his surprised, he felt no sting from the flying shards. Cautiously he lifted his head.

The room was still filled with rosy light. Moving through the light were crystalline forms, similar to that borne by Andris. All were elven but for an elderly human man who held a strong resemblance to Farrah Noor. The ghostly human bowed deeply to them and disappeared.

The elves milled about, embracing each other and rejoicing in their freedom. Tzigone watched with tear-misted eyes.

A light, tentative hand touched her arm. "Ria?" asked a tentative voice.

Memory flooded back, the one thing Tzigone had sought for so long—her name, the name her mother used to call her. "It's me," she managed.

Keturah's eyes, enormous in her white-painted face, searched her daughter's face. "So beautiful," she said wistfully, "but no longer a child."

For the first time in her life at an utter loss for words, Tzigone handed her mother the talisman. Keturah's fingers closed around it, and her face went hard.

"Kiva is near, and with her comes a great and ancient evil." She reached out and touched Tzigone's cheek. "Our task is not quite finished—they must both be destroyed."

She set off with certainty down a series of tunnels. Tzigone glanced at the jordain, and did an astonished double-take at the sight before her. Andris was fully restored, and looked much as he had before the battle in Akhlaur's Swamp.

Matteo nodded to her. "We follow," he said simply.

Tzigone raced after the avenging queen and prepared to face Akhlaur—and Kiva.

# CHAPTER TWENTY

Two armies faced each other across the dueling field. It was as Kiva expected—as it always had been. The warring factions of Halruaan ambition gathered to fight a common foe. Wizards and warriors, private armies and the remnants of Halarahh's militia, they all stood shoulder to shoulder, nearly as pale as the hideous foes they faced.

Akhlaur's undead minions stood ready. Skeletal forms showed through watery flesh that reeked of the swamp. All waited for some signal to begin.

Suddenly Zalathorm appeared, standing before Halruaa's army. He flung out one hand, and fine powder exploded toward the undead army. A wind caught the powder, sending it swirling as a dust devil rose in size and power. The pale tornado raced toward the undead and burst into a shower of flying crystal.

The lich commander shouted an order, and many of the warriors fell to one knee, covering themselves with large rattan shields. The salt-storm, though, struck many of the undead warriors, and all it touched melted like salted slugs.

Their skeletons merely shrugged off their oozing flesh and advanced. Their bony hands unlatched small leather bags hung about their necks, removed vials glowing with sickly yellowish light. The skeletal warriors darted forward with preternatural speed, hurling the vials as they came.

"Deathmaster vials!" shouted one of the wizards. Several of them began to cast protective spells.

The front line charged. Some of the warriors pushed through, shielded by protective magic. Others were not so fortunate. Terrible rotting sores broke out wherever the noxious liquid met flesh. Yet all of them, living and dying, fought with fervor. Their swords lifted again and again as they hacked the attacking bones into twitching piles of rubble.

Arrows rained down upon the undead forces from the north side of the field, which was shaded by enormous, ancient trees. Kiva, who crept along the forest edge, noted the scores of archers perched in the branches overhead. She noted that all were clad in Azuthan gray, and she hissed like an angry cat.

As she feared, whenever the arrows found a target, undead creatures fell and did not rise. Holy water, no doubt, had been encased in glass arrow heads.

The wizards took full advantage of this, bombarding the army with one spell after another. Fetid steam rose as fireballs struck watery flesh.

Kiva's lips firmed as she recalled a terrible necromancy spell she had learned at Akhlaur's side. After just a moment's hesitation, she began the casting of a powerful defoliation spell.

Instant blight fell over the woods. All vegetation withered and died, and leaves drifted like mountain snow. Birds fell limply to the ground, and human archers dropped like sacks of meal. In moments, a swatch of woods some fifty feet in every direction stood as barren as a crypt.

Yet another bit of the ancient elven forests fell before Halruaan magic.

Kiva shrugged aside the pain that coursed through her,

blood and bone and spirit, when the great trees died and the Weave shimmered and sighed. This terrible destruction was but one more stain upon her soul.

The two armies charged, meeting in the midst of the field in terrible melee. A small group of Halruaans broke through, charging with suicidal bravery toward the place where the necromancer stood.

The elf—victim, apprentice, and would-be master of Halruaa's most powerful necromancer—responded without thought or hesitation. Kiva lifted her hands, and red light crackled from her fingertips. It stopped the charge like a wall of force. The warriors were lifted into the air, surrounded by crackling light, their bodies twitching in excruciating pain. The nerve dance was one of the many cruel arrows in a necromancer's quiver. It would not stop the warriors for long, and it would not kill many of them, but it held them helpless for several agonizing moments. Few wizards could maintain a spell in such pain. The moment of invulnerability provided opportunity—it was up to Akhlaur and his lich to seize it.

Kiva turned and fled the battlefield, running for the palace. When she brought Beatrix to this place years ago, she had placed small devices that would enable her to slip past the wards and into the palace.

Whether Akhlaur wished it or not, the crimson star would set this day.

Matteo and Andris raced down the sweeping marble expanse of the palace stairs. They pulled up short as a battalion of militia marched into formation, taking a guard position. Procopio Septus stepped forward and surveyed the dumbfounded jordaini with a faint smile.

"We will hold the palace," Procopio announced. "Someone must stand ready to take over the throne if Zalathorm should fall."

"If all the city's wizards stand with him, the king's chances of survival rise considerably," Matteo shot back. "These men are needed against Akhlaur's army."

Procopio's face darkened. "That is my decision to make. You have yet to learn, jordain, that it is the wizard-lords who rule."

"Do what you will, but let us pass," Matteo said. He drew his sword, and Andris followed suit. "Every blade is needed."

The wizard shook his head. "And let you carry this tale to Zalathorm, like a faithful hunting dog retrieving a partridge? I think not."

The two jordaini advanced.

Procopio sneered. "What can two men do against twenty warriors and a wizard?"

One of the militia—a tall, thick-bodied man—shouldered his way though the group. He bowed to Procopio and drew his sword, as if he intended to offer himself as champion. Before Procopio could respond, the big man fisted his free hand into the wizard's gut. The flair of protective wards flashed, but the man shrugged them off without apparent effort. Procopio folded with a wheeze like a punctured wineskin.

"With respect, my lord," Themo said distinctly to him, "that would be *three* men and *no* wizards."

An enormous grin split the big man's face. He fell into step with his two friends as they stalked down the stairs toward a sea of ready swords.

As one, the men threw down their weapons. Themo's face fell. "Where's the fun in that?" he demanded.

"You're ranking officer now," one of them said to Themo, "and it's treason to fight a commander. There's a bigger battle to fight, but by all the gods, if you tell us to fight Halruaans I'll run you through myself."

The big man grinned fiercely. "I'm guessing Akhlaur's army were Halruaans, mostly, but they've been dead too long to take offense."

At his signal, the battalion picked up their weapons and prepared to run toward battle.

"To the royal stables," Matteo shouted.

They quickly claimed swift horses, mounted, and rode hard for the northern gate. The dueling field was a short ride, and the horses ran as if they sensed the urgency of their riders.

Matteo leaned low over his horse's neck, skirting battle and riding hard for Zalathorm's side. He saw Akhlaur striding forward, a glowing black ball held aloft. Matteo groaned as he recognized a deathspell—a powerful necromancy attack that snuffed out a life-force instantly and irrevocably.

The king swept one hand toward the advancing necromancer. A brilliant light flashed out—as bright and pure as a paladin's heart. It swept toward the necromancer, a light that would dispel darkness, destroy evil.

The black globe winked out, and Akhlaur slumped to the ground. To Matteo's horror, the necromancer's green-scaled faced darkened, taking on the bronzed visage of a newly slain warrior. The wizard's robes changed to a blue-green uniform, mottled with darkening blood.

"A zombie double," Matteo said, understanding the necromancer's diversion. He had lent his form to a newly slain Halruaan. The jordain looked frantically about for the real Akhlaur.

A shadow stirred amid the roiling battle, and a black globe flared into sudden life. It hurtled toward the king. A shout of protest burst from Matteo, but he was too far away to reach Zalathorm in time.

A bay stallion galloped toward the king, and the tall, red-haired man in the saddle drew his feet up beneath him and launched into a diving leap. The black sphere caught him in midair and sent him spinning.

Andris struggled to his feet, his daggers in hand. For a moment, Matteo dared hope that his friend's jordaini resistance would prove equal to the terrible spell, but Andris's hands dropped to his side, and his daggers fell to the field.

Matteo threw himself off the horse and caught the dying man as he fell.

Kiva raced toward the palace. She stopped near one of the trees that shaded the courtyard and began to climb. A soft thump landed behind her. Kiva's wide-spanning elven vision granted her a quick glimpse of Tzigone, her hands darting toward Kiva's hair.

Before the elf could respond, Tzigone seized the jade-colored braid and yanked it savagely. Kiva's head snapped back, and she lost her grip on the rough bark. Using her fall to advantage, she kicked herself off the tree and into the wretched girl.

They went down together like a pair of jungle cats—rolling, clawing, and pummeling. Neither of them noticed at first that Keturah had begun to sing.

Slowly Kiva became aware of elven voices joining in with the woman's ruined alto. She broke away, backing away from the suddenly watchful Tzigone and gazing with disbelief at faces too long unseen.

The song faded. Quiet and watchful, the elven folk lingered near as if somehow their life task was not quite finished.

Tzigone rose. "It's over, Kiva. You've won. The elves are free."

Dimly Kiva became aware that she was shaking her head as if in denial. Yes, these were her kin, her friends. There was her sister, there the childhood friend who taught her to hunt, there her first lover. They were free. Her life purpose was fulfilled, and the proof of it stood by silently waiting for her to understand the truth of it.

Suddenly Kiva knew the truth. It was not finished, her task. All these years, everything she had done—she had believed that it was devoted to the freeing of her kin. But that was not what had driven her at all. Vengeance had utterly consumed her, leaving her less alive than these shadowy spirits.

With a despairing cry, Kiva threw both arms high. A flash of magic engulfed her and she disappeared from sight.

In less than a heartbeat, she emerged from the blink spell, one designed to take her to her one-time ally. She stood at the palace stairs, where a glum-faced Procopio sat and brooded.

He jumped like a startled cat when her fingernail dug into his arm. "Come, wizard," she said in a voice that was strange even in her own ears. "It is time for Halruaa to die!"

Kiva and Procopio emerged from the spell in the midst of an undead throng. The wizard gagged at the stench and lifted one hand to cover his nose.

The elf snatched it aside and pointed with her free hand to the place where Akhlaur stood, limned with black light.

"Look well, wizard," Kiva said in a voice shrill with madness. "He is your mirror. He is you. He is *Halruaa*, and may you all molder in the Abyss!"

She snatched a knife from Procopio's belt and plunged it into his chest. For a moment he stared down at it, incredulous, then he slumped to the blood-sodden field.

Deep in the ranks of his warriors, Akhlaur cast another spell. A terrible bone blight settled on a seething mass of warriors. The undead were not harmed, but the living received each blow with twice the force it might otherwise have had. Swords fell from shattered hands, and men dropped to the ground, writhing in agony as the fragile, jagged shards of broken bones stabbed through their flesh.

Gray-clad priests worked bravely, dragging the wounded aside and praying fervently over the fallen. Wizards, in turn, protected the clerics. A circle of wizards cast protective spells upon a cluster of gray-clad Azuthan priests, who chanted collective spells meant to turn away undead.

The forces of Halruaa, when united in purpose, were difficult to withstand. Skeletal warriors fell like scythed grain.

Akhlaur spun toward his lich. Vishna stood beyond the reach of the clerics. At a nod from Akhlaur, the undead wizard summoned a deathguard—guardian spirits ripped from the Ethereal Plane. These bright warriors glided toward the priests like fallen angels, as formidable as a charge of airborne paladins. Vishna began the chant that could summon an even more dreadful magic.

A dark web formed over the battlefield. As the corpse host spell took effect, the newly dead began to rise and living soldiers, untouched by blade or spell, fell senseless to the ground.

Cries of inarticulate dismay burst from torn throats as scores of living men realized that they were inhabiting corpses. Their own bodies, living but discarded, lay defenseless. Already the undead warriors stalked toward them like wolves encircling trapped prey.

The Halruaan warriors who had not felt the touch of Vishna's spell, who did not understand the spell, rushed to meet their advancing comrades. Not understanding, they cut down the confused and frantic undead. Abandoned bodies shuddered and died as the life-forces trapped in undead flesh were released to whatever afterlife awaited them.

The lich's eyes swept the crowd and found Zalathorm fighting hand to hand against an enormous, bony construct that seemed half man, half crocodile. Akhlaur sped through the gestures of a powerful enervation spell and hurled it at the king. Zalathorm jolted back, his face paling as strength and magic were stripped from him. For the briefest of moments the eyes of the two old friends met.

With a thought, a gesture, Vishna sent a bolt of healing energy toward Zalathorm. At the same time, he sent a mental command to the undead warrior at Akhlaur's side.

The creature drew a rusted knife and cut the tether to the black cube at the necromancer's sleeve. It stumbled forward, bearing the ebony phylactery that contained Vishna's spirit. So engrossed was Akhlaur that he did not notice its loss.

Vishna took the tiny box from the skeletal hand and nodded his thanks. "I grant you rest and respect," he muttered. The skeleton bowed its head as if in thanks and crumbled into dust.

He scanned the battlefield, and his eyes settled upon a small, green-haired female. With a gesture of his hand, the undead commander parted a path through the seething throng. He made his way to Kiva's side.

She glanced up at him with a haughty demeanor and hate-filled eyes. "Akhlaur commands you now. What do you want with me?"

"Only to finish what was begun long ago," he said. "I've come to free you."

The undead wizard plunged a dagger into her heart.

For a long moment she stared at him. Hatred turned to bewilderment, then, to a strange sort of relief.

Vishna released the dagger and let Kiva fall. After a moment he stooped and closed her eyes. He gathered the dead elf woman into his arms and walked into the blighted forest and toward the living trees. There, amid the roots of an ancient tree, perhaps she could find the peace that had evaded her for so long.

At the end of the battlefield, the ghostly form of Halruaa's elves watched with sad approval.

❂

Zalathorm thrust aside the dead crocodilian warrior and scanned the battlefield. The dying light touched the faintly glowing forms gathered at forest's edge. As the meaning came to him, a smile filled his face like sunrise, and an enormous burden lifted from his heart.

He shouted his enemy's name. Powerful magic sent the single word soaring over the field like the shout of a god.

The combatants ceased and fell away. All eyes went to the wizardking. Zalathorm pointed to the watchful elven spirits. "The Heart of Halruaa," he said simply.

Akhlaur whirled toward the spirits of the elves he had tormented and enslaved. His black eyes widened in panic. His webbed hands sped through a spell that would command and control undead, but the elves were far beyond his reach.

The necromancer shouted for Vishna, for Kiva. There was no response.

"Let it go, Akhlaur," Zalathorm said, and there was more sorrow than anger in his voice. "Our time is finished."

He took from around his neck a silver chain, to which was attached a small, crimson gem. "One of our earlier attempts," he explained, holding up the glowing gem. "When our only thought was to sustain and protect each other for the good of Halruaa."

Zalathorm threw the gem to the ground. It shattered, and suddenly the weight of years crushed the king into dust. Where he stood was a small mound of bone heaped with moldering robes, crowned with a circlet of electrum and silver.

A terrible scream came from the necromancer and drew all eyes to the transformation overtaking him. Like Zalathorm, he withered away, but slowly, and he remained alert and in agony, shrieking in protest and rage. His skeletal jaw shuddered with fury long after the sound had died away. Then there was only dust, which blew away in the sudden gust created as every undead creature fell to the ground, released at last from the necromancer's power.

Stunned silence shrouded the battlefield. At last one wizard began to chant Zalathorm's name. The survivors took up the chant, raising bloodied swords and long-spent wands to the skies as they lauded their king for his final victory.

No one heard the small, ragged voice singing a faint melody, no one but the young woman at her side. Keturah's hand sought Tzigone's. Their fingers linked, and their voices rose together in song.

It was not a summoning and held not compulsion but an entreaty. The faint shadows of elven spirits took up the refrain and their song drifted softly over the battlefield to mingle once more with the spellsong rising from the queen and her sorceress daughter.

Finally they parted, revealing the form of Halruaa's king. Gently, as if they were teaching first steps to a stumbling babe, they guided Zalathorm's spirit back to his mortal remains.

The ghostly form melted into the king's body. Slowly, the decay began to reverse. The chanting grew in volume as Zalathorm's subjects welcomed their king back, with wild joy and without reservation.

Keturah ran forward and fell into Zalathorm's arms. They rose together, hand in hand, and Zalathorm raised their enjoined hands high. Her name was added to the chant, for many had seen her sing the king's spirit back to his body.

Finally Zalathorm lifted a hand for silence. "This is a time for truths long untold. I know you are weary, but listen to a tale too long hidden."

He told them all the truth behind the Cabal, the long path to vengeance taken by an elf woman who had dedicated her life to its destruction. He spoke of the brave queen who for years had been trapped between the artifact and the elf, and the daughter who had never given up her quest to find and free her mother.

Finally he pledged to make changes and to pardon the wizards who plotted against him if they pledged by wizard-word to work with him to make Halruaa all that they have ever dreamed she could be.

As one, the people of Halruaa fell to their knees and raised Zalathorm's name into the darkening skies.

Unfamiliar tears dampened Matteo's face as he watched the scene unfolding. "At last she has found her family, her name," he said with deep satisfaction.

"And you?"

Andris's words were whispered and sounded nearly as pale as the jordain once had been.

"I am a jordain, and always will be," Matteo said. "If I can see and sense the Shadow Weave, all the better. In years to come, the king may have need of this."

Andris smiled wistfully. "I was a jordain, then an elf-blooded warrior, and finally, one of three. That was the best of all."

He reached for Matteo. The jordain clasped his friend's wrist in a warrior's farewell, holding the grip long after Andris's hand fell slack, until his own hand fisted on the empty air.

After all he had seen this day, Matteo was not surprised that Andris simply faded away. He watched as a familiar form strode toward the waiting shadows. Andris was received joyfully and without reserve by the elves he had helped to free. Together they turned their eyes toward the first star and rose to meet the evening sky.

Matteo's gaze shifted from the royal family to the stars. Andris, like Tzigone, was finally among family.

The king's jordain rose and quietly walked toward the royal family, ready to serve, content in his own homecoming.

# EPILOGUE

Matteo strode quickly through the city, sped by the light of the full moon and the sounds of battle coming from the dockside tavern.

He shouldered his way into the room and regarded the familiar scene with resignation. A young lad stood on one of the tables, juggling several mugs. A trio of angry men circled, grabbing at the boy's feet. The performer held them off with well-placed kicks and an occasional hurled mug. Several of the patrons cheered him on and even tossed other mugs to replenish his artillery.

Unfortunately, not all of those mugs were empty. Here and there ale-soaked patrons raised angry words and quick fists to the juggler's benefactors. Several small skirmishes provided side entertainment. Bets were shouted, coin changed hands.

Matteo strode into the room and stalked toward a trio of brawlers. He seized two of the men by their collars. He brought their heads together sharply and tossed them aside. The third man, seeing himself alone, snatched a sword from an observer's belt and brandished it with drunken menace.

The jordain's shoulders rose and fell in a sigh. He raised one hand and beckoned the man on. Bellowing like a bee-stung bull, the lout charged the apparently unarmed man.

Matteo stepped into the charge, seized the man's arm, and forced it down. The sword caught between two of the floor's wide wooden planks. The man kept going without it.

The lad, still juggling, hurled all three mugs in rapid succession. All three struck the drunk's forehead. He staggered, fell to his knees and went facedown into a puddle of ale.

Drunken cheers filled the tavern. The performer grinned like an urchin and took a deep bow.

Matteo seized a handful of short brown hair and pulled the "boy" from his perch. He deftly caught the miscreant and slung her over his shoulder.

The cheers turned to catcalls and protests, but by now it had occurred to the revelers that the intruder wore jordaini white. Few of them were drunk enough to seriously consider taking on one of the wizard-lords' guardians.

Matteo kept a firm grip on his captive as he strode away from the docks. After a while she began to squirm. He rewarded her efforts with a sharp slap on the bottom.

"Hey!" protested Tzigone. "Is that any way to treat a princess?"

"Start acting like a princess, and you'll be treated as one."

She muttered something that Matteo studiously ignored, then bit him on the handiest portion of his anatomy.

He let out a startled yelp and dropped her. She rolled to her feet and backed away. "We're even now," she pointed out.

"Not even close! Tzigone, I'm supposed to protect you. You haven't exactly made it easy."

Her face crumpled into a frown. "How do you think I feel? All these protocols and rules and expectations chafe like a badly fitting saddle. And don't get me started on the clothes I have to wear! Shoes, too!"

He glanced down at her small, bare feet, and his lips twitched reluctantly. "I suppose you're not happy with me for spoiling your fun."

"Damn right! You're the king's counselor, and if the

push for a hereditary monarchy comes to anything, you might be stuck with me a very, very long time."

For a long moment she glared at him, then her anger changed to horrified realization. Matteo mockingly copied her expression. They both dissolved into laughter.

He took her arm and tucked it companionably into his. "Since I'm destined to serve as your jordain, allow a word of advice: If you must insult people, pick smaller men, preferably those who like to drink alone."

"Forget it. I've got to keep your fighting edge up." She glanced up at him. "How did you find me?"

"This is Halruaa," he reminded her. "There is no shortage of magic."

"True, but I can't be tracked by magic."

Matteo quirked one eyebrow and glanced pointedly at their moon-cast shadows.

Tzigone's eyes widened in consternation. "The Shadow Weave. Damn! I forgot about that."

"A wise young woman recently gave me an excellent piece of advice. Would you like to hear it?"

She let out a resigned sigh. "Would it make any difference?"

Matteo chuckled and ruffled his friend's tousled brown hair as if she were truly the lad she pretended to be. "Things change," he told her. "Do try to keep up."

# Sembia

The perfect entry point into
the richly detailed world of the
FORGOTTEN REALMS®, this
ground-breaking series continues
with these all-new novels.

## HEIRS OF PROPHECY
### By Lisa Smedman

The maid Larajin has more secrets in her life than she ever
bargained for, but when an unknown evil fuels a war between
Sembia and the elves of the Tangled Trees, secrets pile on secrets
and threaten to bury her once and for all.

*June 2002*

## SANDS OF THE SOUL
### By Voronica Whitney-Robinson

Tazi has never felt so alone. Unable to trust anyone, frightened
of her enemy's malign power, and knowing that it was more
luck than skill that saved her the last time, she comes to realize
that the consequences of the necromancer's plans could shake
the foundations of her world.

*November 2002*

FORGOTTEN REALMS is a registered trademark of Wizards of the Coast, Inc.,
a subsidiary of Hasbro, Inc. ©2002 Wizards of the Coast, Inc.

# Return of the Archwizards

When ancient wizards of extraordinary power return
from centuries of exile in the Plane of Shadow, they
bring with them an even more powerful enemy and
a war that could destroy the world.

## REALMS OF SHADOW

### *An Anthology*

Twelve all new stories spanning thousands of years brings the
war against the phaerimm and the dark designs of Shade to life.
Featuring stories by R.A. Salvatore, Troy Denning,
Ed Greenwood, and Elaine Cunningham!

*April 2002*

## THE SORCERER

### *Return of the Archwizards, Book 3*
### *By Troy Denning*

Tilverton is no more. Phaerimm surround Evereska. The High
Ice is melting. Floods sweep through Anauroch. Elminster is
still nowhere to be found. The greatest heroes of Faerûn are
held at bay, and a flying city has taken up permanent residence
in a world on the brink of destruction.

*November 2002*

Don't miss the beginning of Troy Denning's exciting
Return to the Archwizards series! Now available:

**The Summoning • Book 1**
**The Siege • Book 2**

FORGOTTEN REALMS is a registered trademark of Wizards of the Coast, Inc.,
a subsidiary of Hasbro, Inc. ©2002 Wizards of the Coast, Inc.

# R.A. Salvatore's
# War of the Spider Queen

*New York Times* best-selling author R.A. Salvatore, creator of the legendary dark elf Drizzt Do'Urden, lends his creative genius to a new FORGOTTEN REALMS® series that delves deep into the mythic Underdark and even deeper into the black hearts of the drow.

## DISSOLUTION
### Book I

Richard Lee Byers sets the stage as the delicate power structure of Menzoberranzan tilts and threatens to smash apart. When drow faces drow, only the strongest and most evil can survive.

*July 2002*

## INSURRECTION
### Book II

Thomas M. Reid turns up the heat on the drow civil war and sends the Underdark reeling into chaos. When a god goes silent, what could possibly set things right?

*December 2002*

FORGOTTEN REALMS is a registered trademark of Wizards of the Coast, Inc., a subsidiary of Hasbro, Inc. ©2002 Wizards of the Coast, Inc.